MW01125625

Maurice and Alec in America

by
Fred Carrier

authorHOUSE™

1663 LIBERTY DRIVE, SUITE 200
BLOOMINGTON, INDIANA 47403
(800) 839-8640
WWW.AUTHORHOUSE.COM

First published by AuthorHouse 07/28/05

ISBN: 1-4208-3807-5 (sc)

Library of Congress Control Number: 2005902018

Printed in the United States of America
Bloomington, Indiana

This book is printed on acid-free paper.

The author is grateful to maritime historical artist William G. Muller for permission to reproduce his oil painting of the White Star Liner Olympic in New York harbor for the cover of this book.

Muller lives in Cotuit, Massachusetts on Cape Cod.

Dedicated to the women who have shown me love
in its wonderful ways of giving and sharing
and abiding through adversity:
to my mother Anna,
to my loving wife Constance,
to my precious daughter Laura,
to sister and friend Cecilia,
and sisters Lorraine, Martha and Catherine,
to dear friends Helene and Pilar,
to my niece Linda,
to many others.

And to the men who have shared my venture:
to my father and my brother Joe,
especially to my loving companion and critic Don,
to Jack who shared with me youthful love,
to my special friend Charles,
to Guillermo, a proud youth of Mexico,
to other Joes who are my friends,
and to Michael an inspiring Friend.

To Golo and Ringo for their canine devotion,
to elusive felines Tom, Minou, Neko, Tigger,
Buttercup, Scooter, Lulu and Winnie.

No one could deserve so much love
without returning something of enduring worth.

Foreword

A number of years ago, while visiting in England, my friend Don presented me with the recently published novel **MAURICE** written by Edward Morgan Forster. The first reading moved me to sufficient reflection so that I read the book again, hoping for a different ending that would satisfy my yearning for fulfillment. Needless to say, I was disappointed again. Perhaps it was discourteous that I wanted much more than Forster provided in terms of resolution.

Sensing that some other sojourners would be seeking for more, I thought about carrying Maurice and Alec across the Atlantic Ocean so that they might pursue their lives as Americans, first and foremost because the idea of their continuing journey interested me. Over the years as I thought about Forster's novel, it seemed a shame to lose track of two such likable characters as I felt Maurice and Alec to be. There are not enough lovers in literature who are as fully flesh-and-blood as Alec promised to be, at least to my imagination, or as attractive and vulnerable, yet resilient and bold, as Maurice when he chooses an homoerotic life with Alec rather than a sterile one alone. Their future concerned me and I believe the story of their lives together will interest some small audience because of the commitment they make and hope honorably and faithfully to observe within a society determined to prevent their love. Since I understood something about their fate, I owe it to others to tell their story for whatever pleasure, perhaps even useful wisdom, it may bring to the reader who has some affinity to their plight.

What gave me considerable pause before undertaking this responsibility was my reluctance to tie myself to Forster's coat tails. In no way did I feel able to emulate his style of writing or match his skill as novelist, and even less did I desire to be in his shadow. But I overcame these dilemmas, only after a ponderous process that oft precedes the act of creativity, finally able to set my mind free for something adventurous. Essentially, I resolved on two guidelines that would make my task more achievable while also in the most vital way remaining true to Forster.

First of the stipulations that I vowed, Maurice and Alec would no longer be English, but they would be Americans once they landed on the shore of their new homeland. Whatever Forster might have wished, it is Maurice's resolve to be American and to enjoy a new freedom that would govern my creativity. I had no desire to be bound to English vocabulary, habits or customs that would no doubt have crossed the ocean along with them. Though trained as an historian, even because of the knowledge of how much care that alone would take, I disavowed the formidable task of mastering an English setting, a burden which would surely lead to my failure. Instead, I claimed what poets have often assumed, literary license to create characters who might just as well be American-born, even as I plundered whatever of their history suited the fate my novel held in store for them. To emphasize the transformation they have undergone, I have given Alec a background that suits my experiences and fantasies. Alec becomes my creation, no longer Forster's ideal friend, for aside from being the virile and persistent male of the working class that Forster presents to Maurice, there is little of history or development of character in Forster's novel to either aid or encumber me in my own treatment of Alec. Maurice, on the other hand, retains memories of his English life and occasional contacts with his family, though not with Clive who mercifully disappears from their continued journey.

The second proviso, which links this novel to Forster's spirit, is that whatever Maurice and Alec experience with one another and with America, their story should stamp approval on homoerotic love, not end in a way that Forster scorned "with a lad dangling from a noose or with a suicide pact." Forster wished a happy ending, and this I choose to accomplish for him, not only because Maurice as his romanticized alter ego deserves a faithful and durable Alec, but also because it allays my conscience. Only by carrying forth that aim of Forster's **MAURICE** could I feel entitled to take his characters and make them mine. A happy ending does not mean Alec and Maurice escape the sufferings and anguish of living, nor their eventual dissolution into eternity. What Forster intended for Maurice, and what I pledged to remember with fidelity, was that a homosexual bond of love may prove as beautiful and good and noble as the fullness of love in marriage of a man with a woman. While society through church and state, and through virtue of ideologies which are self-serving, would act as a predator against those who might try to love their own kind through a lifetime, Maurice and Alec must struggle morally and intellectually as they ennoble their own characters and their "marriage" though it be unrecognized and illicit in the minds of others. They would not succumb to social oppression, nor would they settle for tragic heroism. They would, instead, stubbornly make their way through an often indifferent and sometimes hostile world, persisting in their love for one another, hurting and forgiving one another even as their understanding of love undergoes continuing change. My experiences with life do not make such an outcome seem an impossible dream.

In no other way do I feel bound by the original. When Maurice and Alec embark from the shores of England, they leave behind not only England and all that was English in their time, but they take leave from Forster's novel just as if they had stepped out of its pages beyond the confines of what loomed as a penal society for them. Readers whose reverence for Forster's **MAURICE** puts their sensibilities at risk, considering the voyage I undertake with Maurice and a surprising Alec, should put the book aside, or wrap it for a later Christmas present.

Nor have I felt it necessary to be forced into a time-frame that does not suit me which would have required me to consider at length the Great War. That is why I have taken another liberty, to continue their story, hardly a breath being lost by either of them, with a voyage that ensues in 1924. They have not lost a decade of their lives, but time has disappeared without its usual ravages, in this case the carnage of a war that would have likely numbered one or both of them among the ten million who did perish. Maurice is 24 years old and Alec his younger mate 22 when they sail for America. Now, *bon voyage*, Alec and Maurice, and to you as well, good reader, in a literary venture that I hope will refresh and strengthen your spirit.

Chapter 1

Embarking in Search of a New World

I sing ... of bridegrooms,
I write of Youth, of Love, and have access
By these, to sing of cleanly wantonness.
I sing of times trans-shifting ....

Robert Herrick

Tears welled in Maurice's eyes as the great ocean liner Olympic gathered speed toward America. With a lingering look backward he watched the promontory of Land's End, pointing westward, recede into the distance while glimmering lights of coastal towns fell out of sight amidst the darkness of night, along with all of England.

Beside him stood the young man he loved, Alec, in all manliness. They were skippers atop the vast Atlantic Ocean. It was the year 1924, an early October wind tingling their senses to awareness that they had taken command of their fate, so it seemed at the moment. Two youths starkly different in social rank were at one in sharing an excitement that is the prerogative of new lovers setting out on an adventure. Their compass was uncertain, their love untested, with no promise of endurance, yet whose freshness held out hope suitable to their naïve hearts.

Who can say whether Maurice's tears bespoke an effusion of joy from the closeness of his lover, or an utterance of sorrow at leaving family and homeland? Likely their fluid language whispered ungrammatically some confusion of emotions. Surely a sense of loss had a part, for Maurice was surrendering his heritage, all that he had known of station with its privileges. Despite much recent turbulence that had marred the serenity of his life, an upper class existence had brought steady pleasures and comforts. Hence his accustomed ways, their familiar setting, were bound to seem even more precious at this decisive moment than they had been in the living, as he was making the first break with family and society after twenty-four years of dependence.

Yet his rebellious heart, adrift in a small sea of sadness, felt buoyed by a vast ocean of bold beginnings. As the past disappeared, Maurice leaned upon the ship's railing, easing access to Alec's arm which also rested there. Just as he had thrown his upper class standing to the wind, electing to follow an inner voice that unequivocally urged him to pursue Alec against all worldly wisdom, now Maurice, further emboldened by the cover of darkness, decided that amidst great leaps he should take small risks. He allowed himself this first of honest and defiant gestures, something his background shunned, for telling expressions of love between men might easily offend a chance observer. His hand slid along Alec's arm until it grasped his hand. In the bloom of fresh love Alec's hand of flesh seemed sculpted by the great artist of Nature, as beautiful and powerful and as much formed by physical labor as the marble hand of Michelangelo's David. Alec did not pull away, so that their hands coupled one atop the other. A thrill ran through Maurice's body, a shiver not due to the ocean's cold air, but emanating from the depth of his soul confirming this pilgrimage commanded by the architect of his nature.

At least it seemed that clear to Maurice who was the more resolute of the two in seeking some place beyond the reach of family or religion, perhaps because he was the older, certainly because he was already scarred by a lost love. He stubbornly held to that possibility of permanence for this rare kind of relationship.

The resolution to accomplish something new guided his every action, even to the point of seeking a new world which might prove compatible with defiance of the traditions of the old which had become tattered by the recent great war. He was impelled by his certitude that all compromise with the society that had fashioned him into an English gentleman, its privileges coupled with an incumbent conformity, was perilous to a relationship he desperately wished. He had lost his first love through no fault of his own other than the ways society dictated. For a time thereafter his world seemed forlorn and doomed to loveless existence. Then in the most unlikely way a bold sexual adventure captured his heart in the form of a younger Alec who was from the serving class with few prospects. Months of anguish followed that reckless yielding to the flesh. Lost in confused consideration of the possibilities of healing his devastated spirit and fearful of the renewed dangers of a love between two men, his body at last prevailed over all the mind's objections. He owed it to that part of himself that longed for a binding love with another male. And once he yielded to love, he leaped to the conclusion that he owed such daring to Alec as well.

Henceforth he would suffer no mixing of the old world in a new continent that held hope for a democratic liaison. Now, as he and Alec were embarking on their escape voyage, he repeated the dictates guiding this venture. In the quiet of his mind he swore, "I cannot fit in with England as I know it. I have desires the English never pardon. My body and heart cry out, no longer live imprisoned in England! No longer live within the stifling society that denies my existence, deems my nature perverted, considers my emotional self such a corruption that it need be persecuted until my spirit bends. I must live where Alec and I may be equals."

Hence the journey had begun after months of preparation and anticipation. Maurice and Alec were joined with others aboard the Olympic, many who were emigrants venturing new lives in a new land. With this dispossessed lot the young lovers shared a spiritual linkage. They were less bound to those other voyagers, the men of business, or persons of station and means enhancing privileged lives by leisure abroad. Perhaps among these latter there were a few like them fleeing to find a way to love without recrimination and danger, momentary escapees from prohibition and prudery who were living illicitly for a time abroad and at sea. With these unacknowledged few, Maurice shared a sense of abandoning the respectability of a hostile class-ridden society in order to do what was right for his spiritual self. How else could he and Alec have a chance, which youth is prone to grasp, to love and be loved as the heart decides?

*   *   *

A decision had been urged by Maurice months ago to leave England, not in flight, but in search of a place where their love could stand a chance. A memory of erotic bliss stood at the center of such determination. He thrilled again and again when he recalled the boldness with which Alex had seized upon the most unexpected of occasions to accomplish their first bonding. "How did a country lad like that know so much about me?" Maurice marveled at the bravado of a common worker accosting a gentleman in all confidence, somehow knowing that Maurice's heart surged with an overpowering desire that their flesh be united. Alec had without guile or coarseness, without a word or move that when fully understood could be construed as anything but the purest of motives, demolished in one daring swoop the scaffolding of morality and fear which had plagued and paralyzed Maurice for twenty-four years of his life. While the whole scaffolding did not disappear in the tumbling, it was in such ruin that it could never effectively be put together again, for the rightness of that erotic encounter was commanding. Maurice's vivid memory tested that

3

night's fulfillment endless times, measuring its thrilling awakening of flesh and affirming its directive. He pleaded with Alec, for he came to realize that Alec, too, was impelled by powerful desire, that they not let the moment escape them.

"Let us set sail for a life together in America."

It was not the first time Maurice had turned his back on the conservatism of England. When he left the protective walls of ancient Cambridge, aborting the path to a career among the elite, he had entirely by intuition opted for a more rebellious attitude, and so he had made the first turn. Though not a rebel by any convictions political or moral, his sexuality inclined him toward a masculine world where he expected honesty of emotions amidst friends bound by the same passions. In that alone was he a rebel.

Nor was Alec merely a compliant companion in this journey. He had his own sense of adventure. The truth was he reveled in bravado at the easy conquest of a lovely gentleman's body and heart. These were strong inducements to set out for an America that offered him economic opportunity as well as romance. He more than Maurice stood to benefit from leaving an England dominated by an imperious aristocracy. Touting their mission to promote civilization the length of an empire that stretched from Africa to India, they basked in privileges that subordinated inferior races, mirrored in a submissive domestic order of English and Irish workers who, as it were, formed an inferior breed at their service.

Such was the order of men that included his former employers, the Durhams, who relegated Alec, a worker who was an Irishman in his heart, to serve in subservience as long as he stayed in England. His strong hands were assigned to carry out the will of those who controlled the property of England and its Empire. His work had lately amounted to preparing hunts for gentlemen, picking up their leavings, so that they might preserve delicacy of limbs and refined tastes. There was little for Alec to forfeit in loosening chains that bound him to a class of menials. What risk was there in embarking to America and linking his fortune to a gentleman of upright character and undeniable physical beauty? The marvel as he saw it was that Maurice was ready to abandon his privileges to link with him. For Alec had no intention to be less than the equal of a gentleman.

But of course there was risk in a way that Alec could not yet calculate, for while he had known adolescent escapades, he had never before fallen in love. The heart of a man moved by such passion is no different than that of a woman, nor is a worker's different from the heart of a gentleman. To give one's heart in love, though it occur piecemeal, is to give the most precious value that youth has to offer. Yes, even beyond the surrender of

4

the body in lust. Whoever has lived and loved knows what risks the heart entails entrusting itself fully to another.

That two men could fall in love and devote themselves to one another is no fairy tale. It is a story as old as the Iliad's golden-haired Achilles who loved a companion warrior Patroclus. When the body of Patroclus lay slain on the field of battle, his spirit arose to plead with Achilles, "Never bury my bones apart from yours, let them lie together." Whoever feels the touch of poetry sprung from his own experience of love would wish that under the soil of Greece there forever lies an ancient urn, adorned with youthful singers and flute-players, wherein the remains of the two lovers will rest forever commingled. During subsequent ages there have been countless pairs of men who loved each other, and women who loved women, all but a few unheralded because their devotion was as natural as their decorum. Maurice and Alec, though unaware, were thus not rare in their loving, but only in their boldness in setting out to defy the world's wisdom that discretion is the better part of valor.

*   *   *

As Maurice watched with Alec, England became enshrouded in misty darkness. Passengers drifted to dining rooms or to sleeping quarters while the more energetic glided into the ballroom in response to its musical invitations. Maurice longed to cling to England's last sights for a while more, even as distance was broadening the reality of separation. The ocean-cooled air was invigorating. He felt alone with Alec, despite the few passengers who lingered on deck, for he sensed a security in their companionship that he had never before felt. Perhaps it was the vastness of the ocean whose calmness matched his spirit. Perhaps it was a false sense that no man's law governed this floating terrain. Whatever the reason, Maurice was made strong and invincible by his lover's closeness, and he wished to walk the deck with Alec and while away the whole first night at sea.

But it was not long before a stronger emotion prevailed in another direction toward their cabin which for six nights on the ocean would be their private abode, in a way their first home, wherein they could enjoy intimacy of a kind so long denied. They would be where no man could thwart their desires. Bound by love, yet free in spirit, they returned to the cabin.

An hour or two later – time had become suspended for them in their intimacies – Alec adroitly lifted himself apart from Maurice. "I need sound sleep, Morrie," and so Maurice reluctantly yielded to the separation, though he wished never to let loose of the moment or of his lover. Alec bounded into the bed above with a goodnight.

Tired and fulfilled as they were, the creaking and clatter that arose from the tension between ship and sea lulled these two happy mates into dreaminess. Thus ended the first night of a voyage that Maurice would remember as a honeymoon.

* * *

Next morning they found their way to a spacious restaurant a few decks above their second-class quarters. The room was sparsely occupied for it was late morning. Most first class travelers preferred exclusivity in the formal dining room, but an obvious exception met their glances. An impeccably dressed gentleman, one who had taken notice of them at the dock, sat alone. He was pleased to see them entering the room. He greeted them as if in invitation. Maurice bid good morning to the stranger who made a mild apology for intruding, nonetheless urging that they share his table with its commanding view of the sea. Maurice was already moving away when Alec accepted for both of them.

"A pleasure to share a hearty breakfast with someone so congenial." Then, after a long gaze at the water, "How wonderful and grand the ocean appears. Is there no end to it?"

Seeing Alec already seating himself, Maurice begrudgingly followed suit. Their friendly host was John Graham, a New Yorker, an experienced voyager whose business brought him to Europe twice yearly to search for art treasures and furnishings that would adorn the homes of clients. His ensuing talk revealed familiarity with the ship and the ocean, knowledge that was of great interest to his tablemates. Graham proved observant and somewhat loquacious, though from a wealth of experience rather than from loneliness. He was eager to learn about his present companions. He explained that he never wasted an opportunity that might introduce an unusual traveler. "The sea, awesome as it is," thus acknowledging Alec's fascination with it, "no longer offers much new, except at its greatest turbulence. It is people willing to share unusual experiences and inclinations who interest me. I wager both of you have stories to tell."

When Maurice interspersed some fatuous remark about this being their maiden voyage in a way that revealed his thorough middle class Englishness, Graham resumed the initiative. He told more of himself, that he was a seasoned voyager dating to boyhood when his family spent part of every summer in Europe. He had seen his share of historical sites and landscapes. Now in the maturity of life, what compelled his attention while traveling was attractive people, although his business was to collect art works which made each journey memorable.

"I will confide that I prefer the company of men. The ladies are charming, no doubt, but an inveterate bachelor must be careful not to encourage the hopes of those young ladies not yet spoken for, nor of their mothers who are watching for their interests. I, too, am watchful not to encourage false hope since I have no intent to compromise my single state."

He frankly admitted that he had taken note of Alec and Maurice on the dock in Southampton, though he did not say what had drawn this interest. He had observed that the dark-haired lad's speech, with a touch of Irish, and manner were more earthy than that of his better dressed companion. In that instant he decided they might prove congenial company. Now the opportunity had arisen to help fate along. He was further pleased by Alec's ease in accepting the invitation and the confident air with which he casually seated himself to enjoy the sea view.

Not long into their acquaintance Graham revealed a paternalistic propensity, the wish to help naive youth, an attitude uncommon in a man barely forty years of age, perhaps due to his being without children of his own. Before they could order he proffered advice, "Avoid too hearty a breakfast this morning, no matter your ravenous appetites. Seasickness follows indulgence in eating, more than from anything else – except, and happily this cannot be your case, for the female constitution." Both men laughed politely as they sought further insights into life at sea.

"Do you never suffer from the sea? How might we avoid that?"

Graham was pleased to lecture on that bane of sea travel, for he had a lingering claim to the role of physician. He had studied medicine with that profession in mind, though he had chosen not to practice it. He offered a time-tested remedy. "Walk the deck three or four times a day, no matter the weather. I do these rounds without fail, rewarding my diligence by punctuating exercises with some brandy." Pressed for details, he was happy to oblige. "I make several rounds of the ship after breakfast, which I will soon undertake. Nothing hurried. I entertain encounters along the way, rarely declining a word or two, hoping to meet exceptional people. When the ship's horn sounds noon, that's the call to brandy. The rule of moderation I intoned for eating applies in this as well, two brandies interspersed with exercise and good conversation — never overdo that limit. There's a prescription that has kept me from seasickness. In recent years I have increased my pace to a dozen rounds before night." He recalled with a chuckle a passenger who was one of his lucky encounters, as he flattered his present company to be. "He was an athletic American in excellent condition. I trailed along with him on the rounds, but only for a time, as he logged two hundred during the crossing. Forty miles, a record no doubt. Nothing so heroic as that is needed. Young chaps like you should manage several miles a day."

Having convinced Alec, at least, of the benefits of shipboard exercise – Maurice smiled inwardly at the thought that he had enjoyed plenty of exercise the night previous, thus was less persuaded – Graham turned the conversation to other advice that occupied the rest of the time. When he looked at his pocket watch, he signaled the end of the pleasant repast with a last thoughtful sip of coffee. He dabbed at his lips with a napkin. Then, with sagacity acquired from a life of travel, he warned them once again not to succumb to mid-ocean insouciance.

"The lull of the sea soothes one's senses into lazy indulgence which is likely to destroy nature's disciplines. Do not fear that I exaggerate the role of nature in human conduct. Civilization demands much from us that is repugnant to instincts. Yet when it concerns our physical constitutions, nature's voice commands moderation. Nothing to excess is the way to good health. Whether we observe nature directly, or simply follow Aristotle in seeking the golden mean, it comes to the necessity of recognizing our physicality. Maybe we shall discuss this further at our next sitting? Be that as it may, it is the work we perform which demands regularity on land. When we are about our business the clock reminds us of accustomed requirements. Make no mistake on your maiden voyage, discipline is needed amidst all this idleness. Clocks and daylight are disrupted, along with the restraints of ordinary society, so that it falls to commonsense to order matters while adrift."

Nothing more to be said, courteously he bade them good walking and moderation during the day with enough of good food to satisfy the appetite that sea air engenders and that youth requires. He hoped they would meet again the next morning at this same table.

*   *   *

Insouciance characterized the first day on the vast Atlantic. Maurice saw to reserving deck chairs for two on the portside of the ship, as Graham advised, where the wind was less blustery and the midday sun more attentive. That afternoon they stretched out in chairs to enjoy public intimacy that was something they had never experienced on land. Barely inches apart their bodies could touch each other almost as if by accident. How pleasant it was to bask this way on the sunny deck.

Maurice made an attempt to read a book acquired for the voyage, the notorious Edward Carpenter's *My Days and Dreams*. Maurice had been meaning to read the book since he first heard Carpenter's bold ideas within clandestine Cambridge circles. Now the time was right. Carpenter had been a Cambridge don until he abandoned his clerical career in the 1870's to pursue a life among the working class, as well as to fill another need of an affectional nature. His infamous reputation grew as he embraced the cause of the workingman, socialism; then women's emancipation; and going an important step further, the rights of androgynous men and women attracted to their own sex to exercise freely "the most sacred, the most profound and vital of all human functions."

Maurice read in silence, lost in contemplation, Carpenter's thought fast becoming his own. No longer able to contain the excitement at Carpenter's radicalism, he shared one liberating idea after another. He leaned toward Alec to read a passage he thought inspiring, "We have endless lessons of soul-relationship to learn, some most intimate, others doubtless less so, but all fair and perfect" – Maurice read with emphasis certain of the words – "so soon as we have discovered what these relationships really are, and are in no confusion of mind about them. For even those that are most distant are desirable, and have the germ of love in them, so soon as they are touched by the spirit of Truth, which means the fearless statement of the life which is in us."

Alec appreciated that something important was being shared among Maurice, Carpenter and himself. A thrilling journey of mind and sea were in this way joined.

Maurice returned to the silence of reading and thought, every few pages lapsing into dreaminess. Eventually he yielded to memories of the previous night, succumbing to sleep, as he sheltered himself from the cool breezes beneath a warming rug. Alec gently removed the book from a drowsing Maurice's lap. He thought to have a look, fumbling through the pages until he chanced upon Carpenter's depiction of an "intermediate sex" that he could not recall encountering. He pondered the idea – the body of a man containing the disposition of a woman – people neither men nor women in fullness. With irritation he closed the book, then slipped away to make a healthy tour of the ship. Scrutinizing the indolent passengers, their chic clothing, their genteel mannerisms and affected words, all this strangeness led him to wonder whether there were some intermediates among them. He felt uncomfortable so removed from his accustomed social milieu. The sober thought gripped him, what else could his life be with Maurice except estrangement from so much that he knew and held precious? Whatever Maurice's impulses, even sacrifices he might choose,

9

the two could not become an island to themselves. Nor was Maurice a Carpenter able to enter the world of common people.

Thinking of Graham's admonition toward the discipline of work that surely awaited him, Alec decided he had best enjoy the exercise, the air and the sea regardless. Time would tend to things. After a round he settled again into his chair. He sought to reassure himself by an escape from thought into sensuality. He looked at Maurice whose manliness within a man's body pleased him. Under the cover of two warming rugs that concealed any commotions, his fingers stroked Maurice in an intimate way until both were roused enough to savor that contact in half-sleep.

During afternoon tea on deck, Alec unexpectedly dropped a remark.

"Carpenter is right to struggle for the rights of women. Men have unfairly ruled over them. But the intermediate sex he believes in, those neither men nor women, muddles the matter. Men desire women, sometimes men, as the occasion be. Desire seems natural, one as the other. It is women men need for marriage and family. That I know."

Maurice was taken aback by what seemed a rebuke. Not for the first time he took note of Alec's confidence in his own mind. But he was not ready to concede the point lest Carpenter be dismissed out of hand. Too much was at stake, too much lovely hope. "It may be Carpenter overstates the matter," Maurice yielded that much, "yet I find he addresses my feelings." He imparted another of Carpenter's ideas, one that had moved him sufficiently to put to heart, a passage he knew would soften Alec's disdain. "It is the very nature of Love that as it realizes its own aim it should rivet always more and more toward a durable and distinct relationship, nor rest till the permanent mate and equal be found."

Thus the day passed eventfully and uneventfully as if time did not exist, nor any impediment to reverie, at least none for Maurice. Alec laid his concerns to rest for the time being.

*   *   *

Next morning at breakfast Maurice revealed to Graham that their destination was Philadelphia. He explained that his uncle was an officer in one of the city's prominent banks and had written to assure Maurice's anguished mother that the bank would have some suitable place for her wayward son. Maurice rambled on about investment experience in London and his stay at Cambridge, until Graham discreetly shifted attention to the other fellow traveler. Though Graham had proper upbringing, in traveling the world he had not shunned acquaintance with the unsophisticated. It was a credit to his character that he was no harsh judge without a hearing.

He had come to realize it was largely a matter of chance, not of choice, what befell a man, for the child with his given surroundings was father of the man. He did not pride himself that he was better than others, only more clearly fortunate in circumstances of birth that had provided him every opportunity for education and culture. Thankful for those advantages, which rendered him uncommon, he nevertheless exuded a liking for common people that on a rare occasion grew into admiration should he discover a man of original mettle. Even now he was looking.

"What of you, Alec? What brings you west, business or the pleasure of Maurice's company?"

"I should rather say business, since I intend on finding employment in America. I need greater opportunity than any England has afforded me. I follow many Irish emigrants who sought better in America."

"What prospects do you have? Will you stop in Philadelphia as Maurice intends?"

"We travel together being companions. We hope for cordial welcome from the city offering brotherly love, that being what we have heard. As to my work prospects, I should rather ask you, Mr. Graham, what are the chances for a man such as myself with little experience or education? Is America the land of promise we are seeking? I am strong, that you see. What you cannot see is my readiness for hard work. You may guess that I have done so all my life."

Graham had an exaggerated estimation of American economic opportunity. His faith epitomized the wealthy class that ruled America who believed less in democracy than in a guiding spirit of American capitalism, a mysterious force akin to the invisible hand of progress that rewarded hard work and cleverness. Though he had not been called to daily struggle against poverty, he was not blind to the hard contradictions of working class experience that separated hard labor from the amassment of capital. His own social circle more than proved that discrepancy. But his optimism was nourished by the romance of an immigrant nation destined to prosper from the enormous natural resources at its command.

"Yes, Philadelphia is a good place for two young men with a modicum of ambition. Opportunity is there for Maurice with family connections offering a promising start. A position at the bank should bring two thousand a year. Even your uncle will not guarantee rapid advancement, but you can look forward to a steady rise until you attain the social milieu that is your heritage."

"But to Alec's question," and to him he turned, "I foresee no problem in your finding manual work. Philadelphia is an industrial center, not what it was a few decades ago, yet there are Pennsylvania's coalmines and steel mills linked by great railroads to Philadelphia and the ports of the world."

Graham had grown fonder of Alec than even he reckoned, and though he foresaw some dilemmas for the working lad, his paternalism prevailed.

"I hope you will not mind my pointing out that manual labor, which should be respected, limits advancement materially and, it may be, spiritually. Leadership in the business world falls to a small class who are inheritors of property. I happen to be among them. My lineal ascent has been Groton, Harvard, the right friends. We marry at our social level and secure one another's fortune. I am not proud of this, nonetheless thankful. For you without easy entry the surest advance is by education, so that you are regarded seriously. Maurice will no doubt be able to help. If you find interest in the sciences or mechanics, all to the good, for the economy is allied to technology. I do not mean to neglect the arts, for your free spirit needs to measure success in a unique way. None of this should discourage you, only clear your eyes."

Alec thanked him for these ruminations but his mind was where it belonged. He needed quickly remunerative work which was apt to be manual. He mentioned that he had known of men who had contracted to labor before leaving England, and that he might have done the same, though he knew some who had returned to England disillusioned by harsh labor for pitiful wages, nothing to show for their stay abroad. A Scudder relative was an embittered victim of just such an experience. Graham was alarmed by this account for he was aware of the recent restrictive immigration law.

"Make no mention of arrangements for work, simply that you are energetic to profit from America's bounty. Immigration inspectors are likely to be jealous that their fellow citizens have first chance for work. Be discreet, in personal matters as well. Then you will have no trouble, being English. I hope, Alec, you do not mind my including you in this designation, a merely geographical linkage, for I honor Ireland's sovereignty." He offered further assurance, "I do not believe anyone as ambitious and personable as you need go wanting in America. There is a continent to fill out."

Graham repeated a personal preference for New York over any other place. "Philadelphia, to be frank is too homogeneous in its people, largely transplanted from your own British Isles. But a start is needed, and it helps to have family connections such as Maurice mentions."

"I think we will benefit from a more quiet existence in the city of brotherly love," Maurice confided.

*   *   *

Three days out the weather deteriorated into a steady drizzle that was wind-blown enough to drive passengers from the decks to more comfortable inner quarters. Maurice took the occasion to retire to the library to accomplish a letter that he had been meaning to write to his mother. He determined to be more frank in explaining his situation, thereby forcing her to understand the reality of his intention. His own confusing explanations for going to America had contributed to her delusion. Slowly, thoughtfully and, to his mind, considerately, he came up with these brief words.

My dearest Mother:

It has been a happy voyage, I might claim even euphoric, as Alec and I have been the closest of companions, sharing everything travel has to offer. How well we exchange impressions gives me hope for our future. I know that the different backgrounds from which we spring poses troublesome fears for you, but I trust you will not unduly concern yourself, once you understand the matter aright.

There is something I need to make clear to you, though I tried before and failed out of my lack of candor. During the past few years, you know I was miserable after finding myself distanced from Clive. Without fully understanding my nature, I was doomed to suffer from an agonizing chasm of aloneness. Hopelessly, I realize now, I was trying to avoid what needed honesty, my own peculiar nature that desired a devoted friend — a male rather than a female — someone who also needed and sought the same. While it will be difficult for you to understand fully this need you have never felt, one that is perhaps also an unnaturally strong urge in me, I count on what I know to be true, that you love me sufficiently to strive to keep my need paramount against what you must deem more important worldly considerations. Please find it in your heart to trust my explanation concerning matters you do not understand. Trust my judgment, appreciate the friend I treasure, recognizing how much this experience means to me. It is more than some passing fancy. So please do not wish mistakenly, thinking some other arrangement in my best interest, that soon Alec and I should and will go separate ways simply because society poses too many obstacles to the special friendship of men, especially those separated by the gulf between classes. I know as much but this renders me more determined to cope with whatever must be overcome, because for me it is a matter of life, I will not say as opposed to death, but as opposed to a mechanical existence that would not be living.

Be assured that my present contentment is tempered by pangs of absence. I miss you, Ada and Kitty, as well as the home that calls forth many fond memories.

I will inform you as soon as we are settled and I will continue to write you about our travel adventures as well as the mundane experiences.

Now that I have explained the fullness of my situation, I wish you especially peace of mind regarding my welfare. This letter is inspired by the tenderness due to a mother from a grateful son. I remain as I always will be, your loving

Maurice

Pleased with what he had penned, he deposited the note in the writing room mailbox so that another ship could carry it back to England where his mother would come to understand everything necessary. He felt relieved that he had conveyed just the right amount of intimacy, so that only a parent who chose to be obstinate or dominating would fail to grasp things, and Mrs. Hall was neither of those. She was a soft person who preferred to allow the working of time to remedy a mismatch. She had never been willing to try to replace her husband in the authority of command he had exerted.

*   *   *

Maurice justifiably felt a mood to celebrate his honesty and the freedom that it encouraged. He found Alec and suggested it was time for the prescribed afternoon brandy. "Not a bad idea," Alec complied. "We might have the good fortune to run into Graham." Both he and Maurice had quickly grown to like him.

Instead, fortune pulled a different way, as a high-pitched voice surprised their medicinal brandy. "Maurice Hall, of all people! I haven't seen you since London, the concert when we bumped into each other." The greeting came from an old Cambridge acquaintance, delivered in a voice so ringing and so affected in the odd rhythm of pronouncement that it drew the attention of half the room. "You must tell me at once all that you have been doing. And this voyage! What possibly could bring you to sail for the colonies! Clive had you working in London, far from regaling the seas. Trading stocks or some such lucrative conduct, isn't that what you're about?" A kind of non-stop chatter ensued with barely an informative response.

The friend who did not await an invitation to join them was Risley who had been in his senior-year at Cambridge when Maurice arrived. At college Risley talked endlessly, often about Carpenter and other such matters, though to deaf ears as far as concerned Maurice. During that year Maurice fell into the throes of passion for Clive. Risley, who was sophisticated about illicit relations of this sort, witnessed with fascination the incipient charm of youthful Maurice discovering his homoeroticism. When friendship blossomed into Maurice's infatuation with Clive's beauty, Risley, as was his way, pursued every chance to puncture Maurice's romantic illusions, insinuating that Clive was as cold as any fish, warning Maurice that he ought to swim in more teeming waters. On occasion Risley expressed willingness to throw himself into the sea to save Maurice from disappointment. Maurice not only refused to swim with sharks but he came to concur with Clive that a little of Risley went a long way. But here once again they were thrown together at sea.

"A brandy sounds delightful." Risley explained his own presence, that he was accompanying his family to his sister's wedding in Boston. He ridiculed his sister's opportunistic marrying of a wealthy American, the consummation of a strictly worldly relationship he could hardly countenance. "Imagine, I must embrace this ghastly, this boorish man, as my brother-in-law simply because he is a wealthy entrepreneur." After more than enough details Risley turned attention to what truly interested him, his eyes bathing in Alec's masculinity. What was Maurice doing at sea? "And who is this savory travel companion of yours?"

Maurice knew that he did not want to talk to Risley, much less confide in him, but some terse explanation was needed merely to get beyond the moment. He bumbled, "Alec is a cousin I haven't seen since we were boys. We are traveling together to visit some relatives in Philadelphia." Of course the lie was transparent. Alec felt uneasy about it but he played the game silently. Risley was shrewd enough not to act the role of prosecutor though he hoped to have another go at the truth before the ship landed. He bid each of the pair "A bientot" with his tender handshake.

*   *   *

With precaution and an always welcome bit of luck, Maurice was able to avoid the curious Risley through much of the voyage. But Alec was not equally fortunate. The fourth day out Maurice felt indisposed and retired to their cabin after requesting delivery of some medicament to relieve dyspepsia. Though he felt sorry to leave his mate, Alec was ardent to keep to the brisk walking regimen that had protected him from

15

any touch of seasickness. The sun had returned, so now the deck was alive with passengers. Some were sitting or walking together, a few were companionless and pensive as was Alec. Somewhere along his fourth round of the ship, Risley pounced from somewhere as if awaiting his prey.

"I've caught up with you at last! May I accompany you about? I am sure Maurice would not mind, and I hope you do not."

Alec was inclined to laugh outright at Risley's ridiculous dress in white plus fours, fashionable in first class. The baggy knickers displayed his skinny legs to disadvantage. The plaid cap he wore and a sweater draped across his shoulders accented the rather laughable sight Risley offered to someone as common as Alec.

"I will not beat around the bush. I am dying to know! How did Maurice become acquainted with a man such as you?" Risley had no fear that his inquiry would seem rude.

Alec did not know how to be coy, for his wont was to be honest or silent when he distrusted a person. As a boy his mother had been direct with him, and so it was foreign to him to diverge from simple statement of what he knew. Thinking Risley Maurice's friend, he chose to be forthright.

"Far from being a cousin of Maurice, I was gamekeeper for the Durhams, where Maurice frequented. You may not know that he was very troubled this summer. When I saw that Maurice needed a bit of comfort, I was happy to give it."

"Now I understand." Risley surmised the truth. "When I saw Clive he mentioned that Maurice had been depressed. Little wonder! I will never truly understand why Maurice invested so much of his emotion in such a prig as Clive. All those arid ideals! Clive could not recognize a genuine feeling if it smothered him. I tried to dissuade Maurice from entrusting himself to merely a pretty person. What a travesty it turned in the end. You, on the other hand, I quite see why Maurice finds you trustworthy."

Risley was not one to hide his feelings that often spilled into harmless flirtations.

"Now that I recall, Clive did mention a hired hand, not in a kindly way, hinted that something improper occurred. Maurice playing the fool. Clive said nothing about you by name, nor anything of your taking leave together from England."

"That is something came later, when we recognized how we felt about each other." Alec perceived that Risley was stimulated by the adventure that was unfolding, that he even wished a favorable outcome.

"Do you really know Maurice, or the Hall family? You seem so young. Dare I say, inexperienced in affairs of the world?"

"Of course we are not foolish. Young, yes, but not without good sense. We come from different folks, mine who have worked hard with their hands. Yet I have some education, and I intend to be worthy of Maurice. Maurice is as strong willed as me, perhaps both of us foolish due to youth, thinking we can make our own way. That is why we choose a new land. Anyways, we are carried away with our urgings, as you see, for better or worse. We'll make a try of it, and if things go different than our hopes, have nothing to regret for never trying."

"Do you know there are dangers in your plan?"

"I know the laws of England punish what we desire."

"America is no less repressive. Its laws prohibit males from intimacy, publicly I mean. America is worse in some ways, less formal religiously than the Church of England, but more stuck in its righteous convictions. I shudder at its Puritanism, Calvinism run amuck. Even the few days I must spend there for the family's pride, I will feel smothered. I am a hedonist pure and simple" – the words stumbled out of his mouth – "living for the moment."

Risley scrutinized the innocent youth, searching for the strength of character he intuited. "You seem another sort. How wrong Clive was to be deprecating! I suspect you have some calculated view for your future." His tone of voice became unaffected and his stuttering ceased. "I have concern for your safety and for Maurice's. Maurice will be discreet. He is a lovely person who exercises an appeal for me greater than he recognizes. He is more than a pretty face, or that delightful body, though these are nothing to snigger about. Maurice is generous. He has learned from disappointment, and he will be wary on your behalf. If you watch your behavior, no one will suspect you of anything beyond the normal."

There was something disturbing in this advice. Risley himself was a puzzle that left Alec wondering whether Carpenter was right after all.

*　　　*　　　*

When he finally could get away and return to his tired friend, Alec decided to say nothing about Risley, though as chance would have it, he stumbled onto a scene that furthered his indignation toward the privileged class, Maurice too closely linked. Here was his lover railing at a youthful steward who stood in abjection. Somehow the wrong medicament had been sent. The hapless steward pleaded, "I brought what I was given, sir." Taken unawares of Alec's aftertaste from his encounter with Risley, Maurice had no reason to temper his accustomed superiority. In a nasty tone he ordered the steward to open the porthole so that the cabin might be aired. Nor did he display the gratitude owed such service. He continued to complain petulantly, "Well, at least you got that properly." This tone of arrogance bespoke a mastery that Maurice was accustomed to dispense among the Hall women as well as servants.

Alec showed his anger. "The man has only done what he was instructed. He deserves respect, not a rude reproach." Irritation with Risley and talk of Clive had reminded him of the servile role he had performed for the Durhams. He had not forgotten the time when Maurice had treated him in the same manner. He stormed out of the cabin without another word, accompanying the steward while pressing a coin into his hand. Half an hour later Alec returned with the proper medicine. A chagrined Maurice made sure to thank him for the service. Both thought the better of the incident and they were careful to avoid any further irritant for the rest of the day.

That night in the privacy of their cabin, Alec offered a crisp "Good night" and as he bounded for his berth, "You are in bad temper." Maurice was rebuked. That he knew, but there was little of defense. Too proud to pursue his distanced lover, Maurice suffered a disturbed and restless night, alone in his disappointment with himself, uncertain what to do. This uneasiness marked an interruption, the only lull in an otherwise romantic voyage. Wisely, the next morning Maurice acted with decision, waylaying Alec even before he could open his eyes. This time Maurice climbed the ladder to break down barriers. Without words passing that might renew the wounds, a reconciliation ensued as Alec responded without hesitation to pleading embraces.

*   *   *

Breakfast on their last full day at sea completed the restoration of harmony. Graham's presence relaxed any uneasiness that might have lingered. He was their first mutual friend who had won that status because he approved their love whose daring excited him, though it also gave him concern, for his experience showed love precarious even when supported by social institutions and legalities. How much more difficult their outlaw existence! He cared for his new friends enough to wish to help. He had decided to do as much.

"Maurice and Alec, thank you for letting me share your companionship. Romance is always warming to witness, though I safeguard my own safe distance from the vicissitudes of passion. My earlier forays at intimacy left me disenchanted. I have worked out a life of the mind that flourishes during tranquility. I venture intellectual scrutiny is far from your mood while enjoying the tumult of new love?"

Maurice might have resisted such venturing. Alec chose otherwise, troubled as he was by the concerns meeting Risley had stirred. He was seeking assurances.

"Mr. Graham, you have urged us to plumb nature's dictates regarding our physical constitutions. I trust these include the powerful urges associated with the sex organs. I would appreciate your judgment concerning an idea we encountered, one I find unsettling. Mr. Edward Carpenter contends that part of the human species comprises an intermediate sex, a group of people who are neither man nor woman but some of both, having the physical features of one sex combined with the feelings of the other. I could only yield to this strange idea if it were supported by observations of a scientific kind. Is it natural for people to be intermediate, half male and half female?"

"Alec, you are a philosopher who seeks truth without trepidation. This encourages me to honesty. Though I have pondered human sexuality, I have not resolved my own uncertainties."

"I value what you think all the more. Be assured I will subject your views to the criticism of reason and observation. Is not that the duty of a philosopher?"

"Well spoken. I trust, Maurice, you share Alec's curiosity, else I would hesitate to be so bold. When I first encountered Carpenter's view, I agreed. I had observed what he did, that there are men whose feelings are in total conflict with the body nature assigned. I have known men who feel as do women, and I understand the same transgression exists among women. For such as these, their goals are in conflict with gender dictates because they wish to be valued as if they were of the other sex. But over time my intellectual searches have convinced me that humans satisfy sexual passions in endless ways. Individuals vary in audaciousness with countless motivations to resist the restraints society places on imagination and deed. From this I have concluded that every sexual act addresses an impulse from our bodies or minds, for I believe that mental forces, powerful erotic ideas derived from experience, have the same power as physical urges we deem natural emanating from the sexual organs."

"If I understand correctly, that agrees with Carpenter" was Alec's surmise, as Graham continued.

"Carpenter is a man I admire, one who took risks to combat ignorance and bigotry. But I am reaching a different understanding."

"In what way do you disagree with an intermediate sex?"

"I have come to appreciate individual history rather than categories of behaviors. In Vienna a few years ago I learned of an evolutionary approach practiced by Dr. Sigmund Freud. Perhaps you are familiar with his psychoanalysis? He analyzes the sexual character of a person within the family setting, exploring both conscious and unconscious workings of the mind as recounted through memories, dreams and the display of habitual attitudes. Imprints occur while the child is coming to know his body sensually and learning how to relate to other persons who provide satisfactions. The child is taught what must not be enjoyed whether because of morality, religion or gender, all those ways civilization represses deeds and desires. By the time a boy reaches puberty, gender has worked to exact an assigned role that may be comfortable or distressing, dependent on experiences that have shaped the sexual character. No sexual categories fit such a range in feeling and practice.

"I reject the supposition of an intermediate sex. Homosexuality is a phenomenon across all societies. Disparagement of male love defies the long history of human sexual experience, the Greeks and Romans who founded our civilization, when males were proud of natural, deep and enduring feelings toward one another displayed varying ways. Men often took charge of youth to guide sexual and intellectual development. Anthropologists have also found other societies where homosexual relations are part of learning how to be masculine. Boys learn from men who show them the ways of mature virility."

"What is your judgment on those who act as intermediates, who follow their impulses without scruple, but who feel themselves men?" This time it was Maurice asking, as he made clear, "from a moral point of view."

"I deem such behaviors ethically acceptable, as I do all sexual pleasure, with one broad reservation to this liberalism, that no violence or coercion be exercised upon another person, since every sexual act should be an expression of desire. Sexual encounters may be encouraged as experiments, at least when we are young and hardly instructed. Even with maturity there is room for exploration, though I prefer for myself that sexual acts be tangentially related to love, controlled experiments that offer a possibility of discovering the ways of expressing mutual caring."

"I shall have to read more of what Freud has written," Alec promised, but Maurice was still concerned that promiscuity might result from too much excitement of sexual experimentation, distracting from the perfecting of love. Graham hoped to alleviate that fear for he was far from preaching promiscuity.

"Some men will follow errant eroticism, its excitements and dangers. Those who permit themselves every sexual freedom are apt to be as miserable, no less so, as those who repress every impulse. There is good news, Maurice, for that same nature which prescribes our nourishment offers a controlling force to the sexual appetite. Humans prefer deeper love to the excitement of the new. Sexual acts seem initially to be the greatest of intimacies, but in fact they are quicker, and thus easier, compared to discovering mutual intimacy that relates to the intellectual and the spiritual, component parts of character, along with the sexual. Love which we value ideally develops intimacy of two whole persons."

It was getting late into the morning. Graham expressed the desire to see them again, if not sooner, then during the holiday season when he would deliver some prints acquired on this trip to a friend in Doylestown, near Philadelphia. Later that day gifts from Graham arrived at their cabin, exquisite cologne for Maurice and for Alec a new one hundred dollar bill with an explanation for such generosity, "In the event you need to convince immigration officials of your financial independence." Another message to both of them read, "Visit me when you are settled for a tour of New York and renewed friendship. Meantime, as the need arises, do not hesitate to call upon me. With deep respect for your friendship, J.R. Graham"

*   *   *

The last night of the voyage Maurice was buoyant with renewed health and assurance about the future. He looked more handsome than ever in a light flannel suit he had donned for a final dinner on ship. Alec's eyes sparkled, outshining his dull, more rugged outfit of blue serge. Maurice felt the dinner had gone well, that Alec had carried himself with appropriate quietude and pleasure. They returned to their cabin a little past midnight, each certain that, no matter the difficulties experienced because of the newness of their intimacy, the other was fully happy to be there and nowhere else or with none other.

Alec placed their brief estrangement in a perspective Maurice would appreciate, knowing that others like Clive and Risley were bound to cross their lives.

"Maurice – I love you! – and I trust you to love me. But you must not be dense if you choose to be with a common worker. Do you know how it makes my blood seethe when such as the Durhams look down their noses, English as icebergs, at hard-working folk? You become one of them when your background asserts itself in any show of contempt for those who work for your comforts."

21

Maurice knew he had slipped into a violation of his wise prescription not to mix the Old World with the new. He admitted to thoughtless arrogance toward the steward.

"I wish only to be your equal. For all my twenty-four years I have been taught otherwise and it will not be easy to undue. Forgive me."

That having already been done, they engaged passionately in their physical manner, at times rough and at times tender. As the excitement subsided Maurice pledged his troth.

"I wish to be as if married, yours to keep, and you mine."

"Are you daft, Maurice? Marriage is for a man with a woman, to have children. What need do we have of it?"

Maurice readily admitted, "Children cannot come in our case. We must forfeit family to be together. If you have doubt on that, or because of the newness and the strangeness of our love, I will wait until you know for certain."

Once more he enfolded Alec into his embrace and looked intently into his eyes.

"Marriage is union urged by love. I vow to strengthen our love by knowledge of your weaknesses and strengths, nursing the weaknesses and standing with you in your strengths. I imagine nothing more complete than such affection shared with you for a lifetime. If you choose to be mine, our hearts will seal the bargain."

Though it seemed daft at first, Alec knew that he could never love more than he did at this moment. Maurice was worthy of his devotion and needy of some commitment after all that he had heroically left behind. Alec's intuition led him to acceptance.

"I am your partner for life and you are mine."

No license recorded the pledges they made, nor could any encumbering contract prolong what their hearts might not sustain. They went to sleep that last night on the Olympic wed in body and spirit.

Chapter 2

How Maurice Became An Outlaw

The Sun woke me this morning loud and clear,
Saying...you may not be the greatest thing on earth,
but you're different...embrace things,
people earth sky stars, as I do, freely....
That is your inclination, known in the heavens,
and you should follow it to hell, if necessary,
which I doubt.

Frank O'Hara, "Talking to the Sun at Fire Island"

"Handsome is as handsome does" is an old saw that comes to mind with regard to Maurice's youth. He was gifted with a pretty face and a shock of light brown hair, and even as a boy his carriage was lithe and assuming. He bypassed adolescent awkwardness and blossomed early into a gentleman, fortunately without airs or undue delicacy. Not that his body became rugged, for hard work was foreign to him, and he engaged only half-heartedly in sports. But neither was his body too soft, though it inclined that way. So much may be attributed to the work of genes in fashioning a pleasing form.

Fortunately civilization made its contribution in graceful manners that completed the gentleman. He grew up in commodious surroundings with servants to attend his wishes. He had been taught to display consideration for others, thereby warranting from the women who served him an easy willingness to allow for capriciousness on his part or even harmless deviances. It was a lenience that might have been granted through adulthood except for the peculiar bent in the road he chose. Had Maurice been willing to fulfill the role birth offered him, one his father's early death designated, to serve as youthful head of the Hall family, he would have been permitted an occasional dalliance so long as discretion covered any misdeeds. Such private lapses of decorum the English world permitted young gentlemen.

His father had gone to business every day. It was assumed that Maurice would do likewise. After preparatory school his stay at Cambridge was intended as a stepping-stone. Not much was required of this assigned role that an ordinary male would be reluctant to fill, merely to marry a pretty young woman of standing, propagate the Hall bloodline, pursue his profession diligently, and serve England by embracing the orthodoxies of class, patriotism, and public service.

One peculiarity marked Maurice's manners. Consideration was largely displayed toward male members of his own class and toward female household servants. He was a stern patriarch toward his younger sisters whom he viewed as indolent creatures of frivolous tastes whose main occupation was to primp themselves and acquire feminine guile in order to entice men to provide for their wishes. It was only a matter of time before Maurice's disdain might turn into a surly dislike of upper-class women and a distrust of the female sex in general. Even his mother, to whom he was grateful for so much attention, was not spared rebukes for her attitudes and extravagances. Maurice determinedly restrained her whims to accomplish what his father had failed to do. He thought his father someone with little visible passion. Only later did he learn that his father had yielded to illicit passions by taking a mistress. When Mrs. Hall learned of these misadventures, Mr. Hall atoned for his sin by yielding patriarchal rights over domestic finances, though that was not her wish. In anger at such male abjection, Maurice vowed never to succumb to the female, a resolve that turned out easier to fulfill than might have been the case.

Ever since boyhood Maurice had been fascinated by virile men, the younger ones who cared for the house and garden, admiring their muscular movements as they worked and their husky voices as they jested in camaraderie. When his mother issued them orders, the boy watched in awe, imbibing the need to command into his social attitude. During adolescence his interest in these workmen aroused sensations that he barely understood. These inclined him toward physical closeness, but he kept a guarded reserve that might have been misconstrued as dislike. Even when he stared at their bared chests during the work of the summer he intuitively said nothing to suggest his feelings, sometimes able only to mutter a brief instruction. He knew that he had a proper role to sustain toward men of inferior status.

For the first twenty-three years of his life Maurice had stayed within the bounds allowed by polite society. Steeped in Anglican morality, or the memory of it, the young gentleman kept himself pure, unless one wishes to throw into the balance the pleasant activities of a wayward hand which did him more good than otherwise. In his second year at Cambridge, when he was twenty, meeting Clive Durham awakened his heart to something real. He would have been hard pressed to say what it was, enthralled though he was with the beauty of Clive. During the few years of their exceptional closeness that followed, his sensuality remained subdued, masked by ideals that the older Clive drew from Plato. Maurice knew no better. He was not an intellectual able to scrutinize such abstractions. The brain was one of his less developed organs though able to interfere with the others. Their relationship remained sterile because Clive was unwilling to consummate anything explicitly sexual. "It would pull us down," he would say in order to tame the natural impulses that Maurice showed. Clive had other aspirations more powerful, and fears more pressing, for he intended to be at one with society and the law, possibly one day to take a seat in Parliament to serve the conservative cause. He sensibly chose at the age of twenty-five to marry a woman who could further his career and provide Durham heirs.

Maurice was left rejected and battled to struggle with the pieces of his broken life. His friendship with Clive, the formative erotic experience of these years, frustrating as it was proving in the end, retained its hold as an idealized love between men. He needed to be close to Clive, despite the cold and abrupt way in which Clive had abandoned their intimacy, for love could not end this way. Whether Maurice truly loved is beside the point for he was unable to measure the intermix of romance and sublimated sexual excitement that he had enjoyed. Clive had left a sunken wreck behind, more aptly, a man without intimate friendship with another male. Maurice had no one to turn to for consolation, no one who might counsel a sensible course that would not, either from horror or pity at his condition, demand a reworking of what nature and life had wrought. Maurice spent a time running away from the "intermediate sex" that was to be found in the world without, in persons such as Risley, and that he feared might be found within, an identity that repulsed him. Nor was there a woman in whom he could confide, not his mother who already assigned him the position of family patriarch.

When he turned to the family physician for help, confiding "something is wrong with me," Dr. Barry inspected the affected organ and pronounced it functioning. "You're all right. Maurice, you get the right girl—ther'll be no more trouble then." Wither Clive had gone he must try to follow. But the right girl was nowhere to be found. Despondently he turned to a psychiatrist who probed into phobias and illicit desires residing in the troubled unconscious. Maurice was so sick at heart that the diagnosis was quick and clear, "congenital homosexuality" that could only be extirpated by returning to the roots of his sexual self. Using hypnosis to render Maurice susceptible to suggestion, the doctor implanted the image of a woman into Maurice's unconsciousness where her presence was supposed to awaken latent desire. When Maurice was released from the hypnotic surrender he was directed to combat any "poisonous urges" by recourse to moderate exercise. "A little tennis, or stroll about with a gun" was the prescription.

*   *   *

Sometimes bad advice works in mysterious ways to good ends. Hardly enlightened by the psychological counsel, and unmoved by the foreign introduction into his unconscious, Maurice returned to the Durham estate where he was visiting Clive, attempting to sustain the only deep friendship he had ever known. Since Clive was preoccupied with his new wife and with political ambitions, neglect plunged Maurice further into loneliness. He tried to pursue, as suggested, some manly exercise. A hunt was arranged, but at the last minute Clive was called away to some more important matter. Maurice thought of canceling since he was of no mood to take out his unhappiness upon other helpless creatures. As fate would have it, a healthy instinct prevailed that led him to accept company rather than pine away. Maurice sent word to the gamekeeper of the Durham estate that a brisk walk around the woods was all he felt up to that day, but that he wished his company.

Then the unlikely event occurred that changed everything. Maurice found solace in this gamekeeper, an unpretentious youth by the name of Alec Scudder, who gave friendship inappropriate in every way save one, that this earthy lad had perceived the key to Maurice's heart. As they trudged about the fields Maurice showed increasing interest toward his companion and less to the heavy thoughts or the gun he had brought along. He noticed Scudder's bright eyes in a way he had previously overlooked. When Alec expressed his animation for the walk, "Glad you came along, without Mr. Durham," Maurice found the husky voice assuring. What had initially irked him, that a gamekeeper showed no subservience, now comforted him.

"How can you be unhappy on such a pleasant day, roaming the woods? We need no hunt, Mr. Hall. I see that's not what you're needing."

Maurice was touched, and his facial features softened into a gracious grin, "How can you know what I am needing?"

"I have seen you, how Mr. Durham is bad for you. I know more than you think. What you need is fresh company. Enjoy the day with me, that much I'll promise you."

*   *   *

There was much of nature to appreciate in the summer woods that gave way to occasional clearings of high grass and yellow dandelions spotted by fields of wild flowers, and so they shared long silent intervals of watchfulness. They stumbled into a patch of brushes, disturbing a pair of rabbits who bounded away.

"He would have killed one, Mr. Durham I mean, and had me do the bloody task of carrying. But we can let this pair go to find happiness another place."

For his part Maurice was also glad Clive had chosen to be elsewhere. It allowed him to steal surreptitious looks at his guide's face and figure which were transformed by the sunlight. Alec's kindness and directness worked as water sprinkled upon a seed that had been lying fallow. Within a few hours Maurice changed until he felt a surprising tingling of erotic interest in Alec's natural gait and easy banter as he led their way. Feeling their differences lightening, Alec allowed himself to give voice to the slights and arrogances that were his employers' manner in dealing with him: "Scudder this! Scudder that!" Maurice could not help but laugh in sympathy.

Alec had taken him into confidence against risk of reprisal, and had unwittingly touched a deeply buried vein of resentment that Maurice bore for Clive and for the pretentiousness of his class. Maurice could not avoid a tremor of self-loathing, though he was careful to conceal it. He was emboldened to take some risk as well, to ask what pleasures Alec found to assuage his wounded dignity. He had a very good idea what the answer would be for his first sight of Alec had found him flirting with a serving maid, and on another later occasion he had heard the local vicar chastise Mrs. Durham for failure to see to the long delayed baptism of the gamekeeper who needed to be saved from sensuality and carnal sins.

Surprised by Maurice's interest, Alec replied no less surprisingly, "I spend a good amount of my leisure time alone, trying to understand things. Books from Mr. Durham's shelves teach me. True, they are as like to put me to sleep as a bedtime companion might, especially as there isn't else here to provide as suitable."

"You do have days of rest? Do you visit your family or, I suppose more likely, carouse with the local lasses?"

"My body asks fulfillment as surely as does my mind. Isn't it natural for someone young? I need sexual play, the same as you. There is no one here, as I said, that pleases me more than passing. I'm not ready to marriage

27

as some of the lasses wish. Nor might I ever be, at least until I have made something more of myself. Then I might want a family."

Maurice abandoned discretion, for sexual references awakened his daring. Alec, too, was excited that someone of Maurice's distinction was showing an interest in his feelings, and so he offered further revelation that his desires were far from Platonic.

"A man needs satisfaction, that is something matters, and not entirely to be found on his own. I wish for a mate who like myself strives to be clean and honest, not afraid to show spirit. I want trustworthiness before I give my heart completely. So I am ready to wait. At present there is learning to accomplish for I do not intend to stay as I am. You are likely to doubt, Sir, but I spend nights reading till the day's work requires sleep. If desires of another sort delay my rest, I know how to gain satisfaction by my own way."

Maurice was astounded by the discovery that Alec was more complex than he had credited any worker. It was the first crack in Maurice's smugness, only a crack. He had much in common with Clive for they had been suckled on the same fare of class and colonial privilege. Workers, especially the male of the species, were imagined as healthy animals suited to physical servitude and to reproduction of their own kind. Their bodies were tough from manual labor, their minds appropriately vulgar in taste and deed. Yet here was flesh and blood Alec breaking down social separateness, a worker seeking knowledge of the world through books, one thoughtful and attentive to male affections, whether from experience or intuition was unclear, perhaps even preferring a mate to a conventional marriage.

Their whole day together might have been ordinary in certain ways of walking and talking, but one thing was extraordinary. A world of feeling had begun to open to Maurice beyond the intellectual or the esthetic, an emanation from his body and from Alec's. The erotic was becoming a reality of look, of smell, of sound and, just before parting, of touch. As they drew in sight of the Durham house, still at a distance, Alec placed his arm across Maurice's lower back, his hand resting just below the hip, with affection that was as natural as it was bold. With that firm hand enfolding his backside, offering something more than Maurice had known, Clive receded into the past. Maurice had suffered enough of Clive, for the lure had all the while been physical, and ideals of Clive paled by contrast with the harmony of Eros when eye, mind and all the other senses aim to grasp the phallic object entirely. Maurice felt good about himself again for he was alive with feelings. Still hesitant to address his companion simply as Alec, Maurice thanked the gamekeeper for accompanying him that day. Then came one compelling intimacy. He allowed his eyes to cast a lingering look over each contour of Alec's body that plain clothes did not obscure.

Once again Alec understood. He was attracted to Maurice, not by any ideal, but by flesh pure and simple. He knew, as if some sixth sense were at work, that Maurice was soft and vulnerable to any physical display of passion as something he had long been awaiting, though only dimly conscious of it. That night Alec was so bold and so confident as to make an uninvited visit to Maurice's room.

*   *   *

But we are not yet finished with Maurice grappling with the layers of the past. Whatever else, Maurice was not worldly wise. He had been deeply excited by the event but he departed the Durham estate the next morning without a word to Alec. Three days later a letter arrived at the Hall residence. It was from Alec, annoyed at having been treated indifferently, suggesting they meet in the Durham boathouse. Maurice was too frightened to heed the call or even acknowledge it. He suspected Alec might seek some advantage or by just such recklessness expose them both to scandal.

Maurice fell back into the mood of anxiety and paralysis that had afflicted him of late. During the troubled state brought on by Clive's betrayal of their friendship, he had barely managed to escape total despair. Something natural within survived to save a precious part of himself. Perhaps it was the libidinal instinct that respected desire and would only recede into the unconscious in hope of awakening again, but Maurice had little of experience to set a course. Psychiatry had proven wanting, a masquerade of medical science, a disguised accomplice of theology which added sickness to the burden of sin. During lonely nights Maurice desperately sought some means to escape a life without love. He found a biography of Tchaikovsky, hoping the musician's life might suggest some suitable course, but the torment of the one only added to the torment of the other. Then he returned to the romantic tragedy of "Romeo and Juliet" which had planted a seed in his schoolboy mind a decade ago. When first encountering this ill fated love, he sensed that he might face the need to be deviant from the course his family and society assumed for him. Not only did he weep for the star-crossed lovers, but he thrilled to their illicit love and to the heroic action of a bold lover.

This second reading of thwarted love, just before Alec appeared, was to bear strange fruit. Maurice could not know that in some mysterious way the deeper yearnings of Shakespeare were readying the stage for Alec as heroic Romeo. Once events began to unfold at the Durham estate, that poignant drama of Juliet and Romeo cried out to Maurice not to allow a tragic end to a feeling as profound as he felt. What else did the fateful love of Juliet and Romeo bespeak if not a summons to daring and dreadful necessity, a call to lovers to defy imperious society, to cast aside a host of constraints that elevated the many considerations of family, property and religious morality above wayward feelings, no matter how true and pure those feelings felt to youth, no matter how heartless those impediments were to the fulfillment that seemed as imperative as the very nature of the world? That, at least, is how Maurice embraced the fateful drama.

Yet in the days that followed Alec's climb to Maurice, there were dreadful moments when Maurice confronted the reality that Alec was no Montague nor he a Capulet, posing only a family gulf such as faced Shakespeare's lovers. There were deeper, more insidious chasms of class and gender to confound the possibility of a conventional middle class person, such as Maurice knew himself to be, being bound with a rudely educated worker as lovers. Love had been awakened in him by the carnal, by the utter forcefulness of being taken for the first time in his life by the strength of another man who exuded assurance and virility. These are not to be despised. But how much of Alec's appeal was due to this ruggedness which had been carved out of the physical nature of his labor tending the stables for the wealthy? Could the physical passion he felt for Alec's body become the foundation for respecting the wholeness of a person? Even should that be possible for Maurice and, another near impossibility, Alec persist in his demonstrated passion, what about the assignations England had given to men who loved one another as outside the pale of religion, nature and law?

Tragedy and romance, when truth be told, are no solution to life. At times they offer to those imaginative momentary escape, a brief transcendence from personal turmoil. But practical living requires that we find faith amidst a heartless world, strength though our energy be sapped by anxiety, and adherence to the deepest sense of our selves as moral beings against a host of discouragements. Maurice was left wavering between a dream and despair.

*   *   *

Troubled by this sober situation, he made his way to the British Museum to do research into the legal boundaries for someone of his sexual nature. After some hemming and hawing, he was able to explain to

30

the clerk that what he was seeking was the criminal law code of England regarding sexual degeneracy. Fortunately a clerk who was diligent in his duty, neither inquisitive nor judgmental, helped him find access to the particular volume of laws that safeguarded England's purity. He found the Criminal Law Amendment Bill of 1885 whose words cut into Maurice like rapiers to further trouble his heart with images of hard labor as a criminal, merely for loving Alec! He pondered over and over the words of the Act as they might apply.

"Any male person who, in public or private, commits, or is party to the commission by any male person of any act of gross indecency with another male person, shall be guilty of a misdemeanour, and being convicted shall be liable at the discretion of the court to be imprisoned for any term not exceeding two years, with or without hard labour."

Maurice drew small comfort from discovering that the amended act was more lenient than the laws it replaced which had exacted punishments of life imprisonment, even hanging, for the same acts called sodomy. Maurice was in no mood for historical celebration of progress. The laws of England still demanded amputation of his penis, at least symbolically, as an instrument of passion. Was there any way to love Alec without endangering him as well, for the courts of the land were harsh, more so to the poor than to the affluent.

He left the library to wander the lonely streets of London for lack of direction. Passersby were indifferent toward him as he was with their ventures. The sight of two lovers only made his alienation more repressive. He was obsessed with morbid fears of the danger of his yielding to love. He was near fainting with the secret knowledge that he had already done just that, and that disclosure of his crime would mean imprisonment for him and Alec, as well as humiliation for his mother. If all this shame were brought upon his family, he might serve years of imprisonment, and afterward, if he persisted in continuing a ruined life, no matter that it sought its meaning in love, there was danger of the degeneration of his body and soul into an inhuman existence, for such was the proclaimed wisdom of medical practitioners and theologians. Little wonder Maurice's heart was heavy with hopelessness. He yearned for someplace no theology or law could reach, where love could be free from society's intrusiveness.

*   *   *

What we call fate often takes a hand in human enterprises. This mysterious working invokes the world outside our ruminations, often through a stranger unexpectedly presenting a situation that confronts

31

as yet unclear yearnings of one's spiritual self in a way that forces clarification. The new direction in life that ensues seems as if determined by an unknown force of fate.

Maurice had been moving aimlessly through the Bloomsbury district until he found himself in one of those lovely green squares of London. Exhausted mentally and physically, no longer capable of pride or prudence, he sought to rest. He approached a bench occupied by an ungainly man in his sixties whose unkempt gray hair fell across both sides of his forehead.

"If you would be so kind as to share, I am needful of rest." Without awaiting a reply Maurice sank heavily onto the seat as he sighed with unhappiness. The elderly man surmised in an instant that the occasion called for kindness.

"It is not merely physical exhaustion besetting you, young man. Your visage and breath convey the weariness of your spirit that is overburdened. If I may be of help, let us talk. You would do me a favor by drawing my thoughts away from absorption in my own melancholy. Fate may be drawing us together to help each other."

Kindness in the stranger's tone allowed a troubled Maurice to speak with unaccustomed frankness.

"I am discouraged and confused because I am different from most men when it comes to love and I do not know how to find my way."

"I could be more helpful if you find the courage to identify the difference you feel, that which renders you lonely in your confusion. You are right to hold reserve before strangers. Perhaps it will release you to know that I follow the noble sentiment of Montaigne, 'I am human, and nothing human is foreign to me.' All that I am willing to judge harshly is cruelty of deliberate sort."

"That sentiment assures me I will profit from conversing with you. I do not know love's limits when it draws together people of the same sex. What I learned at Cambridge seems of little use when my heart is pitted against the morality and laws of society."

"Ah, a Cambridge man. That we have in common, too, though I studied there long ago." Almost as if he understood everything now, though the fact was he had insight into only one thing, the crux of the matter, he proceeded in a way that was to help Maurice escape his distress.

"It is more immoral to suppress one's own body than to allow it a natural place."

While Maurice pondered the matter, an explanation ensued. "When I was your age, thanks to the impression made upon me by a Cambridge scholar who hailed the humanism of the ancient Greeks, I came to understand that a society without truth and free speaking, especially regarding the passions of love, would stifle my spirit if I succumbed to its dictates. I overcame fright and found another direction."

"But if danger of imprisonment would result from the truth? Wouldn't it be better to live within conventionality?"

"Of course you are right when it comes to imprisonment. One must circumvent the law that deserves no respect. In that most individual of desires, the passion to love, however, happiness may not rest within social acceptance. To live untruthfully is dangerous in its own way. For myself, I had to lay myself open to new ideas once I understood this imperative, even when they exposed me to ridicule."

"Pardon me, sir, I have no heart to offend you, since I appreciate the help you are providing me. But is it your own regret you now express for never having dared sufficiently to defy convention?"

He smiled gently. "You are wise to wonder. I am so drab and ordinary a person, as was true of my youth. I was no free thinker at Cambridge! I have never been a rampant Bohemian. I am discredited on those counts. It took more than studied knowledge of the Greeks to loosen me from a stifling dullness. Yet I owe much to the classics. I dared at least to think and feel. That permitted me to love."

Maurice's rejoinder was quick. "I read some of Plato's 'Symposium' at Cambridge and thought I saw myself there. Presently I have no use for it. Idealism is no substitute for physical love."

"When I speak of the Greeks I refer to the humanism encompassed by all their arts, especially sculpture, not to the rational dialogues of Plato. Athenians sought beauty in the natural, rendered in ideal or perfect form, such as the Parthenon, or the beauty of the human body depicted as Venus and Adonis. Through their eyes I stared into the face of erotic love, which led me to escape the stifling atmosphere of my upbringing."

He paused to receive approval before any further revelation. Maurice nodded his assent, and in that slight encouragement he allowed fate to play its role. Character is also important to the working out of fate. The wise man proceeded apace.

"Believe me, I was young then as you are now, and it was not easy to find my way from the pious simplicity I was taught to the Greeks. When I was fourteen I pondered the whole of the Bible in total immunity to human passions other than seeing them as sinful. I accepted what I was told was the meaning of bizarre texts. Of course I no longer have Christian convictions. One might say I am a pagan, for I consider all that the mind and body enjoy a healthy part of our humanity."

"How did you find the courage?"

"It was a long courtship that always continues. About your age, I realized that I had been living under a tyranny of religion, a kind of obsession that kept me in anguish over what God had made and what God ordained. A tremendous universe was closed to my thinking. Thanks to something beyond myself, to wiser mentors, and the ferment of the Cambridge community, a miracle occurred. The whole range of human experience was gradually transformed by reason into truth that opened to me. I escaped the dullness of conformity. I saw human desires as healthy, not sinful.

"I do not wish to suggest that I unburdened myself of falsity at once. My thoughts were bolder than my deeds. I was still proudly British and in that way separated from fellow races. Athenian dedication to the polis was distorted in my loyalty to national honor. Until 1914 I believed in civilization. Then the shock of war brought a kind of death to me because of such mad destruction of all that really counts. Beautiful young men were destroyed on both sides of battle for inhumane reasons. I could no longer tolerate the hypocrisies of society or of my own life, nor allow any more of the presumptions of society and nation to speak for me."

Maurice was made bold by the spirit of this man who was no longer a stranger, for compassion had replaced time as a measure of trust. He felt his heart lifted from the depths of despair. Without shame he could speak the truth.

"I love someone of my own sex, though society calls it unnatural and immoral. He is pure, honest, a worker eager to learn about the world, the equal to any Athenian ideal."

"If you have found a love where body and mind mix, then it is natural for you. That may be morality, the one you should uphold."

After further dialogue the kindly guide bade Maurice to accompany him a short way through the shadowy park, like Dante's figure of Virgil guiding Maurice out of a circle of hell. At a corner of the square stood a statue of Spinoza with his words imprinted on the base: "A free man thinks of death least of all. His wisdom is a meditation not of death, but of life."

For awhile they stood together in silence that was broken at last.

"It was Spinoza's view that 'Nothing exists except by universal laws of nature.' Perhaps this will help to answer your question."

Then the gentle man departed.

*   *   *

The revelation that "the truth shall set you free" no longer was lost in irony, thanks to a fateful encounter. Maurice decided that he must live as his nature urged, no matter the risks. He had performed criminal acts and would do so again, but they were criminal only because the laws of England claimed power over nature. Not instinct, certainly not the natural laws of the universe, but society had made him a criminal. His desire for Alec was natural because such physical intimacies were as vital to him as any truth to which humans lay claim. Up to now he had suppressed desire, disguised his real self, and performed roles he had been taught were part of being a man. No one had revealed to him that only through love for another man might his spirit soar. This truth would be his uneasy path to freedom. Struggle would be incumbent for the whole of his life, but at this precious moment urgency was necessary if a truthful outcome were to avoid an ending that would be tragic.

Maurice arranged a meeting with Alec. Some bitter words were exchanged, for each had suspected the other of bad motives, but a ruling passion brought them to an inexpensive hotel where magical moments clarified matters, for Maurice at least. Alec was equally pleased with the moment but had scant thought of a future together. He had served Maurice's needs and his own as well. As they were parting, he thanked Maurice as a farewell, nonchalantly mentioning that the next month he would be off with his family to work and live in Argentina.

"We must meet again," Maurice insisted, and so it was arranged that they would meet a week later.

On that occurrence their minds agreed which led them to that October day when they set sail aboard the Olympic.

*   *   *

Smoothing the matter with his mother was difficult. Maurice did not dare confide in her, for he did not trust women. Their way when troubled was to run to a patriarch, attorney, physician or even a priest to seek solace. Such misplaced confidence would endanger his plans. He cast the trip to America in contradictions as he sought to win his mother's acquiescence. At first he posed it as a need for adventure, a year of travel with a friend, some kind of rite of passage. Who was this mysterious friend? He revealed that Alec was a respectable son of a shop-owner, though he withheld the name Scudder or any link to the Durhams. Even this evoked consternation and concerns from Mrs. Hall about improper company for meeting others of influence and gaining benefits of travel. That turned Maurice's explanation into a possibility of a longer stay, a matter of solidifying his knowledge of business. He spoke of becoming acquainted with their Philadelphia relatives. The latter was a ruse, but remembering the closeness of his mother to her brother George, until marriage carried him to the United States, Maurice shamelessly sought some explanation she would tactfully accept. Though Mrs. Hall could barely fathom the root of the matter, she finally yielded to Maurice's persistence. She pressed a large sum of money upon "her Maurice" so that he would travel with proprieties. She wrote to her brother asking him to facilitate Maurice's search for what she considered a year-long position. It remained for Maurice to straighten things with another letter to his uncle in which he forthrightly stated his hope to settle in Philadelphia.

What continued to trouble Mrs. Hall was Maurice's rebuff of her wish to meet Alec. He let slip that "Alec was too busy with work earning his way" to spend time entertaining new friends. Maurice had not arrived at a safe haven. She persisted in a reasonable request until Maurice had to be cruel and peremptory. Now he angrily stated that with all the arrangements to be made for the voyage neither of them had time for such nonsense! What else could Maurice do except leave Alec a shadow figure? He lied about Alec's background. He spoke of their friendship in ways that covered the passion that was at its heart. Alec remained a mystery except that Mrs. Hall knew he was a threat to the hopes she had for Maurice. When the moment came for tearful farewells she had a foreboding in her heart. Maurice would not let her accompany him to the train. "No more tears or nonsense," he insisted.

*   *   *

Surrounded by pandemonium of people and the noise of engines, Maurice and Alec met at Waterloo Station in London. Until that moment, Maurice had queasily contained the butterflies flitting about in his stomach, but he could no longer resist diarrhea that plagued him during tense moments. Alec good-naturedly laughed at his friend's plight. Maurice excused himself once more to attend to his urgent need, returning just before the train's departure.

A two-hour race to Southampton brought them to the dock where Maurice's trunk and one large suitcase were conveyed to the ship. Unused to amenities of any sort, Alec clung to his earthly possessions. So meagerly had England rewarded him for all his labor that everything he carried fit into a single bag. As they approached the ship Alec noticed a gentleman observing him in a friendly way and listening to the excited babble he was sharing with Maurice. He addressed the interested party, "We're off

36

to America on the Olympic!" The man smiled, "I too am a passenger. Let us pray for a smooth voyage" and then he boarded the ship. Both Alec and Maurice were lost in the excitement of the moment as they headed to a different ramp that led to less exquisite quarters than awaited the gentleman who had paid them heed.

Chapter 3

The Apple of a Mother's Eye

From childhood's hour I have not been
As others were — I have not seen
As others saw — I could not bring
My passions from a common spring.

Edgar Allan Poe, "Alone"

Will the man or woman never come to whom love
in its various manifestations shall be a perfect whole,
pure and natural, standing sanely on its feet?

Edward Carpenter, LOVE'S COMING OF AGE

Alec could lay claim to few advantages of birth, certainly not those that heralded Maurice's coming. To begin with, his mother was a poor wisp of a girl who fled her home in the west of Ireland to escape the shame of unholy childbirth. Luckily she had put away small savings which allowed her to depart the barren, rocky land of Connacht which lay remote from any secular humanism that might have eased her predicament. Mary O'Bryan it was who had never traveled beyond the Shannon River. If not quite a miracle, it was remarkable that she managed to flee across the Irish Sea. She arrived in London with red hair and freckled face announcing her native roots. London offered neither welcome nor any friend to assist her way. St. Brigit, however, looked after Mary and led her to Scudder, a man whose heart was not made of stone. In time both Mary and Alec were to become Scudders.

When Alec entered the world it was without a father, nor was any man accorded recognition. Mary was proud enough to bear the child on her own and to settle on his name, foregoing any baptismal blessing from an unforgiving church. Resentment over these rejections gave her reason to deny a man whose only role had been a heedless moment of passion. It was her body that had done all the work in forming the child and her life's work that would see to the upbringing of a man. In due time the child was told the barest details. Though Alec was not the blessed fruit of an immaculate conception, the man who had contributed to his creation remained invisible, for he had not wished to be husband or father. They went without some material comforts that a hardworking father is apt to provide. Young Mary O'Bryan, dedicated to the welfare of her child, did the best she could, but being a woman in a patriarchal world, she was condemned to work for lower wages than were paid the poorest of males. Then the boy lacked a steady male influence, perhaps just as well, for the natural father would have taught him drinking and deserting ways. Scudder and his sons partially filled the breach.

Despite these adversities Alec should still be counted fortunate beyond many children who enjoy the presence of both parents. His mother celebrated him as a blessing, refusing to let resentments against church and wayward men corrupt her motherhood. Mary's devotion laid the foundation for Alec's healthy ability to love unselfishly when he had grown into manhood. Even as the baby lived within her womb, she quietly fell to all the tasks that society divides between mother and father but that misfortune, provoked by the misdeeds of passion, allotted solely to her. So much the worse her foolishness in failing to measure her deed before defying religion and prudence. Still, Mary never breathed a regret at having borne Alec, nor did she become bitter or thereafter dislike the male of the species. She clung to her serenity once, thanks to St. Brigit, she had surmounted the ordeal of giving birth. A brief apology for the absence of her distant family was all she spoke to anyone, the boy included, though this sadness shaped a seriousness in Alec who often asked why they did not live in their native land. She told only half the story, that "our kin live from hand to mouth. One more mouth was more than the land could take. My father had to pay rents to English landlords which ate up any provision for comforts."

Mary's recourse had been the only she could imagine, flight from a hostile environment starved in land and in consolation when it came to sinners of the flesh. Much ado was made by the Catholic religion in Ireland of saints and rituals and evil spirits. Life and death, and all between, were mired in a narrow superstition that had little to assist a girl who had surrendered to the devil's wiles.

*   *   *

Even in the absence of a larger family Alec was cradled with love. It needs be added that this surfeit of attention continued into boyhood. He became used to being the beneficiary of complete attention from his mother who spared neither time nor devotion for him, as she spurned further liaisons with men. Alec was the man of her life. In this way his character was steadily shaped surrounded by security to his worthiness and manliness. He would never fall victim to the kind of masculine arrogance that finds expression in the need to dominate a woman. Fortunately, despite all attention, neither was he pampered into a spoiled child, such as one too often encounters in our times, the child who disdains goods given in abundance for his disposal. Those who never learn that hard work is needed to produce worldly goods are likely to be rude and presumptuous. Alec learned the value by serving as proud helpmate to his mother.

He loved one special woman, and he came to appreciate the role of women as he observed their devotion and their sufferings due to patriarchal ways. He became immune to the rigidities of gender separation of the species. Such generosity of spirit, grown from a seed that often lies fallow in children, allowed him to become winsome in his ways as he blossomed into early manhood. He learned to act as might naturally occur should there ever exist a society where men are not taught to flatter, to seduce, and to abuse women. In this gentleness, spared gender distortion, and in all respects, he was untouched by proprieties or prejudices of ordinary upbringing. He learned to express feelings as they were felt. For all but one discrepancy his mother's native good sense must be credited. As fortune would have it, he was further encouraged in consideration toward others by good and watchful neighbors, especially the Scudders, who offered a lonely mother a needed hand.

Alec did not possess such a pretty face as was Maurice's boon. Admirers more likely noted the coal black hair that casually framed his face than the face itself, or the intense brown eyes that focused amiably. His adolescent form was scrawny, hardly drawing attention, but as he turned fifteen his body developed muscularity and handsome proportion. By manhood he presented a well-shaped physique evincing a strength that stemmed as much from his lifework as his lifeline. Nowadays we attribute too much to the passage of genes. Something must be conceded to their say, of course, but in Alec's case more needs be attributed to the manual labor that accompanied his economic situation. From the age of five he did hard work appropriate to his size, carrying weights, assisting his mother in scrubbing floors or other sundry tasks, lending a hand to the chores of the kitchen; and then when he was fifteen he left school to assume a man's labor, eventually working outdoors. Manual labor demanded efforts and endurances that saw to the hardening of his muscles. In this gradual way his body acquired strength and proportion partially destined, but a destiny that a coddled or dissolute life would have defeated.

Young girls and lads were drawn by his congeniality, but as often by his eyes that conveyed attentiveness. It had become his habit from close listening to his mother to scrutinize any interlocutor as if to signal how much he valued the other. Once beyond puberty, if his sexual interest was aroused, he became familiar to the point of flirtatiousness, showing no distinction among the sexes. His movements displayed the gusto of self-confidence. He would stand with his legs firmly planted, hands thrust into his trouser pockets, adding command to his presence, sometimes to the point of cockiness. This candid show of availability was something his mother tried to ward off for she feared it might impede the boy's moral character. She attributed looseness of sexual conduct to the O'Bryan men whose reputation for imbibing hard liquor and arduously pursuing women had scattered across half County Connacht.

*   *   *

When Alec was fifteen his mother died unexpectedly which rendered him disconsolate, lonely, bereft. The Spanish flu was unmerciful to Mary as it was to many millions of others who perished in late 1917 and during the winter that followed. For the first time Alec was caught in a world without women. He had basked in the warmth of his mother's devotion, but fortunately the Scudders had helped him to learn how men act. He had now to enter the domain where men compete with each other for work, where they dominate one another, as they do women and children. He had to toughen his spirit, resorting as needed to fisticuffs as a means of gaining respect.

He was not spiritually cut off from women for his mother remained as a living moral force. Beyond her steadfast love and good-natured performance of duty, his mother had left him instructions to guide him through life. He should turn to St. Brigit in prayer whenever in need and never fail to thank her. Mary had told him stories of homeless Brigit who in her wandering had learned compassion, especially for women giving birth. Though Mary was no longer a churchgoer, she took him on an occasional pilgrimage to St. Bride's Church in London where he became acquainted through an icon with the gentle face of the saint whose outstretched hands extended compassion. Mostly what abided from this instruction were the personal stories Mary told of how the saint helped her find the courage when she fled her home in fear of imminent disgrace, and again when she arrived in London bereft and alone. She had prayed desperately to St. Brigit who put her into the path of a kind man, William Scudder, who helped her through her condition. He provided a room at the back of his butcher's shop in return for sundry help, though he had three boys who had done the same tasks till then. Mrs. Scudder, a good woman in deed, took pity on Mary's condition, and then for the child whose birth she attended, though she felt relieved when Mary was able to take full employment elsewhere and afford a small dwelling of her own. Not that she was jealous or suspicious. She had put her own sexuality to rest, but she recalled her own experience as a pretty young girl when she had been the recipient of favors from Scudder, how one thing led to another. She did not want Mary to slip into a second folly with a man already committed to a sufficient family.

Even with a little more distance between them, over the next several years Mary continued to receive attention from Scudder, though whether she attributed that as well to her guardian saint we cannot know. She was aware of the man's feelings when visiting his shop for provisions, and she welcomed one benefit that flowed from his visual pleasure: the charges he assayed never added-up to the goods received. Mrs. Scudder also offered needy affection to both mother and boy. From the first she delighted in the infant, and she watched the appearance of the boy's dark hair and eyes that offered an enchanting contrast to his fair complexion. She jested to Scudder, "There is something of mystery in this boy. Then Mary has a right to her secrets." Mrs. Scudder was earthy regarding sexual matters as in all her conduct. Her attitude, conveyed to her sons and to Alec, was not high church or low. Her guidance was simply spun.

"One needs to mingle with all kinds of folk, sexual ways and otherwise, to learn first hand about their goodness and badness. Not marry the first who comes along, God forbid. Better find out where affection is deserved. No shame in learning what the other is capable of or how some intimacies please or not, despite what priests say. They know nothing of these things. It takes bad memories to open our eyes and hearts. My own life could be brought in evidence, if I had a mind to speak."

`But she never did speak more than a hint of her waywardness. Nor did she ever address the slightest reproach about the misalliance Mary had mistakenly entered. If anything, knowledge of men did not surprise her that one had shirked his flesh and blood. It only led her to be more tender to the needs of this fatherless family. Year by year she grew more protective and, in that kind of saintliness that a living St. Brigit must have shown, took the role of mother to Mary. Her experiences with three Scudder boys had enriched her appreciation of the male of the species, which she extended to Alec. On holidays Mary and Alec spent the days with the Scudders. "One more will hardly be noted," Mrs. Scudder assured Mary, "and it will be a good matter for Alec to be around other boys." Mrs. Scudder liked to stroke Alec's coal black hair, pass her hand down the scruff of his neck, and plant kisses upon his cheeks to see them color. She would laugh aloud, "It is a good thing there is no O'Bryan thinking himself father. This boy has something mysteriously foreign." Mary, however, would not lend credence to such a thought.

*   *   *

Eight years passed between Mary's arrival and Mrs. Scudder's death, when Scudder found himself with responsibility for two sons who still remained in his charge. During his trouble he turned to Mary who had come to view the Scudders as her family. Though twice her age he was not long before inviting her to join him in marriage, pointing out the advantages that would fall to Alec. Mary did not turn away Scudder's overtures outright, though out of respect for Mrs. Scudder, she treated them as premature until more than a year had passed. No longer a girl, for adversity and hard work had taken their toll, she clung to her objective to help Alec gain a better life, which she made a condition of any acceptance of Scudder. The boy was in the third year of elementary school where he was doing well in reading and numbers, and on this course she determined he would stay. She knelt before the four-armed St. Brigit's cross of rushes which hung above her bed, praying for guidance. When the inspiration of the saint had become clear, she expressed her conditional acceptance to the man who implored her love. She had become shrewd from disappointment, so she insisted,

"Scudder, I am thankful for your offer to care for me and my boy. I have devoted my life to Alec and will continue so. He will have his education, certain it be, else the name of Scudder will never attach to me or to him. I swore to the good Saint I would not leave him to work his body to ruin for those who are idle. Alec must learn to do the work of the mind and become a gentleman."

No matter that her love for Brigit and these worldly ambitions for Alec conflicted.

Scudder accepted that contract so that the two could marry. He kept to his word for as long as Mary lived which was another six years until her time was cut short by the Spanish influenza. During those years Alec Scudder completed elementary school and when he was twelve went on to secondary school where for three more years he studied geography, the history of England but not of Ireland, and a good deal of grammar and literature. Neither was his education a match for Maurice's, but he was not without the rudiments of literary taste and intellectualism. His schooling came to a halt after Mary's death when Scudder decided it was time for Alec to work for his keep. It was not from meanness or indifference to the promise that this decision flowed. It seemed right to Scudder who treated Alec as he had the other Scudders. Alec was put to long work in the butcher shop for the next few years until he had his fill of the bloody surroundings.

*   *   *

When Alec was seventeen he was employed by the Durhams to tend their grounds and serve as gamekeeper. For the next four years he worked outdoors while his body grew strong. Nor did he neglect development of his wits now that he was liberated from the blood and carcasses of his father's trade. He became a close observer of the Durhams and their society. He rankled at their haughtiness, especially detesting the way they rendered invisible menials such as himself. The resentments he harbored concerned privileges of birth as they were squandered. He was anguished by the indulgences of the Durham women, contrasted with the deprivations his mother had suffered, less from poverty than for yielding to natural passion. There germinated within him, whether the locus was his heart or mind, an understanding that he was biding time, awaiting the day when he would strike out for some role that would honor his mother's determination that he never surrender to serving the idle rich. But he had no ambition to lord it over the poor.

One morning after receiving the day's instructions from Clive who was seated at his desk as befitted the heir to the Durham estate, Alec hesitated in going about his work until Clive noticed there was something more. Alec asked permission to avail himself of the Durham library that surrounded them. Clive was generous, consenting that Alec choose whatever reading might benefit him, though he advised books on practical matters, an advice that Alec felt he need consider. Thus Alec embarked on an adventure of the mind that lightened his manual labor. During years when many a working youth succumbs to the flesh, Alec read far into the night. He carefully removed from the shelves one at a time books Clive recommended, not merely from prudence but to cover the true direction of his questioning. He read enough of each book Clive named to present some clumsy answer, all that would be expected, should he ever be asked about one of the suggested titles, but Clive was too condescending to inquire. Hence Clive did not discover the remarkable youth in his employ.

Alec was awed by this wonderful library, the likes of which he had never perused. There were complete sets of Shakespeare, Dickens, and Austen, the master works of the literary lights of England, and modern playwrights, Wilde and Shaw. Alec bypassed most of these for his sense of the world was neither escapist nor fictional. He knew there would be drama enough for him in time. He was fascinated to find books in half a dozen foreign languages. Why this amazed him he was uncertain, for of course books of weight and esthetic worth were produced by every civilized nation. He regretted that he barely recognized their tongues, though he placed Dante as Italian, Balzac French, and a scientific work German. When it came to philosophy he could not settle on either ancient or modern for the tomes were ponderous, Idealists claiming human history to be movement of Spirit through time, and the Materialists seeking causes and effects through matter in motion. How was Alec to weigh the truth of such sweeping abstractions? With feet firmly planted Alec determined to preserve the power of seeing the world directly with his own eyes.

The closest he came to embracing any writer was Voltaire for his impudence in the story of Candide. The naïve youth, falsely instructed by Pangloss, believes that "everything in the world is for the best." Disaster after disaster occurs, and then a shipwreck casts them ashore in Lisbon after an earthquake has crushed to death thirty thousand people. Pangloss is on a street corner explaining that even this greatest of catastrophes has a benign explanation, when an Inquisitor overhears him. The Inquisition has determined to sacrifice some heretics to appease divine wrath, and so Pangloss is seized and hung for denying punishment for original sin. Candide is only whipped for having listened to heresy, but in a lacerated and bloodied state, he is left in puzzlement, "If this is the best of all possible worlds, what must the others be like?"

Alec searched for knowledge more practical, though he construed that direction in larger scope than Clive intended. He found Darwin's **The Descent of Man** which provided a rude map toward finding his place in the world. He pondered for months massive data about rudimentary structures of various creatures, sense-organs, hair, bones, and reproductive parts, until he had no further quarrel with Darwin that man bears in his bodily frame the indelible stamp of his lowly origin. Alec felt no shame at this, only an increased distaste for human presumptions, even his own mother's intent that he seek a place among gentlemen, dine at their table, so to speak, as if he could or should shed his affinity to the lowly beasts of the field.

45

Pretending to follow the master of the house's direction, he made a show of delving into the history of England, dropping an occasional remark before Clive. Truth was that Macaulay soon tired him with his boastful English pride in parliament and conquest. Alec put that history aside as English self-serving. He recalled an experience that gave him secret pleasure. During the Great War he had heard an Irish agitator charge that "Irish soldiers in the English army are fighting in Flanders to win for Belgium, so they falsely tell us, all those things the British Empire, now as in the past, denies to Ireland." Alec was 16 years of age when this insightful truth brought to his heart a lingering Irish pride of place.

Into his second year of perusing the Durham library, he wandered into psychology. He learned the human mind had evolved along with the body. He was astounded to learn the mind harbors a vast unconscious of strange and forbidden fruit. What turned out to be of compelling interest was the encounter with Havelock Ellis' *Studies in the Psychology of Sex*. True to his youth, when he saw six volumes he thought to begin at the end so that he might reap with less endeavor the conclusions to the work. He carried away the last volume where he became intrigued with a postscript in which Ellis explains that censorship in England forced him to publish the complete work in Philadelphia. Alec's attention was drawn to this particular matter thanks to Clive who had angrily written a note in the margin expressing indignation with the English government for having confiscated the original first volume, which dealt with sexual inversion, and prosecuting the publisher on grounds of indecency. Clive's marginal remarks reflected a more exuberant time of deep passion toward a friend identified only as M. for he had scrawled the sentiment, "Let love shared by C. and M. remain steadfast as it is pure, enduring in its beauty as Ideal, so that it enflame other human souls with a liberating passion." Clive's revelation was adjoined to Ellis's text which read,

"He who follows in the steps of Nature after a law that was not made by man, and is above and beyond man, has time as well as eternity on his side, and can afford to be both patient and fearless. Men die, but the ideas they seek to kill live. Our books may be thrown to the flames, but in the next generation those flames become human souls."

Alec was excited by this reading and delved further into sexual inversion, an idea that was perplexing. Nonetheless he was satisfied that Ellis portrayed all human sexual inclinations in a natural way, as if lawlessness were the character of man's erotic passions. Alec became confident that for many a person, himself for certain, homosexuality is as natural as any other sexual deed. Now he was bolstered by scientifically gathered information to conclude that it is human society that curbs man's nature, generally for worse rather than the better. He had a new curiosity toward Clive, who had hitherto seemed sexless, wondering what expressions his love for M. might have taken.

*   *   *

Among precious bits of advice that Alec received from his mother, second only to reverence for the good saint, she urged another more earthly caution. "Never be misguided by liquor or lust into fooling some girl, trying to gain your way, unless prepared to marry when she becomes with child." This warning stemmed not entirely from her experience, which after all had turned out satisfactorily enough, but as much from her lowly opinion of the behavior of the O'Bryan men. It was not a warning presented grimly, nor with any threat of hell. She had not heedlessly chosen tolerant St. Brigit for patron. She intended to shape responsible conduct becoming to a young man of propriety and to a father. How much this advice contributed to Alec's behavior while in the employ of the Durhams will be left obscure, though he was not entirely forgetful of it.

Yet he did not spend all his free time reading. He had an eye for pretty faces and shapes female or male. He easily settled for what chance encounters occurred with local youth, adventures that came to hand, as opportunity would have it. Those conjunctions when they occurred with the opposite sex were with girls of his class. With males the social line extended once he worked in the country when on occasions a shy son of a gentleman showed interest in him enough to encourage boldness. Whether from youth or deliberation these encounters were dalliances, as he did not throw himself fully into any passion, disappointing not a few of the lasses. Many an attention was accorded him, leaving him at ease with common folk and with young men from all the walks of life.

Some explanation need be given for Alec's behavior that might seem promiscuous, gender notwithstanding, despite Mary's sound warnings. At the time he became a Scudder, Alec at the age of eight was thrown together with two Scudder boys, squeezed into the middle portion of a bed as his sleeping quarter. Master of the bed was the older Robert who was already eager to impress his sexual prowess over the girls of the neighborhood. Thirteen-year-old Denis was ready to explore all possibilities that provided some play. Alec became used to their bodies, finding comfort in the warmth and assurance such closeness offered. He had not previously been around men in such intimate sharing of space or manners.

Even before his own sexual needs took hold he observed with fascination the genital organ of the older brother. He watched when Robert stripped

47

nude or relieved himself with cock in hand. It was innocent knowledge acquired from his first brush with males, opportunity to satisfy curiosity. He took more excited notice of Robert's erections as he lay sleeping when the penis sometimes would spill out of its underwear into the early morning light. Alec became curious to touch it, as if to assess its firmness with scientific precisions, though gently, so as not to awaken Robert. But the older lad was not a log, and once he felt the interest shown by his new brother, he showed him how to more vigorously stimulate that part of the male body. Alec was in even greater awe when he witnessed a writhing climax for the first time, after which Robert returned to sleep in an instant while Alec observed the penis shrink to softness. Naturally before long Alec turned attention to his own small genital that seemed ample for ordinary purposes. He began to fondle it until a time when he discovered his own capacities. These sensations, amidst their happy boyhood setting, were far more exciting than ordinary experiences. There was nothing of abuse in them, only camaraderie in discovery of that most powerful of experiences.

Denis, who knew something about sexual intercourse only in crude words, would jest about the carrying-on of his father with his second mother, remarking upon sounds from the adjoining bedroom. He explained things to Alec in boyish ways. Alec listened with skepticism as little by little he began to piece together what he culled from exchanges between his brothers, for Robert occasionally recounted his sexual exploits. One night the sounds from the parental bedroom excited Denis who began to masturbate. Robert was not yet settled in, and so Denis felt master of the bed. He pounced upon Alec, introducing his penis into the boy's mouth. "It won't hurt you any" was the extent of his consideration. When the deed was complete, true to Denis's promise it had not hurt. "Just spit out" which Alec did. Such sexual play being satisfying, Alec had no reason to deny his brother further pleasure. "Boys do this sort of thing for one another," Denis could assure the younger. Because Denis seemed so grateful and at ease, there followed many similar occasions, until Denis reached the age where his adventures focused outside the home, no longer shared with his younger brother except in telltale ways.

Alec's affection for Denis continued none the less, though his gaze, too, turned elsewhere once he was old enough to seek reciprocity among his peers. At secondary school he befriended a boy his age, Oliver, who showed curiosity for experience, so Alec initiated him into the ways of sexual pleasure as Denis had done for him. For the next few years, until he left school to work in his father's shop, he had a companion who followed him around in a ready manner, worshipping his prowess. Without fully

48

comprehending the matter, Alec discovered psychological satisfaction in holding another person to willing submission. Though he came to know girls sexually, none of that experience supplanted the memories of easy intimacy with the Scudders or the devotion he had gotten from an adolescent friend. These memories would remain true of his mature sexuality.

When Denis went off to war and got himself killed during the last months of the bloodshed in 1918, Alec grieved deeply over the waste of such a healthy life. He remembered their times together, finding in such memories the most precious friendship he had known. For the second time in this year he suffered grief for someone he loved and who had departed.

Not long after he left the Scudder shop and house forever.

Chapter 4

An Interruption at Ellis Island

Not like the brazen giant of Greek fame,
With conquering limbs astride from land to land,
Here at our sea-washed, sunset gates shall stand
A mighty woman with a torch, whose flame
Is the imprisoned lightning, and her name
Mother of Exiles. From her beacon-hand
Glows world-wide welcome, her mild eyes command
The air-bridged harbor that twin-cities frame.

"Keep ancient lands, your storied pomp!" cries she,
With silent lips. "Give me your tired, your poor,
Your huddled masses yearning to breathe free,
The wretched refuse of your teeming shore;
Send these, the homeless, tempest-tost to me,
I lift my lamp beside the golden door!"

Emma Lazurus, "The New Colossus"

An excited shout from the deck awakened Alec and Maurice to the news of New York harbor visible at a distance enveloped in morning mist. A husky-voiced adolescent heralded his discovery as might a latter-day Columbus, "Land! Land! I see America!" to summon others to share the find. Laughter and joy spread among tired travelers relieved to be at the end of a tedious voyage. Maurice and Alec shook loose from sleep so that they, too, could welcome the sight of America. Throwing clothes astride their limbs they hurried onto the deck where they preferred to jostle among youngsters who relished the thrill of newness. Yet they were of age to share other sober concerns with the elders, some of whose faces were marked by anxiety, a few shedding tears of pain at separation from loved persons and places. So much had been left behind, so many loved ones never to be seen again. Yet much was expected from America, not streets paved with gold that legend told, but tangible opportunities to work and the less tangible freedoms to think and love as the heart dictated.

A woman lifted her daughter, perhaps six or seven, as she spoke in German, "You will see the Lady of Freedom's face. She is greeting you." She hoped her child would enjoy choices she had not herself known. Maurice was able to translate the exchange for Alec. They would soon be with her father who had come to America months earlier to work and to prepare for their coming. "Mother, what does that mean, freedom?" The reply was as thoughtful and true as one might offer a child, "You'll feel it here," as she touched her breast. "You will be able do what you please, to go to school and find work, believe what you think true, and marry the man you love." A life was summed-up that easily.

Even as the mist-enshrouded edifices of the city emerged more sharply, to the portside appeared the imposing statue of Liberty. Sure enough, she extended one arm in a greeting that offered a place of rest for a bevy of seagulls and assurance to these weary travelers. Maurice was thankful for the freedom to live with Alec, yet wariness lingered from the past. He would have clung to the security aboard the Olympic for he judged the time at sea to have been the happiest succession of days he had ever lived. Heretofore he had known little out of the ordinary, nothing that could rival the elation of mutual love. His life offered meager comparisons, but regardless, he wanted no countervailing historic scrutiny. He was fully happy for the first time. No one could have persuaded him otherwise, and only a bigot or a cynic would have thought to try. He would remember for the rest of his life this honeymoon across the north Atlantic. In later years, whenever he remembered this passage shared with Alec in exciting, illicit and secure companionship, he would bask in pleasure. It helps to understand what Maurice was experiencing to compare his feelings to that of a new convert thrust into the river for baptism, thinking himself reborn. The water of the Atlantic had blessed and initiated the two lovers into a new life with a wholeness heaven-sent.

Such a mood could not likely last even for those blessed, and it would not in this instance. The world does not exist primarily for our happiness. Those who wish to know some preponderance of happiness may hope for divine favor or what some call kind fate. So much of ordinary life hinges on summoning enough will to endure countless rebuffs to our hope for a benign world. Adversities arise from the harshness of the natural world, or from the social realm of human devices and wills. Marcus Aurelius here should be our guide, "Say to yourself in the early morning: I shall meet today inquisitive, ungrateful, violent, treacherous, envious, spiteful and uncharitable men." That being so, "I will not respond in kind!" Such is the

51

philosophy of Stoicism, but Maurice was not a Stoic, nor would he ever be. Yet even in his philosophical immaturity he was wise enough to savor the bliss of this rare moment. Well that he did, for by afternoon of that very day his tranquility would be obliterated.

*   *   *

Later that morning the boat anchored for quarantine to allow public health inspectors aboard to examine and certify soundness of body and mind of each of the passengers. Their duty was to root out the weak and to discover those whose intentions were suspect. They moved with brisk approval through first class quarters, saving time for closer scrutiny below. Maurice and Alec were lined-up in the main hall according to their alphabetical listing in the ship's manifest. When it was Hall's turn, Maurice was approved easily and respectfully, a courtesy customarily granted Anglo-Saxons. The whole matter should have ended uneventfully for Alec as well, except something troublesome about Scudder had been brought to the attention of the officials. Questions were asked regarding financial surety, work and family background, but it was not clear what it was that the inspector wrote into the notebook he carried and then attached to the ship's manifest. Alec was remanded to Ellis Island for closer examination.

When the Olympic docked Maurice went ashore as an American while Alec was put on a ferry for a trip to the island. Left alone and anxious Maurice fell grip to despondent thoughts. Had someone incriminated their relationship? Surely not Graham, but perhaps a twisted Risley with his loose tongue had unwittingly revealed some hint of their intimacy. More likely, some hostile busybody who had observed something suspicious in their closeness felt it incumbent to warn officials. But why was only Alec detained and not he, too? A nightmare descended over poor Maurice as if a cloud had followed him from England where the whole realm had been against his sexuality. Dread took hold of his heart that their life together might be abruptly ended. Where had his recent bravado gone? He could only hope for divine favor once more. After seeing to the safety of his baggage, he headed to the Barge Office where he took the ferryboat to Ellis Island to await Alec's disposition.

*   *   *

The hours of anxiety Maurice suffered as he waited for the outcome was the harder of fates as time stood still. Meantime, Alec, huddled with the tired and poor, was undaunted, even relieved to be again among common folk. Alec's Olympic experiences had not all been to his liking, times when he felt out of his element. He would not have depicted the week as blithely as did Maurice, though he looked forward to a fresh start in America. Invidious class differences were more pronounced in the 1920's than today, nowhere more so than amidst the hierarchical society of a proud, luxurious ocean liner which places the wealthy atop its world. While Alec had not come uncritically to America, one thing he was sure, it would be different from England where birth alone, which is to say class with accustomed privileges, was the measure of a man's worth. Thus, the first sight of Ellis Island seemed to offer welcoming rather than any threat of rejection. He did not feel anything to hide. He felt no trepidation, nor impatience; rather, he confidently looked to the drama America might offer.

When he stepped off the ferry at Ellis and viewed the colossal main hall, four grand towers adorning each corner of the edifice, it seemed a castle and he a royal personage. Of course, it was not long after entering the grand doorway of that castle when illusions of royal treatment were dispelled. He watched rough handling of the downtrodden until he began to suspect that in certain respects the new world was not going to be different from the old. Uniformed officials controlled the fate of the wretched and the poor who were sorted, women separated from men, their frightened children clinging to one of their parents. Long lines of weary persons were funneled up a staircase to the Great Hall to be scrutinized for the least sign of a loathsome disease. Society had to be protected from whooping cough, trachoma, sexual diseases, and other contagions. Lo to the person who stumbled or appeared too weary to easily make the ascent. Should a hapless person wheeze with labored breath, or look through clouded eyes, or ooze secretions through any of the orifices of the body, that poor person's breast was marked with chalk for closer examining. What followed was wretched separation from loved ones. Even a terrified child might be pulled away, the parents fearful and uncertain as they waited for hours, the worst of fates forcing a return to whence they came.

Alec passed along in a matter of seconds with nary a hesitation by the medical inspectors for he was the picture of vitality. What was in store for him was a different inquisition into his political and moral rectitude, just why is uncertain. He was led into a maze where he waited amidst males tagged with a number that indicated their ship. Under the grand ceiling of brilliant tiles that gave an aura of a cathedral, he watched an old

Jew, perhaps from Russia, reciting prayers to the God who had preserved him from storm and shipwreck and might now be expected to assure him safety on land. For Alec the spacious hall, filled with commotion and a cacophony of strange languages, was conducive to a different reflection. Such a diversity of looks and sounds brought a glimmer of democracy that might emerge out of this confusion of cultures if ever the entitlement of riches were tamed. He wondered if gender might next surrender its perquisites?

With time to fill, groups of men sought camaraderie where a common language permitted a collective satire of indignities of steerage. Otherwise humorless moments became jests for they needed to share some emigrant experience, whether seasickness, the lack of intimacy with wives, or the most recent physical probe of their private parts by officials who bemused themselves at the strange diversity of male anatomy. Alec had been spared rough handling, but he secretly amused that his penis at least would tell no tales, for it was pledged to as much discretion as was his gallantry.

*   *   *

Alec found himself several hours later before the imposing person of an inspector in his blue coat with brass buttons. William Fitzsimmons enjoyed this uniform that signified the dignity and authority of his position. From the ship's manifest he knew he had before him Alec Scudder, 22, born in London, England, of Irish ancestry, embarked from Southampton, intending to apply for citizenship. "What work do you do? Do you have a job waiting for you?" Forearmed by Graham's warning, and served as well by honesty, Alec stated that he had no offers. "Is anyone meeting you? How do you expect to pay for your immediate keep?" Fitzsimmons was amazed when Alec showed him the bill Graham had given him which proved that he would not become a public charge. "I am traveling with Maurice Hall, my friend, both of us bound for Philadelphia where he will be welcomed by relatives." A literacy test was needed, Fitzsimmons having chosen what he considered an inspiring passage from the Bible about "a good heart bringing forth good things". Alec accomplished the reading with clarity, surprising Fitzsimmons and warming his heart.

Fitzsimmons returned to the manifest to scrutinize a notation next to Alec's name. His sober look hinted a good result was not yet assured. The man had his instructions from on high which under glass hung framed on one of the walls: "Nothing is more important than to keep out of the country the anarchistically and criminally inclined and the degenerate in sexual morality." Every inspector was authorized to use his own judgment in matters before him, and Fitzsimmons was up to the task. He had devoted nearly half his life to immigration service during which he had erected a mental platform for scrutiny, so that he was deeply confirmed in his duty to assist entrance into America of industrious applicants, as his own parents had been, while sternly repelling those who seemed likely to pursue immoral aims. His outlook was composed of prejudices, among them memories of the recent war when his dislike for Germans had developed to surpass bitterness toward England's domination as it had brought sufferings to Ireland. Some of his concerns worked against those dissimilar to his own constricted normality, but it was mostly political radicals, communists or anarchists, who were certain to rouse his ire. Not that he met many a revolutionary, but since the Red Scare a few years back he had been on the watch for anarchists whom he loosely understood to be persons who exacted violence against society. Such malcontents should be sent back to writhe in the soil of their birth that had bred such resentment.

The young man before him looked innocent, not someone who as recently as the night past had engaged in "unnatural intercourse" with a gentleman. Alec would have been sent packing had the truth been apparent or his penis boastful of its deeds. Fitzsimmons would have followed his country's laws directing him to act severely in such discovery. But what Fitzgerald was looking for was any evidence of radical political ideology. His own common-sense Americanism impelled him to enforce the law, though his ardor for weeding out radicalism was mitigated by a compassionate spirit of welcoming workers who were simply seeking opportunities for good lives. To his credit he had internalized another order from on high, one hung on the wall near his station for all immigration officials to ponder: "Immigrants shall be treated with kindness and civility by everyone at Ellis Island. Neither harsh language nor rough handling will be tolerated." That spirit operated in Fitzgerald as he moved toward what he perceived to be the heart of the matter.

"Why do you wish to become a citizen of the United States?"

"Because my friend Maurice intends the same, and I want to be with him. Of course I expect to work as a free man." He hastened to repeat, as Graham had advised, "No job has been offered me. I intend to find employment in quick manner so as not ever to be a burden to Maurice or your public."

Fitzsimmons asked about military service without calculating Alec's youth. "Did you fulfill your duties to country during the last war?"

"It was my good fortune not to be summoned, being too young." But with youthful outspokenness, Alec unnecessarily and it might prove dangerously spoke too much. "Knowing what I know of that war, I would not have been willing to serve English purposes. I have never in my life been threatened by any German, nor was ever Ireland, the native land of my mother, under German rule." The hours of idle time spent in reflection while waiting on the benches amidst the camaraderie of men like himself bore unexpected fruit in this boldness.

"Am I to understand you would have refused to serve Great Britain in its need? Would you have failed to conduct yourself in a manly way?"

"England is not my true country, rather the misfortune of exile. I have within me the Irish blood of my parents, and only by unjust circumstance was born under England's rule. Nor do I feel it necessary to kill a man to be manly. I would go to war to defend my own country, but that is a loyalty I never felt while in England. As for a country I choose to be my own, the United States of America, I am ready to preserve its safety against any foe. That was not my cause in England to preserve the rule of England's classes over an empire that included Ireland."

Fitzsimmons did not like talk of class rule, though he could not help but warm to Irish fervor. He summoned his political acumen to discover what kind of American this young-blood might become.

"When you consider the welfare of your country, what does this require of you? Would you be opposed to defending the lawful state? Do you espouse revolution as an anarchist?"

He stared through an ensuing silence while Alec pondered the question, due in part to his lack of understanding of anarchism, and also a matter of habit, for Alec preferred to admit to the truth or to say nothing.

"I am uncertain what anarchism signifies, though I remember hearing an Irish agitator rebuked for anarchist thoughts."

Fitzsimmons' suspicions hung in the balance. Images of Britannia ruling the oceans did not evoke any sympathy. Yet he did not doubt a necessary role for the state, and his duty to serve as its agent, to preserve decency by upholding law and religion and property. He awaited satisfaction. To prod Alec into something more, he pressed for ideological clarity.

"Well, then, if not an anarchist, a communist? Do you oppose the national state and the duties of citizenry?"

"I don't think war benefits common men such as myself. So much more needs be done than killing people and blowing things apart, what military does, usually to control the lands of others made subservient. The United States as a republic of equal citizens suits me. As for proving myself a worthy man, I feel satisfied in that distinction. It is comradeship with others assures me of it. I hope never to have to kill another man to feel that I am his equal." Then without premeditation or guile he added a word that captured the heart of the wily inspector. "My Irish mother knew little comfort in her own impoverished land, much less in England that was no better to her on its own proper soil. Never knowing my father I had to be man of the house from an early age. That is why I would not have run off easily for a cause that was not my mother's or my own. In America I will be a man of my own working with dignity and ready to defend that right of everyone."

Fitzsimmons rolled his tongue across his upper teeth with a slight grin. He was convinced of the youth's worth and delivered his edict with the luck of the Irish, "Alex Scudder, welcome to America! Deserve your new land without discourtesy to the Ireland of your ancestors. Go on with you, you are free to meet your Maurice. Take this advice to Maurice as well, both of you enjoy this opportunity without recourse to radical urgings."

Alex offered a hand which was accepted as he passed through the inspector's post. Then he trod down the staircase, his footsteps falling into grooves traced upon the stone worn by millions before him, wondering what made anarchy so dangerous. Such thought was truncated when he spotted a bedraggled Maurice barely upright upon a bench near the place called the "kissing post". Lifting Maurice so that he could hug him, Alec regaled him with happy kisses upon a happy cheek. In this ecstatic mood they purchased railroad tickets, boarded the ferry for Battery Park which was their entrance to the new world, and that evening they departed Pennsylvania Station on a train to Philadelphia.

Chapter 5

Searching for Whitmanesque America

On City Hall, above our lights,
Penn's statue spreads indulgent arms,
still beckoning . . .
his head in the clouds, his mood
benign, though slum-blocks sprawl,
splotches of rot, across Penn's Wood ....

Our history grows longer, longer.
It's life that's getting away from us ....

Yet there's a spirit in this place
. . . possibilities of grace
like fragrance from rich compost cling
to leaves where our each deed
and misdeed fall. The Seed
stirs, even now is quickening.

Daniel Hoffman, "Brotherly Love"

Their first day in America was near its end as a taxi carried them the short distance from the train station to the Young Men's Christian Association on Arch Street. Maurice recalled dreamily each step in the journey from London to Philadelphia, satisfied that life with Alec would continue to be adventurous, a far cry from the staid existence which might have been his in England.

At the registration desk he implored the elderly clerk, "We are in need of lodging for a fortnight. Something reasonable in cost." Alec chimed in, "We arrived this morning from England and plan to settle in Philadelphia." Pleased that two handsome young men intended to become Philadelphians, the kindly gentleman wished to put them at ease. "You must be tired after such a long journey. Let me get you to suitable bedding as soon as possible.

Do you wish separate rooms or one to share?" Without hesitancy Alec affirmed, "We shared a cabin all across the Atlantic Ocean, and we intend on living together in this city. So it is a room for two we wish, with enough bed space for stretching about." An approving smile accompanied the clerical arrangements before they were sent their way with good wishes. Philadelphia started out the city of brotherly love it was supposed to be.

*   *   *

When sunlight made its appearance through dual windows, neither Alec nor Maurice could sleep any longer, their excitement to see the city overwhelming tiredness from travel. They showered and dressed, then headed to the ground floor to become acquainted with the automat restaurant of Horn and Hardart. Maurice grinned as he manipulated the coin slots that opened doors to coffee, eggs, scrapple, and so on. He found a table where he began contemplating their day's ventures. His proposal to spend the next few days getting acquainted with their new city won easy approval since such leisurely pace posed no economic liability. Grace Hall, wishing that Maurice travel with comfort, had pressed upon him a handsome sum for the journey, a small part of the legacy that was to be his upon marriage. The irony in this appropriate transfer escaped Mrs. Hall, but not Maurice who considered these days the beginning of just such a solemn tie. He was in a mood to celebrate their commitment, not yet ready to make an appearance at the bank or meet relatives.

Alec liked the suggestion that they look about. "Good to see directly where we have landed and learn its limits for expressing our hearts." Determined to find the roots of the freedom they expected, they entered a bookstore where they purchased a guide to Philadelphia's history, and a second book Maurice chose in the spirit of their pilgrimage, a collection of Walt Whitman's poems, his *Leaves of Grass*.

*   *   *

City Hall with its massive tower five hundred feet above the street seemed a likely place to gain an overall view of their new setting. First they walked the square block surrounding this stone structure built in imitation of the fifteenth-century French palace of the Louvre. Then they climbed to the statue of William Penn whose Quaker beliefs urged accommodation with native Indians and a kindly welcome to European immigrants of diverse religious faiths who came to settle on the lands of

Pennsylvania. From the lofty perch high above the city they watched and listened to the clamor of trolleys and automobiles as people moved about their work, immigrants all or their descendents. For the moment Maurice and Alec felt aloof from these practical concerns of daily monetary gain. Life offered larger possibilities from such height of spirit. Alec put his arm around Maurice as they enjoyed the vistas to be seen and contemplated some yet unseen. Yet there was Risley's warning to be reckoned.

"Do you think we will be able to live honest and congenial lives?"

Maurice sputtered something encouraging. No answer could be certain for the history of any people is splotched by oppression. What guarantee for full accord of rights could be expected of a country that had wrested the land from its native inhabitants? They both knew America had not treated its Indians as Penn wished. Or from a society whose economic gain once depended on slavery and latterly on discrimination against blacks? They had seen, only two days in their new land, that the races were separate and unequal in the work they did and in the worth accorded. Or from a patriarchy that denied women the benefits due to equality? Only the hope and necessity deriving from urban mingling of masses of people would provide an answer.

Back to earth they headed toward Independence Hall in a desultory way. They ambled through grand Wanamaker's department store. Exiting onto Chestnut Street they were further accosted by the robust commercialism of banks and shops. They dawdled before store windows whose attractions enticed them. It was already past noon when they saw a modest blackboard advertising Irish stew for twenty-five cents. "Let's give it a try," Alec urged. They sat at a marble-top table. A waitress brusquely plunked the plates down without ado, so that the stew would speak for itself. When Alex wiped his plate clean with bread, she suggested rhubarb pie, a decent finish to any lunch, adding with a shrug, "Customers become more generous after pie." They did not disappoint her, a reminder how easily youth may be diverted from any serious preoccupations to sheer pleasure and good spirit.

One minor incident might have cast a shadow on this pleasant repast except that Maurice and Alec knew it was best to do in Philadelphia as Philadelphians do. Alec tried to hang on to the fork that had served for the stew, "It is good for the pie as well. Why put yourself to unneeded washing?" The waitress insisted in a matter of fact manner, "We have a darkie for that" and a clean fork was provided.

*   *   *

60

That afternoon they resumed their mission at the site where bold colonial leaders decided upon a Declaration of Independence during the summer of 1776. What had led loyal subjects to rebel against their king? Alec recalled from his schooling, "Wasn't there something to do with tea?" Maurice thumbed through the guidebook and began a recitation of its stilted explanation that had more to do with taxes. It started the story in Boston.

"Merchants angry over a tax on tea resorted to incendiary action when a dispensation of the tax was granted to the East India Company so that the company might profit by selling its tea while colonial merchants suffered a loss of their profits. Incited by what they viewed as a threat to their property, a group of irate citizens disguised themselves as Indians, boarded a ship in Boston Harbor, and threw hundreds of chests of tea into the sea."

"That is something we should have done in Dublin! Americans were quicker than the Irish to break British tyranny."

Maurice chided, "If the Irish had rebelled successfully, you and I would never have met. You are my gift from Irish oppression," reminding Alec of Voltaire's satiric tale of Candide. They had more than once ridiculed the absurd argument of Pangloss that everything that happened was for the best because the larger purposes of the universe are often obscured from human understanding. Picking up that theme, Alec spun a syllogistic absurdity, "Which proves beyond doubt that we live in this second best of possible worlds where Irish subjugation was necessary in the chain of events to prepare Alec's romantic liaison with Maurice, else a ladder would have stood unused that certain day." Then he offered something beyond ridicule, "If this were the best of worlds we would have met as equals under different circumstances."

That settled, they were in an adventurous mood, unscathed, defiantly hopeful that America would fulfill its promise. They joined a group of tourists who listened to a recitation of the bold deeds that led to the Declaration's assertion that "all men are created equal with unalienable rights to life, liberty and the pursuit of happiness" and to a representative government. Yet these two special visitors were disappointed, no doubt because they had climbed so high in hopes that morning and through their journey, that official silence on certain injustices was maintained. Alec was of a mind to break the silence. That defiance was something to admire, for prejudice and oppression are oft left unrevealed, or at least unexamined, when gentleness allows society to remain comfortable in a moral vacuum.

"You did not mention, but surely you believe, slavery was a contradiction to liberty. If the honorable deeds done in this hall are to be understood, and this hall revered as a foundation for liberty, we must recognize the failure of the men gathered here who created a government on behalf of some of the people while continuing the enslavement of others."

The guide was surprised but not shaken in his confidence that he was well versed enough in the history of the republic to overcome any such doubt.

"Yes, there were contradictions in establishing liberties, perhaps always will be. Slavery was an institution that could not then be resolved. We respect our founding fathers for their wisdom in not weakening their purpose which was the new nation born in liberty from the despotism of a king and a distant governing body. That was the highest form of politics. No confederation of states would have been possible without acceptance of slavery. The American people were in a passionate struggle against taxation imposed without their consent, and abolition of slavery would have meant the loss of property for many of the constituents of the new nation."

Maurice, at first uneasy with Alec's intervention, now offered one of his own, "Slavery was a denial of precious rights to life and to form loving relationships in the security of not being forced apart. Was there no concern?"

"The first Congress expressed many concerns with a Bill of Rights."

Unsatisfied, Maurice insisted that none of those rights addressed the abuses he cited. He had in heart the limits to his own freedom. Alec got the last word regarding slavery, "Still, the original crime belongs to England."

When the group dispersed the guide managed a private word. "I hope you will not be cynical about progress which is slow. Washington had a plan that would have abolished slavery gradually, but nothing came of it. Jefferson feared for the fate of our country because slavery was bound to bring the wrath of God. But a political way to abolish slavery, it took war between North and South to make it possible. Ever since we have had to struggle toward equality."

The guide need not have worried, for there was too much joy and anticipation in Maurice's heart and in Alec's for cynicism.

*   *   *

That night before lights were out Maurice planned a next day trek to a place that might become a haven to their dreams. They would visit

Camden where Walt Whitman had lived during the waning years of his life. Perhaps there they would discover the spirit of democratic America through its poet.

In the morning on their way to the waterfront Maurice related the links they had with Carpenter who came to America to visit Whitman.

"We follow in his steps. He wanted to learn from Whitman about comradely love, for he had already begun a simple life and taken George Merrill as his lover. When we were at City Hall you asked whether we might be able to live our lives openly. I am unsure. We must try to do so. There will come times we will need to remember men such as Carpenter and Whitman to inspire us to courage."

Maurice's romantic impulses were not untouched by sober reflections concerning a problematic future. Alec loved Maurice more for this reflective insight.

*   *   *

Maurice savored the spirit of Walt Whitman hovering about the ferry as it crossed the wide Delaware River. He and Alec bathed in the feel and scent of the water and the morning mist, just as the poet had done countless occasions. Whitman loved the ferry trips between Camden and Philadelphia, as he had earlier in his life the crossings between Brooklyn and Manhattan, for such passages afforded him "streaming, never-failing living poems."

This moment, once again at sea, was designed for poetry and young lovers. Maurice's heart chose from the book he carried lines that were appropriate. Against the humming sound of the boat engines he recited in the best earthy tones he could muster,

> "Whoever you are, now I place my hand upon you,
> that you be my poem.
> I whisper with my lips close to your ear,
> I have loved many women and men, but I love
> none better than you . . .
> Old or young, male or female, rude, low,
> rejected by the rest, whatever you are...."

Such is the power of poetry that Maurice was ready to embrace equality under the aegis of Whitman. Deflated in his own pride of place he understood that class presumptions, his share of the social accretion from the long past, threatened Alec's hopes in him. A tear, or it might have

63

been a drop of water from the spray, formed at the corner of his eye. He continued from another page,

> "Whoever degrades another degrades me,
> And whatever is done or said returns at last to me."

The ferry docked in Camden, poetry soon left behind. Alec took a deep whiff of air that smelled of tomatoes. "Campbell soup in the making" was the explanation Maurice deduced from the plant visible in the distant, its water towers looking like soup cans and the name Campbell visible. They climbed upward along a street far removed from the suburban tidiness of Maurice's past. Mickle Street was a dingy, smoke-swept lane of mean houses.

"There seems little of the poetic here," Maurice judged.

Alec surprised him, "You may have missed something in the poetry," for he was the better prepared by earthy experiences to share Whitman's embrace of common mankind in its basic conditions, deeds of work or sensuality. Alec reverberated to that same urge "to reveal and outpour the Godlike suggestions pressing for birth in the soul" which the poet expressed.

Whitman's home was a two-story frame house they entered at the invitation of an elderly woman who volunteered her time, as she said, out of love for Whitman's great heart.

"Whitman lived in this house from 1884 until his death in 1892," she explained, and then they moved into the front room where a rocking chair reminded of Whitman sitting at the window to greet passers-by or throw pennies to children.

"Why did he live in Camden?"

"He had suffered a stroke and sought assistance. He came to live with his brother George and his sister-in-law. Not at this address, nearby on another street. Here is a picture of the three of them. When George decided to move to another town, Whitman purchased this house."

While the guide identified pictures of Whitman's mother and father, brothers, and a few friends, Alec moved to a table that displayed *Leaves of Grass*. Pleased with his interest she handed the book to Alec.

"This is an early edition, not a first edition which would be too rare for handling. It contains the poems published in 1855. Whitman wrote many more into his last years."

"Was he a poet from his youth?" asked Alec.

"Perhaps poetic thoughts stirred him as a boy, but he was thirty years old when he began writing verse. He says that of himself, and there is no need to think otherwise. His family background does not explain his gift. His mother was narrowly religious, his father given to heavy drinking. Nothing literary about either of them. In any case, creativity is hard to appraise. Walt's appreciation of literature may have begun with the Bible in his home, or more likely in school, though he only attended till he was eleven. He went to work as a manual laborer, but not for long. His literary work began at seventeen, newspaper reporting, and later editor of the Brooklyn Eagle."

"Did he turn to poetry without training?"

"What training, young man, inspires the heart of a poet? Perhaps you may harbor some gift of tongue with sensitivity to express? Young Walt turned an avid reader, educating himself, preferring European poets but a few American writers as well. If you wish to know his inspiration, I suggest the poetry will tell you."

She took the book and lighted on the passage,

"Through me forbidden voices,
Voices of sexes and lusts . . .
I believe in the flesh and appetites,
Seeing, hearing, feeling, are miracles, and each part
      and tag of me is a miracle.
Divine am I inside and out, and I make holy whatever I touch
      or am touch'd from.
The scent of these arm-pits aroma finer than prayer,
This head more than churches, bibles, and all the creeds."

They climbed the stairway linked by awe and appreciation, perhaps something more, whatever about the man brought a stream of visitors to seek his company. In the front bedroom they stood beside a stark and cold bed. She offered details of his final illness, an ending Maurice did not want prematurely. What about the flesh and love with other males? Surely this was more than a bed of pain during healthier years. Having been touched by Alec's earlier defiance, he was bold to ask.

"Did Walt share this bed with anyone? I understand he favored comradely love."

"He never married, if that is your meaning. Anne Gilchrist tried her best to gain his heart, coming all the way from England after losing her husband so that she could be close to him. Whitman visited her regularly in Philadelphia, spending nights in her home, but his heart must have been elsewhere. He remained a gentleman toward Anne. The only other woman who stayed here was a housekeeper who slept in the back room, a widow who needed his economic help. Nothing of illicit doings. As for male company of romantic sort, which I believe is your question, I can not say if he shared physical closeness in this house."

"I have heard of his extraordinary friendship with a worker, Peter Doyle. I did not see a picture of him below."

"We are instructed not to mention or answer in any way that might disturb visitors. However, just the three of us here, and I sense your interests approving, I shall say more of what I know, beyond the ordinary tour. His poetry seems just such an invitation to share intimate and natural human feelings. He dared to write plainly that he loved Peter Doyle, a rudely educated streetcar conductor, who was a good man. That was at the time of the war between Union and Confederate when Whitman was in Washington to nurse wounded soldiers through their terrible sufferings. Poor man, he needed healing of his own. He would ride the trolley late into the night seeking distraction. That is how he met Doyle who was conducting his trolley. They became close companions and remained so even after Whitman moved to Camden, when they expressed their love candidly in letters."

She looked kindly at Maurice and at Alec in whom she saw an embodiment of Whitman's poetry. When the tour ended, she was happy that she had been brushed by comradely love and given an opportunity to encourage its course.

*   *   *

As they made their way toward the ferry Alec stopped when they saw two little girls at play as make-believe bakers. Their hands and tattered dresses were dirtied from mud pies which were carefully displayed on an old wooden box.

"Do you have a pie of cherries that I might purchase? I have taste for one made by your pretty little hands."

The girls were delighted by such play and agog at the prospect of a transaction. "These are apple, and we've added a touch of rum, that always pleases my father. My mother bakes them so."

"Then we'll have two of apples, one for each of us, thanking your mother for the thoughtful recipe and you for making lovely pies."

He reached into his pocket for a silver coin, handed a reluctant Maurice one of the pies, and took another that he feigned eating, while the little girls howled with laughter.

*   *   *

That night in bed Alec read Whitman's preface with amazement. If only he could remember, these thoughts would stand him well throughout his life.

"Love the earth and sun and the animals, despise riches, give alms to every one that asks, stand up for the stupid and crazy, devote your income and labor to others, hate tyrants, argue not concerning God, have patience and indulgence toward the people, take off your hat to nothing known or unknown or to any man or number of men, go freely with powerful uneducated persons and with the young and with the mothers of families, read these leaves in the open air every season of every year of your life, reexamine all you have been told at school or church or in any book, dismiss whatever insults your soul, and your very flesh shall be a great poem and have the richest fluency not only in your words but in the silent lines of its lips and face between the ashes of your eyes and in every motion and joint of your body."

Alec wondered about Peter Doyle who had worked all his life, whether that had enhanced his role as comradely lover. Why had he not come to Camden to live beside the poet? Not a mistake he ever thought to make! He put aside the book to engage Maurice in athletic poetry.

Afterward came deep sleep, but early morning Alec was lost in half-consciousness, delighting in the healthy urge to "dismiss whatever insults your soul." Maurice lay next to him, fully awake, no longer given to ruminations of poetry but to practical resolutions. That day they must find an apartment of their own. He decided, too, it was time to meet his Uncle George.

Chapter 6

Into the Sinews of Transport and Finance

Walt Whitman, proclaiming for generations hence,
"Just as you feel when you look at the sky, so I felt."

It avails not, time nor place, to the spirit disembodied,
lusting still for comrades copious and chaste.

"My eye fixes upon you sailing the Delaware.
I hover amidst the elements even now,
lamenting a half century wantonly wasted.
I feel the river somehow filthier,
corrupted, not filtered in its flow,
men and women less inspiring of democratic dreams."

Fred Carrier, "Sailing the Delaware"

It was a cool morning in October as Maurice made his way to a trolley that carried him to City Hall. A short walk and he stood before his place of employment, its façade decorated by Corinthian columns carrying upward to a magnificent dome, reminiscent of the Roman Pantheon, but modern in honoring Finance. Maurice entered the bank stiff-necked and starched, ready for whatever endeavors were needed to earn the handsome salary his uncle would arrange.

George Wetherill welcomed him into his office to assess someone he had last seen as a boy. It pleased him that Maurice was a healthy and handsome man likely to do him proud as a nephew. George said as much after less than an hour of acquaintance, much of which Maurice filled reporting on his mother and sisters. When familial questioning was completed, it was time for George to take closer scrutiny of Maurice's ambitions.

"I am perplexed by contrary explanations that have been given for your presence in Philadelphia. Your mother initially informed me that you would be visiting briefly, something of a tour of the business climate so that you would be better fixed for a commercial position in London. No mention was made of your traveling companion. Yet you tell me in your recent letter that you are intending, with a friend, to establish yourself in Philadelphia."

"You know my mother well. She has always spoken of you as her closest brother. As you remember, she is an emotional sort who dotes on me too much." Maurice added, as if he were a man of the world, "I suppose all women are prone to emotional excesses." Striking a tone that he felt would suit his uncle, "I do not wish to cause my mother anxiety over losing a son so far away. Without a business opportunity in hand, much less a promising marriage such as brought you to America, I thought it best to soften her fear of abandonment. When I received your generous offer of a position at the bank, I spoke to her of a year away at most. Let me assure you, man to man, my settled plan is to make this city my home," which settled George as well in the plan he had been considering for Maurice.

"I will write to your mother to reassure her that the course you are on is promising. Time will settle Grace into supporting your career once you are underway with prospects, too, for a proper marriage. "

It had already been decided Maurice would be assigned to a section that handled loans and investments. George explained the responsibilities to be carried under close supervision of an experienced officer of the bank. Hours would be long, diligence expected, but these would bring rewards and advancement. Maurice was awed, less by the sage advice from his uncle than by his handsome and distinguished appearance. George's manner was austere and imposing, as if others had merely to await his command.

"There are two principles which should govern your work," the uncle instructed his young charge. "Safety and profit. First to be considered in the handling of the money of others is safety, just as if it were your own to guard. Next to that, profit." George was rigid in these priorities that valued the careful play of capital. As he led Maurice round and introduced him to the personnel of the bank, he took intervening private moments to repeat variations of that doctrine.

"Our work is quite simple, a matter of clear priorities. Capital first, dividend to follow."

Only one concern ranked higher in George's world than the integrity of the bank, safeguarding family interests. Being able to help someone of Wetherill blood toward a successful career fit well into this moral scheme. That Maurice was his sister's only son added pleasure to duty. During their round of the bank he pointedly showed warmth, putting his arm across Maurice's shoulder once or twice. He was not accustomed to lavish display of affection with anyone, not even with his wife Anne, so this gesture was indicative of his role as sponsor for all to see. George being vice president was an assurance that Maurice would be accepted, though it helped others to learn he had attended Cambridge and acquired financial knowledge working in London.

Thus began for Maurice what would be a lifetime beneficial relationship to the bank. His initial annual salary of $2,000 brought immediate economic advantage and some small pride to be engaged in a career highly valued. To his credit, Maurice was not looking for more than this privileged opportunity of serving the rich. Neither did he lack confidence in his ability, nor the ambition to advance. He resumed the ways he had begun in London of rendering money into expanding capital. His plodding mind fit the demands of this work for he found satisfaction calculating the changing values of securities while investing earnings with perspicacity. Within half a year his steady performance would win appreciation from both clients and bank officers, including his uncle, and a promotion that brought a salary increase.

During the first month after entering the bank Maurice managed to deflect invitations to visit the Wetherills. He pled busyness, not only his demanding work at the bank which entailed carrying business home, but also furnishing an apartment, getting acquainted with the city, and so on. When George learned of Maurice's living arrangement, he regretted a location "the wrong side of Market Street" and questioned whether it was in other ways suitable. "Would not bachelor's quarters be preferable?" Maurice persisted, explaining he preferred to share with Alec, and neither he nor Alec shunned closeness to "foreigners" since they were recent immigrants themselves. Maurice was rightly worried about throwing Alec together with the Wetherills, yet there would be something wrong about his going to their main line mansion on his own, as if he were a bachelor lacking suitable quarters. He did succumb in part to a peremptory note delivered by George from his wife Anne: "We expect to see you at church Sunday and dinner after so that we may welcome you into the family." The most he would agree to do for now was to attend service at St. Mark's in Philadelphia where the Wetherills continued to worship each Sunday despite their move to the green hills of Gladwyne. Alec was not mentioned in the bargain.

*   *   *

In the meantime Maurice and Alec occupied a bare apartment in the Mantua district west of the University of Pennsylvania, located on a street that was neither fashionable nor derelict, one where middle class and respectable working class families mingled. Alec was thrilled with what served as his castle of the moment. Its spaciousness and emptiness echoed their voices and footsteps. He felt himself a prince, a status Maurice was more than willing to accord, though it was a strange castle, a comedown, for Maurice who had previously known only genteel surroundings accompanied by ladies in waiting.

Alec set out to find work suitable to present needs. He walked with Maurice to a news-stand on Market Street where he plunked down ten cents for the Sunday Bulletin. Maurice went on to St. Mark's to worship with the Wetherills while Alec returned home to pore over listings for employment in the pages scattered across the bare floor. Most offered rough labor which did not frighten him, but he discounted office positions, sales, or the skilled trades, drafting, measuring and cutting, printing, and others that demanded qualifications. He noted that not everyone was encouraged to try for even meager positions. Men of color and others were discouraged by specifications "White man" or "Gentile only" which raised doubt America would be fair when it came to those differences that marked his life shared with Maurice.

Placing himself on the market was onerous enough to drive him to seek distraction once Maurice returned and joined him on the floor amidst a scattering of pages. It was too pleasant an afternoon to spend with disquieting thoughts of work.

"Look at this" as he pulled Maurice to a half-page picture of a classy 1925 Cleveland sedan. "Imagine me driving that chassis with you proudly beside me! We could hold our noses high to Uncle George." Such was the second-hand opinion he had formed of George. Maurice grinned at the thought but, the more calculating of the two, he remained cautious as if he were at the bank. "That's worth my year's salary." They turned a page to a more suitable vehicle, a Ford coupe. Maurice was ready for compromise, "Here, not nearly so stylish, but something we might afford." When it came to money Alec was nonchalant, not presumptuous, just so the bills were paid. He should not be faulted. He intended to work as necessary and contribute to their upkeep. It was merely youthfulness to be infatuated by the American emporia of material goods that seemed by right to belong to all its citizens. If equality were not reality in America, at least some sharing in the largesse of goods ought to be.

Maurice knew it would never do to reserve as exclusive any part of his fortune. He proclaimed that what was his was Alec's as well. Theirs was to be a marriage of hearts and fortunes. Still, Maurice kept charge of finances with the final say, not simply because he commanded the larger income, but because he had run the finances of the Hall household and was managing the money of wealthy investors. He felt strongly masculine in these duties, both saving money and occasionally spending generously. He valued the comfortable existence that was his custom, but as strongly, he looked forward to benefiting his avid companion who had never known abundance of material things. Maurice had brought from England a boyhood treasure from his mother, a lacquered box decorated with a picture of companion horses running through a field. Now he took to placing a part of his earnings in it after household expenses were met. He suggested to Alec they draw freely as they needed, hopeful that monthly expenses would not exceed income. What was left at the end of each month would be deposited. Being neither covetous nor prodigal, Alec did not disappoint him, and so there was an accumulation. Maurice promised himself that as soon as Alec was receiving regular wages he would be in the driving seat of a coupe. It would be a way of pleasing Alec, properly caring for him, far from spoiling such a good nature.

*   *   *

In fact work was not long away for Alec. Before he had done more than submit a few applications, Maurice consulted his uncle with the admission Alec was a manual laborer who needed a beginning somewhere. Sure enough help was forthcoming. A concise letter beautifully penned in George's hand was addressed to the production manager of the Baldwin Locomotive Works at Broad and Spring Garden streets, where Alec was summoned.

On the way to an interview he crossed a section of the twenty-two acre plant that employed ten thousand burly men, soon to be ten thousand and one. Alec felt the heat of molten steel from a distance and heard workers shouting above the noise of machines grinding and shaping parts. Baldwin was a marvel of production where coal, steel, and human labor were melded into the sinews of transport as its locomotives carried commerce and passengers throughout the world.

When he entered the headquarters building, the din of production was left behind. As he made his way, he caught glimpses into offices with executives in three-piece suits at mahogany desks under gilt bronze electric chandeliers, betokening the progress of the twentieth century and capitalism. Their munificent dress was properly constrictive to conduce to the attitudes needed in shaping production. As sure as there were times of

72

prosperity, there would be times when a faltering economy required harsh decisions to preserve profits. Then it fell to these managers to provide explanations that made the chronic job insecurity of workers seem as inexorable as nature's upheavals.

Alec had little time to ponder these links of production before complying with its needs. The note from George Wetherill, conveying important connections, led to quick employment. One week later he started for work in the darkness of morning after a happy Maurice bade his lover farewell and turned over to lie abed another hour. From now on half Alec's life would be dominated by paid labor. He reported to the foundry where he was to rub shoulders with barely educated men whose lives were claimed by noise and grime half of every working day, from 7 in the morning to noon, after lunch from 1 until 6. Saturday was half as much.

Strong handshakes welcomed him to the camaraderie of laborers. He was placed under Francis Kowalski to learn tasks that demanded care rather than exceptional skill. Kowalski was in his thirties, with ambitions of his own, for he was the father of six. He worked hard to see to output and encouraged positive morale among his men. He assured Alec that he would soon acquire the skills to advance to a greater role in the line of production.

Alec was not in need of such hope, for he harbored vague other ambitions. Meantime, needing the wages, he intended to do the job well, simple as it was, stirring his imagination with the thought of train engines at work. It was not long before he ceased envisioning the finished locomotive whose power and beauty had brought satisfaction. The daily monotony of hammering out only a small part of a locomotive stifled his spirit and drove him to daydreams, often of Maurice and their nightly fare, or of a future more in accord with his mother's ambition that he become a gentleman. He worked steadily, that much he owed to his fellow workers, though there was no way for him to ignore that he was different. Why were they not more critical of the exploitative system that enmeshed them? As he worked day in and out he remembered with indignation the plush setting of the executives only one hundred yards away but constituting a world apart, the Uncle Georges exalted above the Kowalskis. He could not resign to these stark contrasts between privilege and grime. He had sought a new democratic society but was thrust into an economic system that had class exploitation at its heart. He was not doomed to this underling existence, yet his awareness of the injustices inflicted on masses of workers opened a wound that would deepen and grow into a sense of alienation even from his beloved Maurice.

*   *   *

Within a few months of working at the plant Alec was too weary to hide dissatisfaction with the lot of the worker. Life needs to be for the likes of an Alec more than work and subsistence, even though punctuated by erotic nights. Restlessness of spirit took hold of him. He missed what he had never thought to lack, the Durham estate with its library and time to wander the woods. Maurice sensed danger when he heard this. He sought to fill the void by adding comforts to their domestic lives while some direction might be sought for Alec's deeper expectations. They went shopping at Lit Brothers on Market Street where they purchased a sturdy bed with two dressers, and for the living room a couch and two stuffed chairs. Alec chose a rug, far too expensive, but Maurice allowed this indulgence and another as wise, a Victrola. By week's end persons and goods were comfortably joined, Maurice reclining on the couch, Alec stretched upon the exotic rug, and the Victrola standing on its four spindly legs emitting the glorious sounds of Tchaikovsky's Fifth Symphony. Maurice had chosen triumphant compositions rather than anything weeping. Again it seemed a better world as Alec was swept into a rapturous realm of music that restored his diminishing spirit.

*   *   *

There was uplifting news when a letter from Graham brought an invitation to visit Fonthill where he would be delivering some prints to his friend Henry Mercer two weeks hence.

"Would you come to spend a week end at Fonthill? I have persuaded Henry to extend you the invitation. Be assured it will be a fascinating experience, not least because of the design and decoration of Fonthill, but also because of the opportunity to become acquainted with Henry, its architect and owner. Despite his eccentric reputation, none who know him well would stop short of praising his broad knowledge, artistry and accomplishments. I will add my anticipated pleasure at seeing you again for your consideration."

Graham commented that a few other guests were expected, theatrical performers billed in a new musical at the Bucks County Theatre. There were also included directions to Doylestown where Fonthill was located. The letter was signed simply Graham.

*   *   *

Maurice decided, Alec's wages taken into account, it was time they acquired a Ford coupe. That way they could make their way to Fonthill. He also insisted that Alec acquire some new clothes of style. While clothes do not make the man, they announce his station. Maurice was solicitous that Alec should feel comfortable at Fonthill among men and women of accomplishment.

To break in their new automobile they made a Sunday excursion through the countryside, Maurice yielding the driving to a delighted Alec. After lunch at the Valley Inn on the Wissahickon Creek, a strong sun softened the coldness of the air as they walked several miles upstream. From a height they could see through nearly naked trees the water flowing and a few distant hikers. As they reveled in nature's wonder Maurice took his partner's hand which bore the signs of the earth. Alec thanked him, as he had during the drive, but he acknowledged that important as material goods were they could not put his mind at ease. It was nothing about Maurice. Some further use of intellect was needed if he were to settle. Nonetheless, that night Alec forgot about his work of the next day. He carefully bathed to prepare himself for ardent expression of gratitude to Maurice for all he had given.

*　　　　*　　　　*

Neither earthiness of daily labor nor family could be forgotten, hard as each of them tried to temper any ill effects. Maurice had taken to attending Sunday service at St. Mark's, not from any spiritual inclination, but from bowing to the necessity of meeting the Wetherills, if not yet at their home then in their church. He thought it best to render gratitude for George's help to him and to Alec. On the first of such holy occasions Maurice met George's family, his wife Anne who offered her hand in a gesture of elegance, as did Regina, the older of two daughters, whose husband stood beside her holding their son. Patricia, still in her teens, displayed a nonchalance of manners that set her apart. The eldest of his cousins, Maurice's age, was Andrew who offered an official greeting. Andrew had chosen to become a priest in the Episcopalian Church and had progressed to deacon at St. Mark's, perhaps a year away from priestly powers.

When the service was ended the Wetherills set off in their fashionable car for the suburbs, only after Anne had extracted from Maurice the promise to come soon for dinner. Maurice remained with Andrew who escorted him into the sheltered cloister for tea and raised the question that was troubling him.

"Why hasn't Alec come to meet us?"

Pleased that Andrew inquired, Maurice offered some history, telling why Alec's mother had fled Ireland and raised the boy amidst conditions of poverty in England, how chance had brought about his friendship with Alec, and why they had reached the decision to leave England's class pretensions, though this last matter was presented ambiguously. Though not widely experienced, Andrew could not have missed these outpourings of the heart. Nor did he fail to see that Maurice was drawing a portrait of a man he loved and a relationship that posed objections for his family and society, but this he read as an opportunity for a priestly mission. Andrew had a quality often lacking in a man of the cloth in being readily caring. He had no harsh judgment to render. He made it clear he intended to be friend to both.

"St. Mark's would welcome Alec, though he may prefer a Catholic setting with pope and all."

"Nothing of the sort. Alec is not Catholic, not a Christian at all, for he was never baptized."

This surprised Andrew who shuddered to think a man might be born and raised in England without having been graced with faith in the Christian religion. Surely he must aid Maurice in changing such an unholy state. Settling his own mind in that direction, he embraced his cousin as they parted to show that he meant to be his friend and Alec's as well.

$$* \qquad * \qquad *$$

Alec had also made a friend, Anthony Morelli, another worker traveling the same route to the Baldwin plant. They shared a seat on the trolley one evening homeward, both of them too grimy to be inviting to any other traveler. Their few words, despite the ordinariness, lightened their tiredness simply because they found pleasure looking at and listening to the other. From then on they traveled together to work and back, and before long shared the hour of lunch, causing dismay to Kowalski's crew who wondered why Alec was hanging with a dago. Alec ignored talk among workers who often disparaged others according to prejudices against polocks, wops, micks, spics, niggers, etc.

Alec liked his friend's strong face ready to smile at humor or irony as it came his way. Despite work conditions that might have stirred discontent, Tony's dissatisfaction did not rise to political class consciousness. He was steadied by a simple yearning to get on with his life, to marry his fiancé, Rita, when summer came, to take pleasure with her body, and to get started having children. For years he had been waiting while giving his earnings to his father, an immigrant who had worked and also saved during all his life in America, in order to own a restaurant. Now that "Angelo's" was a thriving business on Lancaster near 39th, Tony's duties to family had been met. It would not be long into the future, his father in his sixties, when he would take over the restaurant as a matter of succession.

Their friendship advanced enough for a tired Tony to confide dissatisfaction of a kind, "I missed much of my sleep last night, too busy beating my prick." Here he was twenty-seven, though engaged to be married, still he had not dented the walls of virginity, Rita's or his. Surprised to hear this, Alec could only ask, "Why don't you and Rita satisfy each other's sexual needs? You are engaged, so what harm?" Tony was careful not to offend Alec who had mentioned the circumstances of his birth.

"An Italian girl is taught not to surrender her purity. Rita is close to her family and mine, and the church. Though I could press hard upon her, we are better off waiting until marriage. What if I ruined her reputation before her family? You told me of your mother. Italians are not unlike the Irish."

Tony asked whether Alec was also inexperienced since he never talked about women in that way. It was opportune for Alec to reciprocate confidence.

"I am wrapped up in Maurice, the way you are in Rita," and he added, "nothing of the virgin left in me."

Tony pondered this confidence awhile until he understood. He felt happy to be so trusted.

Chapter 7

The Wetherills of Philadelphia

Wouldn't this old world be better
If the folks we met would say –
"I know something good about you!"
And treat us just that way.

Louis Simon

Winter was approaching when George insisted almost as a command, "It is time you came to Stone House to be with your family. Anne requests your presence for dinner this Sunday." Maurice did not like the peremptory tone that put him in an awkward situation. He could do no less than meet his family in their domestic surroundings, yet he had no intention of going alone. Where was Carpenter now that he needed him? Maurice half-choked on his response.

"Would Alec be welcome as well?"

Dinner was served at four, cocktails an hour earlier for the men, although Anne made a brief appearance. These were Sunday habits of the Wetherills who began the day at high mass in St. Mark's. Alec had declined to attend church and as begrudgingly accepted the dinner invitation as it had been given.

When they arrived at Stone Hall its pretentious title was not without foundation. Piled high in gray stone the mansion of thirty rooms looked across an equal number of acres. From the terrace where George greeted them a gently sloping hill led to a creek that flowed through a valley marking one extent of the estate. George provided details of its history as they circled the house and then crossed a field to a stone stable where horses were kept. He suggested Maurice come another time to take a horse about. He led them another distance downhill to a large stone cross that marked a memorial to George and Anne's first-born who had been killed in 1918 by artillery fragments in one of the fields of France abutting the Argonne Forest. "Your cousin George was twenty when he gave his life."

The father knelt for a sincere silence. Maurice felt it incumbent to kneel as well, an appropriate honor to a fallen cousin and an uncle who was so helpful, but Alec stood tall thinking only of one more life wasted among many millions of others.

*   *   *

George Wetherill had been born in Sussex in 1865, three years before his sister Grace who was to become Mrs. Hall, enabling her to produce our hero Maurice, nephew to George. George came to the United States to marry Anne Baldwin after becoming helplessly infatuated with her beauty while she was spending the summer of 1896 in Europe. That such a presentable man as George had passed thirty without being betrothed may seem remarkable, but it was his doing to await a woman of beauty matched by suitable wealth. Having found Anne, they were married in St. Mark's Episcopal Church in Philadelphia with high society in attendance, the Baldwins joined by Biddles, Drexels, Peppers and Wannamakers.

A Wetherill family story has it that George, a strikingly handsome figure in his own right, literally lay at Anne's feet in worship on the occasion of proposing marriage, gradually making an adoring ascent, inch by inch, until his lips reached her summit. At that height he did not dare impose a kiss upon her lips, descending to the delicate hand for which he pleaded. Anne had been told all her life of her beauty and treated as a divine creature, so much so that she imagined love an intercourse of vision between beautiful faces. Parts below the neck were merely for procreative duties. Anne could not resist adoration, certainly not in this instance of purity and propriety, and so she surrendered to George's entreaty by offering her hand as a token of acceptance..

In addition to the genes fortuitously mingled by this coupling, it turned out a prosperous marriage for George. Anne was one of the Baldwins who since mid-century owned a company that had launched them into the nouveau riche. During Philadelphia's Iron Age the Baldwin plant produced the engines by which the Pennsylvania Railroad carried heaps of iron and steel for manufacture in Philadelphia's burgeoning industry. As principal heir to the family business, John Baldwin was rich and well established in Philadelphia society, an officer of the Union League of mostly wealthy Republicans. A year before his daughter's wedding to George, Baldwin became a director of one of the leading banks in Philadelphia, furthering his power and prestige.

Through the considerable influence of his new father-in-law, George secured an important position at that bank. Having been placed in this post because of the influence of wealth, not at all unusual, he vindicated this preference by hard work and ability until his election as first vice-president. Thus, when Maurice encountered his uncle that Sunday afternoon, George was a successful gentleman of probity and property who commanded the respect of the community and who in turn relished the virtue of paying tribute to the economically successful. His business life, modeled on adherence to right thinking, had earned him his position of command and appointment, with ability to select trustworthy men who could contribute to the growth of an economy. So it was natural, as the law of gravity guides an apple to solid ground, that the preferences of family connection would draw Maurice into the banking sphere. What John Baldwin had done for George he would do for his nephew.

*   *   *

In the parlor Maurice was greeted with smiles and genuine pleasure, followed by his introduction of "my travel acquaintance, Alec." Anne extended her hand to Maurice, offering merely a nod of acknowledgment when Alec was presented. Her attitude of class distinction derived from a foundation less solid than Stone House's but as intractable.

Anne Baldwin Wetherill was still a face and figure to admire, even approaching fifty, giving credence to the life-size painting done in her youth that presently adorned the living room of their home. That depiction by a gifted artist of renown was destined to hang in the Pennsylvania Academy of Fine Arts so that posterity could admire both art and her stunning beauty. Unfortunately, Anne's beauty was diluted in her living presence by the failing of character that stemmed from being pampered as a child and praised for good looks, so that she became taken with her own physical features to the neglect of concern for others. Even her children were overshadowed in her presence, though Regina vied for attention. Patricia was a disappointment while Andrew in the male sphere had no reason for secondary standing.

George's handsome features were the Wetherill genetic contribution to producing the three children present and the one martyred in France. Regina was as beautiful as her mother and as vain, though she did offer a proper greeting to Alec. Her husband Ronald shook hands vigorously. Patricia was unlike her mother, not only due to adolescent awkwardness, but because she was animated and deliberately rebellious.

Andrew was sincere in greeting his cousin and companion. He furthered this assurance at the table when he intoned a passage from the Bible and started into a special welcome. Maurice and Alec took leave

80

of any piety to scrutinize Andrew intensely, his pleasing voice and look rather than the words. To see him was to languish in his beauty. Andrew had been compared to a cherub while a child, and as a young man his soft, androgynous features invited admirers, women and men alike. One of them, a devotee of Renaissance painting, praised him as a counterpart of Botticelli's Venus. Be that as it may, at the close of his prayer Andrew thanked the Holy Spirit for bringing Maurice safely to their midst. He implored protection for Aunt Grace and her family. Then with courtesy that stemmed from simple faith, he added Alec, that he be strengthened in Christian faith and blessed with prosperity in his new land.

If only the Lord had been watchful this day Alec would have been whisked elsewhere, to a tavern for some brew with common folk or to a game on some athletic field. No such miracle took place. Alec might as inappropriately be dining with the Durhams as with this assembly. Though he had given vigorous efforts to scrubbing himself, his nails showed telltale grime from the week of work. Nor did his dress match the elegance of the Wetherills or Maurice, not even reaching the crisp cleanliness of the servants' uniforms. He squirmed with consciousness of his lower status during a meal that would have suited the best of English tables, served on the finest of china in an impeccable manner. At opposite ends of the table were mother and father. Maurice had the good fortune to be seated between Andrew and Patricia where he felt at home. Not so for Alec, who by the worst of fates was seated next to Regina, as if the devil had planned it. During the second course Regina felt it incumbent to say something to Alec, though true interest in such a common person was lacking to her haughty attitude. All she could think of was to inquire, "What profession did your father follow?" Not because he failed to understand the question, but because he grasped its insolence, Alec showed his irritation. "Religion you mean?" Sorry she had bothered with a person she now deemed rude, Regina corrected him, "No. I mean to inquire into his business occupation." Alec resented this snobbery which he addressed with a loud voice for all to hear.

"A butcher, m'am, he did his own preparing. For awhile I bloodied my hands helping out. Then I decided it was no business for the likes of me."

Ronald, who at times countered his wife's snobbery, knew this was one such occasion to rescue the situation.

"Something like being raised on a farm, I should think, one gets used to slaughter. Did you have a close relationship with your father in his trade?"

Having had enough of the Wetherills, Alec wanted to be sure no one would be denied sufficient information of his impropriety,

"I was a bastard child. Didn't know Scudder as a father until I was eight."

All conversation at the table halted.

Maurice was embarrassed on behalf of Alec, but there was little he could do that would not make things worse. Patricia rushed to his rescue. With goodness of heart akin to Andrew's, she remembered the sermon at morning mass. She looked across Maurice as she called upon Andrew.

"Father Pitts warned us of the miseries that attend riches when their owners offend the Lord with their pride. It gave me a fright. Isn't that right, Andrew?"

Andrew was pleased to be consulted where St. James was at issue. He reached for the Bible to find the passage from James' gospel that was central to the sermon. Studying the text a moment, he paraphrased it in as friendly a way as he could, "Your riches are corrupted and your garments motheaten. You have lived in pleasure at the hire of laborers whose cries are entered into the ears of the Lord."

No one asked for further exegesis. Anne called for the next course while George changed the subject.

*   *   *

Next Sunday Maurice alone joined the Wetherills in their reserved pews at St. Mark's. He was to share their dinner, stopping first at the rectory for conversation with Andrew. Afterward they would drive to the stone mansion.

"It is good to see you for a private word. I miss Alec's attendance. Of course he is uncomfortable with mother and Regina. They are not usually so rude to strangers. I am afraid they feel protective of you, your mother's influence. They feel that Alec does not belong in your company. Both Halls and Wetherills are prideful in this matter, not Christian at all. Is there any way I might make up to Alec?"

"I'll tell him your concern which he already knows. Alec is proud, too. He brooks no arrogance from others. He is alert to indignities. He will accept no inferior status."

"That is democratic, and appropriately Christian. I take our faith seriously that all are judged equal by God. I have attempted to convince my mother that pride of wealth or station should be put aside. Love for all mankind is incumbent on those who heed Christ." Andrew had this way of casting everything into a benign theology of Christianity as pure love. "If only Alec would consent to pay me a visit, I am sure I could right the matter."

"Alec is not likely to come to St. Mark's. He has never practiced Christian forms and he is not keen to do so from consideration for my family. Though his mother was a Catholic, she bore him out of wedlock and became estranged from family and their church which offered no help. Alec has contempt for the church's hypocrisy."

"We must show him otherwise. His anger may put his soul in jeopardy. He needs to be encouraged to seek salvation. This is more important than Wetherill worldly pride."

"I do not think Alec will accept conversion. He blames the hardships his mother endured on superstitions and priests, rightly so. I have amended what I was taught of religion by priests. It was not sinfulness her conceiving Alec outside of marriage. It was natural and innocent sexual behavior that was her undoing."

"Alec and you are right, of course. The Church puts too much emphasis on sexual conformity, not enough on the spirit of forgiveness and compassion. You are close to him, Maurice. While I will not pry into matters you prefer remain private, I hope you will let me assist you. Assure Alec I wish to be helpful as an equal."

Though struck by Andrew's compassion, Maurice wondered what he could know about the world of sexual passion other than its sinfulness. He had only trod the path to priesthood. In appearances at least, Andrew was alike to his mother, handsome, aloof from carnality, certainly not a person in whom Maurice could confide the intimacies of his sexual liaison with Alec. He tried another tack.

"I am growing more fond of your father. He has been helpful to me in my work. We are going to take the horses out this afternoon to explore the valley. Perhaps we had best get on our way."

As they drove toward Gladwyne Andrew renewed his effort.

"You must get Alec to consider me a friend. Urge him to come to St. Mark's, not for mass with the family, but another time so that he and I can talk intimately."

Chapter 8

A Visit to Fonthill

And thus in man some inborn passions reign
Which, spite of careful pruning, sprout again.
Then, say, was I or nature wrong,
If, yet a boy, one inclination, strong
In wayward fancies, domineered my soul,
And bade complete defiance to control?

Lord Byron, "Don Juan"

Fortress and friendship joined at Fonthill,
the first hardened concrete, the second fragile,
like to the first, bold to aspire,
bound to nature's ways immune to fire.

Unlike Icarus, friends with wings steeled
From searchful flight, their strong shield
In honest thought that stays earth bound,
Resisting the fiery clamor of hateful sound.

"Let us be merry and gay with a jug and a jig,
With no room for the dreariness of a prig."
So said Mercer, currying favor of these friends,
And they true to him surrendered to his ends.

Fred Carrier, "Atop Fonthill"

After a two hour drive Alec and Maurice were filled with excitement as their car ascended the long driveway to a garage that stood apart from the Mercer residence. Three Chesapeake Bay Retrievers greeted

84

them exuberantly, and from the doorway of the house a woman called a welcoming which made clear this was not a place that stood on formality. As they walked her way they got their first look at Fonthill, the concrete edifice which would take up much of their visit with surprises, as would its architect, Henry Chapman Mercer. He designed its structure and supervised decoration of its forty rooms with tiles manufactured by a pottery that he operated on the thirty acre estate.

Laura Long, the woman of the greeting, introduced herself with a confident air that gave an impression she held even more importance than that of housekeeper. With sparse comments she led them two flights up a winding staircase to bedrooms adjoined by a common bath, one of the rooms with a double bed as Graham had advised.

"Mr. Mercer and your friend Graham are expecting you after you are settled."

Half an hour later Laura guided them up another flight to the Columbus Room where the two gentlemen sat in a corner of the spacious room beside two large windows that shed plentiful light upon the prints Graham had brought from Europe. Graham happily greeted their arrival and introduced Mercer who stood to shake their hands, gently as befitted a man of 68 years. His hair was gray as was the dapper mustache that framed his mouth with dignity. His lifelong thinness, due to illnesses he suffered and the expense of energy he continued to put into his work, was hidden by a baggy woolen suit hanging loosely on his frame.

Mercer could see his guests were interested in the room they had entered which was adorned by a colorful ceiling upheld by two concrete Corinthian columns. More amazing, pictorial tiles filled the ceiling and walls. Even the floor offered a tile display of coats-of-arms of early American states. Mercer explained that the room celebrated Columbus and the peoples of the New World. As he guided them about the room he wove stories told by the tiles with accounts of his archaeological travels through North America. Along the way of several expeditions he had gathered anything that struck his eye or historical sense until he had a collection of colonial tools and household crafts that were displayed in a concrete museum near the center of Doylestown.

"All my useful endeavors were supported by my Aunt Lela whose imagination stirred mine to preserve our American legacy."

Then he traced with his steps an inscription that bordered the four sides of a floor display:

"Brave admiral speak but one good word,
What shall we do when hope is gone?

The words leaped like a leaping sword:
Sail on, sail on, sail on and on."

He had saved for last Rollo's stairs where his beloved dog had left paw prints on fresh cement, no doubt without a thought of Columbus.

"Was Rollo one of our exuberant greeters?" Maurice asked.

"No, the black one you saw is his grandson, Jack. I will show you Rollo's resting place when we see the tile works this afternoon."

They returned to perusal of the prints that Graham had brought from Europe. Mercer showed one that depicted the bread march of Parisian women along the fifteen miles to Versailles in October of 1789 where they made captive the king and queen of France. The gaunt faces of the women revealed their hunger and the picks they wielded their determination to change the realm to one concerned with their needs.

"We were contrasting these pictures" as Graham held another for display, "Marie Antoinette's Boudoir" where the queen was assembled with a group of aristocratic women listening to music. What captured the eye was the opulence of their dress and surroundings. One might with imagination smell the powder and perfume redolent of privilege and decay, or hear the voice of the queen sighing, "Let them eat cake," after being informed of the hungry marchers approaching the palace.

*   *   *

After lunch Frank Swain who managed the factory guided them through the Moravian Pottery and Tile Works. Its two-story stucco structure embracing an interior cloister resembled a California mission with a tower above the tile roof. As they moved through wings of the pottery, he described the tile-making operation, showing clay grinding machinery, tools for cutting and pressing tiles, and three kilns for baking them.

Then they climbed the tower for a view of the surrounding country. Graham wanted his young guests to know, "Every one of the tiles made here is of Henry's design and Frank's direction. They are widely valued, even paving the floor of the State Capitol at Harrisburg."

"I admire your appreciation of the sweat and toil of workers." Alec was confident that neither Mercer nor Swain would deem his remark youthful presumption.

"My inspiration has been the European pioneers who made Pennsylvania and wrought her fortune, transforming this continent with their tools, clearing the American forest, building the log school house, and preparing the land for agriculture. I respect all the mechanics who devised the blast furnace, the grain elevator, and the oil well."

"Those who build locomotives, too!" Maurice proudly explained that Alec was at such work.

"I appreciate your work which is beyond what I could do. American civilization rests on the efforts of native peoples, then of settlers black and white, and the industry of recent immigrants such as yourself."

*   *   *

As they made their way toward the house Mercer led them to a grove where Rollo was buried. He stood solemnly before the marker as he had done a thousand times. After a long silence he was tender with gratitude.

"Rollo was a beautiful animal from a noble and affectionate line of Chesapeake Retrievers, distinct from the Newfoundland line. A story is told that two Labradors swam ashore in the Bay in 1807 from whence came the Chesapeakes. I have developed these dogs' intelligence and affection, and they have repaid me a hundred fold for my trouble."

*   *   *

During dinner the banter was domestic with Frank and Laura adding to the mix. Graham mentioned a servant problem of his family in Newport, one of the downstairs fellows casting a roving eye on the housemaids, having already sent one of them to the Lying In Hospital.

"I hope you captured his rope ladder" was Mercer's solution, which did not appeal entirely to Alec.

When they adjourned to another room for coffee, Alec remarked on the importance of supportive family. "You are blessed with such a wise and loving aunt. What is her name?"

"Lela – her name was Elizabeth. She died twenty years ago."

"I did not have the good fortune to know aunt or uncle, nor any blood relation other than my mother. Whatever I do of worth will be from her good influences."

Graham sang the praises of Lela who was a strong woman, mixing many traditional ways with progressive attitudes, such as encouraging Mercer while he meandered through his careers. Mercer explained that he had studied law and abandoned it for archaeology.

"Even an interval when I fashioned myself a literary figure had Lela's encouragement. I wrote stories, but without a taste for the stark realism which took hold about that time. I did not feel comfortable adding another American tragedy. We have progressed from caves and what we need is literature that lifts society morally."

Graham chided Henry's liking for the old charm and atmosphere of Victorian England. "We are not going to the devil simply because fashionable women favor short skirts and bobbed hair."

Maurice wondered, too, whether emancipation of the modern woman ought not be encouraged, which brought a retort from Mercer, "I will admire her once she stops slaughtering egrets to bedeck her hat with plumes. The charm and poetry of nature is sacrificed everywhere."

Maurice took that blunt ending as an opportunity to turn to Fonthill. "Why did you prefer concrete in your architecture?"

Mercer recounted how his archaeological studio attached to the family estate had been destroyed by fire in 1912. "I have collections which I want to keep immune from destruction by fire. I turned to concrete to be sure."

"I was wandering through your library," Alec mentioned, "and found one of your verses, about a ruined house, tucked in a book. Was it fire you had in mind?"

"Not when I wrote the poem, for I was young and dreaming of castles in the air." He asked Alec to fetch the book where the poem resided. Seeing that it was a later version Alec had found, he explained that earlier hope had turned to dreadful thoughts of mortality upon the loss of his mother and aunt. "I revised the poem in accordance with my revised spirit," and he read the final lines to corroborate that estimate.

> "Farewell old house, and friends farewell,
>   from here forever gone."

*   *   *

The next day other visitors took up Mercer's morning until they set off early for a theatre excursion.

It was mid-afternoon before the foursome gathered in the garden for tea. Alec resumed the conversation from the last morning on the Olympic.

"I have read the **Three Essays on Sexual Theory** of Sigmund Freud as you suggested, Mr. Graham. I am satisfied his psychoanalytic theory opposes separating homosexuals from the rest of mankind as 'intermediate' or of any special character."

"Like Freud, I'm inclined not to categorize homosexuals."

"And yet," Mercer interjected, "it seems true that men who prefer homosexual behavior are more sensitive than the ordinary lot. I will defer to Graham as our local expert. What, dear Graham, leads to that sensitivity?"

"It comes from their experience of persecution, if only because of forced invisibility. Suppose a male child encounters another boy in a way that is sexually satisfying. Whatever the manner of its expression, that pleasure faces society's disapproval. Remembrance of it will sooner or later be subject to shame toward that secret experience. He will be made guilty and taught to fear repetition of the act lest his masculinity be disparaged by continuing unacceptable feminine attraction to another male. Most of us succumb to conformity in our sexuality. Those few who acknowledge their own homosexuality because of the impossibility of repressing desires too powerful to resist or, it may be, too exciting to sacrifice, must at least censor their public conduct, which brings heightened awareness in sensitivity."

Alec thought it appropriate in the company of men who had never married to consider Freud's premise that homosexual influences were at work in ordinary mental life.

"I am struck by the finding of psychoanalysis that all human beings are not only capable of making a homosexual object-choice but have in fact made one in their unconscious. Does that suggest hidden desires may be the inspiration of friendships?"

Graham thought it best not to follow libido everywhere it might be suspected, "at least for this afternoon," since the dinner hour was approaching. But he leaped at this chance to resolve anew the earlier position he had taken on intermediacy.

"Taking account that there may be unconscious homosexuality in all of us gives more reason to shun categories of sexual separation."

Mercer added some tender logic of his own.

"In any case one must encourage understanding and tolerance of homosexuality. There is nothing to be ashamed about, certainly nothing to be prosecuted as a crime."

*   *   *

That evening Mercer guessed the political affairs of Ireland would interest Alec.

"Do you have special interest in the progress of the Irish people toward independence?"

Truth is Alec had neglected serious political attention to the Irish state, but he was quick to note that it had come to his attention, "Young men are leaving as fast as they can, seeing no hope of employment in Ireland. Had I been there, I would have gone, too."

Graham expressed fear of civil war, "Too many landless and bordering on starvation. The whole economic system needs drastic changing."

"Some say they were better under English rule" was a naïve observation by Maurice that Alec was quick to counter.

"Better the devil we don't know than the devil we do! The Irish can do worse than pursue their unlucky fortune. Even if it takes a hundred years to right the evil done them."

Mercer deplored the Irish Church for backwardness, "even a movement afoot to have the Gaelic language erase everything English."

"That would be a pity" came from Maurice as the last word.

Mercer suggested a bit of Irish music along with whiskey. Laura brought his fiddle and a hornpipe for Frank so they could play some jigs. Whiskey loosened fingers and tongues as Laura sang "Haste to the Wedding" and "Merry Old Woman" among others while Alec tapped his feet. Thus the evening ended in merriment.

*   *   *

Alec imbibed too much of Ireland's spirits, so that Maurice had a time getting him into bed properly. Then he returned to the library where Graham was sitting.

"Not ready for sleep?" Graham asked as he put aside a book.

"I was hoping to find you. You are the only friend who understands our situation. These first months with Alec have given me much to consider."

"Have you no confidence to speak with your uncle?"

"That has not gone well. They are an arrogant pair, my aunt and uncle. Alec has rejected further dealings. I will keep them to myself. Fortunately their disdain has not affected my success at the bank, so long as I keep the relationship with Alec silent."

"Alec told me of dismay with his place of work. He likes the workers well enough, but not the exploitation all around. I suggested that he pursue education, perhaps technical knowledge that would exercise his mind and better his prospects. Do you think he is happy under present conditions?"

"Not happy, truly, but not miserable. We relate very well. Just that the work he does is exhausting, and his mind is conflicted. Still he wishes to carry himself economically."

"It has only been a few months. Hard work will not harm him. What matters is his future in the long run."

"You are right to advise patience. I know I dare not push. There is a delicate balance between two men, neither of us wanting to lose the power of decision. But you need not worry, I will uphold my responsibility to Alec. My ambition brought us to Philadelphia and now we need to find ways for Alec to explore the possibilities."

*   *   *

Sunday afternoon they took their leave, never to see Mercer again. As for Graham, their first American friend, he would be watchful and helpful in the ways already marked out by his affection for them. When Alec hugged him goodbye that was certain.

Maurice thanked Mercer with a handshake, but following the lead of Alec, embraced Graham a little stiffly but with a depth of gratitude.

Chapter 9

Friends of a Kindly Disposition

"On life's vast ocean diversely we sail."

Alexander Pope, AN ESSAY ON MAN

Shortly after the Fonthill visit Maurice received a package from his mother containing foods reminiscent of his youth, English biscuits and plum pudding, along with a gift wrapped in opulent paper to be opened Christmas day, "So that we will share with you this joyous holiday at least in spirit," accompanied by expressions of love from his sisters. This fortuitous touch of home was appreciated, for a tinge of sadness had come over Maurice as the holiday neared, because of the absence of family and English traditional celebration. He had turned down Christmas with the Wetherills, no holiday at all, for it meant being without Alec who would have none of it.

Another petition that came in the mail surprised him, this one from Charles Perry, an executive at the bank, and his housemate. It was no ordinary invitation for it was artfully penned, the work of Albert, and it extended the first request of its kind.

"We fervently hope you will come to our home and share Christmas Eve with us, and with some friends of our generation, as well as a few of yours. Bring Alec, of course. I am eager to meet both of you. Charles and I are hoping to become more intimately acquainted with the two of you."

From their first meeting Maurice had felt an ease with Perry that had grown into curiosity about this fifty year old's private life which centered on a long-standing relationship, its nature uncertain, with another male. As Perry gained confidence in Maurice he parceled out parts of his life story. Twenty years ago he had acquired a large Victorian house and had gone in search of art to add to its distinction. This brought him into contact with Albert who owned a gallery that displayed fine paintings. Perry alluded to an escapade at Cape Cod that had moved their friendship beyond the esthetic, which Maurice surmised meant in the biblical sense.

That had been when each was in his early thirties. Now into their middle age they continued out of sentimental memories to celebrate a month of each summer at their house on the Cape. It was no small matter when Perry extended a vague invitation that Maurice should join them for his summer vacation, but Maurice had remained silent to the idea. Now that Alec was pointedly included, Maurice was excited at this opportunity to meet appropriate friends. Alec was more reserved, expressing doubts about whether these "friends" were appropriate for him. But to please Maurice he agreed to go to the celebration.

*   *   *

A light snow was falling when they entered the Victorian mansion in Germantown. They were greeted in a hallway that without impediment opened into a spacious living room where a dozen guests were already gathered. Many of them held cocktail glasses, a sign that much this evening would be illicit. As the new arrivals were being introduced a middle-aged man sidled up toward Alec. The guest who preferred Alec was Jack Leery, in his forties but closer to fifty, whose body bore signs of middle age desuetude but whose face retained a semblance of faded good looks. Leery's appearance betokened narcissism that had been fostered by the attention his beauty commanded during youth. Nowadays he gained that attention by witty contempt toward gay men who played upon that very feature of beauty which had been his distinguishing trait. As he pressed himself upon Alec, he offered caustic remarks about anyone conspicuous in behavior. Alec wondered why the others bothered with such a cynical person. He hoped to find distance when the opportunity presented.

Everyone's gaze was drawn by commotion from the latest arrivals, a surprising figure of a man in a flowing black cape and a broad rimmed hat, accompanied by a fairy figure of a boy who could hardly be twenty years of age. The spectral figure in black, carrying a mysterious valise, disappeared almost as quickly as he had arrived with an explanation delivered in a high-pitched voice of a woman, **"Excusez moi"** followed by mumbled words about needing to repair herself.

"Winnie," Leery caustically remarked, though without any explanation of the eerie chalk-white face that Alec had only caught with a momentary glimpse. Winnie's companion who stepped into the assemblage was equally striking in appearance, a nymph so wispy as to invite protection, with blond ringlets glued to a perfectly sculpted head, and piercing green eyes highlighted by careful arrangement of make-up. Leery depicted the pair as "Beauty and the beast." Others rushed to offer "Beauty" (whose name

93

was Leslie) graceful hugs and kisses, for they seemed genuinely delighted by even brief contact with such a charming creature of indistinguishable sex.

Before long Winnie reappeared to an obeisant audience that paid homage, for he was fully transformed into a spectacular woman.

"Good evening, gentlemen."

Then Winnie launched into an almost musical performance, for that was her talent as a female impersonator and chanteuse, "**Pardon m'arrivee en retard, non de impolitess, seulement que vous serez satisfait avec mon coiffure et vetements par la vie de plaisirs. Comme heureux je suis des gens de votre sorte.**"

As she went on in this manner, a good-natured laugh spread across the room at the abuse of the French language in such an outrageous display of good spirit. All but Leery seemed forgiving as they rivaled one another in lavish show of affection. Alec was too surprised to care about foreign words that eluded him, as he stared at Winnie's milky complexion framed by bobbed black hair, lips thickly painted brilliant red, silver rings bedecking fingers and ears, such an odd person. Winnie's slim body accented by petite breasts filled every breath of a satin form-fitting gown that might be a burlesque of female vanity. Alec wondered why a man would feel comfortable dressed that way.

Maurice was also appalled. His discomfort was distracted, however, when Leslie greeted him in such a gracious fashion that Maurice felt it incumbent to reciprocate. Awkwardly he embraced the youth.

Leslie took Maurice's fingers into his delicate hand, "I am pleased to meet a gentleman from England. Perhaps you will befriend another exile who left England as a youth."

Maurice wondered how long ago that could have been for Leslie seemed still a boy. But his more baffling concern was over the sexuality of the person before him who might indeed hold some surprises. With quick intuition he decided Leslie was male for when their hands touched he felt a tinge of sexual excitement that he had never felt toward a female. On the way home Alec and Maurice would playfully argue about the uncertainty with Maurice steadfast in his little litmus test.

As they assembled for dinner Leery had no intention of leaving seating to chance, and so he guided Alec to two unclaimed places. What pulled him to Alec was the stirring that a masculine presence aroused. Forcing his conversation upon an estranged youth, on the assumption they shared a preference for manliness and a corresponding deprecation of men who confused matters by thinking of themselves as women, Leery's blasé attitude began to yield to the earthiness that seeped through Alec's sparse remarks. He managed to dissipate Alec's unease by revealing without boasting that he was drama critic for the **INQUIRER,** based upon a career as dramatist that had sparkled for a decade, including a play which had held the New York stage for a season. When his creativity hit a snag, he built a reputation as a critic by reviews that became valued as well as feared. Alec began to relax as he discovered a thoughtful intelligence, though he was still uncertain about Leery's earlier remarks that seemed inappropriate among friends.

When an appetizer was served Leery commented in a gentler tone, as if the curtain had just gone up for a satire, "This is the first course of a comedy, but the whole world's your stage." Alec did not understand what was meant, though he pondered the remark. He knew it was flattering and he welcomed the relief from sarcasm at others' expense. A few servings later, his head lightened by wine, he retorted with comparable ambiguity. "I am no actor, Mr. Leery. Yet I tell you I prefer the comic aspects of life to melodrama." Leery raised an eyebrow, equally perplexed. When they left the table he kept an eye on Alec who drifted away.

Alec wandered into the living room to carefully observe these men who displayed pronounced preference for men. The few women present were less interesting to him, as he to them, for they clearly favored Maurice. Everyone gathered around Winnie who sat at the piano to entertain with some songs that were part of her routine. When it came to carols even Maurice joined the singing.

At a pause Albert caught the group's attention for an announcement, "We wish to present this expression of welcome and support to Maurice and Alec from all of us," as he led Maurice to a painting which, upon unveiling, portrayed a group of males, with only side or back views of their nudity, frolicking along the Schuylkill River. Maurice's emotional gratitude brought applause. Alec was silent, displeased by the commotion, as by the whole evening, which Albert did not fail to note.

"I am afraid you are embarrassed to be the center of so much attention. Forgive us for making you uncomfortable. Winnie, would you resume entertainment?"

Maurice in fact had been doting in the attention that had fallen his way during dinner, as he was plied for as much of the past as he cared to reveal. At times he pontificated: "I did not feel we could live in England comfortably with family pressures so powerful in my case." Thus he condensed their history. Seeing Alec's discomfort, Perry turned gentle questions his way about his American experiences. Alec gave curt responses, but this was generously attributed to his simple background. The group conferred its approval nonetheless. Later in the evening Maurice's pride swelled when he caught asides, "What a charming couple" and "They deserve happiness," words he had never thought to hear.

He found himself warming toward Leslie who approached him again to say how hopeful he was for further acquaintance. When Leslie touched upon intimate details of his situation, Maurice experienced empathy with this creature who seemed bound to suffer torment, but he was reluctant to reveal anything in turn. He did resolve, though he did not say so, to allow a friendship with Leslie to develop, but only to the extent it did not require closeness to Winnie.

*   *   *

Perry invited Maurice to see the house, the last stop being the library where they stood before a large painting by a Dutch Renaissance master. Perry took the private moment to apologize for any circumspection he had shown at the bank. He felt he owed the newcomer candor, but nothing so intimate that required closing the door to the library.

"Please forgive my maintaining deliberate distance at the bank. It was for your benefit as much as mine. It is prudent to avoid arousing interest among our colleagues. Rumors easily disturb our tranquility. I isolate my private life from work, given the unusual relationship I have with Albert. Unfortunately, there are people who object to anything so far from normal. Intimidation is not out of the question."

Maurice squirmed in discomfort at this troubling possibility that had already been raised during their visit with the Wetherills. Would deception have to become his and Alec's way? He asked whether secrecy was incumbent so that their heterosexual associates at the bank, specifically his uncle, would not have to acknowledge Perry's domestic situation. Charles closed the door to the library. He explained that it was not only he and Albert who were leading **de facto** criminal lives, if all were said and known. There were other prominent Philadelphians, even at the bank, who were forced to conceal their behavior to maintain business positions.

"Your uncle is a practical business man who knows the world. He expects decorum from all the personnel and returns respect. He is not a mean person, certainly not. You need not fear him, though you must recognize his requirements."

"Are you saying I must keep Alec hidden from my uncle?"

"I wonder if you understand your position and mine. There is much to disguise among our world of business. Your uncle cannot afford any scandal that touches the personnel of the bank, so it is best that you avoid confrontation. Discretion is surely the better source of valor in our case.

96

Out of consideration for our security we must veil our conduct from those who might be treacherous—yes, there is danger of blackmail, danger from the police. Anyone with intimate knowledge of our lives could choose to harm us. We are outlaws because of whom we love. It does not matter that the law is contemptible. Society has no heart when it comes to business. Men are driven by ambitions and connections. Fortunately, the law which prohibits a relationship such as Albert and I have is only rarely applied, but the threat of its enforcement forces us to live behind a wall of silence."

Maurice was chilled by this frank depiction of how they would have to live. Was America to be no less repressive for him or for Alec than England? His heart sank with fear that hypocrisy and cowardice would corrupt them into such abnegation.

"You and Alec are a splendid couple who deserve every chance to preserve your love within the boundaries of discretion." Discretion was urged again, which Perry expected to be reassuring. He hastened to add that he and Albert had long known the limits of freedom. "Now the subject has been broached, I wish that I could offer complete assurance, but that would be dangerous. Forgive me for persisting in this matter, but there is much you and Alec need to know about Pennsylvania's laws intended to prevent exactly the coupling of young men such as yourselves. Male love is reviled by the state which does not heed separation from the church. Its laws exact harsh punishments that frighten susceptible men away from male love. Even loving men in secrecy, pretending to heterosexuality, may weary a man of clandestine love and incline him into conventional marriage. There are rare persons who resist all the pressures and all the dangers. I like to think of Albert and myself among them, adventurers moved by love to take some risks—you and Alec as well among the daring. Still there is the need for vigilance. There is the risk of exposure. But with discretion, here we are partying in safety. Albert and I have lived together for twenty years in a relationship as solemn as any marriage. So be of cheer, Maurice!"

A sobered Maurice followed Perry to rejoin the party. For the moment he was unable to distinguish where his feelings stood, whether he was outraged at inclusion in such present company or whether he was on the verge of enjoying a sense of relief. At least he and Alec were not alone, for these new friends embraced them as they were, two men in love, without need for pretenses. Maurice looked critically at the guests, as Alec had done, and found irony in the appearance of these men, their sociability casual, a sharp contrast to the warnings he had just heard. Except for Winnie, who was outrageous, the others were commonplace. Neither church nor state was threatened, not by the occasional touching of a male by another. When

97

at the end of the party some of them displayed demonstrative expressions of affection, hugs and kisses along with goodbyes, the earth did not shake. It was gratifying to see the ease with which these men accepted male bonds whether romantic or otherwise. They had fashioned a society of friends comfortable in expressing their interests and tastes. Sensitivity to the arts, but in this they were not "fairies." Fastidiousness in grooming, dress and décor, but neither did this render them "pansies." True they were men who desired men as sexual partners, yet in this they were attuned to their bodies that dictated desire, as did their minds. What was illicit was largely hidden in private thoughts and desires that expressed a daring part of their lives. They concealed their sexual liaisons, actual or imaginary, so that they might pass for ordinary.

Emlyn was one such daring person present, a successful accountant who faithfully attended the Presbyterian Church. No trace of scandal attached to his bachelor existence. His relatives chided him to share his wealth and travels with some deserving woman, more than a few standing in waiting. What belied such prospect was that Emlyn secretly satisfied certain desires which were the core of his erotic pleasure. Once each month he disappeared for part of a week end in Manhattan, returning in time to appear at Sunday church service. The discerning women in the congregation noted his calmness on these Sundays, as if his travel had been spiritual in its compass. Such is the deception that spared Emlyn ostracism, for if truth were told, during these days-after as he sat in church he was lost in a tiredness of sinful reverie, basking in memories of the previous nights of orgy. He had spent his travel at a mid-town Manhattan Turkish bath where hundreds of men gathered. Those who passed the portal of this steamy den excitedly abandoned inhibitions, moral considerations or scrupulous judgment of persons in favor of anonymous sexual encounters. Many like Emlyn would return from the excitement of such nights in exhausted contentment, thus able to bear the dullness of their regular society.

More curious was a pair, Nicholas and John, partners in their law firm of Smith and Smith which was among the most distinguished in Philadelphia. Both were dressed rather too properly for this occasion, perhaps because that was the style preferred by the older Nicholas who was every bit of seventy. The younger Smith seemed half that age. It was odd for love to overlook such discrepancy of age. They would pass for father and son in public, or within circles more ordinary than this gathering. Here they were permitted shows of romantic affection, though in this as well they were true to their station. The older man was courteously protective of the other, escorting him with dignity, sharing private observations that brought grateful smiles of appreciation from his partner and a tenderness suggesting he was neither son nor any ordinary lover, but someone filled with admiration and respect.

They were not inseparable. John made his way to Alec toward whom he felt some affinity. He, too, had come from meager background, but thanks to a helping hand from Nicholas had attained a law degree and was near the top in his profession. He talked of his work and the house he shared with Nicholas near Rittenhouse Square. "We do no grand entertaining, something Nicholas detests, but I would like us to become acquainted. Our house is easy walking distance for you and Maurice, so I hope you will come by. Charles has told me of your background and I think we have some things in common. I owe my success in large part to Nicholas, in case you are wondering." Alec dared not ask about the nature of their relationship, but in time confidence developed so that John gave an intimate account of a love that few understood.

Such hidden history of other guests would have made more than a few of them distinctive if it could have been safely revealed. Herbert, a middle aged civil servant, was exactly as he appeared. After chatting with him briefly Maurice concluded he was both dull and sexless. This had not always been so. In his twenties he had fallen madly in love with a beautiful man who had no reciprocal feelings that were homosexual. When that passion led nowhere Herbert was a lost soul. He rejected any other prospects as undeserving, believing no other man could stand comparison with the lost lover. Unable to bury the past, he at first embarked on the promiscuous path of daily pursuit of sexual encounters wherever or however attainable, no matter how dangerous or brief or degrading, as if the accumulation of male parts and performances could add up to some equivalence of the lost perfection. Then, unfortunately, he was compromised by blackmail which he escaped only after several years of payment when the villain disappeared inexplicably. By then he was haunted by the fear of being discovered – by the police, or his co-workers, or another evil blackmailer. He had grown bitter, unable to face himself or his situation. He resigned from sex except for fantasy, and even at that with only paltry memories, for he dared not awaken desire for real sexual escapades he had known, but only for a man who had never desired him and had long disappeared from his life. The loathing for his nature, and of others like himself, crushed the physicality that had once been alive. After a time he might as well have been heterosexual, except that he preferred the company of settled men such as Charles and Albert. Nothing about him elicited sexual interest from anyone.

Leery had a different story, one that he would tell to Alec at a later time. When the party ended Leery offered a robust invitation, "I want to see you again." Alec was unsure whether Maurice was included. Maurice had received other solicitations on their behalf, and a plea for his solitary company from Leslie.

As they drove homeward Maurice was grateful their company was expanding. He wondered how they might reciprocate the kindness shown by Charles and Albert. Alec chided, "Not with our culinary performances. If we could afford to hire their cook, that would be different." Then Maurice rambled about some of his churning concerns over the warning from Perry. Alec reached over with a free hand to ruffle Maurice's hair. "No need to worry, we've each other. Let me get you home where I'll reassure you." Maurice's anxiety dissipated with Alec's touch. With light heartedness he mentioned a strange attraction toward Leslie, "Something a father might feel for a son." Alec only laughed. "Glad it's not Winnie!"

Alec was happy to be driving with Maurice's hand placed upon his thigh in an encouraging way. There was time for silent thought. He knew Maurice was happy, but still Christmas required something of England, for Maurice missed yuletide traditions, the carolers who made the rounds, the exchange of gifts, festive dinners with family, even midnight mass at the cathedral where the choir sang beautiful hymns amidst decorations of evergreen boughs and holly wreaths. At the least he would please Maurice with a holiday dinner, the best Philadelphia had to offer of English fare at the Dog and Partridge, a tavern reduced by prohibition to serving food alone. The surroundings would be English and the mutton pie hardy.

A light snowfall gave promise to both of a white Christmas.

Chapter 10

Bowing to Secrecy and Sanctimony

Life is a struggle,
like an unending river
and men want to tell me,
tell you, why they struggle
...these comprise my songs....

Pablo Neruda, "The Invisible Men"

Having rejected their holiday invitations, Maurice dined early in the new year with Anne and George an evening they were alone. Anne recounted the festivities the Wetherills had enjoyed, adding how disappointed they all were that Maurice had not taken his place as part of the family. No query regarding Alec was made, nor did Maurice feel it useful to mention anything, though he smarted at the ongoing rudeness.

When they were having coffee Maurice was presented a handsome gift that Anne had chosen. It was a painting acquired from Albert's gallery at his suggestion that its theme and modest size would complement another Charles and he planned for Maurice and Alec. The artist depicted Narcissus, about to bathe, pausing in his nakedness because he is enraptured in his own loveliness of face and figure reflected in a pool of water. Over his shoulder in the murky distance Echo is seen suffering because her love for him is unrequited. Delighted by the subject, and pleased with Albert for coming to his assistance, Maurice made sure Anne knew that it was celebration of the male body that made them companion pieces. He told Anne they would hang on facing walls so that the surrounding presence of beauty would inspire each day—and he added the painting would please Alec. Then he held Narcissus so that the canvas faced an unmoved George and Anne who was ready to listen to what he had to say.

"The artist is timid when art should be bold."

Anne welcomed this immersion into critical appreciation of painting. During travels through Europe she had visited the great museums and she was known locally for her support of art. She asked Maurice to clarify what boldness he envisioned that would serve esthetic purposes. This painting's mythological subject was daring in evoking the powers and dangers of beauty, and as to its success, she admitted being smitten with the beauty of Narcissus just as he appeared. Art is best when it allows the imagination to transcend reality through perception of the ideal.

Mention of the ideal encouraged Maurice to reach for truth in his new certitude of sexuality.

"Narcissus cupping his hands that way to hide his genitals is more a gesture of shame than adoration. Narcissus should admire every part of his beauty, as innocent of nudity as Michelangelo's Adam, but as firm and confident in his prowess as David. Art has no cause to censor merely for prudishness. That would be to forget, beauty is truth."

Anne recalled her aversion to Rembrandt's "Anatomy Lesson" when she had visited The Hague, too clinical a portrayal, though the artist had decently draped a cloth over the private parts. Maurice's allusion to Michelangelo she found remote. From the height of the Sistine ceiling the detail of Adam was miniscule, and as for David, she never did think much about it.

After that Maurice was more than ready to flee.

*   *   *

Trying to accommodate the Wetherills in their pride and position placed Maurice in the discomfort he had thought to escape by leaving England. Three thousand miles of intervening ocean had not distanced family expectations for him. Again the dilemma confronted him, could he be honest about Alec and their loving relationship before the bar of relatives who were his employers and judges?

Charles Perry had made clear that the devil was owed his due: openness was not possible while Maurice was seeking advantages from his inherited place in society. Behavior that was socially opprobrious, even criminal, had to be concealed. Alec would need to distance himself from the bank and the Wetherills. That suited Alec's present mood, not out of his own need for secrecy, but from contempt he felt toward Anne who had treated him brusquely as if he were best left invisible, and toward Regina who had merely blundered into a discourtesy appropriate to her outlook on unequal humankind. When Maurice told him of Andrew's hope to repair the breach, Alec brooked no argument. His mind was made up never to return to Stone House.

"They are your blood kin, no friends of mine."

Maurice's heart sank into this irreparable gulf, as if once again at sea with an unknown course. It should have been simple. They were two males wishing only to be free and open about their love. Yet everything around them presumed a different state of affairs for each of them; and everyone around sounded the same decree. "Don't dare tell us more than we must know and we will not ask about things best hidden, behaviors we know to be unnatural and immoral. Besides, the facts of the matter would only be a bother to our comfortable existence."

*   *   *

Such was the attitude of the 1920's, intensely secretive when it came to homosexuals, unlike the society that was to dawn nearer the end of the century. In Maurice's time a boy would know little of sexual behaviors outside the ordinary. He could not learn of diversity either at home or in the schools where nothing untoward was mentioned, least of all in the churches where theologians offered misrepresentations of nature. How could he come to accept his own differences within hostile institutions that curtailed friendships he desired that would have provided him integrity? Imprisoned within a loneliness of an estranged self, he was left to figure out some way to accommodate a mysterious realm of sexual attractions that set him apart from his playmates, for whatever he was told did not fit his case. If he behaved in any way suspect, a mere gesture or careless word, he might become prey to ridicule.

There were greater fears, that his parents would reject him for acknowledging the truth of his heart, or if he believed what religion told, that a vengeful God might cast him into the fire of hell for sinfulness. Rather than courting such dangers, he might retreat to hiding his own nature that he only half-understood at best. During his growth to manhood he would be confirmed in secrecy as a coat of armor that protected him from forfeiture of the role that could be his within a proudly patriarchal society, as he discovered that employment could be denied him if the truth were told, and a legal system stood ready to imprison him should he in any public way express his honest sexual preferences.

Discrimination was pervasive, women treated as unequal, darker races persecuted and denied advancement. No wonder a tyranny of silence ruled over that other affront to patriarchal presumption, homosexuality. Those different in that way were closeted except for a few artists able to rise beyond contempt, or notorious "drag queens" and "fairies" who contorted themselves into a caricature of femininity that was construed as their special form of "sickness" by the more manly and womanly. Men not wishing to forfeit their manliness and be treated as "queer" only because they felt desires for their own sex found it necessary to relegate their sexual urgings to clandestine and fleeting occasions. Though driven by

103

an inescapable desire for men, they could not satisfy this need by lasting intimacy with other men who shared their affinity.

*   *   *

Whatever the etiology of homosexuality, wherever the source of its grip upon human nature, that society in which our story unfolds generated feelings of worthlessness among many who discovered their sexuality to be different. It was often easier to remain a loner, since there was no safe way to cultivate loving companionship, for any liaison of two men brought danger of disclosure. In some tragic cases men might try to hide illicit desires through a whole life by purging their sexuality of its being, until perchance to stumble into some disgrace. For those defiant who refused to capitulate to the tyranny of heterosexuality, they needed to combat many forms of rejection, escape one way or another the consensus of reproach, and avoid terrorism from the law or the lawless.

Both Alec and Maurice were fortunate in being spared any severe wounds of boyhood that might have bent their sexuality into unattractive ways, though Maurice had come close to resigning himself to a denatured life when for a time he felt helplessly abandoned, until he experienced the power of surrender to Alec. Both he and Alec were strengthened by their meeting, enough to seek a new land, again to wonder what it mattered for their future together that they lived in a country that proclaimed democracy.

Alike to countless unknown others feeling sexual desire toward their own sex, they were expected to act as accomplices in their own oppression. They must spend their workdays passing as heterosexuals. It was not for either of them difficult to accomplish this duplicity simply by displaying those masculine outlooks and behaviors they shared with others of their gender, since a social expectation existed that anyone who was homosexual would be feminine in manners. Maurice was far from that. What he faced each day at the bank was a wall of silence, "the less said, the better" as if not speaking of homosexual behavior proved it was nowhere to be found. Anne's ignoring of Alec pointed the psychological cost for Maurice, a sense of indignity that he might have to live all his life surrounded by a wall of bigotry.

There was a different difficulty for Alec amidst manual laborers, not in acting his manly part, but in how much of prejudice he would seem to tolerate. Instead of outright silence, a loud bigotry was put forth as manliness by some co-workers who knew that to mix with "fairies" endangered a man's sexual prowess over women. Such an image of masculinity resembled the masquerade of the drag queen, in this case a

104

male caricature of his own gender, as if every man were crude, lascivious and single-minded. Alec had lived with the Scudders and he had learned how men act, so that he could play his role without effort, but he had no need for exaggerated displays.

*   *   *

Not long after the evening with the Wetherills, despite being surrounded by the beauty of young boys bathing on one wall and Narcissus admiring his image on the other, Maurice fell to ranting about family. He was fed up with respectability.

"I gave up my family once. I will do it again."

In a spirit of bravado Maurice was sure he had chosen right. He remembered the pain he had suffered at losing Clive's love, and the desperate fears that followed his first encounters with Alec, to the point of considering giving him up. But then the park-bench philosopher had warned him that to sacrifice comradely love would imperil his soul. For a second time he needed to choose wisely and naturally.

Alec was listening to his friend, wondering what lay in store. He also remembered Clive Durham whom he had watched sufficiently to know, as well as Maurice knew, that the public life of social convention exacts denials of the romantic and the erotic, the heart and the body. Alec often reflected on his mother's daring in turning away from family and native land, and he loved the memory of her all the more for sacrifices she had made to raise him free from superstition. Yet he knew it was not right to demand comparable moral fiber of Maurice whose leisured upbringing had never toughened his resolve.

"Your career is at issue, Morrie. I cannot let you think that way. Not when we have no other way of providing. Later you may regret what you have done. Once I have found work that occupies my mind and not just my body, then we may consider some other course. Still the law must be reckoned. Now you need your uncle for economic reasons, and your situation, without Halls around, requires you include yourself as a Wetherill. No place for me there. Don't you see?"

Maurice did see clearly that the exclusion of Alec was expected in this reckoning, but he was angry at having to surrender to the forces of convention.

"Damn George and Anne! Why must they be allowed to shun our existence?"

"**My** existence is what you mean. No secret, property is at root, the concern of most people. We want our share, don't we? As I see it, some think the earth belongs to the chosen part of mankind, the rest say it belongs

105

to all in equitable fashion. Which would be the more natural? George favors aristocrats, priests, bankers, his kind, and that group expects all the others to do the hard work. Myself, I fall among the clods. There are a few women like Anne, while most like my mother scrub their floors, serve their meals, care for their children. Your Wetherills surely have more than anyone should. What do they do in thirty rooms they could not do in three? Still, their duty is to preserve that fortune for the next Wetherills and Halls. Your blood deserves a share of its advantages. George sees how a man's name gives him legitimacy and continuity of fortune. He and Anne know me to be a bastard and scorn my mother. They would not have you follow such example, tying your good fortune to the likes of me. They know where you belong."

Maurice was chagrined to be linked with his own class.

"Their contempt extends to our love which they judge unworthy." Maurice understood more than he had first admitted, but as would remain the case through many years ahead, his will needed strengthening. "They refuse to acknowledge what is before their eyes, men aroused by men. Don't our feelings offer proof? How else are we to know what is natural than to abide by our feelings?"

Alec was willing to enter that nebulous terrain and explore it with earthiness.

"You and I know the appeal of men to men. Simply because we both popped into the world with a penis has nothing to do with the direction it takes. I know mine seeks comforting the way an itch does. I was alike to most boys, providing pleasure on my own once I learned its ways. Assistance was sometimes there, and I was ready to accept opportunities most directions. When first I saw you, an instinct told me I could satisfy your need and mine."

Maurice could not help grinning at this account that came closer to truth than all his education had said. "I hope it was nothing feminine in me!"

"No worry on that, Morrie. Your body is a man's. Yet I am no Narcissus willing to settle for a mirror of myself. You also have softness which needed taking. Your giving your body makes me feel right."

"Since I have little appreciation of women, neither their bodies nor their ways, I must ask what you find of distinction in the feminine?"

"You worry too much that differences are certain. We are none of us all man or woman, but each of them at separate times. I also know soft and tender feelings. When I was eleven I loved my brother Dennis, and I still long for that kind of sexual playfulness that brought him pleasure. Other time my imagination wishes to caress a woman's breast. Most often my penis seeks to penetrate in order to compel another's surrender. It makes my body feel right. I think these are feelings Whitman embraced."

Maurice was amazed that such a young person could fathom the sexuality that flowed into conflicting streams. But he would not be diverted. He asked, "How is it that Anne and George remained rooted in the verities of gender?"

"Pride and social passions work in them, less to do with sexuality which left to its nature is heedless pleasure. They are with society seeking control of mating. But we ought not to be fooled by the hypocrisy of their station. Endless desires are at work in them as occasions offer. Men of George's class do not scruple at using youth, women or men, purchasing among the lower classes as it suits them."

"Yet you advise me to go along with my uncle? Does that not strengthen the prejudices and repressions we loathe?"

"I can not see any other place for you and for me right now. We are in a new land and need to find our way. There is the law to reckon. I did not come to America to live in a prison, nor did you."

"Then I must pay my due to George and Anne. And what about you? Will you compromise some and at least see Andrew as part of the bargain? He is concerned for your spiritual welfare. He has hinted to me that he is ready to accommodate sexual differences, though I doubt he knows much."

Alec in fairness acquiesced in the matter of a visit to St. Mark's as part of their concurrence with silence.

*   *   *

The fateful visit would be a long time coming, Alec busy with work six days of the week and not ready to sacrifice a Sunday to such folly. Maurice continued to urge Alec to come with him to St. Mark's which his uncle favored and where Andrew stood ready to persuade another soul toward salvation. Alec persisted in not going and he was not missed. There was no room for such an interloper at the front of the church.

At church and at Stone Hall Maurice involved Andrew in matters of the heart and soul, even as he grew closer to his uncle. Without recognizing the drift in which he was swirling, Maurice was being pulled toward a place among Philadelphia gentlemen. He was a worthy aspirant for a high place in society: English-American with family connections, the nephew of a rising officer in one of the city's richest banks, and a presentable young man who could attract a wife of wealth and status. Some accounting had to be rendered to his uncle who was clear-headed and watchful of these goals.

George Wetherill was a confirmed Christian but far from devout. He displayed just the right degrees of indifference toward doctrine, but any doubts and reservations were kept silent. Silence serves to cover up many unseemly things. Religion was for him akin to patriotism, just so the world knew where one stood and the church did not interfere with worldly pursuits. George wished his nephew to follow in this carefully advised course. Both had chosen to be Americans, so why should not the nephew accept the importance of being respectable toward the religious establishment?

Maurice acquiesced in this expectation, attending St. Mark's, sitting next to his uncle in the pews assigned the Wetherill family who were generous supporters. Sensitive that he and Alec were sexual non-conformists, Maurice was mindful to minimize suspicions on any other count. Social acceptance seemed worth a small amount of hypocrisy, and he hoped Alec would make a token offering of churchgoing. That way he would not have to remain totally out of sight. Alec was of another mind. He had managed never to enter a church since his mother's funeral. He might be willing in many ways to please Maurice but he was a non-believer. He made blunt distinction between courtesy due to Maurice by prudent silence and outright hypocrisy for the sake of others.

"Churches leave me without illusions. They do not make the world less harsh. Even if I were to go to a church out of genuineness, I would find a place where there are people like me, men who work, with their wives and children. I would want one without priests and doctrines, though such a church does not exist."

Maurice had no countervailing theological position. "It would simply make me happier, more comfortable" was all that he could offer. He was hesitant to delve further.

Nevertheless Alec felt badgered and blurted the truth, "You are tired of apologizing for me."

Bluntness was uncomfortable. Maurice wished acceptance from family and those with whom he worked, but at what price? Apologize for Alec? Is that what he was doing or trying not to do? Maurice felt shamed on this account.

"You're trying to hew the rough edges, to change who I am. I know it is difficult for you. George never says directly, but he has been informed by your mother. It would be interesting to know her pleas. I am sure he is ready to pick the right young lady for your proper marriage, if only you leave behind the impediments due to youth. Your try to avoid that issue is only another half-step in the vain hope George will do likewise. You would need to smooth me over, turn me into an Episcopalian. I might even become cut and mannered to serve as usher at St. Mark's. But where does that lead us? We are never to be proper and never married."

Maurice, thus rebuked, lacked philosophical or moral grounds to argue further. He was not pretending that they become Christians in order to give up their goods. To be the kind of Christian that social circumstances dictated meant giving up the urges and requisites of their own characters. This he agreed with Alec was out of the question. From time to time Maurice would need this kind of calling back to the resolve he had summoned in leaving England to make his life with Alec. There was always danger that tides of ambition or social status would batter the resolve that had to be supported in order to sustain **terra firma** for his and Alec's love.

"I will tell Andrew that you are satisfied with things as they are."

When Maurice took his place next to the Wetherills the following Sunday he felt desolate. Nor did the spirit come to his rescue during the prayers, but afterward Anne took the occasion to offer from Wetherill bounty.

"We have some older furniture in the stable, many handsome pieces still serviceable. Do come by, Maurice, to choose whatever would add to your comfort. There is a piano I would like you to have. I'll see that it is tuned and delivered. This will please your mother who worries for your welfare. Oh, yes, and feel free to bring Alec to help in the selection."

What had brought this modicum of change in attitude? An anguished letter had arrived from Grace Hall asking care for Maurice who had sent an account of his sparse living conditions, though the words had been written in irony lost on his mother. She begged Anne to act generously in her stead, even if it meant extending kindness to Alec. "It is only a matter of time, then Maurice will see that we are right."

Alec was also undergoing a leavening of mood as he faced the complexities of their arrangement. He had been the one to suggest that Maurice sail along the mainstream by remaining beholden to George. Though his own situation was less cumbersome, it was unclear what he might need to do in the way of compromise once his unformulated ambitions took hold. For now, unhappiness needed to be addressed. Maurice's sadness must be soothed, that was the start. By a telephone call to Andrew he arranged to make the long delayed visit on the coming Saturday afternoon.

*　　　*　　　*

"I expect you would enjoy something stronger than tea." Without waiting for a response Andrew poured communion wine into two glasses of fine crystal with words he hoped would provide assurance.

"You see I suspend rules that run against our God-given nature. Why should priests alone enjoy a libation?"

Andrew was delighted to see Alec. He was eager that they become friends, not only because it was important to Maurice's happiness, but also because he felt a strong impulse from his faith and, truth be told, from his quieted sexuality. Halfway toward being a priest he was fully committed to fulfilling the expectations of that vocation. A few years earlier, however, he had laid some grave theological doubts before one of his superiors, misgivings about the Trinity, but he had been assured the important thing was to love and serve God. No need to hopelessly entangle one's mind in theology that could not be resolved.

There was another matter that gave him pause in pursuing his vocation, his sexual leanings. It was not likely that such a beautiful person as Andrew could escape the attraction others of both sexes showed toward him. He had not cultivated vanity about this God-given attribute of good looks, but as overtures came he discovered his body responsive, even when intimacy was pressed upon him without invitation, which happened with males when he was yet a boy. These experiences were not abusive. To the contrary, he saved them as tender memories. He found himself thereafter curious and sometimes willing even after he entered his ministry when approached by a man who was sexually attractive. He spoke of these occasional lapses during sacramental confession, acknowledging sins of the flesh that were "unnatural" acts. He was surprised by leniency from his confessor priests who of course reprimanded him while pardoning the sins as if they were peccadilloes best forgotten. Of course Andrew did not forget, but neither did he feel frightened, nor did he have such strong urges to press his own desires of that sort.

At present Andrew was single-minded that nothing should get in his way to Alec who might be helped to take the path of Christian love. No heavy-handedness in details of theology, no family barrier should be allowed to disqualify him in Alec's eyes.

"It is useless to apologize for my mother's thoughtlessness, or Regina's lack of grace. I hope you will not judge me harshly on their account. I intend to be friends with you and Maurice."

"Sure enough, Andrew. Let us deal with one another man to man. Just so you do not expect me to treat you with considerations as a priest. You are barely older than me, and I have no reason to think you more capable of critical judgment, especially when it comes to sexual engagement. I came to you out of courtesy to Maurice. Do not have high hopes of succeeding with me."

Alec took little time to down his wine and start into a second glass which warmed his heart and loosened his tongue.

"Likely I'll go through life without being christened properly."

Andrew showed no dismay at this disarming frankness. He had overcome the earlier shock when Maurice had first mentioned his friend was without any religion, for he had never thought anyone could live in England and not be a Christian. He was still perplexed why the mother had not seen to it when Alec was an infant.

"I am not a full heathen. My mother's hand sprinkled some holy water on me when she committed me to the care of St. Brigit. That is baptizing enough for me. She was a woman of faith placed in saints who she supposed watch over us. That she taught me, to revere St. Brigit, to pray to her, same as praying to God. Nothing was ever spoken of condemnation for sin or need for rituals. It was not a church she loved for little compassion came our way from that quarter."

"I am more sympathetic with your position than you think. I briefly turned away from the church when I saw its hypocrisy. I was twenty years old when I realized how little the church had instructed my parents to care for those who work with their hands. You have seen my mother's selfishness and heard as much of my father. His religion is far from the spirit of the gospels. It is not creeds he cares about, just so there is no nonsense or exhortation. He worships churches, their structures of solid stone, as if they were part of nature, to be revered as he does banks, attended by the right sort of people and keeping in check the constant forces for evil."

"I have not noticed people who are religious acting any better than the rest. How is it you are different and concerned with the suffering of ordinary people?"

"Christianity ordains love for one another with compassion. My mind does not engage in analysis that requires theology beyond that."

"How can you know what it is for a man to work all of his life and grow old before his duties are fulfilled to his children, or become unemployed and watch their illnesses untended?"

"I have no experience of such deprivations. But I have observed the life of the city and I reflect on human sorrows. Perhaps you can aid me to further understanding? That would give me more opportunity to encourage you in the same direction of salvation."

"It's too soon to worry about my fate in the life beyond. I am trying to understand how you remain devoted to a church complicit with the rich against the poor. Is that not a church derelict in its message?"

"I struggled with those matters, but I could not resolve them. Ultimately I had only my faith in Jesus Christ which overruled other considerations. I believe Christianity was established through Jesus, Paul and the other saints."

"You are not so far from my mother in trusting saints. Too much of superstition for me, Andrew. I warned you that I have no need for religion."

"What if Christianity is the true faith in our redeemer? Would you not find it comforting to believe in Christ as your savior?"

Alec did not find this trend of thought worthwhile to his present comfort or to his ultimate outcome. Better to put an end to the exchange.

"Christianity rid of theology would have more appeal to me. Jesus tells us to love one another. Well and good, I already love Maurice. So I am doing as Jesus urged. If you do the same, and love Maurice, then you may respect what God has made of me."

Andrew was silenced, though he had more he wished to say. He excused himself from the room. Ten minutes later he returned carrying a book.

"Would you take this as a token of Christian love? I accept your friendship and I pray for God's blessing upon your and Maurice's love. God is beyond the limits of our puny brains. It is God who is judge of all things, not the church. We will discuss further when you are ready."

Alec took the offering and reciprocated with his own.

"Now embrace me as a Christian and also as a man of flesh, for I find you honest and sincere."

Andrew signaled his readiness, placing his hands gently to Alec's shoulders trying to preserve respectable distance. Alec wanted no mistake that more than a spiritual liaison was at issue. He pulled Andrew firmly into himself to that they could feel every point of embrace of their bodies. Then he placed a gentle kiss on the other's lips, leaving Andrew not displeased by this assertion of a rebellious spirit.

Alec left with the good book in hand. He resolved upon its thorough reading whenever quiet moments permitted.

*   *   *

On the front cover of the Bible he found a brief inscription, the signature Andrew Wetherill followed by a reference to Phil. 1:6. The passage cited was from Paul the apostle's letter to the Philippians: "Being confident of this very thing, that he which hath begun a good work in you will perform it until the day of Jesus Christ."

The words worked an epiphany for Alec, but not all in the way Andrew intended. The honest hope of Andrew revived Alec's spirit that had been for many months weighed down by hard labor and weariness, and some would add, pushed aside by the sexual deeds with Maurice. Alec was transported again to a time in England, and to the mood of more than a year ago, when he had cultivated learning through the use of the Durham library. He would read the Bible seeking knowledge of the human world as much as the spiritual, exercising critical judgment on every part to better engage Andrew in ongoing dialogue and perhaps to save him. That would be his share of the good work underway.

Despite the heat of the summer, when Alec returned from a day of sweat at work he managed to find a treasured hour each night before sleep. He read of the creation in Genesis, "In the beginning God created the heaven and earth" and "God said, Let us make man in our image." Adam and Eve were familiar to him, but he had never known that while Adam slept God took one of his ribs to form Eve. How amazing it was to learn woman was born of man. He was defiant against this patriarchal transformation of reality. This was something to pose as a challenge to Andrew. He tried to share this discovery with Maurice who was too preoccupied with work of the world to do more than casually dismiss the episode as "a harmless myth, in any case."

Several nights later Alec had arrived at Exodus, and now he stood with Moses atop Mount Sinai, amidst lightning and thunder and smoke. Alec pressed his thoughts, this time more firmly, so that Maurice could not brush aside as just another harmless myth this terrifying appearance of God to issue commands and threats to all who fail to heed his word. What use, he asked Maurice, was this grappling for truth in an old book filled with cruelties and contradictions? In his confusion Andrew was surrendering too much of his nature which would be better satisfied giving of his beauty and gentleness. His was not a figure for sackcloth and torment of the body. Maurice was immersed in some business for the next day, his thoughts too far removed from the Jewish prophets, to do more than mutter what seemed acquiescence in the course Alec intended to follow.

"We must do something for your poor cousin. He seems to be another Candide."

Chapter 11

Life is No Crystal Stair

Well, son, I'll tell you:
Life for me ain't been no crystal stair,
It's had tacks on it.
And splinters,
And boards torn up,
And places with no carpets on the floor –
Bare.
But all the time
I'se been a'climbing on . . .
So, boy, don't turn back.
Don't you fall now –
For I'se still goin', honey
I'se still climbin',
And life for me ain't been no crystal stair.

Langston Hughes, "Mother to Son"

Most of daily life being commonplace, neither exciting in its living nor likely in its telling, details regarding Alec and Maurice's places of work need not by recounted, though such doings occupied a good deal of time. Home was where their hearts were. During the winter of hard labor when the workday was over there were all the little things for them to learn about each other with the difficulty of accepting differences in manners and attitudes.

Domestic life offered challenges that face any new couple, and then some. Theirs was the price of defying convention that assigns domestic tasks according to gender. Who was to play the husband, who perform the work of a woman? Perhaps such distinctions would be better avoided, but was it possible? Maurice came from a society deliberately apart from the experiences of the serving class so that he was twice removed from the keeping of a home. He had never in his life cleaned a room, never done anything to provide directly for his daily needs. Who was going to care for his clothing? Who was to replace the servitude of maids? Fortunately Alec had learned a bit of cleaning, cooking and fixing. He cheerily suggested, "Whoever likes cooking should do it." Of course it was easier said than done, for his job at the plant demanded twelve hours of each weekday when travel was added, and so he got home tired but needy of nourishment.

The day-to-day matters of caring for a house proved a stumble-along experience. Maurice made a valiant go at it. He arranged the bed each morning and when Saturday came he scrubbed floors. Alec might have shown more thanks for these efforts. But whenever Maurice bemoaned his servile role, Alec reproached him, "I don't need a servant, never had one." Maurice persisted in the attitude of noblesse oblige even as he searched for a way of life circumscribed by Alec's long and arduous manual labor. Determined to provide what was needed, he did his best to prepare the evening meal. After weeks of trial, mostly error, happiness eluded him in the kitchen. Alec made caustic remarks after meals. "I shall have to show you how to prepare this." Such discourtesy punctured the slight chance that Maurice might find satisfaction in domestic work done for his prince who had very earthy tastes.

"Why don't we eat at Angelo's?" became a suggestion as frequent from one as the other. Tony had listened numerous times to light-hearted complaints about Maurice's cooking before he came up with what might offer an occasional solution. He invited them to his father's restaurant for Neapolitan food. They would be his guests. It was a way of helping a friend and showing his gratitude for sharing Alec's coupe that had replaced the train to work.

The next Saturday evening Tony placed them at a table made cheerful by a pink and green cloth lit by candle lamp. As they admired a mural of a busy street in Naples that stretched the length of the wall, a first course of fried calamari and olives arrived. Tony was accompanied by his father, Angelo, who welcomed them with a touch of the old world. "You are friends of my son," as he poured a heady red wine into cups from a coffee pot. So much for disguise dictated by prohibition. "Neapolitan food and wine belong together," Angelo assured them. "Don't worry, everything is approved." He nodded his head toward some back tables where two families were gathered. "They are police. They eat here every week."

Angela was on hand to serve them. Tony's sister was a senior in high school who helped when the restaurant was busy. There was nothing "old world" about her except for exotic dark hair and eyes, like Tony's. She flaunted her sensuality as she placed bread on the table or delivered plates.

Alec thought she was not likely to remain virginal as was becoming to Italian girls. Nothing she said, exactly, for her words were respectful, but the ease she took in touching both young men. When she delivered heaping plates of spaghetti, at Alec's turn, her body leaned lightly against his shoulder which left no doubt she, too, wished to please friends of Tony. Maurice was aware of this favoring of Alec. When she insisted they try the rum cake, making clear she had helped prepare it under direction of her mother, they were both enthusiastic, but Alec so much so that he succumbed to a second "not too large" piece in a manner that matched her flirtatiousness. This triumph drew a smile from Angela who said she liked people who shared her taste for sweets.

Their first experience being so pleasant, Angelo's became a haven from some of the discontentment that had crept into their lives.

*   *   *

Spring brought a resurgence of romance as if the outburst of flowers insisted on it. Maurice cultivated this way of looking at things, but their renewed ardor did not last to the summer. The lull was not due to any lack on Maurice's part but because Alec was being coarsened and worn down by the plight of his dreary work, the promise of America gone from his current focus.

It was due to more than drudgery that happiness was slipping away. Not in dramatic ways, but in small disappointments, a layer of resentments was building which, not addressed, would stifle companionship. Maurice suffered from unfulfilled cultural needs that had accounted for more of his pleasure than he reckoned. Alec's background was at issue, though he was eager to experience new realms of culture at Maurice's guidance. He had quickly taken to classical music, Tchaikovsky's symphonies his favorites. He could not help that he often fell asleep from the toil of the day even as he attempted to listen. It was a brutal fact that long hours of work limited esthetic openings, physical tiredness making it additional hard labor to concentrate on foreign ventures. God had done well in the creation by ordaining Sunday as a day of rest for all those who labor in the fields and factories. He might have done better adding another.

Maurice wanted more than Alec's limited leisure time permitted, though he had only a vague restlessness rather than a keen sense of what it might be. He missed a companion to share the indulgent life of the mind, the way he had with Clive. Ordinary evenings, from sheer tiredness, Alec fell into the habit of seeking a "good time" of simpler fare. He wished to eat at Angelo's or to go with or without Maurice to a neighborhood speakeasy where he would find men who shared his lot. Prohibition was only desultory in enforcement, and so beer flowed freely in hundreds of speakeasies all over the city. After a time or two Maurice refused invitations because he disliked the smells of stale beer, tobacco smoke, unwashed clothing, and sweaty armpits. Alec insisted on being with these earthy men who knew in their guts they were demeaned by inadequate compensation and dignity. Even at home they heard the complaints of nagging wives. Alec brought the news to Maurice that after marriage all that love and stuff flies out the window. Among friends these men made humor of sexual fantasies and sometimes vividly recalled real escapades. After such talk they went home reconciled to their toil and cultural impoverishment and to their women as well. Alec, too, would return tipsy to Maurice and fall into bed exhausted.

Maurice was also experiencing less of the physical intimacy that had been the certainty of their companionship. It began to annoy him that Alec was not punctilious about appearances because, as he apologized, he was only going to work day after day or drinking that evening amidst workers who, though they were lax in their habits, offered no pretenses. Alex was not oblivious to Maurice's discontent. He knew Maurice would be pleased if they would simply stay at home to talk and jest. Jest all right, but when Alec did so it now had a harsh edge. He needed to be around more common folk than Maurice.

"Have you noticed the world is cock-eyed? The harder one works, the less one receives of pay." That is something of the fare Alec offered whenever he sacrificed the speakeasy.

"I work hard as well," Maurice insisted, "with my mind and skills."

"Nothing like the sweat from our bodies. Nor do you work twice as hard to warrant your salary, double mine."

Maurice would urge upon Alec a restful and cleansing bath, hoping this would temper his mood and revive his playfulness. He wanted to retire early enough for the kind of sexual closeness that had come naturally at first. Alec seemed to ignore these wholesome wishes, falling asleep if he stayed away from the tavern, neglecting a refreshing bath that might have renewed his ardor. In the morning before departing for the plant he would plant a kiss upon the lips of a pouting or simply tired Maurice.

There was something debilitating beneath the surface affecting them both. That damnable silence was exacting a toll. At work and in their social life, pretense, living a lie, though necessary, was proving distressing. The need to deny what is intrinsic and to live within strictures that society imposes on what it calls immoral behavior was having a corrosive effect. In an atmosphere of heterosexism those branded homosexuals have no easy way to alleviate this scarlet letter pressed upon their minds. Public interaction as a couple was precluded. Their home was the only place of physical intimacy, for it was not a wise or safe thing to express intimacies in the streets of Philadelphia, at the speakeasy, even at Angelo's. The society around them accepted friendship, but it kept a begrudging silence that anything deeper between two males should exist.

Uncle George, perhaps because he knew more than most, stubbornly continued to issue invitations for Maurice alone. There was always a danger that Maurice might take this easier way with another half step toward conformity. Such temptation came unexpectedly when he became depressed from loneliness for the loss of his English way of life. He did not complain, but his moodiness elicited from Alec suggestions that he spend evenings with the Wetherills who were his family. For Alec, the absence of mother and father made his situation less complicated, less painful than Maurice's. Despite the separation of an ocean Maurice was drawn back to the Halls. It was as if his mother were there to remind him, such is your role, such your destiny, as progeny of bourgeois wealth and culture, to extend the business of men and to propagate the species, the Halls in particular. The superstructure of law, education, culture and morality weighed upon him more than he had ever anticipated when he had chosen to link his life to a man instead of a woman. He had set out across the ocean with the naiveté of youth. No matter how resolute he had been in choosing to love and cherish Alec, if he felt estranged in any way from him, the awareness increased of the deprivations he suffered. A part of him that he thought purged would reappear, remindful of family, culture and privilege. Sometimes he struck out in anger at these regrets, and he would accost his upbringing. If only his mother could have said with magnanimity of spirit, "Alec, I welcome you into our family, as a spouse to Maurice," the whole world would have become a warm and sunny place where a God of love might be discerned. Even Uncle George might have bent before such an endorsement.

Alec was also distressed that living with Maurice in a domestic way, he had a secret to keep. He had always been outgoing which enabled him to deal with others in the same accepting way. Now it was different. Whether his fascination with Maurice's body, and by extension with other male bodies, was something of beauty or whether it carried a potential tragic element, it was incumbent that his deepest emotions remain secret. Out of fear or simple prudence he could no longer confidently present himself honestly. A part of his mind wished to be rid of the lie that lay at the heart of their existence.

                    *   *   *

Maurice did begin to spend more time that summer with the Wetherills and with friends Alec did not share. Leslie, who became the prime recipient of favor, was flattered by the attention of Maurice courting him. Every bit of the feminine within him invited Maurice to be at his most gentlemanly. Maurice would arrive attractively attired to pick up Leslie for an evening together, perhaps a drive and then an ice cream parlor. They took to going to movies each week, Leslie selecting films with heroines who defended their purity or suffered for failure. In the darkness of the theatre, the screen filled with tears from betrayal or men's cruelty, Leslie would take hold of Maurice's hand for comfort and never let go until the lights went on. Maurice felt it harmless to provide Leslie the support of a gentleman and as they parted an embrace goodnight that edged on eroticism, his reasoning being that "what is good for the gander is good for the goose" which had reference to Alec's interest in Angela.

It had become their habit to eat at Angelo's Saturday nights when Alec would take effort to scrub himself and dress neatly as much for Angela's sake as for Maurice. After awhile Maurice noted this with a twinge of jealousy. There was no reason for concern. Angela's instincts were sound, so that she was careful to befriend both men she knew were linked by some special bond that Tony had mentioned. She made a point of showing Maurice she liked him as well, though differently. Anyway, Maurice reassured himself, Alec could hardly be faulted for exuding sexual appeal effortlessly.

It seemed different one Saturday in June at Tony's wedding. Not only Rita looked attractive, but Angela as a bridesmaid in a pink gown was ravishing. Outside the church Alec kissed bride and groom, and Angela as well. Then at the evening reception Alec, under the influence of liquor, danced to a romantic melody with Angela and kissed her a second time. Maurice made the mistake of watching.

That night as they lay in bed back to back, Alec in the nude because of the heat of the summer, neither of them gave any sign of sexual interest. Maurice was moved to ask,

"Are you thinking of Angela?"

"Only that she is a goose to be plucked. Not by this gander! It is harmless imagining on my part. Angela belongs with an Italian husband who adores her and will keep her pregnant with a string of babies." In a show of innocence he rolled over so that he could kiss Maurice's neck while pressing upon him.

Encouraged by this affection, Maurice expressed his concern.

119

"What I wonder—I must be frank—do you desire me? I feel I have disappointed you."

Alec felt unhappy that he could only find feelings to say, "I am tired from all the work that takes its toll of my energy." That much was true and part of the uneasiness afflicting him. He knew there was more, but what was he to do when he did not understand? Despite the stifling heat he was ready to rise to this occasion, but for one of the few times Maurice was tired, too.

*   *   *

After almost a year at the plant Alec was in a malaise. He was not satisfied with his work nor had he posed some alternative course that would energize his ambition. Bread alone is meager sustenance for a mind neglected of its own proper nourishment. The corporeal pleasures of coupling with Maurice were tangible, yet a gnawing frustration filled too many other hours of each working day. Alec longed to learn things that his experiences could not teach, at least not in one lifetime.

True, he had made a start, but one that was carrying him in a strange direction. What he had before him was the task that he had appointed himself and the promise he had implicitly given to Andrew. Yet the word that he was reading was more disturbing than satisfying. Leviticus offered mean chastisements and Deuteronomy urged harshness of the sword, matters he meant to pose to Andrew next time they met. He almost abandoned the reading then and there. But a note arrived from Andrew offering a fresher breath. John was cited from the New Testament: "By this shall all men know that ye are my disciples, if ye have love one to another." So Alec continued to read. By the time he reached Psalms it was with a sense of relief, though he found their spirituality excessive, but at least he was halfway through the book. In another few months he was ready to put the Old Testament behind him for well and good.

*   *   *

An interlude pointed him a different direction. Jack Leery had telephoned to invite him on several occasions until he agreed to meet one Sunday morning while Maurice was off to St. Mark's and an afternoon at Stone House. Leery's apartment overlooked Rittenhouse Square where they met. Leery complained at once that it had been too long a wait to see him, but he understood the demands of labor.

"How long will you continue that dreary work of yours?"

"Not much longer. Maurice is urging me to give it up."

"Maurice, yes. How is the dear boy?" There was a ring of insincerity in the query, as there was in the cursory reply, "Maurice is busy." Leery wisely put Maurice aside, at least till lunch, if only Alec would agree to the afternoon.

As they strolled the park Leery did the talking. He mentioned recent travel and a play he had just reviewed, a drama about a hopeless marriage, the woman desperately seeking to escape through an affair with a married man, but when that turns troublesome she takes her life, first delivering a monologue by telephone from one side of the stage to the other where her anguished husband collapses in despair. Leery thought the play too realistic to rise to tragedy. Even worse, the last scene descended into melodrama, though Leery felt it could be reworked to better effect, but then he was not about to do someone else's work. Alec made no response, and so Leery probed,

"As I recall, you prefer comedy."

Alec insisted that he had never meant to slight seriousness on the stage, tragedy being an element in life, and that he was eager to learn from an experienced playwright and critic. Leery invited him to his tenth-floor apartment to have a look at the review which had appeared a few days earlier in **The Inquirer**.

"We can take some sherry. If you will be my guest, I know a pleasant place nearby where we might dine this afternoon."

While Alec slowly read the review, Leery studied him. He had already surrendered his libido to Alec's body and demeanor, but now he found flattering the interest returned to his writing. Leery was ready to dismiss Maurice who had only good looks, not a mind suited for someone as promising as Alec. He was sure something might be done to help balance this inequity.

Alec put down the newspaper. He asked Leery to clarify several passages in the review, especially the final sentence which stated: "Morality triumphs in the end by the supposed heroine's servility to guilt, belittling and betraying the quest of the modern woman. Those who come to the theatre hoping for art to inspire to heroic rather than futile deeds are sent away frustrated."

Leery moved about the room as he expounded theories on drama. Alec at first listened intently until the argument seemed too tenuous, and then he let his attention drift to Leery's fading good looks. What a catch he must have been when his pretty face was in the flower of youth! Even now his hair, light brown with strands of blonde, seemed by its waviness to invite erotic interest. His genteel hands gesticulated, the long fingers accentuating his thinness. These characteristics had helped to shape his character, indirectly accounting for an inappropriate temper that often expressed homophobia, though of course Alec did not yet know the explanation. As an adolescent Leery had responded to male entreaties which came his way through no effort on his part. He yielded more than once to petitions of love, only to his disadvantage, for these claims were illusory and led only to fleeting attractions, until he wearied of finding anything genuine. A quarter century later, when nothing was effortless, Leery was a person who needed male attention, yet he feared casting his own manliness into doubt. He sought company with men like Alec who did not take lightly manliness in themselves or others.

After an exquisite lunch they lingered until the room was near empty. Alec was thinking he might get used to such indulgences. In an offhand way he said he might bring Maurice to this restaurant to celebrate their first year in America. Leery had awaited just such an opening.

"Maurice is not without charms, but bound to such a conventional world as banking, what can one expect from him?"

Alec thought the remark unworthy. He would dismiss it quickly.

"It is myself, rather than Maurice, who should raise that question."

"You are right. What hope is there doing manual labor? Your mind deserves enrichment, as clear to you as it is to me. It would be wise to depend less on Maurice and mark out your future."

"I have a mind alright, but my body currently settles for its pleasures each night. Maurice appeals to me. There are ways I share with Maurice that mean more than you seem to realize. As for my mind, I do not neglect it. I have been reading the Bible these past months."

Leery was surprised at this turn of events, and curious, for he did not sense an atom of spirituality present.

"What has led you to the Bible? Hopefully you feel no need for penance."

After listening to an explanation that told of Andrew's interest in conversion, Leery thought of the perfect antidote that would also give an occasion to share another day with someone he hoped to convert into an admirer. Next Sunday he would be attending an afternoon performance at Princeton that he invited Alec to see.

"A comedy by one of your compatriots, George Bernard Shaw. Maurice may come along if he prefers it to church."

*   *   *

Maurice did not come along, which pleased Leery. That way he had Alec to himself.

Alec was entrusted with driving the luxurious sedan, which allowed Leery to provide a flow of appreciative commentary concerning Alec's mechanical skills, the lovely foliage of early fall, and the wit of Shaw. Unfortunately, as they spent a few hours on the streets of Princeton and at a café, Leery returned to the acerbic attitude Alec remembered with dislike. He rattled off a string of deprecatory remarks against people Alec did not know, which made him increasingly uncomfortable, but then the harsh ridicule turned against people Alec did know, Winnie, Perry and their cohorts. One remark seemed meant to harm Maurice as well. Alec was angered at this meanness.

"I share some of your scorns, but mine do not come from anger. It is becoming for us to think generously of those of like sexual disposition. Considering I love Maurice, I ask you to be less scornful of anything about him others might deem peculiar."

Silence ensued as they made their way to the theatre. Then the curtain rose and Alec was lost in the enactment of "Major Barbara" while Leery, familiar with the play, had else to ponder. He might dismiss this uncultured youth, Maurice along with him, and leave it at that. Or he might persist. His heart already captivated made the choice. During intermissions a more likeable Leery appeared, whom Alec welcomed.

During the drive home Alec was at the wheel, but this time enthusiastically holding his own.

"I didn't make much of the first act, being unfamiliar with the theatre's ways. But my ears perked when the workman Pride took stage. I liked his defiance as evidence he was intelligent beyond any abuse the capitalists intended for him."

"Shaw is a socialist who lets Pride speak his piece. As for my conviction, I stand with Undershaft, Barbara's father. He insists that 'Poverty is not a thing to be proud of.' Employment in his factory will do more for the poor than pie in the sky."

"True enough to my own finding."

"Since you have been reading the Bible, I should think you would find Major Barbara of curious interest. Her bourgeois life as a woman was vapid, but what a preposterous solution she finds, to join the Salvation Army so that she can rejoice in saving souls amidst drumming and tambourining!"

Alec laughed, "I think you will be pleased that I also prefer her father who relishes his wealth but scraps the prejudices of old religions."

"That's Shaw again. Such a relief to know you agree with him. He uses the Salvation Army to show how churches are beholden to rich people who would cut off their money if religion stopped preaching submission of the poor to their helpless conditions. All the repentance and atonement that religion preaches are figments."

"These are matters to discuss with Andrew when I see him. Right now I want to understand more about Barbara's lover."

"Adolphus? He follows Barbara because he is hopelessly in love."

"Adolphus seems willing to sell his soul, to beat a drum for salvation. Not that he believes any of it."

"He is following Barbara to heaven or to hell, though he would prefer a pleasant life on earth. That is why he is ready to accept Undershaft's offer to turn over his considerable business to them, if he will manage the factory and if Barbara is willing to abandon her futile rescue of the poor by preaching other-worldliness to them."

"That explains Alolphus's meaning, I think his words were, 'We sell our souls hourly and daily' or something such. I feel that way myself."

Leery was happy to be taken into confidence this way, even more thrilled that the theatre he loved so much had been the instrument of enlightenment. Shaw had helped to relegate religion to a side matter, and Alec was better prepared to decide what part of his soul he would relinquish in order to pursue practical success. The remainder of the drive was too short to accomplish such weighty decisions, and so Leery suggested tea in his apartment. Alec accepted, though he suspected the invitation went beyond mere ideas, though not on his part. He felt no desires that would harm Maurice and even telephoned him to say that he was having tea with Leery so they could finish their discussion. Maurice, of course, had the patience of a diplomat.

Alec had hardly put down the phone when he determined to speak directly. Though he wanted to benefit from cultural insights that Leery could introduce, these were not worth meanness at every other turn.

"There is something I need to know, did you ever love a man as I do Maurice? Perhaps one you lost and still resent? I am trying to place your anger, to understand your bitterness, because it troubles me how you slight Maurice."

Leery continued to prepare tea while his mind engaged in a swift calculation. Should he let this rare moment pass? He had already decided not to let Alec walk away from his life, and so he would have to tell his strange story. He was certain Alec would say nothing harsh, no matter how ugly the truth, or do nothing complicating. Halfway through the tea

Leery overcame his anguish and embarked on a narration of experiences which hitherto had only been trusted to an analyst.

"I was a lonely boy, and I never had the love and affection of my father. I used to cry about my mother who left my father for another man and showed little interest in me after that. I was drawn to older men, boys really, just a few years older than me. Some of them were attracted to me because I had pretty features. I wished to reach out and put my arms about some of them, though I did not know what would happen, for I had never been intimate with anyone. When I was fourteen I fell in love, the first and only time. It was with my cousin Jeremy who was eighteen, everything of male beauty, athletic, muscular, spontaneous. That summer he visited us while we were in Atlantic City. He spent much of his time on the beach, I think searching for girls. I believe he found some, but I was unclear on these things. I saw how happy Jeremy was and this delighted me. We were sharing a bed. One night I did what I thought innocent, at least it was honest, I surprised him with a hug and kissed him as he lay there half naked. He was not shocked but he pulled away. He told me 'Boys do not love boys' and forbade me to touch him again in any embrace. Then, to my shame, he told my father who was disgusted that I acted in a feminine way. He struck me and demanded I rid myself of queerness. I was disciplined severely."

Leery was sobbing beyond control. He excused himself to leave the room and regain composure. Alec was patient until the narration continued.

"After that unhappy event with Jeremy, I do not recall a single happy memory of boyhood or school. I feared my father, and I hated my mother for abandoning me to him. I was intensely miserable. I needed affection from some one, but I had no way to find it. My sexual impulses confused me. I loathed feelings that I knew to be queer. It was not my body at fault, but the feminine desires in my heart. I still loved Jeremy who had not meant to hurt me, only to help. A few years later he married. I recall even now how devastated I was at the wedding party for I wanted to be dancing with him in place of the bride, to be in his bed forever. I was heartsick and I thought I should shortly die"

"Were there no other men that came along?"

"Yes, I met other men, most of them older than me and willing to take advantage. There were a few others youthful but too frivolous to understand my complexity. Though I permitted intimacy with a number of them, nothing satisfying came of it, for the least display of anything feminine by another man repulses me, and I detest any expressions of it in myself. How can I love anyone since I hardly love myself? It is only my good looks that have given me anything to love. I have seen a psychiatrist over many years, but little use came from knowing the strange workings of my mind. I was led to understand what is obvious to you, that I displace self-loathing onto others. You have seen it and find it distasteful, as you should. I am sorry my jealousy toward Maurice has been troublesome to you."

Wishing to put Leery at ease, Alec thought it best to be honest. "Your sexual interest, clear enough, is no trouble to me or to Maurice. Mind you, I do not encourage anything amorous, but I wish you no guilt merely because of desire. It is the contempt you show toward Maurice that annoys me."

"Thank you for allowing me to share my feelings, as I've never done before with a friend. From the first moment at Perry's party I have been unable to turn my thoughts from you. Not since Jeremy has anyone had this effect. I do believe it is my age giving a warning that you may be my last chance."

They both could laugh at this.

"You see the impossibility of our romantic liaison. Even if you were not devoted to Maurice, I could not be less than manly. Though I wish for you to desire me, I could not be a Maurice. I am terrified of any untoward behavior on my part, any lapse into feminine thought or deed. I would suffer guilt for being the man my father condemned, and I would always dread, even be certain, that you must despise that hateful person I would reveal. This is the ugly truth that rules my heart."

After further disclosures Alec became weary and overwhelmed by the burden of trying to understand this debasement. He wanted to hear no more this evening. Yet he wished to be kind.

"Even with Andrew, a priest, I gave a kiss that he accepted as befitting a Christian. So I have no call to leave you feeling desired in an unmanly way, nor thinking yourself despised. What you have said disheartens me, only because I do not like to see you tortured mentally. I will be your friend if that prove enough. Let me embrace you as men ought to." And Alec proceeded to do just that, leaving Leery satisfied.

Leery was relieved to drive him home and even happier when Alec, thanking him for the remarkable day, suggested another meeting next Sunday.

*   *   *

All was not dismal for Maurice and Alec. They loved each other and shared a bed. Each night had potential, despite weariness and minor

126

irritation. This night was proof, for when Alec returned from his day with Leery he was relieved to be with his untroubled Maurice. He quickly stripped himself bare and forced a surprised Maurice to wakefulness by almost leaping upon him. "I want to hold you" was all he said. That was enough to awaken memories and sensations of their first intimate encounter.

Too often, though, too many nights it seemed, Maurice had only to settle for the comfort of hanging on to Alec until it was clear that his mate had drifted into a sound sleep. He knew how tired the strong body was that he fondled. Whatever petulance he felt at being ignored would subside into empathy for the plight of his lover, so that he could sleep peacefully despite his longings.

Still Maurice was wary about the ease with which Alec fit into the working class almost as a preference. He noticed time and again Alec's discomfort when pulled into his milieu. They had gone to Cape Cod in August as guests of Charles and Albert. It was an exciting time for Maurice who enjoyed lively conversation and parties each night with his hosts and many similar friends. Alec disappeared during these evenings for long walks along the ocean. He was not moody after these walks, merely indifferent to the society that surrounded him at the house. He would await the end of the gathering, energized by the ocean air and exercise, ready to please Maurice. But Maurice was not unmindful that Alec was signaling a different direction than Charles and Albert offered.

Maurice had been thinking, not just partying. He knew something decisive was needed. He recognized that Alec had a mind as capable as any of those at the Cape, only lacking training and nourishment, something not to be found at the Baldwin plant. He would prod Alec to see to his education. During the drive to Philadelphia he did just that.

"It is time you quit the plant. You made good use of Clive's library. I remember how you surprised me with your knowledge. You have told me your mother's hope that you escape working for others, and you can never accomplish that as you are. Schooling is essential. That is what Graham recommended, too."

In that thoughtful moment he touched upon a raw nerve in Alec that called him to honor his mother's expectation that he become a gentleman. Yet Alec did not feel he could fit in with the group they had left behind at Cape Cod. This left him in a state of ambivalence that blurred any vision or decision toward the future. He argued for delay in pursuing education, because he felt uneasy to totally depend on Maurice economically, even for a time, as if some theft of his masculinity might result. Not that Maurice was ungenerous in the matter.

Unexpectedly Leery entered to change the calculation. Alec began to spend Sundays with him, while Maurice attended to God at St. Mark's and to the Wetherills at Stone House. Leery did not dwell on his troubled history, which seemed less troubled once he seemed successfully to sublimate physical attraction into fascination with the whole Alec. He took him to the theatre with determination to concentrate on a promising mind, though he also enjoyed sitting next to a handsome body. Encouragement by Leery on behalf of drama and intellect helped dissolve any uncertainty, so that Alec became less brittle when Maurice urged the opportunity that was theirs. This was no time for false honor, neither by Alec, nor by Maurice thinking his bourgeois class superior. Maurice continued his encouragement during several months as hard manual labor wore down resistance, until Alec decided to begin 1926 by enrolling in the evening program at Central High School.

*   *   *

He filled out forms, presented documents from England, and went for an interview with the school counselor, Mrs. Lippset. She scrutinized his appearance – he had come directly from the plant – which confirmed her prejudices.

"Two years of steady work are needed for you to earn a diploma. To start, a class in English. That way we may ascertain your skills in the use of our language," as if he had arrived from Slobovia. Alec volunteered that he was eager to learn its American uses.

"Since you intend to become a citizen, I will arrange a class in American history so that you learn about the foundations of our republic." Once again Alec obliged. Yes, it was his hope to be a full-blooded American, an active citizen.

"Your education has lacked natural sciences. These are the foundation of modern American industry which is likely to provide you work."

Remembering Graham's urging a scientific bent, Alec welcomed Lippset's direction for his future, merely wondering whether he might prefer the science of biology. He had read something of evolution, and he added, "I have great interest in every part of the human body."

Lippset stared over her glasses in a way that announced she was not to be swayed by such whims. "Physics and chemistry, even better, applied sciences. These are your steps for ensuing semesters, if you have the pluck to continue. Auto mechanics might be appropriate, perhaps working with metals. Industrial skills will improve your prospects for secure employment."

Alec protested, "I should think I get enough industrial skills during the ten hours of the work day" even as he capitulated to the prospects presented. Pleased with his submission, Lippset concluded the interview generously. "I have exempted you from physical education in deference to your daily labor."

*   *   *

Crossing the portal into public high school was reminiscent of Ellis Island. Once again Alec was amidst tired Italians, Polish, Russians, Jews and Irish who could scarcely stay awake after their day of manual labor. Reciting English in American ways was of insufficient stimulation for this lot. Alec was tired, too, but it was no great effort to recite the only tongue he knew. Admittedly his accent needed working over, yet it was nothing compared to the struggle of others to express an elemental thought in a new language.

Alec continued to work at Baldwin through the winter, taking classes two evenings. Other nights, except Saturday at Angelo's, and all day Sunday he spent studying, while Maurice was cultivating his friendship with Leslie. Learning was to Alec's liking, not at all the bitter pill as some would have it, but an ingestion that suited his needs. He was cheated by the text used in history, which had been chosen with immigrants in mind and offered a simple panegyric of American progress as if equality were a reality. When Alec complained of this, Maurice was helpful in borrowing from the Wetherill collection more sophisticated volumes by Channing and Beard. Alec culled from these books a more critical understanding of his new country. He raised questions in class, the eyes of students awakening in wonder, and his teacher thrilled enough to assign him the highest grade. After half a term he was looking forward to greater challenge. He began asking Maurice about Cambridge, especially why he had not stayed on. "More a hindrance to my future it seemed then" was the brief retort. For Alec, with an uncharted future, that seemed an idle attitude. He was looking for more than either bank or plant could offer. The ordeal of attending night school lay in the demands on his time, for he endured a constant round of industrial work and academics with much travel to and fro. At home he was almost always in need of recuperation for the next day.

There was an unexpected diversion Alec welcomed. Shortly into the English class his attention was drawn to a frail girl who spoke with an Irish lilt only when she was asked to speak. He noticed her red hair and pretty face. During the mid-course he made a point of arriving early to class so that he could move to a desk closer to where she sat. She responded to his approach with equal courtesy. Noreen, such was her name, worked as a cook's helper for a Main Line family, the Kleins, who encouraged her education. Her own family lived in South Philadelphia where she spent the two nights of the week after classes. The other days she lived with her employers. One rainy night Alec was pleased to drive Noreen to her family home after class. It was then she shared her intention to make more of herself.

Alec's progress proved swifter than Mrs. Lippset expected, though he could spend only two evenings in class. Maurice could see as much. He tried to convince Alec to give up his job and devote himself to study so that he could more rapidly complete the diploma. Maurice looked forward to their future middle class existence. Alec procrastinated, insisting he should work enough hours to pay for his needs. He had heard from Noreen that her employers were looking for a gardener and handyman who could work several days of the week. Early in June of 1926, having left Baldwin for good, he took the train to Overbrook to meet the Kleins and was given the job with assurances that suited him.

Chapter 12

A Peek into Pandora's Box

What God has hidden is not for men to know.
Aye, blessed is the ignorant man indeed,
Blessed is he that only knows his creed.

Chaucer, "The Miller's Tale"

That is how it came about Alec took up outdoor work again, this time caring for American grounds. The proprietors, Julius and Sarah Klein, presided over a large house that was childless. It would have been empty except that they treated as family a cook, an elderly black chauffeur, Noreen who was an upstairs maid some of the time but assisted downstairs serving meals, and now Alec who would tend to the garden, the coach house and occasional heavy work. All except Alec lived on the premises.

The summer of 1926 could already be reckoned far happier than the previous one, mainly that Alec was satisfied with outdoor work and prospects of education. He was encouraged from every quarter, mostly by Maurice and Leery, as well as Graham whose occasional letter prodded him to use the mind that was his blessing, and now the Kleins. Maurice was pleased that Alec had yielded to good advice and started readying himself for a career.

Philadelphia was in a more than usual patriotic mood as the nation was celebrating the sesquicentennial anniversary of its independence. Three days before the Fourth, a Thursday that was something of a holiday, Alec met Maurice at the bank at noon so they could walk to the waterfront. There was excitement in the air as they joined a growing crowd along Market Street en route to the grand opening ceremonies of the Delaware River Bridge. The oratory had begun before their arrival, but from the fringe of the crowd they picked up words extolling this great technological feat, the longest suspension bridge ever built, or intoning God's blessing, or boasting the commercial destiny of the greatest nation the world had ever to know, as if civilization had reached its culmination right here and now. This was no time for nostalgia, the new was extolled over the old.

"No more use for Whitman's ferryboats," Alec commented.

"Not all the past is done," as Maurice also sounded out of tune with the celebration. "It is an architectural miracle, but I detest bombast about progress when we are still prohibiting liquor and sexual freedom. Damn this certitude of God's blessing! Where is the liberated spirit of Whitman that ought to be along this river?" Not that Maurice's spirit was all that dampened, for no one who looked at this immense structure of steel could fail to be awed. He was as exhilarated as the many thousands who leisurely strolled the span to Camden, once the ceremony was over, gaping at the great steel towers and cables holding the enormous weight of bridge and traffic.

*　　　*　　　*

The next day was hot and muggy as is true of July in the Delaware Valley. They decided to cool off with a swim at a favorite place along the Wissahickon Creek where a huge rock offered a jumping point into a deep pool at a bend in the stream. Hidden by bushes they changed into bathing trunks. Alec joined some teenage boys who were leaping with abandon and splashing about in the water in horseplay. Maurice was more discreet, the effects of his upbringing, jumping only when there was a lull in the boisterous frolicking.

After enough of the water they found a sandy bank secluded from any path where they could stretch out away from the noise. They removed their sleeveless jerseys so that only wet swimming suits hid their bodies, but not the contours of their private parts. Water drops clinging to body hair glistened in the sun. The scene offered an erotic masterpiece. Maurice was resisting stealing a touch when Alec admitted similar desire.

"You are an Adonis. Much better, living flesh, soft and warm, inviting my touch."

Decorum won out, just as well, for one suggestive touch would have furthered an arousal still barely visible that would have betrayed them. Just then several young ladies were coming their way. They were boldly curious in approaching the sunbathers while pretending to be looking only at the landscape which in its own right deserved appreciation. There was little refined about these women, neither their attire nor their raucous laughter at the young men's expense. They let it be known they were out for flirtation. One of them prided herself on being modern.

"Do you have a cigarette? In a rush we left ours behind."

132

As Maurice apologized for the lack, the others chided them with silly remarks.

"Out on a lark, are you, away from your mothers."

Alec had learned to handle such flirtation directly.

"We don't live with our mothers, though I would not mind if mine took care of me. We have our own place, just the two of us. No women at all to bother us."

Puzzled by this defiance, one of them who seemed less modern admitted to her fascination.

"Without a woman about the place, who is it polishes and scrubs?"

"I do it" was Alec's quick reply, though this time gently.

"Then I wish you were my husband."

Everyone laughed, but not Maurice who wished an abrupt end to this intrusion. Rather curtly he changed the mood.

"We are both spoken for and pledged elsewhere," a truth that was enough to send the ladies on their way. In a minute they were out of sight.

"You are harsh with women, Morrie, that is for sure." Alec was laughing at it all. "They cannot help being drawn to you, like the force of gravity. I am helpless, too, near your nakedness."

Alec cast aside discretion. He placed a succession of light kisses to Maurice's face, followed by prurient excursions that missed no parts of Maurice's body. This time arousal broke its bounds. They sought thicker woods to conceal intimacies quickly accomplished.

When passion subsided and they were clothed, Alec gave an assurance that what they had just done was no passing matter.

"Nothing's going to come between us. We're going to grow old together."

*   *   *

July Fourth fell on Sunday but Maurice was of no mood to disrupt a holiday that had been romantic by going to church or doing anything out of sort. He suggested a morning drive about the fields of Chester County where they had breakfast in a quaint inn. They left their car where it was and set out on foot along a country road to enjoy the quiet of their own company except for a few horses who had curiosity enough to poke their heads over fences. After two hours of hiking they were tired, needing to freshen their bodies at home before an evening picnic in Charles and Albert's garden.

Leery was there, Leslie, too, along with others who had been guests at the party six months earlier. This time Alec felt more at ease. Albert made a point of engaging him in private conversation. He inquired about his outdoor work and whether it would allow time for him to come to the Cape during August. Albert was aware of Alec's misgivings about the previous visit, and so he suggested he and Maurice might boat over to Martha's Vineyard to spend a few days to themselves. Before anything was agreed, Leery came over to take charge of the conversation until Albert drifted away. Now that Leery had Alec alone he spoke frankly.

"I missed our Sunday together. When I don't see you it leaves me a Humpty Dumpty unable to pull myself together. I find myself vulnerable, longing for your presence, certain that I have more to say to you. Do you think Maurice would spare next Sunday?"

As if to gain permission, Alec looked toward Maurice who was at a distance beside a fountain whose water was sprayed by a bronze Cupid peeing upward into the air. Through the mist Maurice was illumined by a rainbow and Leslie's eyes sparkled. Alec was delighted to see the two lovely creatures charmed by Cupid. It strengthened his own playfulness as he replied to Leery.

"Andrew has already spoken for the afternoon next Sunday. How would it do another night, one Maurice goes to the movies with Leslie?"

Leery of course would be available.

In a while Maurice came by to say hello and to escort Alec to the buffet tables spread with tempting foods. After heaping his plate Maurice took a chair next to Leery who was with others. Their repartee was swift, leaving Alec unsure and remote. His attention revived when talk turned to a couple who would have been at the picnic except for their recent break-up. Sympathy was generally expressed for Richard and Bruce, though everyone agreed the younger, irresponsible Bruce was to blame for the breech. No one was quicker than Leery to disparage him.

"Why Richard allowed himself to be besotted by Bruce's antics is beyond me. Hysterical effeminacy repels me, even in a woman, but so much more detestable in a man. Richard, like so many men, was drawn to the physical charms of a pretty face and body, as if character were of no matter. Don't you agree, Charles?"

But because Leery looked at Maurice, even as Charles replied that he had not entertained much hope for the couple from the beginning, Maurice felt called upon to sputter something. He had seen the pair only once, yet he was of the general opinion that it is unworthy in a man to forfeit his masculinity. Leery looked then to Alec who would have remained silent, but he felt a need to defend Maurice.

"The object of sexual attraction is something that gets its proper value from the eyes and limbs of the admirer. Who can be certain what love discovers of inner beauty?"

Though his words were oblique, that is all he said.

When the group dispersed Leery lingered a moment too long. Maurice was in such a good mood that he was over-kind. Or it might have been some other motive at work. In any case he offered Leery a friendly opportunity.

"Perhaps some evening you would honor us–not for dinner, we do not have a cook, and I hear you are fastidious. Alec would like us to be friends." He added a quizzical after thought, "I trust that possibility does not threaten your security?"

Then Maurice was pulled away, and Leery sought out Alec.

"What have you been telling Maurice? You have stirred his jealousy."

Seeing Leery livid with anger, Alec was baffled at how his intentions had gone astray. He had meant to strengthen the man's confidence, to help him escape bitterness; but too much sympathy in that direction had excited other emotions. He would not dwell on the rudeness aimed at Maurice, for his own behavior might be at fault. Why would Leery continue to question Maurice's worthiness? Why, indeed! Without proper understanding he took the right approach, as Richard should have done.

"It is not Maurice's feelings that should concern you. You seem jealous that I share most everything with him. What I told him had nothing of ridicule or hardness toward you. Nor could the truth give any cause for jealousy."

Mistakenly Leery felt threatened, and so he was not easily calmed.

"Does it seem strange your telling Maurice might excite his jealousy? Or mine? I value the rare intimacy I allowed myself in trusting you. Though it may seem a small matter, since you abound in intimacies, my thoughts deserve privacy."

"I mean well by you. Just so you embrace Maurice, in order to be close to me."

Leery glared in petulance through a long silence. Rather than leave things uncertain, Alec wanted to set the bounds of intimacy aright. He needed to return to innocence and openness even if it meant estranging Leery.

"I will not be accosted by your suspicions. Jealousy displeases me so that I wish no more of it. It is unmanly behavior on your part."

By then darkness had fallen and a small display of colorful and quiet fireworks was set off. Afterward deserts were arranged and champagne served. Charles, a glass in hand, expressed appreciation to his friends for their company. Leery hastened to propose a second toast. He stepped between the two, daring to put his arm across Alec's shoulder, which drew attention, but that done, he took Maurice's hand into his.

"Maurice and Alec, you have shaken my years of cynicism and led me to become a believer in love. May our friendship deserve your affection and strengthen your bonds to each other."

Everyone was astonished as they sipped the wine. After they dispersed they wondered, Maurice included, at the sincerity of this change in Leery. Alec was left to ponder the insidious ways of foreign spirits, jealousy and spite, which had invaded his innocence. He chose not to share his misgivings with Maurice. He understood Leery had a loathing of being the bitch, alike to the one Richard should have discarded, and that he needed Alec's respect at whatever price, for he had gone too far to safely retreat into past cynicism.

*   *   *

Alec had met with Andrew a few times until their discussions progressed by pushes and tugs beyond the literalness of the Bible. They began to consider whether nature could be appreciated as the creation of a benign God. Alec's sexual proclivities became a focus of concern since much of the Christian view of sexual morality hinges on a teleological understanding of nature. What animals do presumably men should do! Alec had left England for economic chance, but he had accompanied Maurice to Philadelphia out of love and a determination to live together. He had no desire to fall under the aegis of a hostile Christian ideology. Yet Andrew's arguments suited church purposes, as might be expected from one about to be ordained.

Andrew insisted, "Nature is God's design, male and female procreating through all the animal kingdom. Surely a benign creator provided a lawful universe."

"Do not attribute too much godliness to nature. My desires are unconcerned with virtue. Especially absurd is to mangle human sexual desires, the most lawless of all passions, with moral reasoning. If sexuality were strictly moral, as you say, tell me why we are driven by confounding appetites that arise from the body. They are as natural as hunger or pain?"

"It allows the exercise of free will, the choice between evil or virtue."

"Your theology hinges on a tall tale of Eve enticing Adam to an evil pursuit. Seems to me a benign God ought to have given Adam greater discretion that would have enabled him to overcome the capriciousness of the female, rather than leaving the whole of mankind at the mercy of a simple mind that could not resist seduction. We need not consent to God's gamble."

"Your argument overwhelms my simplicity of reason, but not my faith, for I need to believe in a loving God. Why God created the world this way is beyond my understanding. I do not claim to fathom human sexuality, not my own, much less yours. I do not judge in these matters. My ministry is not to prey upon sinners of the flesh. We poor humans need as much compassion as possible."

"That is what I like about you. You are ready to discard dogmatism. I have hope of saving you. Perhaps we ought to ponder the theories of Darwin?"

"Here I thought I was saving you! I have read Darwin, yet I find nature to be other than he portrays it. God's creatures behave according to their nature but within a divine order. Tell me, Alec, what is your way of determining what is natural and what distinctly human?"

"Common sense and science guide me. I know my brain is part of nature as is yours. But I have a mind full of ideas and emotions, a jumble of them. Do you see that a mind is intricate in ways that are far removed from mere mechanical operations of the brain?"

"Of course I accept that distinction, though I allow room for spirit within the mind. Yet I wonder what dictates ought to be derived from nature."

"To argue for or against nature is to set up an idol, even though you call it God. Nature does not have a mind for the moral, nor for the normal. Darwin has shown us otherwise. Nature is heartless, sometimes rewarding the aberrant with survival despite behavior that departs from the usual."

"I do not see where this leads us."

"What a religious man deems sinful is in the mind's eye, neither a distinction made by nature, nor an inborn moral understanding. His understanding of sin is directed by righteous ideas, some of them religion and nonsense. I read in your Bible that the eye that sins should be plucked out. So that we become blind! I also found injunctions to cruelty, priests commanded to slay an innocent calf, as if senseless slaughter of God's creation pleases that same creator. To my mind such views are repellant to any sense of justice. What can such an unholy book tell us of sexual behavior? Are we like to the calf?"

Andrew was overwhelmed and wished to find another course.

Alec persisted, "That is what comes from idolizing nature."

Andrew closed his eyes in prayer until he responded. "You are not far from Paul's depiction of the strife between the mind and the body. Let me find the passage. Here it is in Romans. 'For I delight in the law of God after the inward man. But I see another law in my members, warring against the law of my mind, and bringing me into the captivity of sin which is in my members.' Paul entreats us to please God by overcoming the natural."

"It is not my purpose to reject nature." As if to prove a point he playfully extended his tongue. "Do you see this tongue?" which of course Andrew saw full well though he was perplexed whether to examine it for marks of some sort. "It seeks sexual pleasures, preferring Maurice to a woman. Are you afraid to touch it?" Alec laughed with Andrew who had placed his finger upon the sinful appendage. "Do you think it should be plucked out as your holy text demands? Not only would I be blinded, but tasteless. Is it not better to bend Paul a little?"

Preposterous as was this display, Andrew wished harmony.

"I already take my Bible with a grain of salt. As Jesus bid, I will judge not, when it comes to you and Maurice."

Then Andrew reaffirmed his conviction, "The overall truth about my Redeemer holds fast."

Chapter 13

A Musical Interlude

There's nae lark loves the light, my dear,
There's nae ship loves the sea.
There's nae bee loves the heather bells
As I love thee, my love,
That loves as I love thee.

Swinburne

In most respects the Kleins were an American success story. Julius was disappointed, though, that there were no Klein children because Sarah's body was unable to multiply. He had wished for daughters to spoil, a son or two to carry on the business. Sarah did not so much regret the absence of children, because her outlook helped her transcend the limits of blood and race. There was a whole world of persons in need, some within their own household. She did not neglect extending a caring hand.

One day Sarah explained the roots of her compassion to Noreen. "We come from immigrants who were persecuted in Russia and dispossessed of their property and dignity. It was a terrifying history. Now we have everything here. Not all of it was handed to us. Julius and I worked, and we saved. We are not exploiters. We are grateful to have something to give." She would lend the cook a hand or help Noreen arrange the table because she believed work was part of her humanity. "I was not always a woman of leisure," she would sigh. "Julius means well, insisting I stop working, though he will not give up his business." As she helped at some tidying task she would say to herself, almost as a prayer of repentance, "I was not made for a life of comfort."

Sarah and Julius were newcomers to the main line. Until a decade ago they had lived in the Jewish district of Philadelphia where their families had settled. In the 1870's the Kleins opened a clothing store near Fifth and South with its own sewing room. By the time Julius took the reins it had grown into a large factory. He had learned the business from his grandfather and father, but he was never fully comfortable in the role of owner. He spent time debating with intellectuals who were far from Jewish orthodoxy or class prejudices. Julius himself took the side of workers' rights because of the vagaries of capitalism. It was during one of the strikes in the industry that he became acquainted with Sarah who was active in the trade union movement. He had ignored her when she was a plain neighborhood girl, but now she was attractive in her militancy. She made more sense than any of the intellectuals he debated. It was not long before he proposed to share his life and fortune with her. Their marriage prospered as did the business, but Sarah was unwilling to forget her working class roots, a loyalty that was compelling to Julius, for she would not allow him to do so either. When they took charge of the considerable Klein fortune, it allowed them to dispense lavish philanthropy which furthered the family reputation despite their own anti-establishment attitudes.

Sarah was a smart and a kind woman who gave herself to good causes, one of them the expansion of free schooling that would serve immigrants. She was also deeply sensitive to racial and religious persecution, and so she feared for the impoverished black people who lived at the fringes of the Jewish district. She shuddered at news of lynching and burning of Negroes in the South and she worried over local actions by Ku Klux Klan.

She also devoted efforts to high culture. Both a friend of the Curtis sisters who founded the Curtis Institute of Music and a lover of music, she provided scholarships that went to promising youthful musicians. At the time of Alec's employment, one of the rooms of the house belonged to sixteen-year old David, a talented violinist whom the Kleins had brought from Poland.

From the first Sarah was supportive of Alec's education, as she was of Noreen's. She made a point of coordinating their assigned work to the priorities of the school schedule, as well as limiting tasks so that each would find a few hours of every day for study. A sitting room was made available which Alec and Noreen often found themselves sharing. Alec took cheerfully to this atmosphere which was far different from working for the Durhams. He grew closer to Noreen and the Kleins, and soon to David.

*　　　*　　　*

An afternoon late that summer beautiful music wafted through the windows at the back of the house into the garden where Alec was working. A violin and piano were playing the Spring Sonata of Beethoven which stopped him in his track. It was his first hearing of any work of Beethoven. When the music stopped he clapped loudly so that David and

140

the unknown pianist would know their performance was appreciated. David responded from the window, "We're about to have a lemonade. Join us on the porch."

Alec was smudgy and sweaty when he stepped on to the front porch where David and his friend were seating themselves. Noreen arrived with a pitcher of lemonade and cookies.

"This is Samuel, a pianist, as you have heard." David introduced Alec who extended his hand without apology that he had not stopped to wash. Sam took the hand hesitantly, and the best he could do was mumble something Alec did not hear. Alec overlooked what he construed to be care for the delicate hands of a pianist.

"It's honest work trimming bushes and clearing the ground. Your music provided me a restful accompaniment."

"How are your classes going?" as David turned to Sam to explain, "Alec is making up for lost time in his education."

"I take no classes during summer. But I am studying, natural science, the sexual ways of animals. Far from your interests, I suppose." Alec had not given up extracting a complete sentence from Sam, and so he cut through the visitor's reserve.

"Have you any interest in the reproductive system?"

"Yes, of course." Sam was embarrassed but he tried to correct any hint of brusqueness he did not intend. "I am thankful for it at the least," as a faint smile marked the corner of his mouth.

David intervened, "We are too engaged with music for any personal role in reproducing. All to the good! It would be reckless siring babies who would have to live on music."

"No reproduction for me either, thanks to Maurice."

David had no need to ask, but Sam prodded his friend later for clarification. Sam was pleased with the explanation.

After downing two large glasses of lemonade Alec returned to work. As he walked from the porch through the garden Sam watched every step of his way. David noted his friend's fascination and, as much for Sam's benefit, he called out, "Sam will play something for you, if you like." Not long after, music of Chopin arrived as a gift from Sam.

*　　　*　　　*

It was months later, the first light snow falling as if to announce the upcoming holiday season, when Alec was taking a Friday afternoon respite. He stopped at Horn & Hardart's to await Maurice. Turning his eyes from the book he was reading in order to poke at a piece of cake,

141

his glance was drawn across a few tables where his eyes met those of a youth who was gazing, as it seemed, longingly. It was Sam, David's musical friend. Alec knew the yearning in the look, an intuition that was confirmed by his own bodily sensations. He did not mind the interruption for he approved such innocent exchanges.

"Hello. Sammy, isn't it? Come over and join me. Maurice will be along."

Sam approached shyly as was his wont until some basis for respect might be established. He had illicit desires to conceal from Alec, from all strangers for that matter, perhaps already revealed by careless sensual gazing. Following their first meeting Sam recalled Alec to mind on numerous occasions, usually entangled with bold sexual imaginings during otherwise sleeping hours. Encountering Alec in the flesh was altogether a different matter. His response was hesitant, not because he had doubts about accepting the invitation, for too much of mystery was pulling him toward Alec. He hoped only to disguise his embarrassment at having been surprised in an innocent voyeurism.

"I have a train to catch within the hour," a reasonable explanation if one were needed, since the station was nearby. "Are you sure I would not be intruding? I am a voracious reader myself. When I am deep in thought I resent interruptions." Sam was surely an unusually serious youth.

"Not at all. Take some cake at my invitation." Seeing Sam too self-conscious, Alec guided him to a chair next to his. He placed a chunk of cake on his fork. "Here, have a bite. Don't disappoint me, for I have yet to know a lad who does not like indulgences." Taken by surprise with this flirtation, Sam clumsily swallowed the offering while hoping blood rushing through him was not apparent. Alec ordered another piece of chocolate cake. "If you have no appetite for it, I'll save it for Maurice."

Atop Sam's portfolio resting on the table was a concert program for the Philadelphia Orchestra which prompted Alec to ask, "Have you skipped school for indulgence in music?"

"Nothing so daring as you suggest. I am too conservative by habit." Sam explained that he had permission from his high school to receive piano instructions each Friday morning at the Curtis Institute. In the afternoon he and David would hear the concert.

Alec botched the names Scriabin and Borodin, though he got Tchaikowsky and Stokowski right. "I have little acquaintance with such music, never even attended a concert. I listen to Tchaikovsky since I linked-up with Maurice."

"I am glad that you met Maurice. My home acquainted me from childhood with the classical repertoire. Music is second nature to me. My mother claims I embraced the piano when I was two years old which she believes revealed musical genius. I resist such mystical ideas. Talent is one thing, but genius is half illusion. Without training and encouragement, as I am fortunate to receive, the greatest potential would remain undiscovered. I trust your genius is seeking other interests, things I hardly know," as he noted the book aside Alec's plate.

"Will you follow the piano on and on?"

"No more than as accompanist, for I show more talent singing, at least David thinks so. As you shared with me, I will share with you. My calling is to compose music."

"Will your music be for ordinary people like me?"

Sam held back the thought that here was no ordinary person. He was flattered by the serious interest shown him.

"I am studying composition because I feel compelled to reproduce sounds, perhaps the way others need to father children. I don't think I could be happy any other way. So, you see, my mother was right in a way. Not about the piano, but that my genius lies in creating music. I have not thought of a particular audience other than those stirred by symphonic sound. Nor can I imagine the effects of my compositions. All I know is the poet in me seeks expression that might stir the spirit in others. To reach yours would mean much to me."

This young musician, at first restrained and tongue-tied, now that his deepest self was unloosed, suddenly spoke of the mystery of music. A spontaneous eloquence transformed Sam into an artist. He expostulated on music's magical powers to carry the mind into a realm more spiritual than offered by religion, to seize the heart and enable it to plumb the depth of human feelings. His eyes glowed as he told of his ambition to create art from the wonderful mixture of sound, form, rhythm and idea.

A brief but amazing oratory came to an end as suddenly as it had begun, this time deliberately, for Sam realized he had slipped into a command performance that he ought not overdo. He sought to recapture the physical longing that had impelled this meeting. He could not permit the touch he wanted, but in a symbolic way he picked up the book that had been engaging Alec's mind. To his delight it was poetry he knew of Alfred Edward Housman. The book was opened face down to "A Shropshire Lad" which he recited softly in a baritone voice surprisingly deep and tender, as if in song,

> With rue my heart is laden
>   for golden friends I had,

For many a rose-lipt maiden
and many a lightfood lad.

By brooks too broad for leaping,
the lightfoot boys are laid;
The rose-lipt girls are sleeping
in fields where roses fade.

Rather than respond to Alec's compliment for the rendition, Sam made a puzzled observation, "Are not these lines too sad and nostalgic for such a time of youth?"

"Just so. Perhaps it is for you to provide a lighter song that marks our meeting. You have the voice to please me."

A few casual remarks were exchanged until their time waiting together for a train and for Maurice ended. All that was left was to express a wish to see one another again.

"Why don't you come to a concert?" was Sam's hope.

A quarter hour later Sam was into a reverie that lasted the thirty mile train ride to his family home in West Chester. A way to further their intimacy occurred to him. He would find a more appropriate poem than "With Rue My Heart Is Laden" and render it into music that would please Alec. Nothing so forlorn as lightfoot lads eternally at rest, but a verse with promise of youthful love. Such were the feelings that would continue to stir nighttime memories.

At the restaurant Maurice arrived to find Alec reading the book he had given him. Alec said only, "I had coffee with Sam while I was waiting. You remember, the lad I mentioned meeting at the Klein's, David's friend. Sam is the quieter one, shy, but only at first. He showed me today that he is confident in his music. He has a beautiful singing voice." Maurice ordered a piece of the chocolate cake as he changed the subject. He had more exciting news to convey. Only later did he wonder whether Alec had mentioned Sam's singing on their first meeting.

"Uncle George has invited me to accompany him to New York for some business transaction. Not until the spring. I could bring you along for a splendid holiday without George knowing anything. That is, if you don't mind missing classes."

*   *   *

Several Fridays later an impulse led Alec to the concert with the chance of seeing Sam. During intermission he strolled the narrow lobby

144

of the amphitheatre. Sure enough Sam was there with a group of students who parried over the finer points of the performance. Alec knew his thoughts were too banal to share, and in any case he did not wish the mystery of the music to escape. How could one talk coherently of such ineffable sound? He retreated from the discussion that seemed obtrusive. Just before intermission ended Sam sought him out to arrange a meeting.

Horn & Hardart's, the place of rendezvous, assumed a romantic hue for Sam who made a point of ordering cake for both of them. He was giddy with Alec's presence and could hardly be accountable for anything he said. When an hour had passed, he regretted having to leave for the train. He dared a suggestion.

"Perhaps you could come to another concert when we might sit together?"

"That would be added pleasure."

*   *   *

In the early months of 1927, many Friday afternoons Alec went to sit beside Sam at the top of the Academy of Music. Sam made sure to arrive early enough to hold seats as far removed from his friends as possible. He was in the first surge of love and determined to share without interruption his knowledge of the composers and their works. For Alec it was different. The rich sounds of the orchestra were new, and the esthetic intimacy he was establishing with music transported him elsewhere. Not that he was forgetful of Sam, only that during the concert the vibrations of his heart were attuned to music or to the wish that Maurice were there as well. Sam ventured reminders of his longing, shifting in his seat so that his leg pressed lightly against Alec's. The younger man's heart would be beating rapidly because their closeness and the aroma of Alec's hair offered promise of something unknown. Though Alec was not oblivious, he thought it only a youthful crush that he need not encourage or discourage.

Perhaps Alec should have been more wary, especially after Leery's behavior had sounded a bell of caution against too liberal an attitude when it comes to scattering sexual charms. But Alec had no personal experience of frustrated love such as Leery's. Nor did he know the suffering of being rejected such as Maurice had felt from Clive. Without feeling the pain from lost love it is unlikely anyone would comprehend such perils. A different lover than Maurice, one who was wayward and fickle, might have taught Alec the bitter lesson. That not being the case, Alec took for granted that emotions would find their rational course. As he saw it, Sam, who turned

145

seventeen in March, needed to test the waters wherein his emotions sailed. Since he intended the boy no harm, all would turn out well.

*   *   *

Maurice was in New York for a few days learning something of business, which provided an occasion for Sam to learn something in matters of the heart. Alec, intent on his studies, declined the chance to accompany Maurice. He mentioned this to Sam with the invitation to accompany him home after the next concert to play some music. Sam was thrilled by the prospect. A few days before he wrote to say he would be able to stay in town late Friday and that he was preparing some special offering.

It was an unusually warm day for early spring as they walked three miles home from the Academy. Sam had been restless through the concert. After a quick refreshment, no longer able to contain his excitement, he sat at the piano while Alec stretched on the sofa.

"I have taken some lines of poetry by Swinburne for a song I hope will touch your heart."

He proceeded to sing in varied ways these simple words that showed his own heart captive.

> "There's nae lark loves the light, my dear,
> There's nae ship loves the sea.
> There's nae bee loves the heather bells
> As I love thee, my love,
> That loves as I love thee."

After the music stopped Alec moved to the piano bench where he draped his arms across Sam's shoulders as if to safeguard the musical genius in his grasp.

"Would you sing it again for me?"

This time the song was rendered nervously because of Alec's closeness. Though Alec had meant to show affection, Sam responded otherwise. When the playing ended he leaned back so that Alec could hold him again until, moved by the excitement he felt, he swung round to lower his face into Alec and await a command.

Alec was tempted by this offering, but he stopped to court rationality, which was his preferred approach to human relations. While he wondered whether to encourage passion, he stroked Sam's ruffled hair to show that he was not rebuffing him outright. This turn to scrutiny sometimes

146

failed to imagine another person's passion. Such had been the case with Leery when Alec had vaunted too much the power of reason. Yet, in other instances, as in his daring climb up a ladder to take Maurice, with all the dangers that boldness posed, he had trusted his powers to surmise what was called for and he had acted aright. No doubt, that time long ago he was moved by strong desire that inclined him toward the beauty of Maurice, but nevertheless a long calculation preceded such boldness. He had watched Maurice enough to understand his needs. During their long walk he perceived signals in words and glances that led him to test the matter further. When they were about to part, he deliberately placed his arm around Maurice whose body thrilled at the touch. Only then did the certainty of his powers turn into a passion to rescue Maurice from the coldness of Clive.

In the present temptation, dealing with feelings new to Sam, his own desire was tepid because he was fully satisfied in his sexual needs. Maurice flashed through his mind. Not a reproachful Maurice, but a lover remindful of times his hair had been ruffled at this spot during playful intimacies. Whether these remembrances were the work of conscience or of profound love, the effect was to weigh down Alec's eroticism with sober concerns. Surely Sam would want more than a single gratification, and then covetousness might be unleashed, and unhappiness ensue all round, for Alec would have to say he did not love. Sam might be harmed, Maurice certainly would by restlessness in his lover. Alec knew his desire for Sam was far the lesser passion.

"It is time for us to get some fresh air and supper."

Sam was not offended, nor even evidently frustrated at this abortion of a climax. His youth had always known sublimation of sexuality to musical excitement. The moment of exaltation he had just experienced, as an artist offering his song of love, had been seized with passion by his beloved. Sam was unclear what more to expect. He felt no rivalry with Maurice who had his claims of love. Once they stepped into the street the freshness of the air cooled his limbs. He was overjoyed to be with Alec.

While they ate supper, Alec acted the older man with one so inexperienced. Not disclaiming feelings toward Sam, he explained how his love for Maurice left room only for friendship with others, passionate friendship in this case. Still, the point that needed to be made was that someone else awaited Sam. There was no need to end their unique friendship, but Sam must reserve his emotions for music and for another person sure to come.

"Someone who knows music, a friend to share completely your talents, to travel together, maybe live together."

True, but words were of no avail this night. Sam understood that his genius deserved friends of comparable artistic nature. What he did not know or care to estimate was that the appeal Alec held for him would ever pass. He had never touched another this way, so that he could not now imagine anyone other than Alec, and in his desires he had little but imagination to guide him. It was not a troubling matter. What he had not possessed he did not covet exclusively. As they walked to the train Sam was lighthearted for he knew other meetings lay ahead when they would share concerts. Next week they could have cake and he would take his usual train home to the suburbs. Nor was that all. He did not say it, for he was yet too shy, but tonight and many nights he would find in his fantasies fulfillment of their curtailed sexual embrace.

*   *   *

Upon his return from New York Maurice was jubilant. Uncle George had revealed the purpose of their trip was to acquaint Maurice with international investments as a way of grooming him for that section of the bank's business.

"He has offered me advancement with greater responsibilities and higher pay. You will be able to go to the university without financial worry."

During the weeks ahead Maurice was busy learning his more complex duties at the bank. He still managed to find time to take Leslie to the films. He encouraged Alec to attend Friday concerts even after Alec told him of Sam's romantic infatuation, though he offered advice.

"Handle Sam with tenderness, much as I am doing with Leslie. You underestimate your own sexuality."

Alec devised a plan to wean Sam's erotic attachment by seeing less of him. He would make a point after the concert season ended of being busy during the summer whenever Sam was in town for lessons. A young man such as Sam would certainly find other interests soon.

*   *   *

That summer of 1927 was to be a time of decision for Alec in other ways. Julius took him aside one day to a corner of the garden where they sat upon a stone bench under the shade of a large tree. For months Julius had felt a deeper and more personal interest in Alec's life. The young man was beginning to fill a niche that needed occupying. Though Julius had

148

ceased lamenting the absence of a son, his heart welcomed in Alec some of what he had missed. He put his hand upon Alec's shoulder and held it there.

"I have been wondering about your future now that you have completed high school. You will no longer want to work in the garden. We need someone at the factory to handle personnel matters. I have talked to Sarah who is eager that you have this opportunity. That way you could make your way into the business world."

Alec was moved by this paternal affection. "I never had a father to do as much. I am grateful to you and Sarah."

They arranged for a meeting at the factory to explore the matter.

*   *   *

Unbeknownst to Alec, Julius had come to understand, at least in its broadest and general meaning, what linked him to Maurice. The past Christmas season the Kleins had given a party for their household staff and families. Sarah had to prod Julius to invite Maurice. Julius was reluctant until Sarah nudged him with a hint at their special relationship.

"You know, like your cousin Marvin."

While Sarah and Julius did not talk about the matter, any more than they discussed Marvin, from that time Julius viewed Alec more tenderly, as Sarah already did. They thoughtfully included Maurice in holiday greetings and in concerns for the families of employees. As she did with Noreen, from time to time Sarah would interrupt Alec at his work, not to assist him, but to express empathy. "You let me know if there is anything that troubles you about your work."

One day Sarah shared her sadness with him. "Sacco and Vanzetti are to be electrocuted tonight. They are not murderers, only anarchists who struggle for workers. It is the state that is committing murder." She showed him the morning paper which heralded the crime. Since Ellis Island, Fitzsimmons' warning had all but been forgotten, but now Alec's appetite was whetted for more about this strange anarchism which terrified officials enough for them to murder its spokesmen. Sarah was vague in satisfying his uncertainties, for her tears obscured theory. Best she could do was recall Emma Goldman whom she had seen during a strike of textile workers. "Emma was thrown into jail. She urged us to smash the economic forces controlling our lives. There are times I wish I had followed Emma as my heart urged. Of course I would never say that to Julius."

That night the two men were strapped into chairs so that electricity could turn their bodies to char. Their actual deeds were uncertain, despite much that was incriminating. Bartolomeo Vanzetti had in his pocket when arrested a leaflet advertising a speech he was to give. "You have worked for all the capitalists. Have you harvested the fruits of your labors?" As for Nicolo Sacco, he denied the crime of murder. Much of the last day of his life he spent on a letter to his young son Dante expressing sentiments more tender than criminal: "So, Son, instead of crying, be strong, so as to be able to comfort your mother. . . take her for a long walk in the quiet country, gathering wild flowers here and there, resting under the shade of trees, between the harmony of the vivid stream and the gentle tranquility of the mother nature. . . . But remember always, Dante, in the play of happiness, don't you use all for yourself only. . .help the persecuted and the victims because they are your better friends. In this struggle of life you will find more love and you will be loved."

The next morning Alec and Sarah pondered every word of the newspaper account of the murder of the two anarchists.

*   *   *

During the visit to the Klein factory Alec seemed more detached than usual. He had talked the matter over thoroughly with a persistent Maurice who knew him better than any man and who had taken a firm stand against Alec once again entering the factory. "Not for you at all" was his discouragement.

When Alec declined the position, he explained to Sarah and Julius, "Maurice has convinced me to enter the university this fall. I am not sure where it will lead, but I have decided to pursue knowledge of a different sort than business."

Julius was disappointed but, like Sarah, he knew the longing for the undone. As a way of encouragement, he acknowledged that he would have preferred another calling than the one family expectations held out.

"You tell Maurice I agree with him. You have a splendid future. He is a good man to recognize that and help you find it."

Alec felt good about his choice and about his lover who deserved appreciation all right. He mentioned his resolve to show his gratitude on Maurice's twenty-seventh birthday. The date in September lodged in Julius' mind along with a feeling he would like to do something to assist Alec in celebrating the event. Providence must have supported such a good intent, for a few days later Sarah mentioned news of a family occasion in Cape May during a week end in September which would prevent them

150

attending the opening concert. Julius heard the date, Maurice's birthday, and decided at once to offer Alec two seats in a proscenium box. Sarah agreed it would be a perfect present, and was prompted to another generous thought, "Perhaps we can do something for Marvin, too."

*   *   *

When the sun rose that birthday, Alec only half-awakened his mate who seemed unready to face the fact that as the world counts he was one year older. Maurice languished in the sensuality that pervaded his body as Alec persisted in playful scattered endearments. An appreciative kiss on the backside offered promise for that night.

"I am doing work for the Kleins this morning" as he went off.

When Maurice finally got out of bed he splashed water on his face and hair, looking into the mirror eye to eye at a person who was wearing rather well, if he must say so himself. In another reckoning the outcome was as positive. Three years had passed since the voyage on the Olympic when he had made a vow to love and cherish Alec for all the years hence. There was no doubt in his body or mind about that vow.

That night at the concert Maurice looked handsome to Alec and to anyone who noticed his radiance. They were sharing the box with friends of the Kleins, which put Maurice on guard to display the appropriate decorum. Fortunately no one could see what was going through his mind as it meandered over sensual memories of three years with Alec. He allowed one clandestine touch to convey the sense of belonging to each other while his eyes wandered from the orchestra to the splendor of the Baroque painted ceiling where hung a magnificent sparkling chandelier. Applause brought him back to the end of the concert.

Alec had followed Sarah's advice and arranged a supper at the Bellevue Stratford where they enjoyed quiche, salad and red wine. During a desert, apricot pastry and coffee, Alec reached across the table to lightly touch Maurice's fingers.

"This is a token I wish you to have."

He handed over a small box so distinct in shape that Maurice's heart raced. He opened it carefully to see a gold ring he had never dared to expect, even now uncertain he would have courage to wear it. He was still properly English. Alec, however, with the Irish thrown into the mix, was an irreverent American.

"I would like to be so bold as to put it on your finger right now. Even better, if I could have done so, at the concert before an audience that

151

applauded as much for love as for music." These romantic words were edged with a ring of sadness. "We both know it is better to wait."

But it was not long till they were at home, stripped of concealments of mind or body. Alec took Maurice's right hand, chosen in defiance of convention, and placed the ring upon the second finger.

"Will you wear this? Let it speak to those who notice approvingly. Those who disdain such love as ours are not likely to ask, but should anyone insinuate contemptuously that our love is unworthy, say that the ring represents your dream."

Maurice was in a dream not yet fulfilled but made beautiful by the approving gift from Sarah and Julius, and by the ring that clung to his finger. He held Alec in his arms determined to always act for his happiness.

"My beloved, I proudly take this ring, and yet humbly. You do me honor thinking me worthy. I promise to you, Alec, fidelity and joyful companionship."

The expressions of love that followed befitted the day's celebration. Their private proclamation of union presaged a world more loving in its acceptance of human sexuality that someday would be real, though too late for themselves and for many youth captive to that time and place.

Chapter 14

Removing the Rubbish of the Past

Two Spirits woke me from my sleep this morn;
Both most unwelcome were; for they have torn
Away from me the shady screens of ease
And unreflecting, unself-scanning Peace
Wherein I used to hide from annoy
In years which found and left me still a boy.

The First . . . said, "Look back! and learn
. . . thy youth to its completion nears. . ."

a Second . . . caught all my senses . . . it drew
Its tightening hand of Pain . . .

Scarce worse than the keen hunger-pinch that racks
Numberless wretches all their life. Pain slacks
Its hold on me, only to grasp another;
And why should I be spared, and not my brother?

Wilfred Owen, "Lines on My Nineteenth Birthday"

Alec received a diploma in "industrial arts" and entered Temple University in the fall semester of 1927 with no plan other than to avoid those arts, better called drudgeries. He had seen enough of factory to know the industrial economy imperiled his dreams. Machine production worked miracles turning inert materials of the earth into goods, yet on close scrutiny the dreariness of its processes treated workers as if they were inert as well, draining their life spirit in a way reminiscent of his father's butcher shop where blood had been drained from animals.

Thus Alec adopted the liberal course of study that ultimately disappointed him. He studied literature but had no prospects there. He found philosophy too engaged in metaphysical speculation about man's place in the cosmos, none of it useful in the daily struggles he faced merely to safeguard his love for Maurice. History was disappointing, too, blind as theology as it was presented, too busy celebrating democracy and progress to notice that the American economy treated black people as half slaves and women as play things of patriarchal rule, while church-state cultural hegemony kept helplessly silent what might have been gay. If only history had shown a queer eye it might have helped to direct his disquiet into meaningful struggle, but had that been the case, then this tale would not have needed telling.

No need to dwell on Alec's college years except for the odd direction that he took. Though he enjoyed the surrounding of books, he felt apart from other students who were set on filling a bourgeois niche. During his second year he tired of dabbling. He took a decision not to settle for conventionality in the pursuit of a career to please Maurice, while behaving at the same time radically in matters of love. He did not wish to count profits as was Maurice's task, nor did he wish to set himself apart from hard labor. Only that it took place in an exploitative setting – that rankled him. He would not join the business of exploiting as if it would make him a better man. He would abide by Whitman's democratic and comradely love of men and women. It was a reckless choice that assumed Maurice would trail after him and all for the better.

Thinking to use his time to sort out that direction, he found a philosophy course that examined modern ideologies—liberalism, fascism and socialism. Here might be the chance to learn something of anarchism as well. It was for upper class students, but an imploring note to Prof. Carlton Sanborn earned Alec an interview. As soon as he entered the professor's office he became assured he was on the right pursuit. From the one wall not lined with books he was greeted by Lenin addressing a revolutionary crowd. In a corner of the room on a pedestal was a white marble bust of a face displaying a smile of reason. Sanborn rose from his chair to extend his hand, and as he did so his tall and lank body leaned radically. Perhaps he was an anarchist?

Sanborn gave a sigh of relief to see someone kempt and healthy. "You raised my suspicion of a misfit ready to avenge the oppressed masses. What concerned me was the desire to learn from anarchism, as you put it in your note, 'in order to find an appropriate way of dealing with a society that displeases me.'"

Sanborn liked attractive men who dared to think and behave in unorthodox ways. Now that he saw Alec, he was ready to attribute wholesome intentions to the petitioner.

"Your taste for Emma Goldman and liberating ideas is honorable. But registrars are not as readily inspired by lofty aspirations. Bureaucracy is annoying, but there it is. We can circumvent it, though I need to advance some reason why you should have permission to enter the company of fourth-year students. Would you tell me of yourself?"

Alec was annoyed. "I am twenty-five years of age, not some boy. I know my mind, as proven by the fact of leaving England for a new country. That was three years ago. As for my interest in anarchism, hardly had I entered the gate at Ellis Island, some agent warned me against it. I knew nothing of its meaning. Even now I know only it has something to do with placing oneself against the economic powers that rule society. But I have already done so, working a year in a factory, where I grew opposed to those economic powers. My inquisitiveness has led me here."

"What is it you expect from the study of anarchism?"

"I am not at the university to line my pockets. My friend Maurice would have me do so. He is an officer in a bank and urges me to something likewise, but that disheartens me. I belong among the oppressed by reasons of birth. I want to know whether justice is possible. Though I have heard anarchism decried as the work of the devil, a good lady, an owner herself of a factory through prosperous marriage, has spoken otherwise. She even admits to a wish from time to time that she had yielded to her youthful impulses to follow Emma Goldman. That suggests the devil sides with the exploiters whose company I am not ready to join, Maurice the exception. I need to know why anarchism is feared."

After this outpouring Sanborn enlisted in Alec's causes which he understood to be the liberation of his mind and, intriguingly, saving unknown Maurice from philistinism. What purer use for education than to prepare a man for such worthy goals?

"Forgive me for thinking you a naïve youth. We will make an exception to rules in your case. Thank **gawd** a professor has some prerogative." With this playful use of the deity he pulled from a drawer the Special Permission to Register form that he began to complete, reciting as he wrote, "Mr. Alec Scudder's work in the production line of factories has led him to the legitimate concern that organization of industrial workers should be more rational and in accordance with their Constitutional right to the pursuit of happiness. This course will help him to devise such a theoretical framework " He lifted his pen to offer a smile of reason. "That is an argument no registrar will resist."

Sanborn's loquaciousness carried beyond the form. "If I am not mistaken, ideas are only part of your need. I fear your confusion will increase, certainly your contempt will, when you critically confront

155

capitalist institutions of mass exploitation. Presumably you know Goldman's fate?"

"She went to jail for anarchism."

"That did not endear her to authority. She was the lover of Alexander Berkman who tried to assassinate the president of Carnegie Steel when he hired Pinkerton guards to break a strike at Homestead. Worse yet, she urged men to resist conscription during the world war that she thought imperialist. For that she was deported to the revolutionary Russia. Of course she had difficulties with the new state because communist authority plagued her. The anarchist hates chains of any sort, not only those upon workers' hands and ankles, but those around the throats of those who appeal for equality. Think of the recent destruction of Sacco and Vanzetti! What is one to do? Go to work for capital to enlarge its tyranny? Try to live happily amidst oppression? Not a comfortable resolution for an admirer of Goldman. Is it any better to flail against factory and prison? Resort to violent acts? Prison is likely for such deeds. I hope you see that your craving for justice is admirable but one that must be handled with caution."

Sanborn felt he might have gone too far with discouragement. With a twinkle in his eyes he suggested more pleasant possibilities.

"The political in me wishes to satisfy your intellect, but I have a perverse part that would be happy if you walked out of here forgetting anarchism. Maybe you should heed Maurice. Give yourself to material gain and enjoy natural pleasures."

"Even to enjoy natural pleasures, if you mean sexuality and love to rank among them, it is necessary for me to remove the rubbish of the past."

Sanborn was serious again as he approached the marble bust which was a replica of a work by Houdon. "This is Voltaire who inspired enlightenment."

Alec was pleased to know as much. "I have read **CANDIDE.** I laughed when I found so much of myself in the story. Is that what Voltaire intended as enlightenment?"

"He encouraged the effort to comprehend the laws of nature and their application to human behavior along the principle of the greatest happiness possible for all in society. I am his disciple in respecting science and tolerance. Do not confuse me with the agent who guarded the gates at Ellis Island. I delight in irreverence toward religion and social hypocrisies. If you seek a radical understanding of the world, there is no better basis than materialist philosophy which guided the enlightenment."

When Alec made no sign of trepidation, the flourish of Sanborn's signature put him on the course toward anarchism.

*   *   *

There is a thought put forth by Alexander Pope, "a little learning is a dangerous thing." Such is the hazard of enlightenment that it does not come all at once. It takes hold during illuminating moments after which the initiate wishes to use reason swiftly against great injustices, as if the world can be made better in less time than God needed to create it. When the world fails to budge, then comes impatience toward the small absurdities close at hand that seem more amenable. Such was the case with Alec who presumed Maurice would go along with all the clear demands of reason.

Alec listened to Sanborn's lectures as attentive as Leery at a new play. It is an apt comparison since Sanborn was another frustrated playwright who transcended the sting of unsung artistry by using the classroom as his stage. Perhaps he had deserved greater acclaim from the theatrical world, if not for his scripts, then for his acting, but he gave up before that recognition might have occurred. He switched to an academic career in which he used the stage he possessed to give passion to liberal and egalitarian thought. To keep the attention of youth who might easily be distracted by daydreaming or outright sleep he developed acting skills. He wandered about the auditorium in a peripatetic way, making sly and mischievous encroachments, sometimes brazen bounds that were meant to startle, or perhaps it was only that his long body made his movements less graceful. The texts he cited were often literary, Dickens, Balzac and Zola among his favorites. He was faithful to the spirit of the author, though he interpolated meanings and acted out caricatures of greedy characters that might have come from Hogarth or Daumier. Even the most attentive student could not be sure where the script ended and Sanborn began.

Alec trailed after Sanborn to question whether an idea might justify overturning society, or how at least it might correct the domain within his own command. He heard in a lecture that Locke was the cornerstone of Liberal positioning:

"The state of Nature has a law of Nature to govern it, which obliges everyone; and reason, which is that law, teaches all mankind who will consult it, that, being all equal and independent, no one ought to harm another in his life, health, liberty, or possessions."

Alec was not only a good listener, but a lively respondent who drew proper deductions. From the history he knew of Ireland pillaged and Africa enslaved, he was scornful. "Where was English respect for the

157

natural right to liberty? Even now, what natural right to property prevails while the mass of men are wage slaves?" That was Alec's reasoning after only a few weeks of lectures, before hearing from Marx or anything of anarchism. His radicalism was incited by Rousseau's critique, "Man is born free, yet everywhere he is in chains." Alec shook his head in pity for hypocritical mankind.

Sanborn took from a shelf the **Discourse on the Origin of Private Property** and handed it to him.

"Rousseau has turned many a man into a socialist."

That night Alec could not sleep, too excited by an explanation of the source for human misery. Rousseau's words were so powerful they must be true.

"The first man who enclosed a piece of ground with the claim, this is mine, and found people simple enough to believe him, was the real founder of civil society. How many crimes, how many wars, how many murders, how many misfortunes and horrors would another man have saved the human species who in pulling up the stakes or filling up the ditches had cried to his fellows: Beware of listening to this impostor. You are lost if you forget that the fruits of the earth belong equally to us all, and the earth itself to nobody."

Alec was about to cry aloud at this discovery of truth, "There is the answer to every injustice. Let us pull up the stakes!" But that would awaken his poor mate who had to go to the bank early. He wondered, besides, if Maurice was ready to join a declaration for full equality.

He waited till the next day to find Sanborn, "Is it not soon enough to pull up the stakes that unfairly divide the earth? Must we forfeit our humanity for property?"

 Sanborn was pleased that he had measured his man accurately. From now on he lectured with an eye to Alec as he stripped bare the claims of the Old Regime to divine rights. He invoked Voltaire's ridicule of these monstrous pretensions of nobility and kings, their claims sanctified by bishops doubly implicated in deception, from the arrogance of their own noble birth which was proof of being selected by God, and from their more sordid selection by the king to do his bidding as princes of the church.

Alec thrilled to Sanborn's radical analysis.

"That unholy alliance of church and state corrupted natural rights. Absolutism and religious fanaticism drove Jews from Spain and Protestants from France,' as Sanborn's body writhed with their villainy. "Tartuffes! They condemned to flames those who dared question the dogmas of the church they themselves disbelieved."

He paused to let puzzled students question one another on this reference to Moliere's Tartuffe. Then he implored with a calm voice,

"I address you as incipient philosophers to note how preposterous are any claims to rights beyond reason or empirical basis, as if God ordained the masses be plundered by the powerful. Such absurd claims are made even in our time, their inherent logic the possession of property and power as a gift of nature, and not contrived by economic advantages abetted by state power. We may deduce from this historical analysis that for injustice to continue the mass of people must be kept in ignorance so that they will work in order to surrender the bounty of the earth."

Now Sanborn added the smile of reason and enlightenment.

"Yet we need not despair at the long suffering of our fellow humans. Change is part of human direction. Reason pursued astronomy and physics during the seventeenth century as Galileo looked at the heavens to discover the earth moved. Newton formulated laws of attraction and motion. Discoveries of rational relationships throughout the universe encouraged men of trade and professionals to seek liberty to pursue wealth and knowledge which turned their minds against the restrictions of the church in favor of truths derived from nature, where Locke discerned natural rights. The revolutionary era spurred by this Enlightenment demanded restoration of natural rights."

Sanborn relished accosting the church. He was one with Baron d'Holbach who was bold to say. "We find in all religions of the earth, a God of armies, a jealous God, an avenging God, a destroying God, to whom lambs, bulls, children, men, heretics, infidels, whole nations are sacrificed. The zealous servants of this so barbarous God even think it a duty to offer up themselves as a sacrifice."

To Sanborn's mind, there was only one possible conclusion to his lecture.

"All national institutions of churches appear to me," in the words of Tom Paine, "no other than human inventions set up to terrify and enslave mankind and monopolize power and profit."

For several weeks afterward Sanborn elaborated the historic course of liberalism along the line of its principle, "All men are created equal with natural rights." This slogan was at the heart of revolutionary attempts to realize the political and social embodiment of natural rights in France and America. These revolutions fell short, and it became the plight of the poor to discover the right to life needs assurance of means of subsistence. That became the work of socialist theory to advance the cause of security in bold ways, none more prescient than the materialist exposition in **The Communist Manifesto.** Sanborn cited Marx and Engels, "In every historical epoch the prevailing mode of economic production and exchange, and the social organization necessary to it, results in a history of class struggles between exploiting and exploited, ruling and oppressed classes." Each ruling class defines its ideology that becomes the cultural superstructure, so that "The ruling ideas of each age have ever been the ideas of the ruling class," who sanctify their exploitation in the name of God and nature.

Alec was immediately at home with Marxism: all that comes from the earth, the land and its produce, the ores, the timber, the harvest from the seas – all these rightfully belong to men who share the work and should equally share the wealth. That much was clear enough to his heart and to his head.

Matters became ruffled with the long awaited anarchism. Bakunin praised the bourgeoisie for their revolutionary moment advocating liberty, equality and fraternity. But, during the nineteenth century, these principles deteriorated into dogmas once the bourgeoisie established a regime suited to their property. This was no more than Marx had declared. Bakunin, however, separated from him on the ways of the proletarian revolution. Marx envisioned a workers' state moving toward equality, but Bakunin feared a proletarian state would betray the masses because "The State has always been the patrimony of some privileged class." The directors of the state would be corrupted into an exploiting role. Bakunin desperately sought the dream of anarchism, full liberty and economic equality from the first moment of revolution.

*   *   *

It was the final lecture of the course, only one more thing to do. Sanborn would offer Alec an explanation of the agent at Ellis Island who so feared anarchism.

"Anarchism is an impossible dream. Yet its exponents are feared by the powers of the state. There is good reason. The anarchist is a deviant, allied to the criminal as an enemy of society."

Together they walked in silence to the office where they sat near smiling Voltaire. Sanborn made light comments about his leaving for Mexico to spend the summer in a remote province. Would Alec come that way so that they might deepen their friendship? But Alec was grappling with a more immediate dilemma that finally he declared.

"I am a deviant. Perhaps I should also be an anarchist."

Sanborn offered no quarrel, only that he wished to remain part of this conversion. He wished to guide it safely lest it end in futile sacrifice of any kind. He offered to gather readings from his collection. Alec was instructed to return in a few days to receive them.

*   *   *

That is how Alec came to spend the summer of 1929 falling in love with Emma Goldman, with no obvious threat to Maurice, for it was not her body but her mind that fascinated him and the life she led in ways that crossed his own. She had emigrated when she was sixteen from Russia to the United States where work in a factory turned her into a critic of industrial capitalist society, as it did Alec, once she recognized, "The average worker has no inner point of contact with the industry he is employed in, and is a stranger to the process of production of which he is a mechanical part. Like any other cog of the machine, he is replaceable at any time by other similar depersonalized human beings."

Goldman's early marriage and divorce increased her awareness of the plight of women and nourished a powerful wish to satisfy her nature against institutions and limits.

"Poor human nature, what horrible crimes have been committed in thy name! Every fool, from king to policeman, from fatheaded parson to the visionless dabbler in science, presumes to speak authoritatively of human nature. The greater the mental charlatan, the more definite his insistence on his prejudices."

Alec heard echoes of **Candide** in these jibes. He thrilled to her sweeping anarchist vision.

"Freedom, expansion, opportunity, and, above all, peace and repose, alone can teach us the real dominant factors of human nature and all its wonderful possibilities. Anarchism stands for the liberation of the human mind from the dominion of religion, as well as liberation of the human body; and a social order that will guarantee to every human being free access to the earth and full enjoyment of the necessities of life, according to individual desires, tastes and inclinations."

She meant for women to have the freedom to love outside marriage.

"The demand for equal rights in every vocation of life is just and fair; but, after all, the most vital right is the right to love and be loved."

She extended that same encouragement to homosexuals when she came to the defense of Oscar Wilde as "the victim of the horrible crime perpetrated against all homosexuals." She disassociated with the doubts of other radicals.

"Any prejudice or antipathy towards homosexuals is totally foreign to me. On the contrary! Among my male and female friends, there are a

161

few who are either completely Uranian or of bisexual disposition. I have found these individuals far above average in terms of intelligence, ability, sensitivity, and personal charm. I sympathize deeply with them, for I know that their sufferings are of a larger and more complex sort than those of ordinary people."

Alec was fully won to her side. He knew it was necessary to fight the burdens of the past which hold us all in a net.

Chapter 15

A Youthful Indiscretion

Now therefore, while the youthful hue
Sits on thy skin like morning glow,
And while thy willing soul transpires
At every pore with instant fires,
Now let us sport us while we may.

Andrew Marvell, "To His Coy Mistress"

That summer a letter arrived from Sam who was eager to share his happiness with Alec. The letter was postmarked from Milan after "a voyage that was dream-like, one that may be reminiscent of your passage with Maurice. When you told of that experience, an attempt to comfort me that as much lay in my future, I believed your story the stuff of novels and operas. Having now enjoyed gaily such days and nights with Carlo, I am in a blur as to dream and reality."

Alec had learned some time back of Sam's friend, another student at Curtis, who had become his roommate. Now he and Carlo were traveling companions, as the letter explained, spending the summer at Carlo's family villa.

"Despite much bustling of relatives and gatherings for enormous amounts of food, there are long stretches when we are not interrupted. We share impressions of literature, music and the nearby landscape. We find time for composition. Carlo is devoted to opera while I prefer the lighter touch of song." Then he added tenderly, "My heart is no longer laden with rue, so that I am able to cherish the memory of 'There's nae lark loves the light as I love thee.' Carlo is a cheerful sort, though an excitable artist, more so than me. What it all amounts to is that he is quite perfect. At close range, his defects disappear from delights."

The news from Sam stirred memories which blended into Alec's fascination with Goldman's views on sexual freedom. He was groping with her argument, "Marriage and love have nothing in common; they are, in fact, antagonistic to each other." For all practical purposes he was married, thus far in a monogamous way. He did not feel imprisoned though Maurice wore his ring. In fact, he reveled in the pride of possession, Maurice belonging to him, no doubt about that. It was not love he doubted, but it made him uneasy that Maurice persisted in seeking approval of their relationship elsewhere, as if impositions of a watchful society would bolster their monogamous loyalty.

*   *   *

It was a mid-July evening when Maurice was going to the movies with Leslie. Alec could go along, but he said he would rather take a solitary walk along the river to indulge some quiet thinking. As he walked under a bright sky he wondered how free love might apply to his situation. If only Maurice could endorse the attitude of Goldman, now his, "Love, the strongest and deepest element in life, the freest, how can such an all-compelling force be synonymous with that poor little State and Church-begotten word, marriage?" Why silence his stirring doubt that monogamy was not natural in shutting out the excitement of endless possibilities of sexual attraction? Why should both Maurice and he not taste generously of love within that one boundary of natural freedom set by mutual attraction? Maurice's playfulness with Leslie gave him no concern, no reason for it. He was ready to measure matters by his own complete sense of security.

Such thoughts were interrupted when a student with a book bag across his shoulder came sauntering along. The youth was silhouetted against the brightness of the sun at the western horizon that offered a halo to innocent Eros. They exchanged casual greetings as they passed each other in opposite directions. For a time the lad's face lingered in memory, an inviting image of loveliness, but it was forgotten after Alec continued up river where he sat upon a rock to watch the sun disappear. Before light was gone, however, the lovely vision was renewed for he noticed the same youth who had been following. Alec invited him to share the rock. There was nothing of seduction in the suggestion, only the mystery of physical longing. When darkness marked the release of clandestine affections, Alec took the boy's hand and guided it to what they wished of shared manliness. Then Alec led their way into a secluded area where he leaned against a tree to give his permission.

"Do as you desire" was his instruction as he opened the front of his trousers.

When the deed was delightfully done Alec said his thanks.

He returned home and slept soundly with peaceful dreams, not even waking to greet Maurice who thoughtfully undressed in the dark.

*   *   *

The next morning when they awoke Alec announced he was an out and out anarchist. Maurice was used to surprises, but this one might be dangerous.

"We are not even citizens. Is it wise to deny the United States government? Isn't that what anarchism does? "

Alec alleviated this concern. He knew they needed to stay within the law for in a few months they would take the oath of citizenship.

"Don't worry, not a bomb-thrower, just disposed toward freedom in every way natural. I am no longer willing to respect laws or culture or alienation that comes from class separation."

Maurice was practical by instinct and by the conditioning of work at the bank.

"What will you do for work and income?"

"Don't get so far ahead of me. Do you recall the words of Carpenter you offered me during our ocean voyage? Now I have some words I hope will stay with you, something of Goldman" which he read.

"In freedom love gives itself unreservedly, abundantly, completely. All the laws on the statutes, all the courts in the universe, cannot tear it from the soil, once love has taken root. Love in freedom is the only condition of a beautiful life."

Maurice approved this thought, but he was cautious to avoid anything anarchist.

"That is beautifully put, a sentiment I hold. But is there anything wrong wishing that an institution of society recognize our love as genuine and worthy?"

"We might be happier as two of love's renegades rather than as beggars."

Maurice was no dullard, but he was not ready to give up on an institution which held out promise, though perhaps falsely, of monogamous love, the only kind he believed could last. The best he could do was listen with patience to someone he loved and knew to be honest.

*   *   *

165

That was not enough. After this unsatisfying reception to his announcement Alec wished for a kindred radical spirit. He thought of Sarah. When Maurice was departing for some task, Alec mentioned he was going to do some work for the Kleins.

He arrived that Saturday afternoon only to be disappointed that the Kleins, taking their cook and chauffeur, had left that morning for vacation at Cape May. Only Noreen had stayed behind to look after things. Alec knew of these plans, as well as from previous years this was their custom, yet he had forgotten. Whether forgetfulness of this kind may be attributed to meaningful mistakes that mask deeper psychological impulses, as Freud contended, or whether occurrences of this kind be better left to inscrutable Fate, as many novelists indicate, an innocent visit by Alec took unexpected turns that ultimately proved fraught with consequences. The kindred spirit he sought not being there, there was only Noreen who was far from anarchist political inclinations. All she was able to offer was good-natured company. Their casual conversation turned an unexpected visit by early evening to more intimate exchanges and, without either intending it, something more.

Till now they were friends working in the same household, but there had been nothing of intimacy. Alec viewed her sympathetically as someone overcoming the same ignorance that had shaped his background. He was taking strides and he wanted her to do as much. He encouraged Noreen, often as they studied in the same room, support she welcomed even when his closeness distracted her from books. She did not count their friendship romantic or problematic, for she had little sexual understanding, and she knew little of the relationship of Alec to Maurice other than males could be attached to males.

This day Alec was happy Noreen displayed her charm in ways he had never seen nor imagined. No wonder, here she was in charge of a house, generously dispensing its comforts. She suggested supper on the porch. Alec accepted, gentleman enough not to mention Maurice, as he wished to continue their pleasantries. While Noreen prepared the food, he needed to telephone Maurice who would be awaiting him. Not used to deceiving Maurice, he offered no real explanation for the delay except to say that he was having dinner at the Kleins. It was not literally a lie.

Through the meal they talked and laughed while daylight disappeared; and so too did any reservations that had marked earlier hours. Night added to a sense of freedom. Noreen could never be bold or presumptuous, but her interest was more than affection as her body warmed to Alec's physical presence. She was willing to expand the promise of the moment when Alec in an offhand manner expressed surprise that he saw for the first time her maturity as a woman. Unsure though she was of the practices of seduction, she displayed a radiance that came from her new-found power, though it was strangely coupled with vulnerability, for she knew she was ready to be led. Why should she not trust Alec at this moment when he, too, might welcome greater closeness?

It was not a romantic impulse that rendered Alec susceptible, nor was it duplicity, only that anarchism had loosened his mind along with his trousers. Various other reasons far from rational theory disposed him to succumb to desire at least this once with Noreen, though he could not have calculated the forces of attraction that had long been at work in the recesses of his mind. Noreen's hair, her fair skin spotted by freckles, her slight build, and her disposition to be attentive to his wishes, all of these appeared against distant memories of his mother when they had been devoted to one another. Alec meant to be protective, as he had been of his mother, but this night he was too elated with his own masculinity to be fully watchful and to spare Noreen disappointment, given that his heart was not available for the long run. The anarchistic ideas regarding free love gave him the last push to pursue desire for this once with Noreen.

When supper was long finished she took his hand as if they were lovers and led him up the grand stairway to the second floor and then by back stairs one more flight upward to her room. There was no shyness to impede their passions. Noreen shed her summer apparel after Alec displayed his readiness. They touched approvingly, Noreen asking only one precaution, that he act gently. Alec was proud of his virility, not so much as to mistake the newness of this experience. He waited until she surrendered herself without any promise of tomorrow.

When excitement had subsided, as they rested side by side, Noreen asked whether he might stay the night.

"No, Maurice will be awaiting me, and I do not wish to disappoint him."

Noreen did not take this special friendship as a rebuff. She had given her body without the implicit promise that goes with courtship, and they had not spoken of any significance of sexual liaison. Alec had offered his body as well and, it seemed, part of his heart, no matter what Maurice meant to him. The truth was Noreen was swept up in the emotions of her first carnal knowledge, overwhelmingly joyous, so that Alec held an unrivaled place.

*   *   *

During the weeks the Kleins were away there were more meetings with growing abandon. Then the Kleins returned, an impediment, and when Alec did not press for her company, another impediment occurred. Noreen had not anticipated what a hold the body would have on her, that images of Alec would arouse powerful desires for his presence. She learned too late that a need for Alec awakened a claim for primary possession, whatever other claims might be pulling him from her. She knew Maurice stood in the way of their full consummation. But how could a man fulfill the role of a woman? She was cautious not to complain except to express uncertainty. She found Alec at his work one afternoon, and when he asked about her feelings, she spoke of doubt. "I have not known any other man with intimacy, and so I am not sure of love. We have never spoken of it and I have no reason to expect it." Alec was relieved to hear this, for he felt comfortable with his special love for Maurice. He did not hear her hope for tranquility which required an assurance of love, since he had no expectation with Noreen other than sexual pleasure as long as free love held sway in his mind, an instance of Alec's penchant for logic which led him to measure the passion in another by the limits of his own.

When Alec failed to address her confusion, Noreen's doubts became demanding of a resolution, though she voiced her protest faintly. "When I hear your feelings about Maurice, they are so certain, it makes me less clear of my feelings toward you." She placed her fingers upon his face in desperation. "Forgive me, I feel so alone. I do not hold it against you, only it makes me wonder whether we would be better to change our ways with one another."

She did not press, and neither did he, for further intimacy. While a few months passed Alec kept himself busy outdoors so that he did not notice her sullen mood. Then Noreen surprised him with plans of going away.

"We have never spoken of love, but I need to mention it. I am thinking of taking a different position. Sarah has told me of an opportunity in Baltimore with a good family. Being uncertain of your feeling, only a strong hand would decide me against that move. It seems proper to ask so that I do not mistake your intention."

"I have a passion for Maurice," was how Alec responded when he knew their friendship could continue no longer. "My passion is for his body and person."

Free love had run its course because Alec had entered this affair less out of hot-blooded passion than from a theory that sexual liaisons may be of benefit beyond simple gratification. He presumed Noreen would go forward to some other man more suited to marriage. Why not with experience on her part as more than likely would be true of any man she met? As for the gain he would realize, it would be to satisfy a curiosity whether his virility would fail with a woman after long satisfaction with Maurice. It was egoism to test the matter, reprehensible with someone innocent as Noreen.

If only the mutual attraction that brings sexual liaison would always be matched by mutual disaffection at the conclusion. Then disillusion would set in, rather than the suffering that follows the rejection of one by the other. Alec knew Noreen had wished their union, though it be brief, but he should have reminded her another person held his heart. Instead, he deluded himself that he had tender regard for her. This vanity led him to a regretful act. Then again, a more beautiful view urges itself, that his behavior be seen as offering himself in love, however fleeting the attachment of body and heart, a gift that would remain overwhelming in Noreen's memory through all of chaste monogamous life that was her destiny.

By the turn of the year Noreen was gone to Baltimore with only occasional letters to remind him of what might have been. In his imaginings Alec at first conjured a little girl resembling Noreen and a boy like himself. That picture did not prevail because his love for Maurice was stronger. It dawned on him he had slighted Maurice, jeopardizing their secure love, had it become possible for him to love Noreen more. He settled on simple regret that he largely kept to himself, "Why can't we enjoy sexual pleasures without possessing one another?" Marriage was not needed in his case. He wondered why Maurice valued it so, but as matters stood he faced a conundrum, "I guess there is no way love can be free of complications."

Chapter 16

Mrs. Hall and Andrew to the Rescue

Let America be the dream the dreamers dreamed.
Let it be that great strong land of love . . .
(Though) America never was America to me.

Langston Hughes, "Let America Be America Again"

No further adventures in free love, but another crisis loomed that might upset their relationship. A letter from Maurice's mother announced she would land in New York early in September "to try to rescue my Morrie from the other side of the Atlantic," as she quaintly put it.

Five years had passed since Maurice left England. Mrs. Hall was not getting any younger, and she missed her Maurice terribly, as she often complained to Ada and Kitty. They urged her to cross the ocean to see her wayward son that she might exert a mother's wholesome influence. Was it not her duty as the surviving parent to enlist Maurice in preserving the respectability of the Halls? Surely their father would have taken charge sooner. True, Grace had not misspent these last few years. Not only had she succeeded in seeing Ada prosperously married, but now Kitty was promised to a successful man. Yet there was Maurice nearing thirty years of age. It was past time for him to do likewise, assume the position of spouse so that he could produce a male heir to carry on the Halls.

Despite all that Maurice had written in explanation of why this might not be his destiny, it was far from enough to convince any of the women of his family. Mrs. Hall was not a stubborn woman, but all that she knew of the world, and in this matter it was all she needed, added to her resolution that Maurice must assume his role as the head of his family. Because of how little she really understood of anything beyond her upbringing, it was easy for her to persist in rebuffing Maurice's protests. She insisted to Ada that she knew Maurice better than he understood himself. As for Alec, she knew him not at all.

170

It was not religious scruples that troubled her, for Christian morality spoke in too many tongues to command her convictions. Railings of priests against sodomy, that it was an abomination in God's eyes, she dismissed as prattle. Male affection for male had its place, and it was common enough as far as she could tell, even admirable as when Maurice had been inseparable from Clive. The ways of satisfying human sexual passions struck her as in the order of importance of gastronomic pleasures. Certain restraints were needed. She had not been able to retain her maidenly form by indulging in either excess. Though she had nothing of personal adventure to draw upon, her observations of married acquaintances proved all was not as it was supposed to be. Besides, she was not so self-deceptive as to forget the reasons that had led her to marry Hall. His awkward person had hardly held interest for the few fantasies she had indulged as a girl, and neither had his ranging body excited her eroticism beyond the brief flickering of curiosity and mild surprise. Very soon his bumbling deeds in their marriage bed had doused any romantic flame before it could have ever grown to be consuming. None of this mattered much, for no romantic hope enkindled her stolid imagination when she yielded to the proposal of marriage, more at the urging of her father than the suitor, and thus was filled of sort the chasm that existed in her feelings where adventures or amorous urgings might have been supposed. She was neither disillusioned by marriage nor ever enchanted, least of all by the advances of male arousal. She performed what she believed duties as requisitioned and produced three little Halls. Sometimes she wondered if Mr. Hall fueled his passions elsewhere, but then she laughed at unfounded suspicions. It was well into her marriage when she discovered there was another woman. Revelation of carnal infidelity brought no jealousy but surprised her with a sense of relief that sexual commotions were completed since her expectations had long gone. What mattered was her husband supported his family bountifully while preserving the outward show of proprieties. For this he deserved her acquiescent silence.

Grace Hall's letter offered other reasons for her visit than that she missed Maurice "more than you realize." Stone House was readying festivities to honor Andrew who was about to be ordained into the priesthood, and she had not seen him since he was a boy. Then, too, Maurice's approaching twenty-ninth birthday ought to be celebrated amidst family, no mention made of Alec except for a curt notice, "Anne and George have invited me to stay with them and I have accepted rather than inconvenience Alec or you."

*   *   *

Maurice was fretting at a rescue that suggested no leeway from the Halls. Instead, a chilly wind from England had blown the message, "don't tell and we will not inquire, but we patiently await Alec's disappearance." Prejudices of this sort unchallenged might last all his lifetime. It was already five years since he had taken residence with Alec, but still no recognition was accorded by either Halls or Wetherills. At first his letters had confided what tact permitted, but his mother showed no interest in Alec or in his own most intimate feelings. His letters home became less frequent and less revealing.

Maurice was petulant with his mother's pronouncement not to inconvenience them during her visit. "She does not wish to confront our way of living. Better she stay with George where our living arrangement will be hushed." But Alec disagreed on this one-sided arrangement of hospitality. Not that it was his pleasure to share quarters with Grace Hall. He jested he would "rather take a vacation to Ireland for that month," but he relented when Maurice was miserable and needy of help.

"Morrie, you are going on twenty-nine, your mother twice that age. I think we are all old enough to deal honestly with each other. Tell her and the Wetherills, I will not be at Stone House for the celebration. We will accommodate your mother here within our family when she wishes."

They prepared the second bedroom, carefully removing every trace of secrets, including a photograph of Leslie that had been given Maurice to treasure but had been placed out of the way. They purchased an expensive bedspread the dark blue color he knew his mother favored while Alec painted the walls a complementing light blue so that the room would be welcoming.

*   *   *

Maurice went to New York to meet the ship and spend a few days showing her around. The evening before the landing he saw Graham who grasped the delicacy of the visit. Maurice was in such uneasiness that Graham volunteered to escort them around the city for a day and arrange a dinner in one of the finest hotels, even to bring a woman as table companion to make it more comfortable for Grace Hall.

Thanking him for his help, Maurice confided a failure of heart.

"I am in a state of anxiety, not sure how to handle the Philadelphia part. Alec is trying to be helpful, but he insists on openness, though he promises consideration. I am too old to ask her approval, perhaps she too old to grant it. What can she understand?"

"She knows more than you realize," and he advised Maurice to find much time to be with his mother away from the Wetherills. "There is a hold on her heart that keeps her silent. She will not give up the boy she remembers, nor acknowledge the boy you once were was father to the man she does not want to know. Be patient, but give no quarter on moral grounds or social conventions. Alec is right asking openness. Let her see that your relationship is genuine and decent."

Thanks to Graham the New York part whirled by successfully.

*   *   *

For at least the beginning of the Philadelphia visit, Maurice thought it easiest to deposit his mother in Gladwyne. Anne met them at the train station with her chauffeur, but Maurice insisted he would walk the mile home. Arrangements were made that he would be at Stone House two days hence for his birthday and stay the night. Thereafter, his mother understood, a bedroom awaited her in his and Alec's home when she chose to occupy it.

Ten days later, midway through her visit, Mrs. Hall brought a small suitcase into what Alec dubbed "The Blue Room." This was the manner he chose, gently satirical but not resentful, what one might hope is genuinely American. Earlier that morning he had purchased a bouquet of American flowers which he placed on a table beside her bed. Maurice was by then sufficiently relaxed to place beside the vase a photograph of Alec and himself which framed their happiness.

Once she was settled they conversed or, better put, they listened while she recounted news from England. Five eventful years had to be covered during which Ada had married and given birth to two girls whose first words and steps and succeeding behaviors were related. Next there was an account of two of Kitty's failed romances, and the accomplishment, which gave her great relief, of being engaged to a successful man of business. Even so, there was an unresolved matter. Once the marriage took place in the spring they would occupy the Hall house with or without her presence. Whether she would continue to live there was uncertain, but Maurice offered advice that it would be better that she not intrude upon newlyweds. This brought a wistful remark from Mrs. Hall, if only Maurice had spared her this dilemma. Perhaps it slipped out, so complete was her assumption that happiness rested in a secure middle class style of living, the path being respectable marriage with or without love, when she uttered the wish Maurice might yet produce the first male heir of the family, but that he had need get started.

173

This brought a smile to Alec, "England would be more fertile ground for that."

Maurice grimaced to show his displeasure with that direction. He would settle matters with his mother as soon as there was the chance.

Alec suggested supper, an invitation to Angelo's. They had arranged the best family setting they could. Tony and Rita were there with their first son who was two years of age. Angela was not present to add luster for she had married and lived some distance, just as well for Maurice. Their appetites were hearty as befit the food, except for Grace. Alec noted she was ill at ease with the company, and so he took efforts to please her with numerous polite questions which got her to share small talk from England.

It was a warm night, good for walking, and so Maurice accompanied his mother homeward on foot while Alec lingered with Tony.

"Did you enjoy our family circle? Nothing like Stone House, but I thought it all quite wholesome."

The most she would concede was she was pleased to be with him. That night she tossed in her bed with little satisfaction.

*   *   *

Confrontation and clarification were essential lest the visit end as estranged as it had begun. The dreaded moment came when Alec had reason to be away an entire day. He had work to do for the Kleins and that evening he was accompanying Leery to the theatre. Maurice used the opportunity to take his mother for tea in the Crystal Room to set an English tone of restraint. Even so, the calm was shattered.

"Mother, I must assert what should be obvious. Alec is of permanent importance to me. I wonder at your obstinate avoidance of this commitment we have made, as if my happiness is of no concern."

"What do you mean? My deep concern for you has led me across the ocean to see to your respectability. Now that I have met Alec, I see he is attractive, and in some ways winning, but with little accomplishment professionally. Where can this friendship of yours end? It is time Alec find a common girl and go with her."

Maurice was astonished. "Do you believe I would be happy to lose Alec?"

"He would be your friend, as Tony is his. Your welfare requires that choice. George is sure a career in banking awaits you in England. It is time you observe what society and your family expect."

Grace Hall's concern went beyond her own term on earth. Her son's future was at stake which made it right to be blunt.

"If you stay with Alec, when will you marry and have a family?"

Maurice had traveled too long, too far a journey to relapse into uncertainty, even to protect his mother. She presumed to love him and surely did in her way. Suddenly her opposition was no longer silent. He regretted he had not been more forthright, that he had been too ready to accept her silence for acquiescence ever since that letter written on board the Olympic, thinking to spare her further indelicacies. Now he was caught by her directness. His instinct took wonderful command as he replied adroitly,

"When it becomes legal to marry Alec. That is when I will marry."

Mrs. Hall was taken aback. "But you will regret you don't have children" was her admonition.

"I already do," Maurice concurred, but such was the consequence of his status.

Maurice was not about to gainsay the desirability of a family, something he had worried about often. He feared and regretted a family might be necessary for Alec who would not easily be contained within a dualism whether man with man or man with woman. Alec's nature was not likely to be satisfied with romance. He was fully loved and would not be looking elsewhere. Moreover, he had pledged himself to Maurice, which was an accomplished matter, unnecessary to repeat or guarantee by fanfare. But Maurice knew there was restlessness within Alec to leave a mark on the world. He was not able to sift through his mistaken concerns. Children, could they have some, would extend their love into a new generation. The possibility of marriage and children that was on his mother's mind was therefore of gravity to Maurice as well. All he could stammer was a disclaimer.

"But I have principles of my own!"

Poor Mrs. Hall was perplexed at this rejoinder, and it did not help at all that he repeated his distress.

"I do regret not having children. But that can't be helped, can it?"

Maurice was heartsick at his mother's grief that he would never have a family of his bloodline. His anger surged to think she was saddened because he loved Alec. How selfish to demand he produce grandchildren for her satisfaction, no matter that it meant a supreme sacrifice of himself. How could she withhold approval of his nature and crush his self-esteem? What kind of world was this! Instead of grief, should she not be joyous that he had found Alec to love and cherish, and preside over a family celebration such as had honored Ada and would honor Kitty?

She persisted against a sense of defeat, "That is the way we must live, as instinct ordains and society prescribes," and in a feeble effort to comfort him, "the only way which gives our lives meaning."

"My instinct convinces me otherwise."

*　　　*　　　*

Maurice had some necessary business at the bank, which relinquished to Alec the duty to spend the day with Mrs. Hall, the last time he was likely to be alone with her during her Scudder-Hall visit. She would be returning to Stone House for festivities around Andrew during the last week of her visit. Alec decided to show her the Pennsylvania Academy of Fine Arts which he had come to appreciate. As they walked about the gallery he led her to several favorite paintings. His commentaries and courtesy pleased her, though she preserved an emotional distance. Not satisfied with this stand-off, Alec decided on something more robust than tea while they awaited Maurice for dinner.

"I know a place where we can have some wine, if you would."

Alec's company had relaxed her into a mood of less formality, not to be taken as equality of friendship with someone so different. Nonetheless, she had been humbled once she despaired of winning Maurice to her wishes. As the wine took effect she permitted herself the frankness of someone who had no more to lose.

"I am to blame for not marrying again when Mr. Hall died. During adolescence Maurice lacked a man to influence his behavior."

Having become that man, Alec could afford to handle her regret gently.

"What Maurice desires of male companionship is not a failing, certainly not yours, and none of his."

"Why do I feel a loss, as if Maurice were gone? I do not mean offense to you."

"Perhaps it is your ambitions that are lost?"

She could not hold back tears which were the culmination of long grieving since Maurice had left England and of the last quick death of hope of Maurice marrying and taking his appointed place as head of the Halls. These expectations were asunder. As she stood up to retreat from a public display, her body convulsed. The only compassionate thing for Alec was to support her strongly in his arms. She did not repel him. For the first time she appreciated Alec who eased her desperation with his well chosen words of assurance he would care for Maurice, even as he was caring for her.

"Of course Morrie is happy with you."

She returned looking proper and Alec ordered the glasses refilled.

"Maurice would be satisfied to become a father. That is something I desire for myself. Neither of us is acting in defiance of that natural course. There are feelings we have for one another that stand in the way. It is more important to Maurice to be with me than to realize the advantages of returning to England. His feelings cannot be opposed, not out of love at least."

She was more ready to listen.

"Will it comfort you that I love Maurice as much as any woman might? I cannot say whether in the same way. But he will not be alone while I am living."

"It is helpful that you behave manly with one another. I would not want Maurice to lose that aspect of himself. Perhaps you think me limited in understanding, hopelessly unimaginative. A woman of my age has no view other than marriage of a proper sort. Of course men have always sought adventure. Women have learned to avert their eyes from such diversions after marriage, as I did regarding Mr. Hall. I thought Morrie might bridge his needs by marriage and the occasional infidelity."

"Maurice could not be happy with the kind of marriage you prefer for him. He is a man – have no fear of that – only he needs a man. Do not think it pride, but I mean to be honest. I am the man for him. If you mean to assist his happiness, it's best done by acceptance of his heart which has decided. We are pledged forever. Nothing inferior to marriage in our promise, only that society threatens us. That ought to be your concern."

*   *   *

The following Saturday Andrew was ordained and Sunday he presided at mass in St. Mark's before full attendance. Though Alec was not in favor of preaching, he was there with Maurice. Andrew had sent a special invitation because the sermon he was preparing on "All Men Children of God" was derived from their conversations about Christianity and "that other matter." Andrew promised "not to speak long, nor to cite the Bible more than once or twice, and then not on any matter you contested. Most certainly there will be no sacrifice of a lamb. Not even for the reception."

When Andrew entered the ornate pulpit his eyes found troubled Maurice who sat next to his mother, Alec at her other arm. To start he conjured an image of David as a boy singing, not to be counted a reference to the Bible, for the episode was from the poetry of Browning. He added lyricism of his own that sounded a different Andrew.

"Oh, the wild joys of living. How good is man's life, the mere living. How fit for all of us, creatures of God, to use the heart and the soul and the body, all its senses, all in joy."

The tone was unlike anything Alec remembered of their talks. Yet as the oration continued there was sameness of Andrew's theology that God gave us life, and genius, and intellect that we might fathom the mystery of existence. It was far from satisfying Alec but as bold he ought to expect from this initiate into a church that thought its mission divine.

"Every man must find a life peculiarly his own, for we live in a time of progress. The Church provides rules of duty but it does not find docile followers because the modern man appeals to freedom. That individuality must be held sacred by our faith so that we be spared the hardened hearts of the Pharisees, who brought before Jesus a woman taken in adultery, citing the law of Moses that she be stoned. Jesus repelled this harshness of law and spirit. 'He that is without sin among you, let him first cast a stone at her.' When the condemners left in disarray, Jesus acted gently to the woman, 'Neither do I condemn thee. Go and sin no more.'"

It was Andrew's first use of his Bible, one he felt Alec would appreciate.

"This forgiveness of a sin of the flesh I believe is an inspiration from Jesus to seek love with body and soul joined. God gave the body and bade us to love one another. It is sexuality that most immediately urges us to this love."

Alec recognized their exchanges about the body as a source of truth.

"No doubt we err along the way as we follow the body. Every man's youth offers enough for God and man to forgive. But where love is, God is present. By experience that brings deeper love, and other times suffering and disillusion, the love from the body cultivates the soul. The soul strives for the larger life of man to love all creatures not seen which is our faith that all are children in the image of God. We must exercise freedom and rationality, not fearing or condemning the body, so that the soul may fulfill love by natural devotion for our brethren."

For the remainder of the sermon Andrew deplored the kind of righteousness which benights the mind in prejudice. Few in the congregation understood fully, and some who did were not ready to heed the judgment, but Andrew won the day because he radiated the joy he felt as priest and the sincerity of his mission to love all children of God. Then he allowed a second and last reference to the Bible, staying true to his promise.

"Christians in the courage that comes from freedom show their faith by loving all God's creatures and not sitting in judgment. Is there not a caution from Jesus, vital to the application of the laws Moses conveyed, to 'judge not' lest we be judged unworthy by our own sins?"

No words could have been more apt, though he had prepared most of his text long before Grace appeared. Was this not proof of the mystery of grace? Just the day before in the rectory while congratulating the new priest Maurice had lamented, "if God is in his heaven it is time he guide my mother to love Alec." Andrew prayed afterward that he might be an instrument of God. He replaced a different Biblical injunction in the sermon, lest he go beyond two citations, with the "judge not" passage that spoke to the Halls.

*   *   *

Dinner was festive at Stone House with Andrew the main feast. Maurice was more at ease than he had been for weeks. Andrew provided further balm to his cousin when Maurice was ready to take leave. Accompanying Maurice to his car he embraced him in the robust manner Alec had shown, not anything Wetherill.

"I will convince your mother. God will work wonders."

Later Andrew sat with Grace on the patio under a sky replete with stars.

"There are stranger things on this earth than two men loving one another."

"Is it not our Christian faith to deplore sins of the flesh? Marriage, I was taught, sanctifies the carnal act. Now you are my priest, and I see you love Morrie. I wish you to tell me how I am to behave. He would have me accept Alec. That goes against all my fears for Maurice, less for his soul than for his security, given the ways of society. Do help me out of this dilemma."

Andrew had prepared his advice. He knew Maurice was resolute and Alec a worthy man. The truth must set his aunt free.

"The mother of Jesus did not turn away from her son though he was judged a criminal. She transcended the precepts and the priests of her own religion."

Grace Hall cried quietly this time, cleansing her mind of pride. Andrew said they ought to pray, and he took her hand and led her to the grave of his brother with its stone marker. They held each other silently in thought. As they returned to the house he urged,

"Do the only thing which suits you as a mother. Love Maurice, he is your son in all his weaknesses. It is the love Jesus condones that stems from our human nature. Maurice and Alec wish to be together. That is for God alone to nourish or deny."

*   *   *

Maurice accompanied his mother to New York one day before her departure. It was a different Grace Hall than several weeks ago. When she and Alec said goodbye she had not repelled his embrace, albeit her physical response was lukewarm by contrast. Still Maurice was gratified at the sight. He was more satisfied when she asked Alec to look after her son and to grant her further chance to know him.

"I hope you will come with Morrie to meet his English family who will be more gracious than the Philadelphia contingent. Please do not wait long."

They spent the day in a hotel, venturing out late afternoon into Central Park. She explained arrangements made with George to transfer a considerable sum of money to the bank and to Maurice.

"It is from your father who intended it as your marriage right. God knows, he was not scrupulous about marriage. Neither is Andrew with his peculiarity of religion such as I have never heard. He managed to turn my Christianity topsy-turvy, to unsettle attitudes I have held all of my life. He tells me I ought not to behave as someone aggrieved—and I will not. In any case my objections to Alec are practical."

Enough had been said about other disadvantages, and so Maurice addressed real dangers.

"We are careful in public behavior and in a few months we will be citizens. What else are we to do without losing integrity?"

When parting was near Maurice promised to visit England, though at no specified time. Perhaps Alec would come as well? Not likely, since his memories of England were embittered by the class system and he could hardly look upon the Halls as family, though her change of heart made it possible. She insisted Alec was welcome wherever she settled once Kitty married. Maurice seized the opportunity to thank her for the monetary gift and for coming. He, too, had experienced a change of heart.

"No matter what your doubts, accepting Alec lifts a burden from my heart. I love you all the more."

"Then I comfort myself for doing the right thing."

This exchange was a token of their love no longer estranged.

Chapter 17

Too Unhappy To Be Kind

. . . I see
In many an eye that measures me
The mortal sickness of a mind
Too unhappy to be kind.
. . . all they can
Is to hate their fellow man;
And till they drop they needs must still
Look at you and wish you ill.

A.E. Housman, "A Shropshire Lad"

As soon as you're born, grown-ups look where you pee,
And then they decide (what) you're s'posed to be.

Peter Alsop, "It's Only a Wee Wee"

Against George's advice to invest his legacy in stocks, Maurice leaned a different direction toward real estate. Wishing to seize the good fortune that had presented itself, he craved a piece of solid earth with an imposing structure upon it to give a stake to the Scudder-Hall future. That seemed the best he could do in the way of family. He turned to Mr. Huston whose praise he had heard from Perry for guiding him to the house he owned. A man in his eighties, Huston had since given up his own agency, but he continued to conduct an occasional sale because work had kept him healthy. He studied every property he promoted inside and out, its real values, and all about the surrounding neighborhood, and drew satisfaction when he could lead a client to the right place.

Maurice excitedly mentioned he was seeking a house of Victorian fashion, one close to Charles and Albert, though Alec showed less enthusiasm in that direction, something Huston observed when he invited a look around Germantown. After several disappointments Maurice became fascinated with a house that was grand and odd with three towers and other quaint features.

Alec showed only remote interest. "Can you really afford this? What will we put into all this space?"

Maurice sought to justify an otherwise selfish extravagance, countering the tone of Alec's question with buoyancy. "It is a wedding present, you see, for you as much as me. We should have a house suitable for all our lives. My father expected the Hall house would be mine." Then he turned to Huston, "We will purchase outright and still have resources for furnishings and for Alec's education yet to be completed."

Huston wisely steered them away from the dilapidated three-towered showpiece as too expensive maintaining. He found another less showy that might have done except modern edifices had encroached either side so that the Victorian spirit was diminished. Then Maurice liked another house that preserved its surrounding within an acre of trees that deterred Alec.

"I have no intent of becoming the Hall ground keeper."

Huston all this time was unraveling the mysteries of his clients. A few days later he telephoned to say he had located something that might suit them. They agreed to have a look. As the car climbed a Manayunk hill their enthusiasm mounted, but then it waned as they saw the house at the corner of the first cross street. It was not the house which fronted uphill that disappointed, but across the street was a short block of colonial row houses. This sight did not please Maurice. He remained disapproving as they examined two lower floors. When they climbed to the third floor it was Alec who showed delight for the first time during their search. "What a wonderful place!" he exclaimed, as they entered a room stretching the back of the house lined with windows except for double doors that opened onto a porch overlooking the spires of a church toward the Schuylkill River with a sweeping view of the industrial town below and at a distance an arched stone bridge that carried trains across the valley.

"Imagine awakening to the light reflecting from the river." Alec had designated the sunlit room as their bedroom. With further command he contemplated their future, "I might find work below," as he pointed to a lane that led from the gate of the garden along the cliff past several houses to a wooden stairway descending to the street.

Mr. Huston discreetly left them on the porch to contemplate that possibility.

Maurice jested that the small garden below would not need a caretaker. He added as a slight concession, "I could take the Reading to the office each morning and read the morning paper." That being said, some doubt lingered which he did not put his finger on. What displeased him not surprisingly pleased Alec, that the row of modest houses on the street defied class separation, that Manayunk itself posed uncertainties of a working class milieu where men who lived in these houses worked in factories.

"I would be more comfortable using my legacy for something more fashionable, perhaps a brownstone on a square."

That brought the rejoinder, "Did you not represent the money as a marriage gift? That seems I should be taken into account."

No further talk ensued of Maurice's legacy. They would live in Manayunk with its mix of common folk and finer breed, the likes of Alec and Maurice, where they could awaken to the glow of the river and imagine themselves commanders of the valley below. Arrangement was swiftly made for a cash dispensation with ownership to be transferred by the end of the month.

*   *   *

A guardian angel must have been watching over Maurice during this fateful time that the stock market began to collapse in October of 1929. The big drop did not catch Maurice by surprise.

"The market is adjusting, long overdue. I have been warning clients," as he sipped his coffee while perusing the morning newspaper. "Real estate is timely, property that won't disappear. George would have had me invest in the bank," which brought only a disinterested nod of approval from Alec.

*   *   *

That autumn was taken up settling into a new house as Maurice, often with Leslie's assistance, engaged in a frenzy of acquisition to furnish it appropriately. Alec laughed at this marriage gift that brought remarkable behavior by Maurice whose every workday promoted capital investment, yet here his speculation was on their long future. Maurice acknowledged being stung by his mother's urging to get about making a Hall family, preposterous advice in the direction she envisaged, but not without merit in another way.

Alec decided to contribute to that end. He surprised Maurice when he brought home a handsome newcomer. "This is Oliver" as he introduced a pup as uncertain in pedigree as his own. Chance along with calculation had entered into this expansion of the household. Hearing of Mrs. Hall's concern, Tony had put him in touch with someone who had one pup remaining from a litter, an enterprising one who at first sight grabbed Alec's sleeve and would not let go. Alec did not let go either, for this rascally persistence won him over, reminding him of Oliver who had followed him about as a teenager. Not that there was other resemblance of canine to man. Oliver the dog was black and brown, likely German shepherd infused into a wide assortment of genes. He did give promise of being as loyal as his namesake, and likely of playful character, unless some meanness spoiled it. In a short time Oliver found a niche in the Hall-Scudder family.

* * *

Winter brought further excitement. Having fulfilled the five-year residency that was required to become a citizen, they appeared before a judge with Leery and Charles witnesses to their good moral character. A few months later they stood in a federal court with hundreds of immigrants to declare loyalty to the United States of America. Alec and Maurice were full-fledged citizens with rights and duties.

Other than waiting five years, Americanization had come easily, near painlessly, except for the loss of family that was stronger in Maurice's case. Neither of them knew the bewilderment of immigrants who could only use a foreign tongue. They suffered no insults, for they were not "micks" since Alec was too English for disparagement, nor "dagoes" or "hunkies" or "spics" and above all they were not "niggers." Their speech marked them in a way that brought respect. Alec spoke with more common vocabulary and voice, as he absorbed American words and ways quickly, so that he seemed more American than Maurice ever would be. He was ardent to practice American democracy because he felt equal to the high and the low. When he met another immigrant he was eager to share impressions of their new country. It was easier for him to assimilate since he was less British, and never much Irish.

Maurice would retain a touch of Cambridge and British upper class speech and manner all through his life. Despite living with Alec, he held the working classes in proper distance. Class informality ran against his expectations of deference to breeding, education and culture that accompanied wealth in England. Sadly, what he did assimilate readily

184

was American racial prejudice that extended beyond Negroes to everyone other than northern Europeans. Imperial Britain had deeply embedded in his consciousness a disdain for any culture that did not embrace the values and manners that were his own. It was not entirely a matter of color, for he had viewed the Irish as primitive, but that was before Alec. What saved him from outright bigotry was his determination to love Alec as an equal. The England of king, peers, and privileges disappointed him for the barriers it posed to their full union. He had left England and he thought all that tied him to England. It was harder than he expected due to the family connections established in Philadelphia.

In another way they were fortunate, their conduct did not render them transparent in their preference for the male body, so that they were not branded "inverts" or "fairies" except perhaps behind their backs. America seemed to accept their relationship, albeit unwittingly for the large part, and for the rest, mutely acquiescent, hardly appreciative. Nowhere on this earth could they be free to find the full humanity they deserved.

*   *   *

New Year's Day of 1930 found them giddy with citizenship.

"It is time we act Americans straight away," Alec jested as they walked briskly from the Reading terminal toward Broad Street on the way to Philadelphia's traditional Mummers Parade.

Maurice took genuine pride in their new country for it had been good to them. A glancing look at Alec reinforced this satisfaction, for his muscular body was magnified by a bulky navy blue sweater of Irish wool, along with the companion scarf of emerald green wrapping his neck in a warming hold. These were Christmas gifts from Maurice who liked the way the scarf undulated in the tailwinds of excited motion that brought a glow of healthiness to Alec's face. They were this morning optimistic, unaware of the challenges the American dream would face during the years ahead. As often the case, happiness hinges on not foreseeing every misfortune which stalks.

As they arrived at the Bellevue Strafford Hotel the parade approached up the avenue led by a squadron of mounted police whose captain sat astride a white horse. Maurice stood across the street from the stately hotel where in an upper suite the bank was hosting a party with a lavish table of food and drink. He had displeased his uncle by shunning the habit of Philadelphians of his status to prefer the view of the parade from the warmth of the hotel. Maurice insisted on being with Alec.

The bystanders who lined Broad Street were gleeful with fancy string bands and the all-male burlesque. This was, after all, the Mummers' raucous day for queer toggery and strutting. Heralded by a string band, Uncle Sam came by in satin robe with a cloak red, white and blue, that trailed half a city block, more appropriate to the King of France, with a hundred page boys cavorting gaily under the train they carried. The procession was cheered hour after hour for outlandish fantasies that tweaked royalty and foreign ways. Tsar Peter the Great was escorted by peasants, strangely garbed in blouses of gold color and trousers red velvet, dancing incongruously in happiness about the throne of their master. Hilarity greeted a barge that sailed by carrying Cleopatra, an obese drag queen pampered and regaled by royal guards. Later the Prince of Wales danced happily while hunting for "big game" in Africa, the "natives" bowing to his royal person which dwarfed miniscule lions and elephants.

One panorama was not genial, as far as concerned Alec. It offered a travesty of native Indians scantily clad with headdresses of colorful feathers, cavorting riotously to wild music. Every so often their savagery was accentuated. At a signal from their chief they performed a synchronized ritual dance, each savage waving a tomahawk in search for some civilized scalp. Alec found the panorama vile, as if Indians had never been victims of genocide but had merely made room for American progress. It was a far cry from Mercer's appreciation of the pre-Columbian era. An outpouring from Alec questioned why even in jest people felt it right to degrade the existence of others; why they found it amusing to dehumanize those who followed other creeds; why their lighter skin led them to abuse darker races; and, alluding to their fragile glass confines, why so many resented those who marched to a different gay drummer?

Serious thoughts were laid aside to enjoy dinner in town as entitled Americans. When at home again Maurice suggested they listen to music. The miracle was that the anguished sounds of the Pathetique Symphony, sorrowful and desperate, did not leave them dejected. Somehow they were strengthened in the resolve to live freely and kindly. With dimmed lights they celebrated their love.

*   *   *

It was months later that know-nothingness reached their door. Just when they were feeling at home, a pleasant morning turned sour. Maurice was troubled all that day over the rudeness of a neighbor.

Returning from the morning round of dog and man, Maurice stopped to chat with Mrs. Sipolski across the street when she inquired into how things were going. She had taken a shine to Maurice for his handsomeness and looked for any occasion to engage him in talk. Maurice obliged her, but he became distracted from the watchfulness due Oliver who had crossed with him and was entertaining his natural pleasure of spraying a pristine bush two doors from the Sipolski house. This occurred all in sight and reach of O'Donnell, who was touching up his modest garden. By every legal right the bush belonged to O'Donnell, sacrosanct as every square foot deeded him, a legal point never in contest except **de facto** by hapless Oliver. Unlikely that Alec's anarchism had rubbed off on him, but whether that was so or not, Oliver had grown sufficiently confident to throw his weight around, usually in play, but now regardless of the rights of private property. This impudence turned O'Donnell a scowling red in apoplexy.

"Why is your god-damned dog running loose!"

Not only the dog was untethered, but O'Donnell's tongue, which unleashed accusations beyond the present misdemeanor.

"This neighborhood was better without faggots!" The charge was shouted for the neighborhood's benefit, and afterward under his breath the irate man continued in outrage. "They respect nothing" as he indicted their defiance of the laws of God, nature and private property. How neatly these three pillars of righteousness aligned in his judgment.

Oliver disliked this unneighborly outburst, though whether he was included in the charge of unnatural is impossible to say. Nevertheless Oliver bared his teeth and growled without contrition. Before the incident had time to escalate, the man disappeared behind a slammed door, leaving a dumbfounded Mrs. Sipolski. She gathered her voice to assuage the hurt she perceived.

"Don't let him bother you, Mr. Maurice. Such as the likes of him never cared for God. It is wild talk out of envy of your success." Mrs. Sipolski attended the same church as O'Donnell. "The man shows no respect even for his Mrs. I will leave more unsaid." She cupped the canine face within hands that showed the drudgery of raising seven children. "No more peeing there," and extending the remark beyond Oliver, "Take care where you pee. Many of us pay no heed, but others are looking to find a quarrel."

*   *   *

Maurice was upset through the day. By evening his anger left him unsettled as to his place in the community, exactly what prejudice intends. In discomfiture he recounted the episode to Alec who had left home beforehand. While the altercation was small pickings – if one could truly live by the adage, "Sticks and stones will hurt my bones, but names will never hurt me!" – it was a warning how fragile is serenity within the human scheme of things. Maurice was shaken that the meanest of sorts may vent anger at small provocations, even another's difference. Alec consoled his friend with the conjecture that O'Donnell was accustomed to fastening on to anyone he thought weaker, and that likely would be a dog, a woman, or someone whose nature marks him as vulnerable.

"For God's sake, he is no more a man than either of us. I am no fairy."

It was strange Maurice appealing to God, though only in a manner of speaking. Sadly, he spoke as did his assailant. He distanced himself from fairies, demeaning them, capitulating to the bigotry which had a claim on his own feelings. Truth was, Maurice did not feel kindly toward men who mocked the conventions of gender.

Fortunately for O'Donnell he was too old to be thrashed, which checked Alec's initial impulse. Discretion may be the better part of valor, but it offers a painfully slow remedy to the point of seeming no remedy. It hurt him to see Maurice licking his wounds. Though Alec was not a Christian commanded to turn the other cheek, he was inclined to play the part of Oliver, to soothe Maurice's wounds, putting his tongue to the eyes, the ears, and finally the lips of his troubled mate.

"Such presumption to think us fairies," Maurice continued less angry, "We live respectfully, nothing outlandish in our behavior. We behave normally."

"O'Donnell has eyes, not much of a mind." Then Alec threw out a bit of flattery, "He does show intelligence envying your good looks and English manners."

Maurice's calm was restored so that he could expound on his indignity.

"Winnie's flamboyance is disturbing because it confuses things. Leslie is different. I do not consider him a fairy. Though he seems feminine, it is guileless, nothing confused, simply that he likes being treated as a delicate creature. I wonder about such queer differences – remember the intermediate sex that Carpenter described? You rejected it out of hand. I would not cultivate anything feminine myself. But why is it we prefer men? Hopefully we are not fairies for that."

"Don't torture yourself. There is no reason for recriminations. We should be proud of who we are, not apologetic to the likes of O'Donnell, not to Uncle George or anyone. We need never doubt our preferences for they make us who we are, and we ought to grant the same latitude everywhere. I could no more be happy acting as a fairy than being alike to O'Donnell."

"There is so much lovely in Leslie that I would spare him any disparagement or any reason to conceal his nature. Must tenderness be deplored in such a person? Need we hide our tenderness along with our sexual behavior?"

"We need only keep private the bare essential! Even so, some will understand our direction living man to man. Mrs.Sipolski would protect us as her children, says we need looking-out for. O'Donnell is the sort who cannot imagine other than his way. He thinks his meagerness all there is to masculinity."

They both could laugh at that claim as preposterous.

"Having a wee wee has nothing to do with what excites it." Alec alluded to the term of affection his mother had used when his was small. Now his penis had grown to a cock, one more discriminating. "Like Oliver's tail, each cock wags differently."

"You are right," Maurice grinned. Then his mood was serious again. "But I feel defenseless when faced with contempt. That is how women sometimes feel."

Alec was pleased with Maurice's unusual empathy for women.

"You are right to recognize women's plight. They face contempt every day from religion that preaches God created man to act straight-forwardly, guided by the dictates of his penis, and made women a weaker sex, the easier for them to succumb. No wonder the modern woman gets angry. We ought to ally with her anger for we suffer similar oppression, as if God was so bumbling as to devise an inept scheme that failed to instill heterosexual feelings he wanted of us."

"I deplore priestly trickery. Yet there is something extraordinary about our feelings. Nothing I wish to change."

"No requirement of any exclusive status, not even that of homosexual, far as I can accept. The camaraderie men prefer, I prefer – the things they do, the ways they talk, the feelings they have – all these I know the same. That I find pleasure holding the male body is natural for me, perhaps as natural as any sexual act to anyone. This means no scorn toward women. I enjoy their company and am pleased they enjoy mine. I could be a father if it did not require losing you."

Maurice was unable to leave the matter. His heart ached for an end to hostility from society.

"We are married in every way but law and public proclamation. Wouldn't our lives make more sense if we were recognized as properly married?"

"Don't be daft, Morrie. We are happier than most people, and in most respects less encumbered. Why long to put a legal fine point on who we are? Marriage is for having children and settling property on them. Look a your mother's dilemma about the Hall name and house. Have you forgotten Goldman? We can do without hocus-pocus of religion."

Alec rejected the label homosexual because he did not feel apart from other men or from women. Alike to his rebellious Irish ancestors he would not live outside the pale, nor was it right any man be forced to do so. To submit to being homosexual would be to accept a self-image debilitating to the full humanity that anarchism upheld as a courageous ideal.

There had been enough seriousness, and so he playfully wondered whether Oliver might be a case worth consideration. Had Oliver been cast into intermediate status in defiance of nature? "Surely he would have been heterosexual had we not changed his direction."

"Oliver has not been ruined for his nature does not reside entirely in his testicles. Otherwise we have made a sorry mess mutilating them."

Maurice never cared a whit for philosophizing, but he did suffer an obsession with marriage. He was not yet finished with serious speculation.

"Suppose," he asked Alec, "you loved a woman. Would you shun marriage? Not at all! You would do the same as every heterosexual, march through a church to hear a priest summon divine blessing to man and wife joined. Those gathered would cheer the couple."

"If I had married a woman the way you picture, it would be to have children. You know that is not for us. From what I have seen, church ceremonies do not erase desires that men feel. Since I would still be Alec, my desire to bed other men for pleasure would be there. For occasional lapses I would not be deemed homosexual, as far as society concerns, but a heterosexual, a husband, a father, and occasional wanderer. That is a truth society silences, male adventurism is not satisfied within monogamy. We would do well to forget seeking a church's approval. We have enough of a struggle to withstand inducements and coercions thrown our way, and to hold on to the adventure of a unique love."

Not that he was won over entirely, yet Maurice felt better that Alec was firm.

*　　　*　　　*

News had come of Mercer's death through Graham who would attend the funeral at Fonthill. Afterward he wished to visit them.

He arrived bearing a gift that would have been Mercer's but now would best serve living friends. It was an eighteenth century print that apart from its classic Roman setting needed explaining. At the foreground Horace was on the banks of a river watching the field workers gathering grapes for new wine. Under the picture was the caption: "I am like the bee that busy works on the sweet wild thyme around the groves and banks of wide-watered Tiber." Horace was a favorite of the French **philosophes** because he delighted in the simple pleasures, living as sweetly as any man, while shunning luxury and extravagance.

Next morning Alec walked with Maurice to the train that carried him to his work at the bank. Near the station he made a purchase, then with fresh bakery sweets in hand returned to Graham for breakfast. The bright sun tempered the cool air so that the porch setting, with coffee and pastries, invited a mood such as Horace enjoyed along the Tiber.

"What is this about your tiring of study? Maurice has told me that much. All this despite excellent grades which ought to be encouraging."

Alec admitted he had less direction than ever at the university despite Sanborn's winning him to philosophy.

"I drifted into philosophy encouraged by my professor. I do not see where it leads other than unrest. Anarchism has stirred my anger at the political and economic systems. There is a personal stirring, too, as anarchism has led me to sexual restlessness. Perhaps it would be better I return to common labor, though I suspect my discontents would be greater."

"Such resignation doesn't suit you. You are ripe for the Irish cause of liberty. How could you settle for less in America? What has happened to your optimism and the ambition to fulfill your dream that I learned about on the Atlantic? Tell me."

"I have gotten my mind tangled. Injustice all around needs changing. I feel the dissatisfaction but I do not have a plan for acting. Maybe too much of philosophizing."

"Yes, that perennial question about injustice, what is to be done? There is a famous tract by Lenin asks that question. His answer was revolution directed by a party of dedicated leaders. We do not face the tsarist tyranny he hated, but there is plenty of stupidity and selfishness to oppose. No shame in radicalism that seeks enlightenment, but even your Voltaire lamented near death that the world he was leaving was no better than he had found it. Do you think he was right?"

"He was no small part of that movement of enlightenment. As for the sum of justice that resulted from so much reasoning, that moral calculation is impossible to reckon. I suppose Voltaire right in regretting lapses in justice."

"Can we reckon *Candide* on the positive side of the ledger? Does not its wit and wisdom encourage greater efforts toward justice?"

"Just laughing at Candide, thinking of him as myself, makes my thinking clearer. You are as usual reasonable and encouraging."

"Alec, I know your intelligence. You ought to acknowledge good fortune, being in the company of Maurice, and use it to advantage for education whether philosophical or other. You and Maurice will benefit and social good will come in ways you can not presently see. What is your objection to the university for a few more years?"

"Simply that it troubles me to strive to enlarge our comforts, Maurice's and mine, when it entails exploitation of others."

"That's an honest response, though I see your situation a different way. Allow me to remember Mercer who was blessed by good fortune and, like Horace, chose pursuit of knowledge. Look at his legacy, enough to furnish more than one museum."

Graham wiped his eyes with a handkerchief as he added, "Moral truth ought not preclude expansion of your mind."

"I hope to do some good in the world."

"You are already doing something, Maurice and you, building a life in defiance of prejudice. But still you need to find work consistent with your concern for justice. Have you thought of law?"

"Never imagined such pursuit, but I will look into it."

Thus a seed was planted, and before many weeks had passed Alec was thrown into an ugly encounter with crime that pointed him toward serious consideration of the judiciary as court of justice.

*   *   *

That evening they dined in a restaurant along the river that enabled reflective conversation which their guest enjoyed on land as he did at sea. Graham asked whether their life style had caused any commotion. Maurice started with the happy news his mother had come to terms with his partnership with Alec. Then he enlisted Graham's support regarding the unpleasantry with O'Donnell. As he detailed the incident his narration was flawless until his tongue stumbled over the word "faggot" which still wounded him.

"I was indignant to be called a faggot. I was angry and uneasy, and remembering the ugliness I still feel resentment. That strong an emotional

192

reaction may be hard for you to appreciate, never having been a victim of bigotry."

"Not quite so. I will tell you about the time I faced danger for similar reason, though I fled the scene before scandal touched me. During the war thousands of sailors were trained in Newport. Many were looking for recreation and there were boisterous parties for men only where questionable things occurred. I was never at the center, but at one party I did allow a sailor to approach me sexually. It was only after the war the navy began an investigation of homosexuality in its ranks. Some sailors were arrested and the brig of the USS Constellation in Newport was full of men awaiting court martial. No one was safe who had been at one of the parties. I felt endangered, and I did not wish to be forced to testify against some innocent sailor. Without telling the truth to my family I left to live in Manhattan. I understand your dismay."

"Alec helped to calm me," Maurice continued. "Though months have passed, as I vividly recall the words, I shudder that others assume the right to condemn Alec and me. My rationality is generally strong, but that attack has left me with uncertainties as to Carpenter's intermediate sex. While I want no part of that strange group, homosexual love sets us apart. Alec rejects the possibility outright."

"I think Graham should hear my thoughts directly," Alec interrupted.

"Just because we live outside convention does not mean we must accept insults, thinking ourselves fairies or faggots, nor even those categorizations of the homosexual which cloak inequality in scientific terminology. These would limit our humanity. I have been following the ideas we discussed at Fonthill years ago, which have led me to believe nothing is gained of understanding or pleasure by denying even a bit of the full range of sexuality. Too much is made of the 'normal' which is a quantitative assessment of what people do, no more made right by the plurality of number, any more than a preferred taste in eating is made healthy for its popularity. It may be that what people do not eat would be healthier than what they do."

Graham smiled and interposed, "Quite an unusual way of putting it."

"I think Maurice and I ought to stop envying those able to marry. Marriage was designed to thwart adultery by women, to legitimate children for transfer of property, which is not our concern, and to discourage public homosexual expression of love, which is our concern."

Graham's heart reached out to these two young men amid their adventure.

"You have challenged every conventionality I might hold, inviting me to judge the bounds of natural sexuality, notions of religious morality, and practices of marriage. Quite a menu! Allow me to limit my remarks to your personal affairs. My conscience permits no utterance that might hurt you, for I wish the happiest outcome for your bodies and hearts. I encourage your love. My presence is assurance of it. That is why I agree with Alec that you need to reject disparaging ideas and despise institutions that limit your rights. The law is an abomination, an intrusion into private sexual behavior. It will be a long time to change. You must hold to your choice, privately as proves necessary, for the love you feel is right. All else is artificial."

"Thank you for your friendship. Fie on those who would love us to change us!" That was Maurice's renewed defiance of family or foe. His resolve had been strengthened for the struggle they all knew would continue tomorrow and after.

Chapter 18

Mayhem and Murder

Miniver loved the days of old
When swords were bright and steeds were prancing:
The vision of a warrior bold
Would set him dancing.
Miniver sighed for what was not,
And dreamed . . . .

Edwin Arlington Robinson, "Miniver Cheevy"

Hold fast to dreams
For if dreams die
Life is a broken-winged bird
That cannot fly.

Langston Hughes, "Dreams"

During the middle of the night a frantic knocking that had a sound of desperation awakened Alec who hurried down the steps to the street door where an hysterical Leslie threw himself into his arms. Something terrible had happened. Maurice arrived to see Leslie sobbing convulsively. Words would not do, and so he stroked Leslie's head awash in sweat and soothed the face drenched in tears while Alec lent a strong, comforting hand as they awaited an explanation. When it came it was more terrible than they had feared.

"Winnie is murdered! I ran away and left him threatened by a bully. Now he is dead."

*   *   *

It was the next day before the bare facts of the murder unfolded. They learned the grim details from John Smith, their lawyer friend, who had taken the case in hand. Winnie and Leslie had been drinking at an accustomed speakeasy which had a back room where gay clientele mingled with a more earthy crowd. It was the sort of place that offered opportunity for sex-seekers to meet money-seekers in trade. One of the young hustlers named Gary, unlettered and unkempt, showed a rough interest in Winnie whose acquaintance he had courted earlier, even visiting his apartment once or twice. This time he was rebuffed more rudely than was Winnie's custom. Not only did Winnie refuse him a drink, but he loudly rejected any attention, "I am only able to respond to gentlemen." When Winnie left with Leslie to walk homeward, the young tough followed them in anger for his manliness had been threatened. A heated exchange of words ensued before Gary viciously assaulted Winnie. Leslie was frightened by the quarrel, so that even before the physical assault commenced he had fled in panic. Some time later he went home where he found the police and learned the awful truth that Winnie was dead. Again seized by panic, he rushed to find a haven. It was Maurice's embrace he sought.

*   *   *

There was nothing to do but take Leslie in since his family was distant both in miles and understanding of their own kin. Maurice needed to be at the same time tender and strong, and he would have to guard against Leslie's vulnerability until a time might come when the forlorn youth would replace a lost protector or learn to do without. Alec would lend a hand toward this recovery.

In the months of grief and anger that followed, work helped to restore some order to Leslie's life. Daytime he went to the small business that employed him in center city where sympathetic co-workers helped distract his mind from the violence and hatred that terrified him. Evenings Maurice and Alec comforted and encouraged him. Come the week end they guided him about in practical ways, seeing to a haircut or purchasing a pair of shoes or some other task he would have neglected. Saturday nights were spent at the palatial Nixon theatre under the splendidly painted ceiling as the mighty Wurlitzer organ introduced a double bill. When the house darkened it might be Laurel and Hardy providing antics only a sourpuss could resist, or a dashing cowboy forcing justice upon the frontier town. More often tears streamed down Leslie's face while tragic heroines, Garbo and Swanson his favorites, were abused and abandoned by villainous men. These films worked their catharsis, and afterward the three young men would move to the ice cream parlor nearby to recollect their emotional reactions and laugh at themselves.

But bedtime was the loneliest, the most frightening time, except that the two friends did not stop short. Leslie could be found snuggling between them, Maurice holding him closely until his guilty conscience was salved sufficiently to allow him to drift into sleep. Often those first weeks the troubled boy would awaken from a nightmare and Maurice would comfort him without disturbing Alec.

Even generosity of this measure has its bounds. Maurice soon moved to the middle position that allowed Alec and him intimacy after Leslie was asleep. Leslie learned to feign sleeping so that two lovers might enjoy one another.

When morning came Alec was first to rise and go about his business. Maurice and Leslie would linger until preparation for work required getting up. What started as a way of helping Leslie cope with anxiety drifted into something more. Maurice found himself aroused when he held Leslie who welcomed any security he could find. One morning Leslie removed his pajamas as an invitation to Maurice who responded vigorously. Afterward Leslie turned to face and thank Maurice, "I have found a gentleman. If only Winnie had been as fortunate." Maurice did not have the heart to reject this sincere admission.

Later he needed to confess to Alec that he was not made of stone, which of course Alec well knew.

"Perhaps I have encouraged Leslie to think of me as his lover. Once you leave the bed he presses into me needy of loving. My cock has responded."

"He is deserving of love. Do you have a mind for it as well as a cock?"

"My mind is mixed, a part favorable to giving comfort. Leslie is the closest I'll ever come to being with a woman. But you know it is not a woman I prefer. Just that I wish to help him."

"No harm in it then, is there? Comfort him awhile. He will need another arrangement when the trial is over. If he clings to your attention after that, then we'll have to deal with it."

Maurice was relieved at how easily Alec had accepted this attention to Leslie. He was certain he could not show comparable latitude.

"I am curious, don't you feel jealousy? It would upset me if Leslie favored you."

"I'm glad you feel such need. I think of myself as anarchist with hopes for free love, yet I enjoy possession. Emma Goldman urges free thought, but she herself suffered from the indifference of her libertine lover. Sharing sexual favors is not the best way to cultivate love. This being an unusual situation, I see it as kindness on your part."

As if to prove the point, that night Alec initiated intercourse with Maurice while Leslie pretended sleep. In the morning, after Alec had left their bed, a satiated Maurice held Leslie who could not forget the night's lovemaking, so that his tears flowed lightly, something Maurice noticed when the boy turned toward him.

"I am indebted to Alec for letting me be here. That is because he loves you, and who would not? I must take care not to love too much. What I need is to become whole. Someday, when a time comes, I will comfort you."

Maurice was aware that Leslie was helping him even now. He had awakened a long-ago desire for the tantalizing beauty of Clive who had thwarted sexual passions, left them suspended, insisted they await legitimate expression in heterosexuality. Leslie by surrendering his beautiful body had proven mysteriously healing. Maurice wished Leslie to claim his credit.

"I have never told you about Clive who seemed the most beautiful person I had known. I thought he loved me. He resisted my approaches so that I never had sexual satisfaction. Clive preferred talk of ideals that I did not share and rejected me in favor of a woman."

Maurice told his recurrent nightmare of Clive taunting him. Alec coming along had put to rest any conscious longing for Clive, but there remained a festering wound in another part of the mind that disappears with waking. Maurice felt that burden was lifted now.

"Until this morning I could not have told you this. I had no idea to articulate, only a buried weight in my heart. Clive seems no longer beautiful, but selfishly ugly. I have tasted your beauty which is generous."

It was many days hence until such generosity helped overcome the anguish that beset Leslie. Alec was helpful, sharing Maurice. He also aided security in another role, again and again affirming to Leslie, "You are not responsible for the violence. It was Gary who did the terrible deed, his twisted mind that needs correcting."

Leslie knew this was so, but his guilt that he had deserted a helpless Winnie could not succumb to impeccable reason. Instead, his anger mounted against Gary and the society that fed Gary's ignorance, hatred and violence. He wanted an execution even against Maurice's reminder that he would find love more easily if he could get beyond revenge. Leslie was quick to tears in any case, but on many occasions it was gratitude that overwhelmed him. He would hug Alec in thanks and Maurice in love.

*　　　*　　　*

Before the trial began Alec paid a visit to John Smith who was informed on the course of the criminal investigation. They settled into soft chairs in the living room of the house that belonged to John, for Nicholas had passed away. A clean-cut man brought in tea.

"This is Jurgen who has come from Germany so that we can live together."

Jurgen exchanged a few pleasantries before excusing himself with the explanation he had no interest in criminal proceedings. He had his own work to do, and he was also keeping an eye on a dinner he was preparing. John offered an invitation, "There will be plenty if you care to join us. Jurgen is an exquisite cook. Why don't you call Maurice to suggest he come directly from the bank?"

Returning to the business at hand, John related that the charge was second degree murder because of the compromising circumstances of Winnie's life style.

"There is likelihood the jury will sympathize with Gary. It would certainly balk at convicting him if capital punishment or a life-long sentence might be imposed."

Alec was baffled that there could be any doubt that crushing a person's head with a lethal object that in fact brought death could be anything but murder impure and simple. He expressed his confusion. For the rest of the afternoon they talked without interruption except for a telephone call to Maurice. John took pains to explain that criminal prosecution and defense were never simple whether from ambiguities of the statutes and precedents, uncertainties of evidence, ruses and deceptions by the prosecution and defense, the public images of the abused and accused, the quality of justice exercised by the court, and the prejudices of the members of the jury.

"Gary, you will see, is his own best defense."

"I had not thought of justice as a game of cat and mouse."

"Much in law is procedural, slow and intricate. Disputes are better settled away from the courtroom. Murder is a different case, once it gets into the public eye. There is a political need for the prosecutor to seek vengeance, or in this case, render a result that shows sympathy as the public prefers."

Maurice arrived for cocktails that created a relaxed mood. Everyone was relieved to hear Leslie had found a new and older friend who was protective. Jurgen and Maurice hit it off at once. They reminisced about Germany and England, their upbringing and education and appreciation

199

of culture. When Maurice explained reasons for leaving his homeland, Jurgen offered an intriguing account of his own belated emigration. He was a visiting professor at Princeton when he met John. The next several years he spent part of each summer as a guest of the Smiths. He took John's hand as he explained, "I grew fond of dear Nicholas who treated me graciously. It was only after Nicholas died that I decided to move to Philadelphia."

*　　　*　　　*

When the trial began Maurice was there for the opening session while Alec persisted throughout as he became fascinated with its workings. He reported events to Maurice and to Leslie who because he was a witness could not be in the courtroom. Just as well, for Alec was able to leave out brutal and bloody details presented as a matter of fact by the prosecution: blows to the head after a loud quarrel, the weapon a heavy vase of cut glass, police summoned by neighbors, the accused found in the apartment where the victim lay dead from a crushed head, and the accused the only living person present through it all. There was no work for the prosecution other than extracting its case from the mouth of the accused, for not only had he admitted the assault, but he took the stand when the defense counted on winning sympathy from the jury.

The young man charged with murder seemed incapable of such a monstrous act, his face without a hint of criminality and his appearance dignified by a dark suit and tie. He had been coached to walk humbly, to smile in a calm though not indifferent way. Placing his right hand on a Bible he swore to tell the truth which he did over two days of questioning by his own attorney. Then the prosecution cross-examined. Did you follow the victim home? Did you force your way into the apartment? Did you intend malevolence? Did you take the vase and strike the victim blow after blow? Yes to all of these incriminating questions, leaving no doubt murder had happened. The only question was whether it was first degree deserving of execution.

There was one part of Gary's testimony that won favor with the jury, his becoming blind with rage when Winnie taunted him with the insult, "You are not a man." The jurymen, all men clad in coats and ties—there were no ladies since both the prosecution and the defense agreed the deeds were improper for ladies to hear—were not indifferent to the code of male honor.

Leslie was given his turn in court as the one eyewitness to the quarrel inside and outside the tavern. Early during the trial his testimony was

200

crucial to establishing the prosecution's case. Later he was recalled to rebut what Gary said. He was adamant, Winnie had never said to Gary, "You are not a man." Leslie clearly remembered Winnie pleading, "You are not enough a gentleman for me to entertain you" which was clearly the case. Leslie brought tears to Maurice, who made a point of being there, "Winnie was not that kind of person who was interested in sex with just any man, certainly not someone crude. She dreamed of chivalrous love, like Miniver Cheevy, the hero of a poem. Minnie, that is how she called him, longed to be a knight but was misplaced in a world that had no knights, no damsels, little of chivalry. Winnie felt herself mistakenly placed in a man's body. She longed for courtesy, for romance with a knight, for a graceful man to carry her away to another place and time when everyone would be considerate and appreciative of people like herself. Once when we went to a costume ball in Atlantic City, Winnie felt we were in a dream, not to be threatened or beaten by anyone or the police. Does such a dream deserve her life be cut short?"

The defense whittled away at what was its strong point.

"Why did Winnie invite Gary home if he (or she) did not find him gentlemanly?"

"It was the effect of liquor. Winnie made a mistake thinking Gary a gentleman. He only came home with her the once. The next day I saw bruises Gary inflicted during that night. Winnie cried, not because of the pain from the bruises, but because of the horrible mistake she had made out of desperation. She swore never to be with anyone like Gary again. That is what she tried to tell him the night of the assault."

*   *   *

As the defense presented its story Gary became an innocent young man lured into expectation of money for sex. Not an honorable activity, but one the world tolerates because of the weakness of the flesh, a foolish, immoral yielding to a despicable act because of economic need. Then the murdered woman, or man – the attorney deliberately mixed genders to confound the all male jury, speaking of the murdered woman, then changing as if by mistake to man, or it might be in reverse order, all the time maligning the victim by insult added to insult. Winnie, as he called himself, had loitered about an illegal place of vice for the purpose of enticing another man to commit a crime. The elder Winnie knew the younger man's weaknesses, for he had exploited his strengths at least once earlier, luring this hapless youth to act against nature. Not a man himself, certainly not a woman, only disguising himself as a woman in order to deceive others, Winnie provoked violence by impugning that same manliness of the other which he had stolen on an earlier occasion for illicit sexual exploitation. A foul insult for any man, an impossible one for a youth so misled by his upbringing as to be uncertain of his role. Gary was confused and became crazed with all this deception. Prior to that incitement he had no premeditation to violence when he entered the tavern. The older Winnie, even if unwittingly, said things that were most violent. This verbal attack provoked violence that came back upon him.

Step by step the defense replaced the focus on words that precipitated the eruption of violence.

"How did the encounter begin which led to the unfortunate death of the strange person who called himself Winnie?"

"I was drinking beer next to Winnie dressed like a woman. I knew Winnie was a faggot. I had been with him before, only for money. He called himself Winnie, but no one was fooled. I don't like to speak this way. I am sorry he is dead. But he wasn't pretty like a woman. He was laughable. I was only interested in money. He showed a billfold with plenty in it to pay for drinks – he was with this friend, also a fairy – I thought he would enjoy my company as he did before."

"Did Winnie invite you to share his company?"

"He stood next to me. I know what he wanted, so I hustled him, nothing wrong in that. He had flirted with me. He had paid me for what I could do. He knew what I wanted, the money for my consideration. I put my hand on him as he likes it."

"Where was that?"

"You know, his rear. After him urging me on, he changed, as if it was a joke. He pushed me away, said I wasn't man enough."

"What were his words that offended you? Tell the court his exact words."

" 'You are not man enough' is what he said. That is what angered me, a faggot like him saying I did not act like a man! I couldn't think straight. When he left with his friend, I followed them out. The other faggot ran away. When Winnie screamed again I wasn't man enough, I punched him, not so hard. He had no right treating me that way, urging me on, knowing I was in it for the money, insulting me. He threatened to call the police on me."

"What was your state of mind when you feared the police might come and take Winnie's side?"

"I was angry. I thought, that queer, I should bust his head and take the money that was mine by right, the same he had paid before."

"Please tell us what happened next."

"I followed him where he lived. I had been there before. I knocked at his door. But he wouldn't open it. I got mad and kicked his door until someone complained. Then he opened the door, but the way this queer stared at me made me bust in. He ran behind a table, knocking it over lamp and all, screamed and tried to call the police."

"Did you stop to think, were you able to think?"

"This got me madder. I decided to mess him up for fucking with me. So I beat him, this time a good beating. He picked up a heavy vase that was on the floor and swung it trying to hit me. I grabbed it out of his hands. Without intending to do him in, I hit him harder than I should."

"Since you did not intend to do him in, why go on beating him? What were you intending?"

"Bloody him up so that he would learn not to fool with me. I might as well go all the way, do a good job on him. I was in trouble already. I hit him on the head with the vase, not thinking. By then the police had come to arrest me."

The next day the defense searched for mitigating circumstances that stemmed from the pervasive brutality in which Gary had been raised.

"Did your father treat you violently when you were a boy?"

"No, sir. He only beat me when I deserved it."

"How often did you get beaten?"

"No more than once a month. I hurt enough to remember that long!"

"Did your father use his fists to beat you?"

"At first he used his belt. When I got older he punched me. Forced me to put up my fists and try to defend myself."

"Were you able to ward off his blows when you were fourteen or fifteen?"

"My father was too big a man and too strong. I could never lay a hand on him. If I tried, that made the beating worse."

"How badly were you hurt from these beatings?"

"Broken teeth. Once I thought my arm broken. Never had to go to the hospital, though. Just bruises my mother remedied. She told me not to fight for it did no good."

"Was your mother speaking from her own helplessness? Was she beaten by your father?"

"He was rough on my mother, too, when she quarreled. But I don't hold it against him any more than she did. Sometimes a woman needs reminders."

"Did your behavior improve so that the beatings stopped?"

"No, sir, but I learned to protect myself. My father taught me how to fight and to punish anyone who tried to take advantage of me."

"Is that what happened when Winnie attacked you?"

The prosecutor objected to that suggestion of attack.

"When Winnie insulted you verbally, did you feel it necessary to punish him, as your father punished you?"

"My father told me when I get into it with somebody, not to run, but fight, no matter what it takes. I respect him for that advice."

"Did you understand your father to be instructing you to resist insult even to the point of killing?"

"I can not say so with certainty. He told me he once came near killing a man who made false charges against him, that he felt no shame and didn't have any more trouble from him."

*   *   *

Alec confided to Maurice – out of hearing of Leslie – that he felt sympathy toward Gary who might be worthy of rescue. Surely the jury ought to explore for any reason not to waste his healthy body which, no doubt, was linked to a diseased mind but one that might still learn gentle consideration of others. Not that the crime lessened in horror, just that Gary seemed himself a poor soul. What kind of home produced such lack of regard for human life? Why did Gary loathe himself so much as to be dangerous? Was it possible some great misunderstanding lay at the heart of the deed?

"He committed a criminal deed, but Winnie being dead, what gain is there destroying another life?"

Though not astonished by such reasoning, Maurice made the objection, "Would not Gary likely enact violence on another person, perhaps someone like ourselves?"

"I will not say otherwise, but looking at him – you have not heard him as I have – there is something that could yet be made decent. He is quick to anger. That way I am as guilty as he is."

"But you have not murdered anyone, not even Uncle George, thanks to your mother who showed you love and encouraged your self-respect. I fear Gary is beyond help, or redemption, as religious folk would have it."

"I believe there is something of enlightenment needed in all of us. Not redeeming people, for saintliness is beyond my understanding, more for Andrew to contemplate. But the law should take into account people who are innocent in their misunderstanding of themselves and in their ignorance of others unlike themselves. Graham suggested I consider legal study and now I am considering that prospect."

*   *   *

During closing argument the defense cleverly claimed two crimes had occurred. The second, Gary's, was provoked by the first.

"Only one crime is charged and being tried today but, gentlemen of the jury, remember the prior criminal activities by Winnie so that you are able to properly judge whether criminal motivation and intent existed in the heart of the accused. He had entered a familiar speakeasy for pleasure and, when money was flashed before him, he was ready to pursue economic benefit as he turned to someone who had earlier taken advantage of his pliable sexuality. The supposed victim is not present to answer for his crime against the order of nature, yet you and I know that Winnie initiated all that followed. It began with heinous invitations extended to a confused youth who, in response to a promise of money, yielded to the perverted desires of an elder man he trusted. As to the second crime, all Gary did was try to repeat the act for more of the same money. When he was harshly rejected, his manliness scorned, the result was a violent reaction. Any man would defend his honor, though we hope with some measure of consequences. Gary knew no recourse except what had been demonstrated all through his life by his father and condoned by his mother. Gary's was the second responsive crime, one of passion, committed almost as an act of honor in the attempt to rescue his natural manliness."

The prosecutor could only repeat the words, "You are not a gentleman enough" to remind the jury Winnie had tried to extricate himself from a deplorable situation. What was further true was that the violence stemmed from Gary's inability to hear the words spoken by Winnie which were a plea to be left alone. Instead, he heard other inflammatory words that had not been spoken. That is why, placing itself in the heart of Gary, the state asked for conviction of murder of the second degree, since that crime did occur, and must be punished to preserve the safety and decency of society.

The jury was quick to render a guilty verdict with a recommendation of leniency in sentencing.

*   *   *

On their way to the courthouse the day of sentencing, Alec wondered aloud for Maurice's benefit why men like Winnie wanted to behave with outrageous femininity.

205

"If Winnie had not pretended to be a woman we would be going about our business as usual. So would he."

Alec thought absurd the congenital inversion theory of the day. His gut instinct told him otherwise. The idea of a feminine mind coming into the world in the wrong biological setting of a male body offended his reason. What on earth was a feminine mind if not culturally shaped? It was one thing to be drawn erotically to the male body that was like itself. Had not his brothers taken liberties with him when he was only ten and then gone on to fulfill their roles as men with women? Had not his own experiences with them and with Oliver helped him to understand sexuality apart from cultural mystification?

Maurice concurred, "Desiring the male body does not impose a feminine mind with all its wiles and enticements."

* * *

When Gary's sentence was assigned it was five to ten years of imprisonment. Leslie heard the news and cried through that day. His confusion of anger, fear and grief persisted for a long time, but he was too charming to remain unattached. A few months later he found a haven elsewhere with an older man who took a fancy to him and welcomed him into his home even as he encouraged more circumspect behavior than Winnie had shown. Leslie was sobered by the tragic event, no longer as carefree and gay as before. Listening to Maurice's advice, he appreciated the protection and affection of a man of maturity.

Thus the tragic event came to a close, if that term can even be used for traumatic events whose repercussions do not cease until all who have been touched by horror and violence complete their term on earth. There was one unexpected aftermath in the Hall-Scudder house. Not much later a handgun was placed in the drawer of a table that sat next to their bed. Alec insisted on its purchase.

"We were both handy in the hunt awhile ago. We need to practice firing so that no one dare break into our house to do violence."

Maurice thought no harm in having the weapon for defense of home, though he was dismayed to know security from attack was so spare an element of American civilization as to warrant this degree of protection.

Chapter 19

Law Triumphs over Anarchism

But yield who will to their separation,
My object in living is to unite
My avocation and vocation . . .
Only when love and need are one,
And the work is play for mortal stakes,
Is the deed ever really done
For heaven and the future's sakes.

Robert Frost, "Two Tramps in Mud Time"

It was a quiet evening at home when the telephone rang, John Smith inviting Alec to a lecture by defense lawyer Clarence Darrow, notorious for saving the lives of child murderers Leopold and Lowe, more so for his role during the "monkey trial" in Tennessee. John Scopes had purposefully violated state law that prohibited the teaching of evolution in public schools. William Jennings Bryan, three times a candidate for the presidency, turned the trial into a public spectacle when he intervened to uphold the Bible as total truth. Darrow rushed in to defend the truth of scientific evidence and to ridicule the willful ignorance of Biblical fundamentalism. He scoffed at Bryan as he questioned, "From where does man get the selfish idea of his importance? He gets it from Genesis, of course." It would be better to recognize our kinship with other animals because "No one can feel the universal evolutionary relationship without being gentler, kinder, and more humane toward all the infinite forms of beings that live with us, and must die with us."

Seven years after those trials, an April night in 1932, Alec sat beside John in a packed hall. It was the same Darrow who did not mince words as he excoriated the mean spirit of vengeance of the "criminal injustice" system which ignores the complex of causes that control what men think and do.

"If men are not free agents, how can we hold them responsible for their acts, even those we deem criminal? Who are we, anyway? A child is born into this world without knowledge. He has a brain that is a piece of putty. He inherits nothing of knowledge or ideas. Society plants seeds in his mind, telling him he must do this and must not do that. Before any of us knows better we are all not very much but a bundle of prejudices. We are prejudiced against other people's color. Prejudiced against other men's religions, against other people's politics, even against people's looks. We are full of prejudices which control our behavior."

That was the gist of his lecture urging scientific analysis of human behavior and sentencing aimed at reforming miscreants. Afterward he took questions, mostly erudite, but a few angry denunciations of his disdain for religion. An elderly man, likely a minister or a judge, irately pronounced that punishment for transgressions was embedded in the fall of man. Darrow ridiculed the belief in original sin as "silly, impossible and wicked – a very dangerous doctrine."

Toward the end of the session Alec posed a plaintive concern.

"Do you advise someone like me, confused, yet considering training for a lawyer, to pursue that career? Is there any good might come of it?"

"Young man, my life has been marked by futility with the law and with a society that condones human suffering. Times I feel quiet desperation, for I believe our species is doomed to be predatory upon the weak. You ask me to tell you what you ought to do. The cynic in me says you will arrive at despair through your own choosing. If you are gifted with talent in words and vision, I advise you to be a poet. There may be more of use to be done that way. Inside many a lawyer is the wreck of a poet. We show bravado without literary talent. If poetry does not claim your voice, it is alright to ally your ideals to legal combat against a society which is often criminal and ought to be on trial. When I was in law school I was told falsely that the courtroom is a holy place, a temple of justice, where all its officers were sworn to pursue the truth of what actually happened and what is demanded by justice. Now I know neither the law nor its practice are that pure. Even so, the accused need to be helped, for some of them are akin to wild animals whom we may help free from captivity to face another day, though their fate may be to be slaughtered after all."

*   *   *

That night Alec dreamed he was delivering a final argument before a jury, Gary the wild animal he was trying to rescue. His lawyer words were

208

intended to hold back the spear of vengeance. As only in a dream he was able to hear his own summation.

"Somewhere in the infinite processes that go into the making of a man something slipped – was it a father's brutality or a mother's misplaced love toward an unworthy and abusing spouse? Or had the community taught him to hate other races and those whose sexuality made them queer? Perhaps it was because Gary's boyhood occurred during the Great War that he learned from his country killing is honorable? No one can truly fix all that is to blame. This young man was not the maker of his own beliefs."

Alec offered as a last plea, "What good can it do for this court to add its own hate and cruelty to the crimes already done?"

Everyone was in tears. How ennobling a lawyer's work could be! As a suitable climax the jury responded magnanimously, sparing severe harm to Gary, and remanding him to the care of men like Alec who would tame him to love and to work within a just society. Such was the stuff of dreams.

*   *   *

The same night Alec was dreaming of himself as an advocate for sane justice, John Smith was sitting in his study into the early morning, ignoring Jurgen's call to come up to bed. John arrived at a decision to do for Alec what Nicholas had done for him. He would guide Alec to a career that would nurture his intelligence and egalitarian leanings. First he would write the dean of Temple Law School asking for a personal meeting to press the case. Alec would receive a bachelor's degree in June, and if he were willing, he could begin legal study in the fall. More than talk would be brought to bear, for John resolved upon a generous bequest to the Law School to establish a scholarship for exceptional students, Alec to be the first swift recipient.

John's dream would come true, perhaps Alec's as well.

*   *   *

At the commencement Maurice was as proud as any parent, doubly happy as a lover. He had steadied Alec's course through the curriculum, and though he had little regard for the practical use of so much philosophy, he was certain their middle class life would grow better once the economy resumed its growth, which surely it would.

He had arranged a gift for his baccalaureate, a three-day holiday at the shore. After the ceremony, their bags already packed, they needed a brief stop at home for last minute matters. Maurice gathered the bags while Alec checked the mail. He was glad to find a greeting from Noreen which he put unopened into his pocket. With joy they embarked to the Atlantic, to the island of Brigantine, where a suite in the island's grand hotel awaited. A few hours later, at a twelfth-floor window they stood together surveying the vast ocean and several miles to the south, Atlantic City.

Late afternoon they walked the shore accompanied by seagulls and waves which washed over their bare feet. Curiosity took them several miles northward beyond the settled area to an inlet that set Brigantine apart from other land. Following the inlet they discovered the deserted western side of the island where they found a private cove that Alec turned into their own nude beach. They boldly made love with nature blessing their enterprise. Then they crossed a wild growth of foliage to the eastern shore that had started the walk, returning into the sunset just as the light disappeared.

The next two days they repeated the walk and all else, again with nature's support of warm sun and cool breezes off the water. They talked incessantly, their ideas flowing from hearts overjoyed with the remarkable experiences they had lived, the most amazing how they had met and dared to come to America. They thanked fortune that had brought true friends, thinking of Graham and Smith. Maurice recalled that his father, too, had blessed them with the gift that had strangely aided their union. They could not avoid the tragedy that had befallen Winnie, though they found relief in having helped Leslie.

By Alec's decision one matter was unspoken, his anarchist behavior which he felt was in the past. From time to time reminding letters came from Noreen, never frequently, until only a Christmas greeting was likely. She had married within a year and a boy was born named Benjamin. Alec thought it strange Noreen gave no account of the man she married and also that she continued to work in the household as before. That was her same address, but he attributed it to concern that her husband might find cause for jealousy. No need for such indirection, far as concerned him. He was fond of Noreen but happy the past was closed.

Maurice had met Noreen and knew she was a simple Irish girl who worked for the Kleins and that Alec encouraged her schooling. He thought nothing of it when she left for Baltimore. As for occasional correspondence, which Alec shared readily, nothing in whatever Noreen wrote suggested more. Nor did Alec feel need for revelation. Anarchist deeds were better relegated to silence now that his course was changed. Why awaken phantoms that could hardly be understood by someone not an anarchist and so inclined to marriage as Maurice?

Shortly after arriving in Brigantine Alec found a private moment to read the latest note. She congratulated him for a college degree and wished him well in finding suitable work despite the hard times. She regretted her ambition had been waylaid of necessity, but it was not so much a complaint. "Raising a child is a fuss. Yet I have never known such tender love as I feel for him." She mentioned that she hoped to visit with her family, not till Christmas, and likely with Ben only, when she would welcome seeing him. Alec resolved to encourage such a meeting. That is what he told Maurice when he showed him the note.

The holiday over, Maurice back at the bank and Alec doing summer gardening for the Kleins until he would embark on law school, their happiness seemed complete. Their love seemed as certain as it had been the day they boarded the Olympic.

*   *   *

John Smith's efforts met with success. For Alec the next four years centered on law school situated in the Public Ledger Building near Independence Square. Most of his nights drifted away in classes or in the library studying case after case dealing with torts, contracts, commerce, taxation, domestic strife, criminal acts, libel, and sundry litigious disputes. During all of this tiresome mastery of fact and precedence, he worked dutifully despite much dullness. There was little occasion for displaying his philosophical bent until moot court during his third year. He was assigned to defend an eighteen-year old man accused of kidnapping his sixteen-year old girlfriend so that they could marry in another state where the age of consent was lower. Alec carried the defense so well that a few of his professors thought his work brilliant, though he lost the case.

During those years of study, Maurice devotedly would come from the bank many an evening to meet Alec for supper and then see him into the Temple building. Maurice had escaped bank closure and the depression with only a diminution of salary that left them still comfortable. Financing of Alec's study posed no burden thanks to the first scholarship to honor Nicholas Smith for "steadfast contribution to the education of deprived youth." Alec worked the summer of 1932, earning $20 a week that Maurice insisted be used for books and sundries. Subsequent summers he held a position as clerk at Smith and Smith which took care of his expenses.

*   *   *

The next four years were dedicated to the notable accomplishment of preparing for the bar as Alec worked doggedly with Maurice as his helpmate.

Were these happy years? Certainly Maurice would have said so, had he been asked. His purpose was to help fashion Alec into a lawyer in every way he could. He relished the role of "man of the house" which fell to him because of earning and paying for household expenses. He tended to the bills and took full responsibility for supervision of house cleaning and the care of his own and Alec's clothing, even at times putting out what ought to be worn. He saw little of Leslie, more of the Wetherills. He made few demands on Alec, one being that they spend time during each summer with Charles and Albert at Cape Cod. Maurice did enjoy such gay company.

For Alec it was less certain how those years should be characterized, only that the notion of happy would be imprecise in application. Not unhappy, either, but there was much tedious about law that kept him busy round the clock. He lost sight of ideals, his anarchist heart in abeyance. To his way of thinking it was too much trivia, except for a rare lecture or case study, until all this fuss day after day made him discontented.

Maurice was there to remind him of practical gains that would come from finishing the task. It was Maurice in a reversal of roles who acted as philosopher of sort, chiding that "It may seem the worst of all possible worlds right this day, but then you need to recall your work at Baldwin."

Alec laughed at the notion even as he drew emotional support from Maurice's attentive presence, especially his faithfulness in coming each evening before class for supper, no matter that his reward was a mind dulled with facts or preoccupied with an assignment. When they ate or when they "slept" together, Maurice was patient in listening to cases that had interest only because Alec was at hand. He tried to interject common sense into their discussions, as if he were the Greek chorus in a drama. No matter that these remarks were usually pithy, the good heart of Maurice was busy at work.

Of comparable importance to the wisdom of Maurice's love was that however late the hour, once Alec's study ended and he got into bed, Maurice took pains to rouse himself and refresh his body. Afterward he would offer affection that might only be to rest in the embrace of his lover whose tired body and mind fell quickly into sound sleep. Alec drew comfort from such possession colored with subdued eroticism. Whether out of gratitude for such devotion, or from a lapse of philosophical exactitude, Alec's sexuality falteringly settled into a way no longer anarchistic.

That is not to say these years were all tranquil and routine. There were occasional reminders of the tragedy that besets human existence. Theirs was not a time to live openly without fear. That was impossible for gay people.

*   *   *

Two years into his law study, the summer of 1934, John Smith assigned Alec to assist in a case he knew would stir him to good work. A police raid had been conducted on a bathhouse that accommodated gay clientele. Formerly a church, the bath had been converted to other rituals where men could find sexual release in private rooms. As a rule the police ignored the business in return for handsome payoffs. The night in question, for political reasons, the police arrived without warning, brutally striking patrons, knocking some of them down and denigrating the dozens arrested as fairies.

One of those accosted told his story to Alec. "I was trying to get into clothes as a policeman pounded on the dressing room door shouting at me, 'Come out here, Maude!' He let me dress, but then I was forced to walk outside through a hooting and jeering crowd where I was placed in a paddy wagon. I spent a terrifying night in a crowded cell." It was Emlyn telling the story. He was charged with "degenerate, disorderly conduct" which was a misdemeanor subject to a $25 fine.

Was it worth Emlyn contesting his clear infraction of the law prohibiting sexual acts of the kind he often committed? His name had not been printed in the newspaper. Lafayette Baths was in New York city and word had not gotten beyond there, at least not yet. What was damaged was not his reputation, but his sense of security and well being. Wisely or not, Emlyn handled his sexuality by just such clandestine release as when he was arrested. He had gone as was his habit to a bathhouse where there was a knowing staff, to find a haven that allowed openness with other patrons, to feel positive about homosexuality, to be effusive while safe from robbery, blackmail, beating or arrest.

John put Alec in contact with a court official attached to the presiding judge. Alec spent a day traveling to New York by train where he met the officer, an experience that transcended the classroom. His client was offered an out. Alec returned and talked with John about proprieties, then to Emlyn about practical concerns. An exchange of $200 was at issue in order "to expunge the record" and make everything disappear. Emlyn leaped at this escape. The crime disappeared, but Emlyn remained wounded, filled with fear, and left to figure out how to lead his troubled life.

Alec was left disheartened at the meanness of the law and the ways of extortion.

*   *   *

To return to happier moments, 1932 passed without Alec seeing Noreen who might have had a change of heart, preferring to forget what had happened between them, but during the holiday week of 1933 they spent an afternoon together. Noreen had written to say she would be visiting her family and would be at the Kleins for their usual staff party two days before Christmas. Her brief letter brought surprising news that she was separated from her husband. No explanation was given, only assurance she was securely situated in the house where she worked and being treated as family. She hoped they could see each other so that he might meet Ben who was three years old.

When the holiday came it was good to see Sarah and Julius again, even more so Noreen, although she did not appear well. Alec's heart jumped when he saw Ben who was pretty with black curly hair and a complexion as pure as milk. The boy was quiet though alert, his eyes reacting to every word and move of Noreen. Alec took them into the room where he and Noreen had studied and found the big box that he had placed there, one Maurice had carefully wrapped. It delighted Ben when he found inside an electric train, the engine marked Baldwin, with freight cars and a caboose.

After the party Alec drove Noreen to her family home where he asked about her tiredness, which she accounted to the strain of travel, and about the break-up of her marriage which she was reluctant to discuss. They parted with a kiss that lacked passion. He offered more lavish attention to Ben.

"You have the most wonderful mother in the world," and having been told that such was not the case regarding the father, he thought to offer something special. "Your mother is willing that I be your godfather. What do you say?"

Ben, of course, had no understanding of what it might mean, only that he welcomed male affection.

"Will you live with us or be far away?"

His heart touched by this simple yearning, Alec replied, "When you are old enough you will come to stay with me and Maurice for long visits."

214

He kissed the boy's lips to show how males might relate.

There would be more meetings, during Christmas season in 1934 when Noreen brought Ben to meet Maurice. While Alec lavished affection on his "godson" including gifts Maurice shared, Noreen helped with arrangements for a meal that had been cooked by Mrs. Sipolski. Everything went so well, a year later they repeated a holiday, this time with less caution. Noreen stayed overnight which allowed Ben to reap attention from Alec while she got to know Maurice better. She showed warmth, more so toward Alec, which Maurice saw and approved since it was clear how much Alec liked the boy. Sharing this way gave a touch of family to a special holiday.

*   *   *

By then it was 1936, still not a good year for the nation's economy. Yet Maurice advanced at the bank because of retirements and, as George emphasized, because of the confidence he had encouraged among clients through turbulent years. He was put in charge of investments with a salary increase.

It was another proud moment that spring when Alec received a degree in law. He passed the bar examination that summer and accepted a position with Smith and Smith.

Chapter 20

A Friend in Need

That John Smith, plebian, who forty years since
Walked Broadway barefooted, now rides as a prince,
Having managed, though not overburdened with wit,
But rather by chance and a fortunate hit
To take a high place in Society's rounds.

Horatio Alger

Alec joined the Smith firm at a salary of $100 a month, which was fortunate, for unexpectedly he fell into new responsibilities. Noreen wrote to say she had to see him on a matter of great concern to him as well. The day after Thanksgiving he met her at the 30th Street Station when she arrived. The moment he saw her frail body and desolate look he knew his life was about to change.

He took her to a restaurant, the one Leery had introduced, where Noreen explained the purpose of this visit.

"Ben is your son. Did you not suspect?"

If Alec's life would change because of that knowledge, it did not displease him. He easily accepted the revelation.

"I took immediate liking to Ben, but I thought it due to his being yours. Now I am told he is both of ours, I will be of help caring for him. But why have you waited this long to tell me? Was it consideration for your husband?"

"There is more to tell—never was a husband to show consideration. There was only you, the father, that I considered with my silence. Knowing you love Maurice, I left you to be happy with him, as it seemed to be."

Alec responded sadly, "We would have helped, Maurice and me."

"It is not too late. More than ever I need you," as she began to cry.

Alec did not yet understand the full truth, only that she needed assurance she was no longer alone.

"I will do anything for you and for Ben. Stop your tears and tell me what help you need."

"I am going to need you to take Ben and care for him the way I would wish myself to continue doing."

"Take him from you? I would never be able to do something so cruel."

"It will not be cruelty, but kindness to me and especially to Ben."

It was time for the full explanation of dreadful news. Noreen was fatally ill, her breast afflicted by cancer, and disease was spreading through her body. She had at most a year remaining. When she first learned of the disease she was too stunned to think or act – that was months ago – but now her concern had to be for Ben. That is why she desperately appealed to Alec.

"I do not want my family to take him. Their home would be a bitter place for the boy who would have to pay for my misdeed. Even though my father does not know I never had a husband, he sees Ben in evil ways because I never had a proper church wedding and ended in divorce." Through her tears she uttered the hope, "You could keep Ben from the narrow views that come of Irish suffering. For you to take him and see to his education, that is what I want for him, the only dream I have left, if only Maurice is willing to see Ben as yours and his."

Much more was said of Noreen's tribulations which would have been worse had not Sarah prepared the way. There was no husband, but Sarah had provided for the expenses of Noreen's childbirth and arranged work with a family she knew willing to offer them a place to live. That domestic security might have continued except for the grave illness which seized Noreen. Now she was terrified by what lay ahead for her body and more so for Ben. What was to happen to him?

Alec lamented that she had not from the first approached him honestly. He learned that Sarah had recommended such a course, but Noreen in her youth and uncertainty insisted on secrecy. Now she pleaded the only thing she could, that the way she chose had been the best she saw, and it was too late to right the past. There was no use for recrimination or regret by either of them. Her dishonesty had compounded his own to Maurice. When finally regrets were put aside, they reached a concurrence of what needed to be done. Noreen was near exhaustion.

"Will you stay the night with Maurice and me?"

"I would, except Ben is awaiting me. My arrangement was only for the day, to return by night."

217

"Put your heart at ease, I will do what is needed to make Ben my son. I will also see to your care in our house. Maurice is a good person who will approve. You and Ben will move to Philadelphia."

They parted at the station, Noreen relieved, Alec in dismay. It was just as well Noreen had not taken up his offer to spend the night for there was much explaining owed to Maurice to pave the way.

*   *   *

A grim, determined Alec had his mind made up. Benjamin was his son. This peremptory certitude was grounded neither in the rights of blood nor of possession, but it flowed from a powerful conscience. He had not been a father to the boy during nearly seven years and not a true friend to Noreen. He recalled uneasily his mother's judgment that an absent father was no father at all. Yet Benjamin's mother, Noreen, had chosen to bequeath to him the role of her successor. This stirred his already troubled heart into the deepest concern for his own son's plight, facing the imminent loss of his mother. He remembered how grievous was the aloneness that followed his mother's death. He could soften the boy's painful awakening to a world indifferent to our dependence on those we lose. It was too soon to speak of loving Ben, only he was sure that guarding the boy's welfare would enhance such feeling.

Just how should he go about securing the relationship of father to son? He made an appointment with John Smith whom he could trust to be empathetic to the situation at hand because of his own Horatio Alger story. Allusions have been made to the strange and questionable relationship of the Smiths, but it is time to tell that story fully. At seventeen John had been rescued from the streets by Nicholas Smith who over the next three decades was his patron, bequeathing his name along with a sizable fortune to John as his adopted son. Along the way there were whispers and innuendoes accompanying this set of events. Alec had heard various distorted versions from supposed friends of John. It turned out that few people knew the truth, and Alec became one of the few who heard the story directly. John told him of early hardships which provided a strong link between them.

John left home at the age of fifteen, heading to Manhattan for the kind of excitement that contrasted to the small town he departed. Determined to make his fortune, during the next two years he drifted into one sexual dalliance after another, with men or women as opportunity presented, for he discovered that a handsome youth, which he was, offered something of value in trade. It was a way of supplementing what otherwise was the limit to his meager legitimate income set by the lack of other skills. He exchanged his favors for money, always careful to reach a monetary contract in advance of providing satisfaction. But he did not enjoy the labor that often was distasteful because his sexual inclinations were toward gentleness. Wisely, he carefully stored half the returns from his prostitution for some better future. With few scruples about these exchanges other than the provisos of fair trade, he put even those few reservations to rest by arguing that what he was doing was beneficial to clients and only a temporary aberration on his part.

And so it turned out when a street encounter presented wealthy Nicholas Smith, a frail and diminutive gentleman of the Victorian Age who asked little in return for his generosity. As part of the unwritten contract John was expected to display good character and discretion, and need engage in nothing actively sexual until it stemmed from his own good impulses, and even at that it required little more than that the youth's male organ respond to warm attentions. John was plucky enough to seize the opportunity posed by this fortunate hit. He spent several nights with Nicholas in one of the fashionable hotels of New York and days visiting shops to acquire a tasteful wardrobe at the generosity of his benefactor.

Though Nicholas was thirty years older than the boy-man he had rescued, John was not offended by the discrepancy in age, since it was matched by an equally vast discrepancy in position. To the contrary, as John experienced affection from a gentleman, he basked in this unaccustomed favor and thanked fate for singling him out from the thousands of other young men who, facing similar poverty, would have jumped at the opportunity. Many of the other boys he knew welcomed overtures of this sort, generally rougher in their enactment, settling for far less, though not many of them would have been able to respond as graciously as John did.

By the time Nicholas was ready to return to his Philadelphia home on Walnut Street, a lavishly furnished three-story stone dwelling, he was smitten with John's looks and good character. John accepted the invitation offered him to live with Nicholas Smith who was a prominent lawyer and social reformer. To the outsider this kind of relationship could not hold much promise, the discrepancies of age, education, social status and economic control seeming too great. But there was something unseen by outsiders. Nicholas was from the first tender, his embrace tepid, which made it easy for John to be considerate to his patron. Nicholas valued good qualities in the young man who proved intelligent, sensitive, appreciative and honest. Like Mr.Higgins with his Eliza Doolittle, he set about polishing the rough jewel fate had placed in his hands. In ensuing years John became a lawyer with connections that Nicholas facilitated, so at the present juncture he was certain to know how to secure Benjamin's future, just as his benefactor had done for him. Nicholas, as his years on this earth were waning, took the precaution of legally adopting John as his son, henceforth John Smith, making him heir to a considerable fortune. The son presumptive drew up the papers himself and guided the legal process to its happy conclusion. No legal complications arose after Nicholas' death as no distant cousins or claimants appeared able to swoop down upon his fortune.

*   *   *

John welcomed Alec into his office without a clue to the purpose of their meeting except that it concerned a personal legal matter. He would be glad to help, for he admired in Alec some of his own background of poverty and the deserving of favor from another well-placed. He was ready to empathize with a disconsolate Alec who sank into a chair across the desk.

"How may I help you? You mentioned a legal matter of personal importance. We can put aside our formal relationship. What you say is between two good friends."

"I have learned that seven years ago I fathered a child, a son I wish to claim."

"What is his mother's wish? Does any other man have a stake in this?"

"The mother is favorably disposed to my being recognized as the father. She came to me with that request, since she has a fatal illness and does not wish the boy to fall into the hands of her family who are narrow in outlook. She prefers the boy share the manner of life Maurice and I are able to offer. As for legal encumbrances, there is no husband, no other claimant than a family that cares nothing of her predicament. They believe her married, though the boy has known no legal father."

"What is the nature of the mother's illness? How much time do we have to take the proper action?"

"Noreen, that is her name, says she has at most a year before the cancer does its deadly work. That is why she came to me with information about the boy. Until a few days ago I knew him as her son, a lovely boy whom I treated affectionately those few occasions I saw him."

"What is your boy's name? We may start to speak of him as yours."

"Ben, whom I wish to make a Scudder. I hope he will acquire much from the Hall side as well. Ben is sweet and soft-spoken because he has been only with such a woman who has taught him gentle ways. Noreen wishes Ben to have advantages that I would provide."

220

"Does Noreen understand the bonds that exist between you and Maurice?"

"She knows we are loyal in our affections toward one another. She also respects that we would confront the world honestly in the matter, if we could."

"This will be an awkward question, but I must ask you one time and once only. Much as you care for Noreen and the boy, is there any doubt of your paternity?"

"One look at him and you would not ask. No doubt on Noreen's part and I have none. He is a Scudder to be sure. The wonder is I did not see it, for I had been with him enough to know."

"Alec, it was a legal question as well as something to be asked in friendship. Should the advice turn legal, you would be ill served did I not establish this fact."

"It does not matter, since Noreen has come to me out of desperation. I would help her even if it were otherwise. But the boy is mine, that I am sure."

"The situation is clear as far as the law is concerned. Do not think of trying to adopt Ben. If you petition for adoption as a single man, or reveal your life with Maurice, the petition will run afoul of the legal system. There is only one way to secure custody. That is to marry Noreen, go through a proper ceremony, preceded by acknowledgement the marriage was consummated long ago. Noreen will swear to parentage, you the birth father of Ben. It will be necessary you live with Noreen as husband and act as father. No one will ever be able to challenge your right as father."

Alec had suspected as much.

Nor was he surprised at John's next question, "What will Maurice think of this?"

Chapter 21

A Sorry Scheme of Things

Ah Love! could you and I with Him conspire
To grasp this sorry Scheme of Things entire,
Would we not shatter it to bits—and then
Remould it nearer to the Heart's desire!

Edward Fitzgerald, "Rubaiyat"

Maurice's heart ran cold when he heard what Alec had in mind.

"I must marry Noreen, the only way to assure my custody over Ben. Surely you understand the predicament. Noreen is dying and the boy needs care. She wishes to bequeath him to me. But being the natural father is not enough when it comes to the law, at least in our case. Help me so that the outcome will be best for all of us."

That statement was as matter-of-fact as John's legal advice had been, as if only a legal dilemma had to be dealt with, and not the fragile human heart. For more than a week Maurice had been under the strain of a broken relationship that had been his life's measure. Hearing from Alec that he intended to marry another did not help Maurice escape his overwhelming confusion of emotions. Though Alec had repeatedly protested his love, and had done so again along with an announcement of this stark decision, too much had been swiftly revealed of the whole sordid intercourse for words to soften Maurice's anguish. Anger and jealousy blinded him to every other consideration than that Alec had broken their faith and would complete that betrayal by marrying Noreen and commingling his body with hers, as he had done before, perhaps as nature in its indifferent way would have it. The two of them would draw together as husband and wife for the parenting of a young life. That life was a gift from Noreen such as could never be his to match.

What seemed necessary and noble to Alec, the one good thing he could do to relieve Noreen's pain, and the only way to secure Benjamin's future with him, found philosophical common ground with Maurice that nature and society confounded human aspirations for happiness. Alec was struck by the cruel indifference of the natural world that takes a mother away before the child is prepared to fend for himself. Maurice's heart also assayed the cruelty of the natural world, heedlessly appointing death, but his despondency hated also those social dictates which, claiming alliance with inexorable nature, erect a domain of gendered denial and discrimination. He was denied what he longed for, that which a brief moment of passion long ago was about to hand to Noreen. How unnatural to his heart was this scheme of things. He and Alec, joined as in marriage by mutual will and desire, could not merit approval from the institutions of society, nor could he realize his mother's wish that he discover the profundity of life in children of his own with a hold on the future. Biology worked against such an outcome because he loved a man. It seemed a trick of nature upon his heart, mind and body. He and Alec were unable to accomplish what Noreen and Alec had done without any purpose other than might be ascribed to a fleeting sensual moment. His desire for fertility with another man might be disharmonious with the physical universe, but Maurice held firmly that the universe was perverse, not his feelings.

Alec was not oblivious to the anxiety besetting Maurice, but he had gone through life without suffering jealousy, and so he did not understand the power it had to demonize a person in its grips. He pleaded his love over and over, begging forgiveness for mistakes of the past, while at the same time offering a defense of the course he had worked out, adding to Maurice's weariness with the whole bloody mess.

"It is a legal matter which John advises to assure Ben will live with me after Noreen's death. Otherwise Noreen's family could challenge my right. John says their claim would prevail in court. The only safe course, the only one he is confident would withstand challenge, is that I marry Noreen and live with her. You know I haven't been a father to Ben and have no other claim to him than to establish myself as a father by providing for him and his mother as a husband."

Maurice shouted, "I know that our lives, if subjected to legal examination, would ruin every chance that you would be recognized as his father." He was verging on hysteria as the ground was slipping from under what he had thought to be secure domesticity. "I hate the discrimination we have suffered. Twelve years together counts nothing, as if our love had no right to exist." He could not hold back tears of anger, "And it is you who brought this upon us! How could you have deceived me in such a callous way?"

"Please, Morrie," and Alec took his hand as if to renew earlier vows, "recognize that my love for you is still paramount. It does not please me the oath we made to each other must be cast into legal obscurity because of what I have done. But what is the good that can come from recrimination if it paralyzes our decision? What I did with Noreen was wrong. Strike me for it if you must. Still the deed is in the past, and Ben has been on this earth more then six years. It is Ben whose plight is urgent more than yours. You need to overcome the hurt and help me think clearly and act rationally. My fears for the boy override any indignity you and I suffer because of disapproval of homosexuality. There are other pains at work. I am sick at heart to know Ben lacked a father for all his years. Now the boy faces the loss of his mother."

Maurice was trembling and pulled away even as Alec continued to plead.

"Listen to me and trust what I say. We need to outwit the law. When Noreen dies—and that time is at most a year off—Ben will be ours. Not only mine, but ours. That is what Noreen has chosen, knowing that I have cast my life with you, for she respects you as a second parent. You also remember your mother's wish for you to have a family. I know you hoped for that with me but thought it a necessary sacrifice. As fate would have it, for us to raise Ben would satisfy all our wishes, even my mother's for me."

Part of Maurice admitted to the soundness of this reasoning, but whatever in him strove to be rational was overpowered by turbulent emotions of having been deceived. He could not stave off anger at Alec for concealing so long this sexual adventure with the bitter consequences now thrust upon them. He had been betrayed, not for thirty pieces of silver, but for a woman's flesh. Alec was following the same path as Clive, though in a circuitous way. To worsen this descent into self-pity, Maurice succumbed to homophobic doubt that a male's love was ample ground to deserve a healthy man who wanted children. His youthful years of indoctrination, religious and heterosexual, awakened the specter of abnormality as the nemesis of his worthiness. He rapidly slipped into contempt for the incapacity of male love to give Alec what he wanted. Noreen had accomplished that naturally, almost without a thought, as he saw it, or at least without much thought from Alec.

So much anger and doubt was accompanied by the powerful fear that he would be alone in misery. A feeling of helplessness overcame him that he could ever be happy. He had lost Alec, and now the good part of himself was slipping away. He could hardly recognize himself.

"Alec, the Maurice I wished to be is destroyed. What you ask of me, no matter how reasonable it seems to you, is beyond what I am able to give. I am not exceptional in strength or courage, only a selfish human being made jealous and insecure. Ironically, in these feelings, I am as normal as everyone else. The thought that Noreen will sleep with you in our bed torments me. I am filled with hate, and yet I can not hate you. Better that I see myself as a wretch who does not deserve you. Everything seems hopeless when even you cannot help me. I shudder at Andrew's insistence that God loves his creatures, when God is merciless to me."

Alec disliked such ravings as distracting from a predicament demanding gravity, but here was Maurice collapsing into religious and psychological obfuscation.

"There is no need to lacerate yourself for what I did. Self-reproach and religious cant are useless to the deeds we need. It was not God who brought us to this rift, only my behavior, call it adventurous or call it heartless. Your feelings need tending, which I will see to once we reach understanding of how we are to proceed. We both know what is necessary. I want this boy as mine, a Scudder, and I want you to do your part. One day you will help to shape him into a better kind of Hall. If we don't succeed at keeping him, all my life will be tormented. I can't let Noreen die without knowing I will take care of our son. I have already done too much harm. Tell me what good it would do you if I should lose Ben? Though your heart does not presently join with mine, I need you to forgive me and to be strong so that you can support what is necessary. You may feel lost, but I know you as the same Maurice who had the courage to leave England so that we could be together. Now, will you be as brave again to do what love demands?"

But Maurice was not strong at this critical moment when clarity of heart and mind were obscured by anger and fear. So great was his loss that he could only rant about the betrayal that had occurred seven years ago.

"How could you deceive me so long?"

Alec admitted the error of thinking himself adventurous and moving in directions for which he had not foreseen the consequences.

"I am recalling events as honestly as I can. Forgive me, but I did think sexual experience with Noreen was an innocent pleasure. There was no thought of betrayal. I loved you then and I will always love you. When Noreen and I realized our mistake, and I convinced her it was you I intended to love, there was an end to anything sexual. Noreen was wiser and decided to leave. I knew nothing of any child. It was a year later she told me of her marriage and when the child came I assumed it was another man's. I thought Noreen and I might never meet again. What point was there to confess what was finished?"

But deceit is not easily absolved. Maurice was even more infuriated as he ranted at Alec's new-found honesty.

"Noreen has a place in your life that I can never hold. She will be your wife and she is already the mother of your child. How can I mean as much to you ever again? I will always be inferior because you chose to make a child with her."

Alec was exasperated seeing Maurice reduced as a man. He too was weary and wanted an end to reproaches which he knew were justified.

"For God's sake, Morrie, I fathered a son without intent. Not a crime, nor any sin, for we refuse to think that way. I was dishonest with you, and to Noreen as much, then to the boy that I have not had a chance to acknowledge. I regret that outcome. Now that I understand what I did wrong, I am trying to right matters. I don't want to be a father like mine who never cared for what he sired. He never showed me a man to admire. Here I have a chance to be a father because of Noreen's desperation and trust in me. She has not asked that you disappear or that I stop loving you. She gives us both the chance for a son. Could you not appreciate that as a gift to you as well?"

These dictates of reason had to be repeated. But they failed to prevent Maurice deteriorating into a pitiful state that only a complete change of heart by Alec could have halted. That change was impossible for Alec who was resolved to do just as he said. Instead, he was weary and unable to put up any longer with hysteria which was being tried as a weapon against his resolve.

"Remember that it is Noreen who is dying and not you."

Maurice, swept up in his own ugly mood, burst into tears as he uttered something unforgivable. Nor could jealousy or dejection make it right. He screamed pitilessly words that taken literally were demonic.

"Noreen can go to hell, for all I care!"

Alec heard these words as a heartless judgment for a sin of the flesh that was as much his. It seemed the devil had taken hold of Maurice and was emanating from his shriek as hell's curse, damning Noreen's soul into everlasting torment. As if to forestall such a terrible fate, Alec struck in anger before any humane sentiment might hold him back. His fist crashed into Maurice's face, the only physical brutishness committed in twelve years together. Perhaps the devil had seized hold of him as well. Alec did not draw back from this violent negation of love, nor did he repeat the physical blow. What he did was as wicked, except that—leaving the devil to his own due—like Maurice's words his were not premeditated for cruelty. Still, his words violently inflicted a wound that might never heal.

"You are right that the Maurice we both want has disappeared! I despise you as you are now. Selfishness and hate have consumed you. Noreen is a good woman. She mothered my son without ever a demand upon me or asking anything from you. She has offered to accept you as a parent because she knows of our commitment. It will be long before I forgive your harshness. "

When Maurice did not reply, Alec added a judgment that was intentionally hurtful.

"I can not be like you."

Maurice's body throbbed with pain more appropriate to a battlefield where men wound each other. Alec's words cut to the quick, remindful of words of long ago when Clive defended his preference for a woman, "I was never like you." Alec, too, was different than Maurice, more manly in desires. Maurice was defeated and once more must surrender to the bitterness of what was happening. There might be some salvation later on, but it was one Maurice could not see. He must come to see in Ben the incarnation of what he loved in Alec. But for the present his body and mind were torn with passions that thwarted such hope. His worth was in question, whether Alec loved him, and whether he was deserving of his love. All he could do was collapse in a heap onto the knees of Alec who had sunk forlornly into a stuffed chair.

Maurice needed rescuing as much as did Noreen.

"You see how queer I am, more than you bargained, and more than you are able to love. I am insanely jealous. Only Maurice matters! I loathe myself for being what you despise." Then he lapsed into silence, and only after much time had passed did the devil within him seem exorcised. He was spiritless as he offered the only decision left to him, "I will do whatever you ask."

Alec was disheartened and angry, despite his demand being met. Maurice's surrender into abjection was pitiful. Alec stroked the head cradled in his lap out of duty. Maurice felt as much as he folded in exhaustion. Alec let his own troubled head sink back into the soft cushioning. The chimes of the clock betokened each passing quarter hour, once, then another time, and when the hour sounded Maurice stirred, wakening Alec who now sounded more gentle.

"Why do you make yourself miserable? Have I suggested that you are unworthy?"

When no response came, "What I did with Noreen is no reason for your hating yourself. It was my lapse, only mine, not yours or Noreen's. I did harm to both of you and, as it turned out, to Ben."

Alec was spent of all emotion or reason, except the good sense that he need no longer repeat that the needs of Noreen and Ben must be paramount. All he could do was help Maurice accept a fait accompli and the terms of its resolution. Suffering was the price of his youthful indiscretion.

He could not provide Maurice's battered soul with true relief, and so his apology rang hollow, but what was in his heart might much later prove of importance.

"I know you doubt the things I say, after what I have done. I cannot say that I am sorry for my anger. I defended Noreen as I would defend you from meanness. It is striking you I regret. That was cruel, as mean as your judgment upon Noreen." Alec's eyes moistened, something Maurice would remember. "When our passions quiet, and you are able to measure what I did, and see some innocence on all our parts, in the sexuality not meant to harm, but beyond that, Noreen taking responsibility for her child, and belatedly my taking responsibility, and now you assuming responsibility to someone you love, then you will find encouragement. No matter, you are not dispossessed from my heart. Marrying has to do with Ben. This terrible estrangement between you and me will pass if you hold nothing against Ben."

It was not meant as an ultimatum, but it came from a mind that was determined.

"For us to heal, you must accept the boy as my flesh and take him to your own."

"I will do as you ask, what you have decided must be done," a beaten Maurice responded.

Then Alec placed his lips to the wounded face of his lover.

*   *   *

Two months later Maurice was retracing his way across the Atlantic, this time on the Queen Mary, back to an England he no longer cherished. He had been contemplating such a trip in any case. His mother was gravely ill, and arrangements were made that he leave his work at the bank so that he might spend some final time with her. All was uncertain regarding his return. Needless to add, his mind and heart were overburdened that Alec was about to marry Noreen and she to live in the house where he and Alec had shared their love. Though he had agreed to this course of events, it would be too much for him to witness their unfolding, and so his departure to England took place two weeks prior to the Scudder wedding.

Chapter 22

A Dangerous Journey Back To England

He felt that chilling heaviness of heart
Beyond the best apothecary's art,
The loss of Love . . . .
No doubt he would have been much more pathetic,
But the sea acted as a strong emetic.

Lord Byron, "Don Juan"

The voyage back to England was one long nightmare, some of its terror emanating from the accretions of the unconscious part of Maurice's mind, and other anxious strains fed by consciousness of deceptions and broken vows. Alec was not alone in dishonesty, though his act preceded another of a different kind. Maurice, too, betrayed the promise given to Alec to love even in the worst of times, succumbing instead to that mortal enemy of love, jealousy. In the grip of that devastating emotion, every thought that seized his mind was falsely understood because reality was refracted through a prism of anguish and anxiety. Events were remembered in distorted form because his self-image as a devoted lover, encouraged by love from Alec, was damaged and cast into surreal realms of shame, guilt and loss. The awfulness of being scorned reawakened and intensified the self-loathing of early manhood that had fallen into long sleep. Was it wakefulness or a nightmare soon to end that he was unworthy of Alec's love?

Lost in an abyss of worthlessness, Maurice dreaded acts of further rejection he knew were imminent. Worst of all imaginings was Alec sharing a wedding bed with Noreen, the very bed that was his as well. That other moments he dreaded might never occur, that some of them enacted might be construed as acts of kindness, as Alec understood them, did not ease the festering wound at the fringes of confused consciousness. Thoughts of Alec's intimacy with someone other than himself induced anxiety that nearly crushed poor Maurice who was alone in wretchedness.

It was no avail that among all the generations of lovers who had preceded him, many had suffered the same condition. Maurice had now to be numbered among the ranks of those myriads of troubled souls who, having loved with full confidence that their love was undying, found themselves rejected in favor of another. He was at sea amidst this pain of egocentrism, in need of finding his humanity anew. Either that, or the healthy and loving person that had recently been Maurice would vanish.

*　　　*　　　*

The borders of the fractured mind are crossed silently, precious sleep conveying us haplessly into foreign territory where exotic phantasms, creatures beyond ordinary acquaintance, babble mysteriously, or in speechless ways pronounce profound insights. Their messages may be as riddled as those the oracle at Delphi delivered. In this tortured realm of dream-consciousness that Maurice suffered, Alec was no longer the Alec he had trusted for a dozen years. He was there, approachable, yet beyond reach because of the scorn he displayed toward the wishes put for his disposal. Maurice felt enormous fright as he sensed an impending fall from grace. In his nakedness he reached out, a gesture reminiscent of Adam finding inspiration from the finger of the father God, but Alec ignored this beseech. Alec did not recognize the imploring hand because his attention was distracted by the imposing figure of a woman, perhaps a goddess, who summarily beckoned, seducing him. There was no subtlety in her call emanating from the lower portions of her figure. The apparition loomed more statuesque than human, a warlike Brunhilde commanding Alec to grovel in subjection before the configuration of woman. Maurice felt unworthy in her sight, cast aside, Alec assenting in the scorn with which they conjoined in banishing him. His only hope was that Alec as male would turn his way, choose him again, so they could together be banished. But Alec scorned Maurice who was neither man nor woman. He rushed to the goddess, fell prostrate, and wrapped himself in adoration round her thighs and buttocks. Maurice plummeted into an infinite chasm that awakened him drenched in the sweat of fever.

*　　　*　　　*

Maurice sought escape from the chill of the February dampness and from himself in one of the ship's bars, but he was unavailable to the cheerful companionship that offered itself. After a few drinks he hurried nauseously toward the deck. He spewed his vomit into the sea. The rough waters conspired with his turbulent emotions, forcing his wrenching body to emit the physical contents of its unhealthiness. For a time his thoughts were distanced by sounds of his own vomiting, the pungency of its smell, and the unpleasant aftertaste. Some spill that reeked of alcohol spattered his chin. As he wiped the spume away his senses confirmed the disease which gripped his body and sickened soul. The reaches of his mind were at one with his body in attesting to utter sickness.

*   *   *

The borders of the fractured mind are invisible, with no signs to announce demarcations between the real and the imagined. What domain constitutes reality, whether it be memory or dream or the corporeal immediacy, becomes uncertain. During daytime Maurice wandered the ship unable to escape himself. In the afternoon sun two young lovers strolled the deck hand-in-hand, heart linked to heart, totally enraptured in their moment of infatuation. Maurice followed at a distance, leashing his step to their company. They playfully leaned into one another, they laughed, the young man whispered into the ear of his beloved in order to nibble an erotic kiss, and she touched his cheek to signal acquiescence. Maurice's voyeurism continued for a long time until the couple disappeared into the interior of the ship. Emotionally exhausted, he found a deckchair where under a warm cover he lapsed into another dream, this time one marked by recollection rather than nightmare. Alec was resting beside him and, as he had done long ago, reached beneath their blankets for some intimate gesture that betokened erotic embrace.

So it went for the several days of the voyage, alternations from waking dismay to troubled dreaming. There was no rest for poor Maurice who did not know whether he could live without Alec.

*   *   *

As the ship's horn sounded the approach to safe harbor, he remembered Southhampton on a fairer day of departure twelve years earlier when dreams of consummation and fruition of love brought elation. Escaping the coldness of England, its pedigreed snobbery left behind for a promise of freedom, he and Alec had leaped at a wager of love. In their innocence a world of beauty seemed then to open before them for the taking. The loss of that world in the despair of the present brought great questioning to Maurice. Had he loved enough or too little?

*   *   *

Maurice had been in England not even a fortnight when a quiet wedding took place in a south Philadelphia Catholic church. It was in March of 1937 that the ceremony was attended by Noreen's family and a few of Alec's friends who put loyalty to Maurice aside. John Smith was there approvingly, Leery, too. Andrew came as a friend and a stand-in for Maurice's better self. Tony was the best man and Rita had been requisitioned for bridesmaid.

It was not the joyous event a wedding ought to be, too poignant for the betrothed when the words "till death do you part" were intoned, and for others informed of the circumstances, an event bittersweet because, though it put the stamp of approval on a husband and father, it might have been Maurice standing there beside Alec. There were even a few harsh witnesses because Ben was the occasion rather than the fruit of the sacred rite of marriage. Among those offended were Noreen's parents who felt a strain of disgrace because the child was the product of a deed not ordained by priests. Alec saw as much and hated every moment in the church. Running through his mind was the troubling judgment, "There is nothing sacred here, nothing sacred about marriage. If only Maurice could understand this." That thought overwhelmed any other, except the promises exchanged during prior days, Noreeen's that she would ask nothing of the marriage for her own pleasure and that she would hold to gratitude so as to burden him less with tribulations, and his own that he would see her through the ordeal and afterward provide Ben a father. When he cast his eye on the seven year old boy handsomely dressed in his new blue suit, seated beside his grandmother in the front pew, Alec felt his private vows were worthy and that he would honor them with Noreen's help, and then with Maurice's.

Chapter 23

A Change in Heart

What though reason forged your scheme?
'Twas Reason dreamed the Utopia's dream:
'Tis dream to think that Reason can
Govern the reasoning creature, man.

Herman Melville

It was some weeks later, after many days with his mother whose life was waning, that Maurice's nightmare dissipated with only the slightest of heralding. Conversation with his mother had not been a cure, though it contributed in small measure. His presence through hours of silence had brought distraction to her, and despite his preoccupation with his own unhappiness, comfort to both of them. He chose to be thankful for that much. Nor did the imminence of her death elevate his thinking to a plane where philosophical resolution occurred. It was a mystery to Maurice, almost a miracle, as if divine power had lifted a punishment, how his mood alternated. Despite attempts at explanation by science and psychology, it remains a mystery how disorder of the mind and heart ever resolves into acceptance of oneself in a clearer light of reality.

The change occurred as sudden as a fever breaking after a gruesome night of uneasy sleep. All Maurice knew was that his mind found ease again as he sat there looking at his mother sleeping. He was glad to be beside her, who had given him life, to witness life's cycle completed. Here she was humbled by mortality, which turns all to dust, and yet she found security knowing she had done everything she could for her children, even in the end accepting Alec. Then Maurice understood the verity of the principle, to give is better than to receive, because offerings from one's heart are more controllable than demands placed on another's emotions. Suddenly it all seemed simple. His mind unclouded, his heart released as from a prison, his emotions were once again within his own power. Hope revived and strengthened into a certainty that he needed to watch over

Alec and be with him till his dying day, or if the order were reverse, to have his presence for his own end. What more legitimate test of love need he exact? The marriage of hearts he claimed with Alec was not a legal or emotional prison. If he mistakenly persisted in judging Alec beyond forgiveness, their love would fall into a heap of shattered legality which had never been theirs to uphold.

He leaned over to place his lips on his mother's forehead before returning to his room in haste so that he might reinforce this healthier frame of mind.

*   *   *

Reverently he retrieved the letter Alec had placed into his hands just moments before embarking. Now that the evil spell was broken, he was able for the first time to read the words as Alec had meant them. Maurice had anxiously violated the instructions on the envelope that specified the letter was intended for reading after the marriage of Alec Scudder to Noreen three weeks hence. But once aboard the ship in the privacy of his stateroom, Maurice had waited not even an hour, ignoring the stipulation, reading with incomprehension as far as his feelings went.

This reading, months later, he was able to understand the words differently.

My most beloved Maurice,

The marriage is completed as you read this letter.

I know your heart is troubled because I have legally married, something you wanted between us. Though I do not share your sentiment for ceremony, I wish circumstances were such that we were turning your dream into a deed. For now, I ask that you trust and believe what I have done is decent, not an inconsiderate act toward you. I am no saint, you know better. My way is to act stubbornly with reason and passion once I believe it will serve good purpose. Surely you recall that impulse on my part, a foray fraught with presumption, when I allowed passion to rightly direct me to our first encounter.

Marrying Noreen comes from a different conviction not comparable to our beginning. I mention the way you and I began our liaison so that you carry its memory through your troubled journey. What I do with Noreen comes from a totally thoughtful motivation. I have taken this last chance to honor her wish that I be a father to Ben. Let me explain to you in a way that will assist your understanding. I am haunted by my mother's words that I never abandon a woman I have placed in need. It is as if my mother were allied with Noreen's request that I care for Ben beyond her ability to do so. How could I refuse their joint entreaty?

My endurance will come from being a father, with help from Noreen, learning ways to help Ben, readying him for manhood. You will share this work with me. Then I will be a good father and faithful to you. Is that not what you have always wanted?

Noreen is soon to die, probably before this year is out, else my choice would be impossible because I could not leave you for a lifetime. When we are reunited, neither of us will be the same because the suffering Noreen must undergo will change me, as your sad journey to England will change you. Sharing death has to be sobering.

I urge you to place our separation into perspective that allows you peace. My thoughtless misdeed that made Ben is reproachful because of the unhappiness it has caused all round. I wonder, though, what use there is in your clinging to a morality coming from heaven? We must reject the supposed ways of God since we are excluded from so many of them. We ought to root our happiness in truth close to the earth. Like trees we are bound to the soil, though less firmly. Trees lift themselves to the sky in need of air and light. But as mortals, we vainly attempt to soar beyond physical limits to an unknown space that eludes us. Better accept the earth and humans as they are.

Nothing I have done, nothing I will do, belies my commitment to you. From a strictly sensual consideration, your flesh complements mine perfectly. If a physical bond is not sufficient—since clearly I did share my body with Noreen—I remind you that we also share a dream that will remain true so long as we choose to live it. I would not know happiness if you could cease to love me. My share of the dream makes such a breach impossible. I will be faithful and confident. On this point I am an idealist and dreamer.

Do not doubt I suffer loneliness from your absence. I selfishly think you belong to me, unlike the anarchist I once thought myself. But I learned at law that possession is a large part of any claim. While I can not hold your body though my heart cries out for you, it hurts both of us that you are alone. Hence I recommend free thinking guide your stay in England. Should companionship worthy of consideration offer itself, do what pleases you. You need not guard your body as a monk. Simply hold it in trust, as it were, for me to reclaim.

Feel secure that I will look to Ben for my male companionship. He will need all the time I can give for comforting, and he will be watchful how I attend his mother.

Your presence will be remembered as I tell Ben stories of you, and remind him that the future includes you.

Hold this letter, as if it were my heart in your care, knowing that I love you and await your return, when we will be companions again.

The letter was signed Alec, the date February of 1937.

*   *   *

Maurice was able at last to purge his evil spirit with tears that fell upon the letter. He cried aloud, for he enjoyed the sanctity of his room where neither shame nor pity could intervene. Almost as a prayer the words came of their own, "I thank you, my savior, my joy, my star. I love you. My God, I love you!" It was Alec at the center of his devotion. Not any divinity, but a flesh and blood Alec. His fear of losing Alec was gone, impossible as that would have seemed only yesterday. His mind was free of self-pity, his body overwhelmed by desire for intimacy, which he satisfied in the way that stood at hand, even as in imagination Alec took complete possession of him as for the first time. Then Maurice slept in reverie.

When he awoke all was not well, for he was not satisfied with the course love had taken. He was lonely because of the distance between them of space and sea and circumstance, but he was no longer alone in the direction his life ordained. He would before long cross the ocean again for good.

He need now return to his mother who was facing her own reckoning.

*   *   *

Important words were exchanged between them during the little remaining time. Before it was too late she expressed the wish, "If only Alec were here to comfort you. I was stubborn and foolish not to acknowledge his importance. Why did I not see sooner how wrong it was for you to follow my direction? Will you forgive me?"

Maurice was released from the burden of guilt and anger. He held his mother's hand gently as he poured out news about Alec and Ben, and how the three of them would become a family after all. She expressed satisfaction, though she did not inquire about the plight of Noreen, for her weakened attention turned to others of the assembled family.

Several days later she slipped away forever. Maurice wept in a wrenching way that could not have been foretold. No map of life directed this outcome, though it was part of a chain of events that included Alec's youthful indiscretion that led to the birth of a boy and an honorable denouement on both sides of the Atlantic, the mother's death-bed acknowledgment of Alec being a critical link in a still unfolding story.

*   *   *

Two letters crossed somewhere on the vast Atlantic ocean during the week before Mrs. Hall's death. Maurice, the person of old, wrote the day after his reawakening that he would return home as soon as it would not compromise Alec's pledge to Noreen. He was not sure how long his responsibilities would keep him in England. He added a remark that worried him after sending the letter for fear it sounded bitter.

"Your suggestion that I not be an ascetic, guarding my body from sensual satisfaction, is generous. You know I am needy of the sort of assurance you suggest. If only we could help one another in that way. But I feel the shadow of death as you do. I find this bad ending to life confounding and enormously tragic. When I think of holding another person physically, as the way to overcome such sad confusion, it is a reminder of your embrace and understanding that I need. Since you are not here, satisfaction with someone else amidst this sadness is uncertain."

Maurice need not have worried that Alec would find any point of dissatisfaction, for he took joy in that part of the letter which expressed forgiveness. He had forgiven his mother and now Alec.

"I love you with a discovered appreciation that what you are doing for Noreen, and for Ben, comes from the same integrity that allows me to love you. You are not a thoughtless transgressor, though that image haunted and frightened me awhile. I know and love you as a seeker of love, and a giver of love, along uncertain paths. Otherwise you would not have forged a life with me. That is the truth. As for my part of the dream we share, it is intact. I know you will be the honest companion of my life and Ben our son."

The letter from Alec that had passed his own at sea arrived shortly after his mother's death. Alec expressed again his own loneliness, that it was all he could manage to display cheer each day, Noreen's strength waning, her end no more than months off. Maurice felt sorry for his lover and for his immediate circle too beset with sadness.

*   *   *

There was more for Maurice to endure. His mother gone, he faced another wait. He wisely swore he would never indulge in the wish for Noreen's death. A more generous impulse to take the earliest boat back to America was too fraught with complications that might hinder rather than help the denouement. Instead, he would write frequently to Alec with encouragement. He would need to find some way of renewal for himself, perhaps to follow the healthy advice from Alec and restore some pleasures of the senses.

As fate would have it, someone who might be an attractive accomplice very soon presented himself.

Chapter 24

An English Affair

... yet not hopeless quite nor faithless quite,
Because not loveless....
Searching my heart for all that touches you,
I find . . . love's goodwill.

Christina Rosetti, Sonnets

Since my young days of passion—joy, or pain,
Perchance my heart and harp have lost a string,
And both may jar; it may be, that in vain
I would essay as I have sung to sing.

Lord Byron, "Childe Harold's Pilgrimmage"

At the memorial service for Grace Hall, a friend of the family who felt it necessary to reintroduce himself approached Maurice.

"Peter Arnold, a long-time acquaintance of your mother. You don't remember me, do you? Our fathers worked together, our mothers were friends. You were away at school much of the time, though we did play occasionally. You left a lasting impression."

Learning that Maurice had recently returned from America after a dozen years, Peter surmised he was unlikely to have close friends in England. Here was an opportunity to offer company to someone he had reason to remember fondly.

"Will you be on your own?"

When Maurice said he would, Peter was direct as needed. "Perhaps I can help you through this awful time? I will telephone when you have had a few days to rest."

Maurice hardly gave it a thought.

Several days later it was a different matter, for Maurice was indeed feeling lonely when Peter telephoned with a graciousness that could hardly have been discouraged without deliberate rudeness. Maurice felt no need for that. Instead, he accepted an invitation to dinner with someone who promised good company and upon whom he had left such an impression. Though he barely remembered their dealings as boys, he had a faint sense of something unusual between them. In any case there was much to commend a personable man such as Peter.

From the moment Peter arrived to escort Maurice he was especially considerate for he sensed a double loss to be assuaged. At the time of Maurice's departure to America he had picked up telling remarks between Grace Hall and his mother, nothing positive in the way of information, except that his mother expressed sympathy with the Halls for something illicit on Maurice's part. He had hardly judged Maurice, except for a curiosity regarding what adventure he was having. He even felt a slight jealousy because during their boyhood play the sight and touch of Maurice's body had brought a tingle of excitement to his own. Now he was kindly disposed to know Maurice better and help him through any difficulties.

As they settled in a restaurant Peter could see that light banter would not do. Maurice was too somber and guarded for that. Yet it was too soon to inquire into deeper troubled feelings, and so Peter began a brief domestic history of his own, emphasizing his present status of bachelorhood, though week ends were largely taken with parenting, something he made a habit of doing since a divorce a few years ago. He had married when he was twenty-five, the same year Maurice left England. A few years ago he initiated a divorce in which he surrendered custody of his children. This experience left him a different person, uncertain about long-range intimacy, though he took pains to demonstrate that he was not embittered. Presently he was enjoying company with women and men, though without any commitments.

"I have obligations enough with three children. My income is sufficient, but I do not wish to add anything more of responsibility to a wife who might want children of her own. I am distrustful of a serious emotional commitment, given the sorry result of my marriage. In any case, work and trying to be a decent father takes most of my time."

Though Peter was not ordinarily loquacious, this running commentary lasted through most of the meal. Maurice displayed enough interest to keep Peter going until it was past time to invite something from Maurice about his course of events during the dozen years since leaving England.

"I have wearied you with so much talk of myself. I was relieving you of any burden to converse, thinking your mood might prefer silence on your own part. Yet I also want to know more about you without prying into your privacy. How did you fare in America? I do remember at the time you left there was a stir in your household and mine about what our mothers agreed was a misadventure, though I was left to surmise what you were doing. Afterward I heard nothing further."

Maurice was not as direct, for he thought his situation more complex than he need explain. He did not want to entrust intimate details to a near stranger. Only when Peter asked, in a way that sounded nonchalant, how he had avoided marriage, did Maurice allude to a lasting affection toward someone who was currently tied to another, not mentioning it was a man whom he loved.

"Well, then, I am a friend who can help you feel less the separation. It is not easy to find compatible company when one is wounded and uncertain about the future."

Peter ordered an after-dinner liqueur to accompany what promised to become serious conversation.

"I will say another word about myself, to show the confidence I place in your discretion, hoping this will put you at ease. I only got my head together after years of confusion due to estrangement and then the divorce. My feelings are deeply loyal, as they were toward my wife. I fully trusted our relationship. But midway in our marriage she had an affair with another man, a younger, unmarried man, who fell in love. He cared for her in ways I was lacking. She was honest about it all. They wanted to be together. You know how hard it is to break emotional dependency, and so I suffered for two years until I realized I had to let go. I could not accept second place sexually, especially when it became clear she was indifferent to my attentions. There is some hope, perhaps, knowing that after several years since the divorce, now I hardly miss her. I continue to regret I can not be with my children each day. I see them regularly each week end."

Peter was discreet and did not question Maurice. Instead he talked about work and the children until Maurice's attention was waning. Peter asked if they should end the evening.

Maurice insisted otherwise, that he was listening to everything with interest, only that he would rather not discuss his personal affairs until they were better acquainted.

"I hope you will not construe that as disinterest in you. Far from it, I hope that our interest in one another will increase. As you have perceived, I need an intimate friend."

Peter was pleased with this acknowledgment, and to show his willingness for such an outcome, he made further conversation about the political excitement being stirred by Herr Hitler's demands for revision of Versailles. Maurice admitted he was not paying close attention to European affairs, though he wondered whether England should accommodate Germany's reasonable demands in order to avoid war.

"Hitler is far from reasonable. He is deliberately provoking nationalist hysteria with tirades about Germans being a superior race. Nazi flags and uniforms are turning Germany into a militarist state with an eye to an empire in the east. It is the Czechs and Poles who will lose their freedom in order for the master German race to have a European empire. Then the Russians will be next, I venture."

As Peter elaborated on the danger, thoughts ran through Maurice's mind that he kept to himself. He thought of Alec who, if he were here, after agreeing on the deplorable nature of Nazi ideology would pointedly ask whether Indian and Irish independence were less important than the rights of Czechs and Poles. But Maurice did not wish to risk offending a likeable companion. Instead, he accorded with Peter's liberal ideas while he indulged in appreciation of the man's good looks. He knew, too, that Alec would encourage an interest in what appeared to be Peter's virility.

Later, Peter pulled his car in front of Maurice's house and gave sign of lingering as he stretched his legs and leaned back on the seat. Maurice could almost hear Alec encouraging some invitation to intimacy. He relaxed into a resting position. Peter seized this opening to take Maurice's hand without looking at him.

"The person you love, Maurice, I presume is a man. You have no need for mistrust. Everything will be kept in confidence. I have liked you since we were boys, though you did not notice, and I only wish to help. Perhaps touching you will be comforting, though I need to know whether I am on the right track."

Finding no reasonable objection other than discretion, and certain he wished to keep this new friendship with a companionable man, Maurice decided to risk something.

"Yes, it is a man I have loved since leaving England. Surely you understand my reluctance to confide this delicate matter when I already am vulnerable."

As he said this, Maurice did not remove his hand from Peter's, but deliberately leaned back into the seat as he closed his eyes. After a few minutes he felt relaxed enough to continue.

"As you said, the future is uncertain. Yet the present is clear enough, for I know I love Alec and I am sure that he loves me. There are complications to work out."

Even this small degree of confidence from Maurice had a strange effect on Peter that he wished to share. He lifted Maurice's hand from the seat where it was resting within his own and brought it to his place of excitement where he held it firmly until he leaned to kiss Maurice just below the ear.

"Let us save further conversation. I hope you enjoyed being together as you know I did. I'm busy Saturday with the children. We could spend Sunday together if you like."

Maurice said he would like that.

*　　　*　　　*

Peter taking his hand and placing it as he did had set off a torrent of memories that ranged over all his youth. That night in sleep, Maurice was once more the boy plagued by torments of longing and flight, the adolescent who had resisted powerful urges from his body in order to appear normal and to function so. He knew no other way than to flee desire. When he saw young men of beauty he was almost made ill by the need to repress his feelings. In this taunting recurrence of memories there was a concatenation of images from his youth, but one in particular persisted of an exciting boy who kept taking Maurice's hand and leading it to an untouchable place. In the dream he pulled away in desperate fright from the genital liaison his senses wanted. Maurice awoke, knowing it was Peter in the dream, that it was not all dream.

Much of the night Maurice tossed only half in sleep. In consciousness he knew Peter was exciting, virile and apt to be persistent as long as he was not rebuffed.

With the light of morning he remembered something Nietzsche had advised, that one should attempt serious thinking only in the fresh air. He took a long walk through London, observing many plain people going about ordinary lives. There were some lovely persons, too, who caught his eye. "I don't think I've lost my attraction toward males" became a resolute idea, though it was not Peter who first came to mind when his subdued eroticism stirred. It was comforting to know he was settled on Alec, though of little comfort he was far away. If only he could feel Alec, all would be settled.

Where could Peter fit into this?

*   *   *

Sunday morning they walked through Kensington Gardens viewing the spring flowers as they followed the south side of Serpentine Lake. The setting encouraged Peter's confidence.

"You have wondered what feelings I have for women. To be honest, my sexuality is a puzzle. A pretty face is enough to arouse me. Do you remember how you attracted me from the first when you were a pretty boy? I tried with you, I would have done anything you permitted, but you showed no response. When I was in my teens I was overwhelmed by sexual excitement without discrimination, so long as someone looked pretty. I don't like to say it, lest if offend you, but I think of prettiness as a feminine attribute. As it turned out, my first serious opportunity was with a girl when I was sixteen. We did it regularly. I don't think our sex had anything to do with love, just something we both enjoyed. After we drifted apart there were several other women. None of them led to love on my part."

"What about your wife? How was that different?"

"That started with a lovely face as well. I enjoyed touching her and she responded hesitantly. She was guarding her virginity for marriage. She wanted to be a mother more than a wife and I wanted regularity in sexual deeds. I thought myself ready to be a father. After we were married, I can now see, we did not develop much in the way of friendship. She was disappointed when she discovered I was not a happy social person. Not the talker you see me now. I loved her, in the way of being faithful, but we never shared much except the children. After three children, she found that was not enough. Then she began to complain of frustrations because there was little communication between us until I no longer listened. Another man came along who appreciated her in ways that were important to her. Once that happened there was no stopping. I could only make our lives miserable by opposing divorce. They are together, with my children, and one of theirs."

Maurice was perplexed by sexual ambivalence in a male. He understood the male desire for children but nothing more of their interest in women. It did not bother him that Peter thought his face as pretty as a woman's, but he did not want in any other way to be so compared.

"I am curious about your inclinations toward women. I am innocent of any knowledge. I appreciate a beautiful face, but beyond that, feminine attractiveness eludes me. I fall outside the bounds of prurient interest. Alec feels otherwise, of course, else he would not have impregnated a

244

woman. Now your history adds to my need for understanding a taste I have never indulged."

By now they were approaching an end of the park where each Sunday morning speakers pronounced on many topics. At one make-shift platform, surrounded by several men in black shirts holding banners proclaiming racial purity, a leader with a shrill voice spouted hateful ideas that smacked of evolutionary geopolitics as if nations were alike to turtles.

"Every animal mates only with his own species according to nature. This basic law of racial purity is valid for our species, and for each nation, imposing an evolutionary duty to preserve the race from pollution by different and inferior kinds. For Aryans the grave danger comes from the Jew who is a parasite, one without a national territory, predatory upon other purer peoples. Who has not seen the lurking Jewish male youth always waiting for the unsuspecting Aryan girl so that he can defile her with his blood and steal her from her people and culture?"

As they moved on, Peter spat on the ground to clear the poison of Nazism. Maurice seconded the rejection with astonishment at such claptrap. They left the park by Marble Arch and walked to Edwardes Square where they entered an elegant restaurant for a wholesome English dinner of roast, vegetables, potatoes and Yorkshire pudding. Afterward they walked some more, seemingly aimlessly, though all the while Peter was leading the way until they arrived at his dwelling as the evening was fading. He suggested they go upstairs for a time before he saw Maurice home.

*   *   *

They shared some wine as they relaxed on a couch, Peter close enough to put his arm around Maurice.

"I like you, you know. I am ready to pick up as we were when boys, to see where affection leads, whenever you give the sign."

Maurice did not pull away, and so Peter placed his lips to Maurice'e ear as he had done previously, but this time his excitement was clear to see. An uncertain Maurice became taut, unable to respond in kind. Hoping not to offend Peter, he blamed too much alcohol. Otherwise he was willing. Peter jested to make light of the difficulty.

"I am not a predator. Though I nibble at your ear I will not eat you up!"

Even as he said this, he invited Maurice once again, taking his hand as he had done before and leading it to the bulge of his crotch.

"Just so you know that I am a supplicant."

245

They rested that way for a time, Peter patient with his excitement, Maurice uncertain. Then Maurice was glad to leave. The taxi he called was waiting below.

The next morning, very early, he knew he needed affection, and so he telephoned before Peter could go off to work to tell him so.

Later that day he wrote the accustomed letter to Alec to tell him about the new friend who was helping him to cope with the sadness of separation.

*   *   *

In the weeks that followed Peter did not unduly press his desire, though he expanded his affection to Maurice's lips. Before each separation he held him tight enough for there to be shared sexual excitement. Maurice responded to this attention that made no immediate demand. As he tried to explain his own reserve, without discouraging further overtures, he found that he was confiding more about his years with Alec. The account expressed his feelings of satisfaction with details, but how of late his love had been frustrated. Often as he related Alec's sexual misconduct, he slipped into reproach, though it was clear that he loved Alec.

Peter could comfort Maurice's hurt feelings, because he had learned from his experience with divorce to be lenient in judgment, and because he had no motive to take anything from Alec who was doing what was needed to fulfill his fatherhood.

"The man was curious, and that got the lot of you into trouble. Since he is trying to love the child, you ought to do as much."

Amidst heartfelt pleas that what he most needed was a relationship with Alec that would henceforth be exclusive of adventures, Maurice acknowledged that Alec urged him to find good company as he could during their time apart. Peter was candid in embracing the suggestion. Why should Maurice not add sexual satisfaction to their time waiting which need not threaten his return to Alec? When Maurice insisted he did not want to encourage feelings that would likely end in disappointment, there was always a cheerful response from Peter.

"I see no problem now that we understand each other. I respect your commitment to Alec. I encourage you to offer the same devotion for Ben. Loyalty is among your charms. You know I have responsibilities and commitments, not as great as Alec's, but I lack his courage. I am not seeking the complications of loving a man and trying to live two men together in a society that exacts awful penalties for it. If I marry again, it will be with someone unencumbered, someone clear of heart enough to want commitment. What I seek with you is different. You are alone presently and sexually needful. I anticipate your body with a sexual excitement that I have not felt since you were a boy. There ought not be promises that will take anything from Alec or intimidate you by any claim from me. I will enjoy you as you feel, in love with another, yet troubled by his inaccessibility. You can use me for a time and appreciate that I care for you. Why should we not enjoy the physicality and friendship that will give us pleasure as long as it lasts, especially since Alec wisely wants that for you?"

When Peter promised, "I will see you off to Alec and America when it is right for you," this attitude resolved most of Maurice's tension, though he was content to bide the time as spring turned to summer.

*   *   *

"I am taking the children on a holiday to Brighton. Would you join me?"

When Maurice agreed, separate quarters were arranged for the children and their guardian, and another to be shared with Peter.

The first day at Brighton was a family outing on the beach. Only long after dark did Peter and Maurice find time for romance. All the time Maurice was building his anticipation until they took a playful swim that was invigorating. At midnight, in wet bathing suits they huddled between two blankets on a deserted beach.

"Your body is ready. Let us wait no longer."

Maurice said yes as Peter took charge of a sandy coupling.

When their first liaison was long accomplished, they returned to the room where they took showers. In the comfort of their bed they repeated an act of love that was remarkable for Peter who had never known male intercourse. For Maurice there was being possessed with such tenderness that despite his misgivings he would be ready to yield again.

*   *   *

The next day Peter was with the children while a tired Maurice sat on the beach faithfully writing to Alec. He would post a letter that afternoon.

"Writing is difficult today. I am alone on the beach where an occasional breeze deposits miniscule pebbles upon the page, enough to distort my penmanship. More than that, a mood of nostalgia weighs on me. Not a

247

feeling of loneliness, for I trust in your affection, and Peter will be with me soon. Rather, I am overcome by a deep recognition of how much and in what ways you have shaped me into dependence on your love. Since I do not regret this state, neither should you, except for regret of separation which is bound to cause so much pain. I will make good use of this holiday, observing Peter's behavior with his children, contemplating my future with you when I will be what you and Ben need."

On the other matter of issue Maurice was sparing.

"I hope you are pleased that I am accepting Peter's attentiveness to me, though it gives me queasiness. I wish I were beside you rather than anywhere. The truth of my heart, the nostalgia for being again in Manayunk, is that apart from you I am not completed. Everything I feel and do in the meantime is filling in absences and needs."

*   *   *

Nonetheless several nights running Maurice engaged in sexually satisfying encounters. He liked the way Peter told him of the beauty of his face and body in ways that were seductive.

Yet each morning when Maurice awoke his first thought was yearning for Alec. So it was true what he wrote, he did not feel completed apart from Alec.

There was no sense in dwelling on a missing lover, except when writing letters, because he did not wish to slump into spiritless waiting for a time that could not be appointed. He was thankful to be with Peter who seemed happy with him without commitments. When they were alone their conversation flowed easily, sometimes in serious vein, but more often finding reasons for humor.

*   *   *

In the months that followed Maurice shared Peter's bed. Not every night, for they were careful not to make it seem like marriage, though there were hints of it. By the start of winter there were occasional weekday mornings Maurice prepared breakfast—as he thought, and as he remarked, a preparation for the time he would be with Alec and Ben—then after seeing Peter off to work, tidied the bed and tended other housekeeping before returning to the Hall house. Peter reserved much of each week end for his children, but Sunday night for Maurice alone.

Maurice wrote almost daily to Alec to keep him informed of settlement of his mother's remaining property now that the house was Kitty's. He always noted the sadness he felt missing Alec and Oliver, and awaiting Ben. As for the English affair, the most he revealed was acknowledgment that he was fond of Peter and enjoyed his company. That curtailment he thought the right approach, for honesty ought to be measured differently than under ordinary circumstances which he hoped would soon be restored. Meantime, until he was at home when he would confess the truth, it was carefully considerate of Alec's hopeless situation, as Noreen's suffering worsened, to refrain from depicting his own sexual exploits, no matter that Alec had urged him to just that.

Such conduct raises a touchy ethical question, is truth literal or something more? Maurice never doubted the veracity of his heart. He clung steadfastly to memories of Alec rescuing him and thereafter directing his sexual course into utmost dependence. That bondage of desire as it grew rapidly, that surrender of freedom, had yet been liberating from the hopelessness of unmet sexual longings. Alec had instinctively acted to release Maurice from attachment to Clive who had been awarded the pinnacle of beauty and who offered rebuffs to Maurice's physical yearning. Real and vital sex with Alec had knocked Clive off that pedestal. Thanks to Alec, there was even further release from thwarted longings of a troubled youth, so that Maurice could see a handsome male without a heartsick feeling. His eroticism had settled with certainty—not just on someone of strong and worthy character, though that was a necessary ingredient—but on a body with natural beauty, especially its genitals, which in Maurice's vivid sensual recollection preserved their thrilling and compelling bondage. He knew where truth resided, and so did Peter. He was captive to that yielding. Henceforth anyone other or anything other was mere substitute. That was the truth conveyed to Alec.

*   *   *

News of Noreen's death came early in 1938 as the winter was waning, and later a letter from Alec paved Maurice's way home.

The end of the affair was different than either had expected. It was Maurice whose heart was heavy when the time came to say goodbye. For someone like Maurice, who needed to belong to someone, whose heartfelt trust was in fidelity, there was sadness in abridging intimacy. Habitual mingling of flesh with Peter had brought joy, and without any notice of its increase, deepening concern for his welfare that had grown into a dictate of monogamous love.

Peter made the separation easier than it might have been, for he remembered his first promise that temporary would be sufficient. Though he felt disappointment, he assured Maurice that return to America was the ending both of them knew was right.

"I have discovered I could love you, but there is too much in the way."

Maurice could only acquiesce.

"I am no longer English because I belong to Alec who is too bold for this society."

Maurice expressed what he felt as gratitude in a strange way. He offered a pledge of fidelity that only Peter could understand, loyalty to Alec as his deepest love, but the preservation in memory of Peter who would remain a source of strength and satisfaction.

Peter provided a final consideration to their affair, accompanying his anxious friend to Southampton where for the second time Maurice began the journey with Alec. This time the joy of returning to his lover was lessened by battered feelings from the knowledge of death and separation. Maurice wished, as no doubt Adam must once have hoped, that he were able to return to the innocence of youth—and who would not wish the same for him and for oneself?

Chapter 25

The Scudders

Ye wise men, highly, deeply learned,
Who think it out and know,
How, when, and where do all things pair?
Why do they kiss and love?
Ye men of lofty wisdom, say
What happened to me then.
Search out and tell me where, how, when,
And why it happened thus.

Cited by Schopenhauer

For nearly a year after the wedding Noreen lived, though less and less during her final months. Only Alec took note of the advance of disease because her illness was such that it was not apparent to casual observers as she tended to necessary public tasks. When she could no longer maintain appearances, she confined herself to the house, putting greater burden on Alec who cut his legal work in order to tend to family needs. Against advice from the doctor she continued taking Ben in the morning to the Catholic school halfway down the hill where he was in first grade, and meeting him at the end of the day to escort him two short blocks to the stairway that ascended the hill to their home. Ben playfully accounted the day at school, Noreen listening as cheerfully as she could, but exhausted by the climb which drained every bit of strength from her body.

Scudder family life was far into the year 1937 quiet and satisfactory which allowed a diligent Alec to learn the role of the wage-earning father. He spent days at his office or arguing a case in court, but John Smith made sure he was relieved of undue demands or complex litigation. Every evening was reserved for dinners Noreen prepared. Alec made a point of asking Ben about school so that he could encourage the boy's accomplishments. While the dishes were washed, Ben finished schoolwork, if he had dallied during the afternoon. There might still be time for the three of them to

251

listen to a radio program. At bedtime Alec would place a goodnight kiss on the boy's lips. Noreen would go with Ben to accompany him in prayers and to read a story, sometimes falling asleep beside him.

Alec deliberately put aside legal work each week end so that he could be with his new family and do household chores. Every other Saturday he took to washing the car. The coupe that had been Maurice's and his had been replaced by a four-door sedan appropriate for a family. Ben helped to soap the car and then as a reward for his work received instructions, "Sit at the wheel while I finish the job. Here is the brake. That is the gas pedal." Sometimes Alec would shout to the pretended driver, "Don't go over 25 while I rub it dry." When work was completed the driver would be switched so that they could head for a soda counter along Main Street.

Sundays fell into another sort of routine. At Noreen's behest Alec accompanied her to high mass at Saint John the Baptist Church beside the school. She dressed in finery according to season, and Ben's blue suit matched his father's. Noreen's pride to be with two handsome men offered her relief from preoccupation with her fate. Alec was also distracted from the ceremony which held no interest for him. The statues of saints scattered about the church carried him back to unpleasant pilgrimages to a London church where he had knelt beside his mother who bowed remorsefully before such images. Even then he had resolved to leave such pitiful behavior behind. But during Noreen's present crisis he did not think it right to refuse his company. He reconciled his presence in a church despite disbelief because it pleased Noreen that he was there. He had only to look at her to see she was comforted. Whatever other blessings flowed to these churchgoers, afterward they took a ride in their spacious sedan and went on to some restaurant where a pleasant dinner awaited. Later afternoon they went to a movie matinee to delight Ben.

Though her Catholic faith did not run deep, Noreen wanted something to be left the boy other than the memory of her glum departure. She hoped that attending mass and Catholic school would provide Ben spiritual support upon her death. When she prayed with him she conjured a heaven where in the company of angels she would watch over him. The first angel she counted on for Ben was Alec.

When she discussed these matters with Alec she oft repeated her wish that Ben continue in a religious school.

"I worry about his faith, that he sink into a sad outlook after losing his mother, and have no saint to help him. We vowed when we married in a church to raise him Catholic. Though you are not a believer, and I have not been faithful, will you see to it?"

Alec had no heart to argue otherwise.

*   *   *

Something less spiritual bothered Noreen, a matter of such delicacy
she hesitated to raise it, but as the time of her death was nearing she did
ask Alec how Ben would be affected living with two men who loved in
ways beyond society's acceptance. She tried to mitigate any offense that
might be taken from the utterance of common prejudice.

"You know I have given Ben to your care, not just because you are
his natural father, but because I trust you more than I do my family. I also
respect Maurice who means so much to you. He will help you to take good
care of our son. Only I wonder, is it not natural for men and women to
complement each other? Will two men have undue influence leading Ben
counter to his own nature?"

It was not as if Alec had not posed the same question to himself. He
had worked out an answer he hoped would assure her. His fears for Ben
lay in another direction.

"Do not trouble over it, you have already done your influencing. No
doubt things will be different when Maurice is here with me. There will be
no gender distinctions in our household. But Ben will not be without the
influence of women as if we lived in a monastery. He will be with the nuns
each school day. Your mother and sisters will also have their part."

Alec tried to educate Noreen about the mystery of sexual
preferences.

"Maurice and I are both offspring of ordinary parents," which he
thought good evidence that sexual disposition is not something straight
forward from instruction or demonstration, nor the fault of discrepancy.
The most he would concede was, "I never had the benefit of a father such
as I intend to be. Perhaps that will be of account in the boy's case."

Noreen acknowledged her shortcomings of education, nothing beyond
the commonplace. Now a shortened life would curtail any chance to
learn from diverse experience. She admitted she had not the least idea
whether the sexual feelings she or anyone possessed came from nature
or nurture. What she knew with certainty was that the outcome of Ben's
sexual feelings was a matter beyond her ken or control. Insofar as it was a
direction for him to choose, guidance would soon rest in hands other than
her own. Better Alec's than any other.

Following her right instinct she requested, "Show me patience and
kindness through this last ordeal that remains for us. Your tending to my
needs, and the mother I have been for him, will guide him in the ways of
love. When I am gone, it will not harm him to see there is another kind of
love you feel for Maurice."

Though she was comforted, Noreen had another fear, the same that concerned Alec, that the mean and punitive ways prevalent in society toward homosexual love would afflict Ben.

"No matter what Ben's ways, there will be much prejudice about you and Maurice. My own family is narrow, and there are many in this world heartless toward sexual conduct they don't approve. Having Ben out of wedlock brought me condemnation. Ben will learn how unusual you and Maurice are in your ways of loving. It hurts me that he will hear his father ridiculed, and that Maurice will suffer unwarranted hostility, when both of you deserve respect."

Alec was quick to agree that Ben would encounter misrepresentations of homosexuality.

"That is why I suspect the Catholic indoctrination he will get in the school and church. Most religious are assured their thinking comes from God and are too ready to inflict harm on men like me. But I have agreed to continue his learning at the school he attends. I will see it through. Just so you know that I will teach Ben philosophy so that he learns to think clearly, to shun common prejudices, and in good time to formulate an outlook that suits him."

"I hope Ben will love a woman, and you and Maurice."

"Ben will see for himself how Maurice and I act toward one another and toward others. We have to be honest and firm in defending ourselves. Not that I have always been so, but I will be tender to you as my wife, and he will remember how I treated you. He will honor women because he honors you. When Maurice is here, it will not harm Ben to see sensual affections of other sorts, so that when his own feelings come to the fore he will treat them as deserving. That is how he will learn what is true to his nature."

Some weeks later Noreen was resting with Alec seated beside her bed. He launched into what had become an ongoing detailing of his plans for the boy. In short time a weakened and weary Noreen was lulled into sleep. Had she been able to hear what was said she would have mostly approved.

"It is important that Ben be told the truth about sexuality as soon as he wonders enough to ask. Such instruction will be in accord with my understanding of things. I approve sexual enjoyment and will encourage him to explore for insights of his own. When his body and mind mature sufficiently to prompt questioning, I will be attentive to his nature, as will Maurice. No doubt he will suffer his share of rebuffs and disappointments due to his own choices, and maybe because of the deeds of his parents judged by meanness of some."

When Noreen stirred to show she was listening, Alec broached the most imminent concern.

"Before Ben gets to explore sexuality, he will be forced to face your death. His little heart will be overwhelmed with loss and uncertainty. He will struggle in his mind's solitude, but I will hold him until he feels secure again. I have no dogmas to offer him, no religious truth to impose. He must go on without comforting answers or find his own. Awareness of suffering is the way to sympathy and compassion for other creatures, how the spirit grows, just so there are many joys of sensuality to nourish it."

Noreen half listened to Alec reciting views that were shaped by Freud about the sexual instinct being bisexual and ready to respond in a welcoming way to whatever is of pleasure, and the importance of a mother's behavior in the formation of a child's capacity to love, such imprints forming layers of the unconscious. These were Alec's searches for understanding that were soon to be shared with Ben.

She nodded approvingly as she whispered, "I am confident in your reasoning. You will help Ben to discover even more on his own." Then she rested with consolation that her boy would draw more satisfaction from life than had been her allotment.

*   *   *

The bed Alec slept in, with Noreen for only a few months, was Maurice's. It was replete with erotic memories of all that he had done with Maurice. Alec was never able to detach it from those exciting events.

Yet the rest of the house took on important new memories as Alec learned to love Noreen, differently than he did Maurice, but no less concerned for her welfare. No matter how lonely he sometimes felt, he did not regret his present role as husband, nor did he fail to honor the past. Maurice was central to his erotic attachment. Atop a chest of drawers that held his belongings a photograph of Noreen and Alec's wedding half faced another of a handsome Maurice together with him. There was no competition of these loves as they were directed to Alec, or of Alec for them. As if to moderate any such pulls, a charming picture of Ben stood between.

*   *   *

Eventually Noreen felt it necessary to move to another room of her own because her body needed stillness as she often lay awake in discomfort and anxiety. It became a room half hospital where she could suffer unseen.

Left to his own bed, Alec felt he had begun the return to Maurice. Though generally weary when he retired to a night of needed rest, he could only find sleep after satisfying himself with his hand as he fantasized about the past and future. This offered him momentary relief from the grim present he was witnessing of pain and anguish.

He sought his friends who offered help, Tony bringing his boys to play with Ben, and Andrew coming by to comfort Noreen. John Smith was careful that Alec not be overburdened by legalities come the week end. It was Leery who proved Alec's confidante. They met occasionally for lunch but these days it was Alec who poured out his anxieties and longings. Leery proved a patient listener, finding Alec attractive as ever, but when he heard of going to church because Noreen wished it, he feared Alec might be slipping into metaphysical thinking. Several days later there arrived by mail a copy of "Major Barbara" that was inscribed, "Lest you forget that wonderful lesson" which Alec took as a warning against hoping for more than this world had to offer.

Of course the greatest comfort came from Maurice's letters which, though sent regularly, arrived irregularly. Sometimes three or even four would arrive in the same mail. Then Alec would find time to himself, in his room at night or even at work, so that he could hold the letters close and dream of his lover. These intimate links of words and sentiments sustained him during each day's cares for he went on believing that the world so sad yet held recompense.

*   *   *

As the end neared Noreen was too weak to make her way to meals below or partake of the food. Alec set up a smaller table a few feet from her bed where Ben and he could eat within her view if not always her company. She smiled as she could and talked softly of their interests so as not to trouble the men of her life. Then a time came when it became clear she was no longer able to be with them in any degree of consciousness.

These last days Alec put aside his professional work and when he was not sitting with Noreen he hovered over Ben. There was morphine to silence the ordeal of the patient but there was no such relief for Alec. As if the scales of justice were balancing, Alec suffered in dread akin to Maurice's ocean voyage. But such a figure does no justice to Noreen who bore it all so silently.

At bedtime Ben would kneel beside Noreen's bed so that she could touch him as they prayed. Alec stood apart to allow them intimacy, though he was close enough to hear her words that repeated such thoughts, as much for the boy's ears as any, "Dear Mary, heavenly mother. Lead Ben to Jesus and to love Alec, his father on this earth, and Maurice as a good man." She thanked God for Ben and Alec, and more than once she added Maurice into the reckoning for she counted on his caring for Ben. After the boy made a closing sign of the cross and kissed his mother's cheek, Alec would lead him to his bedroom where Oliver kept him company for the night.

She did her best, as honestly as one may address a seven-year old, to instruct Ben regarding prejudices he was bound to face. "When people ask about Maurice, say he is your uncle, but that he takes care of you like a father. Say no more, no matter what you hear. Be sure to respect and show thanks to your father. He loves you and Maurice will love you likewise."

At the very end she whispered, "Remember, even though you do not see me, I always love you. I will be happy knowing your father will see to your good. Trust him and tell him what you are thinking and feeling."

Her last meaningful words to Alec, despite their sadness, were meant to be encouraging.

"You are the only man I have loved other than Ben. Please take care of our boy."

Not long afterward, aided by morphine, she slipped into a coma until death released her spirit from the cares of this life.

*   *   *

There was a church funeral because Noreen wanted some blessing upon her soul. Poor Ben was dazed and baffled by the terrible events. So too was Alec who found that he was battling the premises of mortal life. It was too far removed from his heart's wishes that a boy could be left without a mother who had for all her years been devoted. There was no comfort to be found in religion or science. What seemed of immediate purpose was to hold Ben and assure him that he was in hands assigned to the task by the very mother he loved.

Tony insisted Alec come to spend some days with his family, for Rita's cooking, and so that Ben would be with boys. Alec partially accepted the hospitality, daytime only, for he thought it best at night to be with Ben in the same room that he had inhabited with Noreen and soon Maurice. They would talk or read, and after Ben had silently prayed, Alec would kiss him and hold him in affectionate embrace until the time of sleep. He thought

257

of Maurice, remembered him doing the same for Leslie. He could not help but wonder how closely linked are the expressions of love whether filial or any other kind. He was confident Ben would benefit in all love's domain from this affection which was so badly needed by both.

Following the funeral he waited some days to inform Maurice by telegraph, preferring it to the telephone, so there could be no instantaneous response in the sentiment of the moment. He instructed Maurice to await a letter that would soon follow containing an important proposal.

Chapter 26

A Proposal of Marriage

My true love hath my heart, and I have his.
By just exchange, one for the other given.
I hold his dear, and mine he cannot miss.
There never was a better bargain driven.
His heart in mine keeps me and him in one.
My heart in him his thoughts and senses guides.
He loves my heart, for once it was his own,
I cherish his, because in me it bides.

Sir Philip Sidney, "Arcadia"

With Noreen gone, loneliness and exhaustion enveloped Alec who wished Maurice to rush back to reclaim his place. His needs had never been greater, for watching the wasting away of Noreen cast him deeply into grief, while Ben needed comforting that Maurice could help provide. He wished to pick up the telephone to urge his desperation, but that would be unseemly after all he had forced upon Maurice, in effect sending him into exile across the Atlantic.

During the months since that rude and dismal departure, Maurice had written copiously of his longing that their lives be rejoined, but all Alec had time to reply were factual letters that briefly recounted the woes of watchful waiting. Only once had he poured out his love, and that was the letter he had put into Maurice's hand at the dock as he was returning to England. Therein he stated everything he had to say, as far as he could imagine. After that his emotions were sparsely expressed because he falsely thought it would be easier for Maurice to make a better accommodation if he were not drawn into Alec's troubles. Now, an eternity of experience and emotion later, when he was ready to close the gap, it would be presumptuous to think there was not much they had to say and resolve.

He sent Ben to spend Sunday with his grandmother so that he could write a careful and necessary letter that should be above all honest. The end he had in sight was Maurice becoming part of a new Scudder family. That afternoon he wrote such a letter.

*   *   *

My dear Maurice:

I address you in the hope of taking us back to the time we first came to know one another, you were sir and I an underling. That is not to discount all of the feelings that have grown between us in the years since, nor do I approach you as anything but equals. Only that it seems we need start afresh, with the innocence and hope we once had, as if just setting out across the Atlantic – if that were possible, which it is not. There are different circumstances than our first start. Yet the decision is as momentous for we need to risk everything in order to live together.

I will tell you what I wish. Then it is for you to decide whether to start the journey anew.

It must be obvious, even an ocean apart, that I am no more the carefree lover who thrilled you aboard the Olympic. For years hence I come with a dependent Ben who is mine to nurture and safeguard. That is what I mean to accomplish. I hope you will join me in this task by accepting Ben as our son.

No longer in our first voyage, this time I am beset with sorrow. I grieve for Noreen who lost everything on this earth. Her death perplexes me more than I can understand. For how long I will be weighed with sadness I can not say. There is no comfort from Andrew and his theologians, nor any from worldly philosophers. Grief must run its course, for I wish to remember Noreen. Helplessly I watched the painful struggle she endured without losing sight of Ben's welfare. I will remember her as Ben's mother and be grateful to her for a priceless gift.

I am restless that you come home. I wish it were at once. But when I stop to reason, it is better for you to carefully consider, as you must have done already many times, what changes and hardships will face us. You will have to cope with the grief that afflicts Ben and me. Mine will be diminished with your presence, but not gone, and what about the boy? For a time you will have to live with our dark feelings that may revive troublesome doubts of your own. Do not misunderstand, I will be thrilled to hold you again each night with excitement.

But there is another price for you, that you never allow jealousy to erupt violently in times you are disappointed with me or with Ben. You must be certain that my desire for Noreen was never the powerful passion that *drives me to claim your body and your heart. I beg your forgiveness for making our lives complicated. Still, I insist that you never scorn Noreen who entrusted Ben to you as well as me. That is the only way to help Ben who will grow to love you in her stead.*

If these emotional demands are too much, it is better you stay in England awhile longer until they are resolved. You might cultivate your friendship with Peter who seems a good man. You are fond of him and he has helped you to be calm. There is a chance you take in either direction.

I offer this proposal by letter so that you can contemplate your interests and mood. I am not being gallant, though there is a part of me that way. It is, rather, that I know full well how quickly physical attraction might pull us together. I do not want you acting on that impulse and coming before you are ready. That is not what is good for you or for Ben or for me.

I need your trust. I have mended things regarding Noreen and Ben. When it comes to the ways I deceived and surprised you, it needs repeating now, and however often a sense of betrayal troubles you, I regret my dishonesty. What I did with Noreen I thought a harmless adventure, though it has not turned out that way. I should have told you from the start what I did. Then I would have heeded your displeasure. Encountering your pain years after has convinced me that libertine sexuality does not suit us.

If good can come from bad, we have the chance to begin again with greater prospect for we have come to be forgiving. There is a beautiful boy, from my flesh in a way of speaking, that same flesh you have caressed. Ben will be yours, as if we made him together. We shall train him into a man.

When you used to speak of marriage I made light of the idea. My mood has changed. Though I care nothing for ritual, I propose marriage. We can agree to a union of love in which we accept the weaknesses of the other and encourage the strengths. In that way, and every useful way possible for us, we will be married if you wish. Nothing could make me happier than such a commitment. I will never again deceive you.

If only this entreaty could be in the youthful spirit of joy and simplicity of our original venture! But we are encumbered by disappointments. The burden is not without benefit, for we are both wiser with passage of time. I have learned to express love in ways I did not earlier imagine. Yet I am as certain as during our first year together that it is only to you I could make the promise to be a faithful life companion and it is only from you I wish that same promise for myself and Ben.

I have reason to hope you will act boldly, as you did on our first venture, so that we are reunited as soon as is practical for you. There is a marriage bed needs using, though at present Ben and Oliver are keeping your place. They will yield it because I need you next to me.

Alec

*   *   *

Maurice did not hesitate to make arrangements for his return to America in the spring of 1938 before war engulfed Europe. The Hall property had long been settled. Maurice's heart was decided, but he did not want to botch the matter of separating from an intimate friend.

The end of the affair was different than either he or Peter had expected. Maurice's heart was heavy with departure. He did not know how to leave a lover. It was easier for Peter who had never wanted anything complicating because he was not recovered from disillusion after believing marriage would last, only to find he was mistaken. For Maurice there had never been abandonment, something Peter understood from the start. Maurice's love was no mistake.

"You are a man I could love," he assured Maurice, "But there is too much in the way. I am not sure what lies ahead for me. I enjoy our intimacy, but I respect your heart and will find satisfaction knowing I sent you back to Alec ready for him."

Maurice had gained a deeper understanding of Alec's adventurism. He was surprised and uncomfortable that he could love two men at the same time. He wished to remain close to Peter, to see him through his uncertainties, but his heart had long ago yielded to Alec and it was Alec's needs that dictated what his course must be. Peter made it easier by assuring him he would remember their intimacy joyfully.

Their last night together, Maurice's heart began its mending. He made love with Peter, believing it their last time, enjoying lavish words of his beauty accompanied by excited deeds. Yet Maurice's thoughts were already distant. Alec had invaded his mind with anticipation. It gave him strange security to recall he had never when intimate with Alec thought of anyone but him. Still he held Peter to his body with affection.

Early in the morning they drove to the station and Maurice said goodbye.

"Thank you for a special friendship that I must carry to another land. I am no longer English. I belong to Alec who is too bold for this society."

Chapter 27

Raising Ben

Lad of Athens, faithful be
To thyself,
And Mystery.
All the rest is Perjury.

Emily Dickinson

Maurice's return brought joy nearly all round, most demonstrably to Oliver who quickly forgot the year apart, least for Ben whose heart was unclear. Noticing some hesitation, Maurice was unsure where he stood with the boy. His first day home he was relieved when Alec, eager for privacy, saw Ben and Oliver to their bedroom earlier than usual. There was no mistaking Alec's welcome to their bed of old where he was exuberant in restoring that passion which had initially drawn them together. He took liberty of possession as he had done aboard the Olympic. Their hearts were transported to that voyage of blissful memory, the doubts and fears that then existed forgotten because replaced by new ones.

But any hope for a honeymoon was a thing of the past if only because of Ben's presence. There could be none of the insouciance of an ocean voyage, no carefree breakfasts with Graham, nor any leisurely lolling away of afternoons reading and resting in deck chairs. Ben was used to rising at a certain time, going off to school and returning in the afternoon to the care of a parent. His needs had to be met, including the supervision of homework and an evening family meal. These considerations and other arrangements Maurice wished to help accommodate.

After a few days Maurice returned to the bank where changes had occurred requiring him to adjust to different personnel. Not that there was any doubt of his status, for his uncle had been elevated to president, which counted importantly in Maurice's favor. George was more remote than in the past, less at his desk, but Charles Perry was close at hand to help in day to day work. He and Albert also extended support beyond the bank as they tried to cushion the domestic demands on Maurice. They insisted on helping with Ben, as they had done toward Noreen's end, which freed a week end of the resumed Hall-Scudder domestic life so that Maurice and Alec could spend time at an old inn along the Delaware River.

Whether the inn's claims of having harbored illustrious colonial personages were true or not, it did not matter who had long ago rested within its walls to Alec and Maurice. Just so the four-pillared bed was strong enough for their vigorous play and nearby were woods to walk. They hiked Saturday morning in settings reminiscent of their first conversation when they had feigned hunting on the Durham grounds.

Maurice had to bare his secret.

"I need to tell you of Peter."

"By all means, whatever you wish to say, but don't feel guilty. We can dispense with sacramental confession, leaving that to Andrew. You will not be blamed for overcoming the hurt and loneliness you felt. I am pleased and grateful to Peter for helping you through an awful year. You are returned to me more loving than ever."

Maurice was put at ease.

"We are both thankful to Peter. He knew, as you did, how desperate I was for intimacy, yet he was patient and persistent. It was last summer at the seashore that I embraced him. It took me time to follow your sound advice because I am not adventurous in love, not seeking sexual experience for titillation. You recall my attention to Leslie when we invited him into our bed. I delighted in his body, yet it was half-hearted on my part. The same was true with Peter, though his sexual ways are like to yours."

"Do you miss Peter's physical attentions? Is there anything more for me to do?"

Maurice laughed aloud, though reassuringly, "This is no complaint."

"You have shown too much excitement in bed for me to doubt. Just that I am curious if I might be a better lover, if you will guide me, adding a bit of Peter to my ways."

Maurice might have laughed at this way of putting things. Instead, he set the matter right. He explained how he prized the Alec who had climbed to his room, taken possession of his body and then of his heart. That perfect moment he had dreamed about all the year apart.

*   *   *

As they paused at a lovely spot aside the Delaware River, Maurice's thoughts flowed to the lusty advices of Whitman. He had carried his copy of the poetry to give him strength to speak forthrightly of what had occurred in England and to assert his hopes for their future. He found in the **Calamus** collection which is called after the flower of that name, "Come, I am determined to unbare this breast of mine. I have long enough stifled and choked," as he began culling lines that expressed tellingly both the poet's and his own lover's spirit.

> *"In paths untrodden,*
> *In the growth by margins of pond-waters,*
> *Escaped from the life that exhibits itself,*
> *From all the standards . . .*
> *Which too long I was offering to feed my soul,*
> *Clear to me now standards not yet published,*
> *I proceed for all who are or have been young men,*
> *To tell the secret of my nights and days,*
> *To celebrate the need of comrades."*

"That is a good beginning to our resumed journey as comrades," Alec said. This encouraged Maurice to continue.

> *"O here I last saw him that tenderly loves me,*
> *and returns again never to separate from me,*
> *and this henceforth the token of comrades, this calamus-root shall*
> *interchange it youths with each other."*

The calamus is a flower whose tendrils entwine for strength like "two boys together clinging" or "a leaf for hand in hand, you natural persons old and young." Whitman took his pen in hand to depict such love and to decry the separation of "two simple men I saw today on the pier in the midst of the crowd, parting the parting of dear friends, the one to remain hung on the other's neck and passionately kissed him, while the one to depart tightly pressed the one to remain in his arms."

Maurice chose a poem to speak such love.

> *"When he whom I love travels with me a long while holding my hand,*
> *Then I am charged with untold and untellable wisdom.*
> *I am silent, I require nothing further,*
> *I cannot answer the question of appearances,*
> *But I walk or sit indifferent, I am satisfied,*
> *He ahold of my hand has completely satisfied me."*

Alec took hold of Maurice's hand, the ring he had given him in place, their acknowledgment "he ahold of my hand has completely satisfied me." They walked in thoughtful accord for miles along the river.

*   *   *

With hearty appetites they opted for an extravagant dinner at the inn, purportedly colonial in fare, which went so well Maurice hesitated to undo its romantic direction. But he was determined not to put off exposure of unspoken doubts hanging over their happiness. Alec needed to bare his soul. Maurice asked about Noreen's end, painful as it would be to hear, and even more painful for Alec to tell. During the detailed recollection of the somber scenario Alec was brought to sobbing by the terrible end.

"I witnessed the rapid destruction of Noreen's body and, near the end, of her soul—for she was driven to paranoia by the suffering. She succumbed to fear that she was being punished for her sin. Yet it was not her sin, but mine."

Though he had listened silently, Maurice could not hold back reproving Alec for any assumption of guilt. All the anguish Maurice had suffered in England was not without some humbling of its own. He had made up his mind not to wallow in self-pity. There was no room in his mind for condemnation of sin.

"What if Ben were to do the same someday and place a woman in predicament? Would we not understand? Noreen did nothing sinful, nor did you. I will not have you bear such torment. We have experienced too much joy as outlaws to ever be harsh toward sexual ventures. I love you too much to let go of youthful innocence."

How grateful Alec was that Maurice had transcended narrowness of judgment, thanks in part to Peter.

"What I said of sin comes from the pain of suffering by the innocent, I mean Noreen, which is beyond my comprehension. For the moment I slipped into Noreen's way of speaking. I know sexual joy is healthy and not to be condemned. You and I ought always be youthful when it comes to that."

They returned to their room where, ensconced in their four-pillared bed and Alec again comfortable within Maurice's forgiveness, they were able to recover the lusty sprit of Whitman. This week end at the inn would hold a tender place in their erotic memories, subsidiary only to the untouchable Olympic voyage.

*   *   *

It was a troubled Ben who faced loneliness far too early, barely eight years upon this earth, deprived of the only steady companion he had known. Alec was able to comfort him, but he had still to make up for the lost years of fatherhood in winning the boy's trust and affection. A start had been made while Alec cared for Noreen during her waning days, that example more precious than any words could speak. Still, with Maurice back into the picture there was bound to be insecurity for Ben who had never had to share a parent.

There was no need for Alex to explain his feelings for Maurice, something Noreen had already told their son. She assured Ben he would be fortunate to have a second guardian akin to a father, though she cautioned him never to mention anything more than that Maurice was a "good friend" who shared their home, and in equally strong tone, "You must never be ashamed of your father or Maurice, no matter what anyone says." Alec's intent to lead Ben into philosophy was of little comfort to Noreen because she knew from her own family and worldly observations that bigotry was common when it came to male love. Ben would need as he grew into a man to stand against the bigotries surrounding sexual convention, lest he feel shame for what ought to be appreciated, if only Maurice would be won to the role of caring parent.

Maurice was outwardly recovered from the anger and the jealously he had felt upon learning of Ben's existence and the despair when Alec married. Yet there was still deeply buried anxiety to be laid to rest. Though he had brought reason to bear and found grounds to accept Alec's conduct, the scars of the mind do not ever heal completely to the point of total forgetfulness. Beyond that soreness of heart, he felt a nagging anxiety and uncertainty he could win Ben's love. It would be easy to be a congenial companion as before to Alec, even easier his sexual partner. Yet more would be needed than taking sexual repossession of one another. New expectations would be pressed upon him by a family of his own. Without understanding why it had to be so, he knew that change would come through his dealings with Ben in everyday situations. The way to bind their hearts as never before would be Ben.

*   *   *

Such opportunities presented themselves readily. It was not long before an evening came when Alec was busy with legal papers, and he was quick to chastise the boy over some minor annoyance, too much lively play while Alec was trying to concentrate. There was only a brief reprimand, but Maurice deplored this show of anger against the innocent.

267

Alec's tone of voice reminded him of the bitter incident when he had fallen victim to violence. He gently led Ben away, Oliver in tow, to help him to quick forgetfulness by play.

Later he reproached Alec, "We ought not show anger over irritations," and then he pointedly added, "Your harsh words carry horrible memories for me. We must never allow violence into our house, not even in words."

Alec had anticipated that he would need forgiveness again and again from Maurice. He called to Ben who returned sheepishly, and with the boy as witness took Maurice into his arms.

"I struck Maurice once in anger. Maurice has forgiven me, but he saw my harshness which has hurt you and him. I need you to forgive me. I promise never to act in a mean way. It is wrong to hurt anyone. Do you understand this, Ben?"

Ben nodded thoughtfully that he understood. He had grown close to Oliver and would never think of hurting him.

*   *   *

Not long after this Alec announced a decision he had been pondering during the time Maurice was away.

"I am going to open an office of my own here in Manayunk. I have talked to John and he will assist the move."

To Maurice's practical queries Alec answered that he wanted to be closer to home so that he could keep an eye on Ben. Besides, he was not satisfied serving the corporate world which provided the bulk of income to Smith and Smith. Better to serve individual justice.

"It will be tight at first. Rent to be paid, and I will need a part-time secretary. Likely income will hardly pay for these. I will have to hope some small clients will come along. John will refer some cases."

That summer a sign went up on a building across from the Terminal Hotel along Main Street: *Alec Scudder, Attorney at Law.* Thus began a round of divorces, wills, collection of debts, traffic accident injuries, petty crimes—with small profit to show. Some months later, when one of Alec's cases got attention in the press, it marked an upward turn in his career. There was more humor and poignancy in the case than anything sensational. A young man, rising to a dare while intoxicated, robbed a local gas station with a toy gun. That it was prank was evidenced by his demand for only one dollar! Equally telling, the robber had talked casually with the attendant, a former high school acquaintance who after filling the gas tank had cooperatively handed over a dollar. The crime was nevertheless filed as "armed robbery" and could have had serious implications. Alec was able to get the charge dropped in exchange for a public apology and community service which won plaudits from the local paper. After that, the Scudder practice grew quickly to the point he needed a secretary and a junior partner.

Meantime, finding more time at home was still not easy.

*   *   *

Maurice was ever watchful and growing more protective of Ben. Some months had passed when Alec was slouched in his favorite chair after supper either dozing or lost in thought. Ben was standing at a distance, remembering earlier reprimands, uncertain whether to approach his father or in any way to seek consolation for something troubling him. The boy's heart was longing for his mother. He had not yet learned to address Maurice with such concerns. When Maurice came from the kitchen and noticed the sadness, he brushed his hand across Ben's forehead as if arranging his hair.

"Alec, Ben may want to be with you."

An awakened Alec reached out to Ben, "Let us go for a walk with Oliver." Outdoors in the coolness of night their mood grew more collected around the grief that had to be accounted.

"Look how happy Oliver is. Life is sad some time, even for Oliver when he has an upset stomach or when he is alone too long. I know you are feeling sad. I lost my mother, too. I was older than you. Still it hurt to be without her. I thought I would always feel loneliness. But I knew my mother wanted me to seek happiness and so I welcomed it when it came. Now I have Maurice, and I have you and a happy Oliver. That makes me happy. Do you remember your mother telling you that she wanted you to be happy with me and Maurice? Do you remember her saying that she would be watching over you? Do you know the kind of person she hoped you would become? Not a sad boy, but one who would study at school and enjoy play, and be secure with me, and Maurice, too."

Ben did nothing to show his appreciation of these words except to surprise Oliver with a hug.

When they were at home after a long walk, Maurice sat Ben down in the kitchen, "time for ice cream." Plates were provided, Oliver included, for this was no occasion to skimp. Then Maurice saw to bedtime preparations and read a story until Ben fell asleep.

*   *   *

Thus Ben grew accustomed to listening to his two fathers as they fashioned themselves into a family. Much of the evening the boy belonged to Alec but the afternoon after school to Maurice. Ben would accompany Maurice on grocery trips along Main Street. One afternoon while Maurice was making selections at the butcher shop, Ben stared at the carcasses of what had once been living lambs or pigs.

That evening when Maurice served supper Ben avoided eating the meat on his plate.

"No appetite?" Alec prodded. No response came, and as the meal continued there was concern in the air. After another prodding, Ben gave an explanation.

"You told me it is wrong to hurt an animal."

Ben had awakened to the grim discovery that what was on the table had once been a living animal who deserved affection and tenderness. He did not wish to eat such wicked fare that required killing an animal as precious as Oliver.

Alec decided equivocation or any lie was not right, even less in this case, as he recalled his own repugnance to the Scudder butchery. He had not been able to answer himself why a human being should add unnecessary violence to a world already beset with natural calamities. Eventually he had settled on utilitarian argument that beasts devour one another, and so it was natural for man to do the same. But now he wanted to nourish Ben different than his own youth, with a diet of consideration and compassion, in the philosophical light that humans could be more than beasts, though their arrogant claim to moral superiority could not be established by killing animals for pleasures of the palate. He took Ben's plate, removed the bloody token, and piled an extra heap of mashed potatoes where dead flesh had rested.

"There, nothing bloody on your plate. You need never eat anything that comes at the expense of an animal's life."

He cleared his own plate of the meat.

"You can have a bigger portion of sweets," was Maurice's contribution to a wholesome outcome.

It was only after Ben had been put to bed Maurice expressed some doubt about this moral instruction due to Ben.

"It is going to be even harder to raise Ben than I feared. I hoped treating one another kindly, with proper respect to others, would be enough. But now compassion for animals as well! We have a sensitive boy in our hands."

"His loss has imposed anxiety regarding death. Why should animals die any more than his mother? If we are to encourage him, we need to show consistency in what we say to him and what we do. You heard me forego violence in our lives. I have had the last of meat!"

"At his age I had no scruple about animals. Even now I do not feel remorse about what I eat. I suppose English customs abetted by Anglicanism helped me avoid such dilemmas. Maybe Ben needs that amount of religion? Perhaps I could take him to the Episcopal Church each Sunday? Andrew would certainly take to him."

"Religious school is enough. I never promised abundance of superstitions. There will be no more priests to tell him our sort of love is vile while they do violence to God's creatures in the name of God."

"You are right. Yet we both had boyhood instructions of saints and religion. Did it harm us?"

"I do not know that it did me harm, but it did no good. None of that malarkey is for Ben. He deserves knowledge that will help him to understand nature and human behavior. How will fear of an unknown God benefit him? Better that we forego violence and respect living creatures insofar as it lies within our power, and admit to him that we have only good sentiments and our own use of reason to offer. I am ready to encourage Ben's sympathy with animals in refusing to add to their suffering. He sees the hypocrisy of loving stuffed animals and eating real ones. Helping Ben, we can improve ourselves by leading lives as peacefully as possible. Do you remember our first walk together when I seduced you from Clive's bloody grip?"

Maurice welcomed the lighter touch. "I am ready to give up eating rabbit."

Alec was not jesting. Meat disappeared from their joint table. The line was drawn so that eggs and dairy products accompanied whole grains, vegetables, legumes and fruits, as well as the sweets every boy enjoys. Maurice relegated his meat eating to times when he was out.

*   *   *

This brought fathers and son closer as did other occurrences. Alec was taking a bath one evening after a long day of work, a habit he had acquired to please Maurice. The door was partly ajar so that Ben watched as his father reclined in the tub. He stood there for a time before Alec noticed him.

"Come here, Ben." As the boy did so, Alec splashed water upon him clothing and all. "Join me in the water and I'll wash you clean."

Ben quickly stepped out of his clothing, as if he had been awaiting the invitation, and climbed into the oversize tub. The two splashed so noisily it drew Maurice's attention. He had supervised Ben's baths many times—never like this—as for the first time he viewed Ben simply as a charming boy, not a troubled one.

Alec got to the serious bathing as he soaped Ben from head to toe with a running commentary on the virtue of cleanliness. Then he took his own penis in hand to roll back the foreskin to show how cleanliness of that body part was gained.

"Hold your cock firmly while you clean it."

Alec asked whether it felt good handling himself that way and if it brought sexual thoughts.

For Ben the word sexual had little meaning, and that little was far from erotic. He had only curiosity, not yet having found such pleasure on his own and with only the vaguest idea of what interplay of penis might occur with another person. But he did as his father instructed, took his miniscule cock into hand and cleaned it roughly, a good practice for what the future held of interplay.

When they were rinsed, Alec toweled the boy dry while Maurice was watching approvingly. He provided a tender hug to the boy.

"I love my Ben, I love you as your mother did. Maurice loves you, too."

Maurice stepped forward to provide the boy a hug. Then he gazed at Alec's nudity, at the source of his fatherhood, with a surge of erotic feeling.

Later that night he lamented to Alec, "My father never told me he loved me."

"Nor mine."

*   *   *

Maurice came intuitively to an awareness that one of them had to provide a kind of nurturing that would act in place of Noreen. Two fathers were fine, but there was need for a mother. The way society was structured someone had to tend to the minute tasks of daily living and see to the care of the boy's body and mind from waking to nightfall, accompanying hand in hand the journey through childhood. Not that two people should fail to cooperate, but the timing of those services was not that of the industrial or professional world.

Maurice saw quickly enough this was not an assignment for Alec who was better suited for society's image of a man. Alec had lived up to gender expectation by fostering a child and marrying. As was customary for men, he was away from home for long stretches doing the work of the world. There was no easy opportunity to see Ben home from school or

272

supervise his day. It fell to Maurice with banker's hours to provide what was needed.

Circumstances dictated that he put aside his reserves about the feminine gender and discover whatever he could to support his role as a nurturing parent alike to Noreen. There is no use to argue that such arrangement was arbitrary, more so in the case of two men raising a child. Social convention presumed there would be a woman, a wife, who would be carrying another child within her womb while at home watching over a brood. All of this was a social construct that in our own time is being altered. But in the days when Ben was a boy, Maurice acted as any man or woman ought to do. He did not complain of tasks that he faced each day because of the presence of Ben, nor explain that he was troubled along this lonely path, for he did not dare to confide in Alec his misgivings about the loss of his manliness. He ran full force into his own misogyny. The thought of being akin to a woman was confusing. So much of his life had been constantly proving himself a man that it was like clinging to life. His understanding came slowly and painfully that his fear of acting like a woman was the dreadful legacy of homophobia, both his and Alec's. He had to overcome the dread of being less than fully male, if not a fairy, yet something queer, neither man nor woman but some amalgam that stripped the attractiveness of wholeness. Alec preferred a man, and Maurice might suffer in standing.

Less a rational solution than a pull at Maurice's heart eventually decided the matter. Day by day Maurice learned to address each occasion as he gave care to the boy whose dependency grew apace. Eventually Ben's needs prevailed. Maurice slipped into a new calling. He loved Ben more and more until without reservation.

Maurice remained Maurice, however. He drew the line when it came to cooking, as much from pride as ineptitude. He found a neighbor, Rosa Francesca, who came each weekday afternoon to prepare a meal. It was wonderful to come home to the smells of Rosa's cooking, with lots of vegetables and cheese as she was instructed, except that she slipped some meat into the pot for flavor, removing the evidence for Oliver's pleasure. She even made bread once a week and more often earthy pies which so pleased Maurice that he paid her more than had been agreed, so much so that the woman insisted on coming with two teenage daughters to do housecleaning on Saturdays, which had not been part of the bargain. What else could Maurice do than reward her even more!

Not only eating but order improved in the Hall domain in ways that would have pleased Noreen. Rosa saw that things were done, not just cooking, but things Ben ought to do. He learned to work and took well to discipline. Saturday mornings he liked to watch the girls at their work and lightening their task by offering a hand. Though they laughed to themselves, they found him too earnest to tease, and too charming not to fawn over him. With only their noticing, Ben's sexuality was leaning their way.

*　　　*　　　*

When Ben's ninth birthday came in June of 1939, Maurice took care of the arrangements for a Saturday afternoon party. A few girls who lived nearby and some boys who were his third grade classmates were invited, among them a special friend, Jimmy, the one Ben preferred above all the others. The Friday afternoon before the party Ben brought bad news. Jimmy could not come to the party, the explanation being, "His mother said she did not trust a house with two men living together," nothing else specified.

Maurice was consternated but he calmly asked, "What do you feel about that?"

"He said he would come, anyway."

"No, Jimmy cannot come to the party without his mother's permission. You tell him he would be welcome, but that he must obey his mother. I don't want you to feel angry or hurt because your father and I do not live as most other people do."

"My mother told me I should never be hurt by bad things that were said about my father or you. I just want Jimmy to know only good things happen here. Then his mother will know."

Ten children came to celebrate the birthday, and when the party ended they returned happily and safely to their homes, all the better for the frolicking of an afternoon.

When Ben was back at school come Monday, Jimmy had a gift for him, a set of colorful marbles for the games they would play during the summer soon to begin.

"You will come to my birthday next year. It will be better than this one."

Thus Ben was learning from Maurice and Alec to treat humankind tenderly, in a way that, were it common, would promise a more peaceful future for our species.

*　　　*　　　*

Whatever the ways that were helping Ben develop good character, his small quest for harmony with nature and man was in stark contrast to the harsh realities of the surrounding world. Countless millions were out of work and victimized by war as Japanese armies took hold of China. In Europe, most spectacularly in Germany, economic desperation and confusion led to angry readiness to follow nationalist movements that saw the fault in foreign enemies and the solution in war for territorial plunder. Sadly but truly, humans had found no other way to treat one another.

A dark mood descended upon Maurice as the clouds of war enveloped England. When German bombs demolished London he was glad his mother was no longer there to see it. His concern for his sisters and their families made the war a personal affront. There was also Peter who had warned during the Munich debacle, "Poland will be next, you will see." But Maurice had returned to America for his own brighter prospects and had put aside the dire prediction. When that scenario came about for Poland, and France was overrun, a letter from Peter told of his enlistment in the Royal Air Force to do what was needed. "I am worried for my children, all of England's children. We are not willing to accept Hitler as Europe's despot. No matter what the sacrifice, I am ready to fight, and if need be die, for a liberal Europe. England will forestall complete German domination until your country comes to our side."

Though he also deplored Nazism, Alec was more detached from the war. He sympathized with Peter's anguish and did what he could to give comfort to Maurice, but his assurances were tinged with skepticism.

"Too many empires are at issue for the war to be one good side against the other bad. Hitler is out to plunder the Slavs, just as Peter says. There can be no doubt. But then I think of how filthy England's hands are as well. Churchill can boast about freedom, but India's not free. As for racism, think how English and French drew a color line across Africa in order to exploit the continent. Not that we dare throw stones, for Jim Crow rules our country to enforce inequality of the races."

Maurice made no argument in reply, only that it made him sad to watch the havoc as it was portrayed in the press and newsreel. Since his recent stay in England he had felt more English and, no matter that it might sound a contradiction, more American as well. His stake was at home in America, but a fraction of his heart lingered with the English people and their humane values.

After Pearl Harbor in 1941 there would be a different attitude from Alec who saw the United States and the Soviet Union joined in a democratic cause that might undermine empires and encourage freedom of all peoples. If that amounted to patriotism, still he wanted Ben to know the ways of nations at war including his own. In newsreels and movies there were sadistic Japanese soldiers whose ugly grins seemed to celebrate cruelty, and Germans who knew nothing of compassion for those they conquered. It took much explaining to counter dehumanization of whole nations. That task fell largely to Alec, Maurice being too partisan. Bit by bit Ben was exposed to philosophical reasoning.

*   *   *

Ben was soon a reader and not of children's books. He began to peruse the library which lined the walls of the back room of the second floor. In this he was encouraged. Consequently he spent a good deal of time to himself acquiring a vocabulary well beyond his years. Though he was precocious in many subjects, not surprising since he overheard much political and critical thought, sexuality passed him by. There were few romantic books on the shelves, none in fact that interested him. Because his body was slower to mature than most, he gave little heed to things he heard from boys who knew everything there was to know. He heard but ignored the occasional slur on homosexuality. Alec and Maurice behaved so naturally that he had little reason to question. He became during these years an attractive boy, quiet and thoughtful, more pleased with a serious book than horseplay.

*   *   *

Each generation wishes to avoid the mistakes of the past, particularly those which they continue to suffer in the form of personal anxieties and self-doubts. With great precaution the younger generation acts to counter the wrongs they attribute to their parents. If they succeed in avoiding old prejudices and behaviors, they are apt to make their share of new mistakes. Such are the uneven ways by which the claims of progress go forth.

The time had come for Ben to more fully understand his maturing body and the pulls of sexuality. It was for Maurice and Alec jointly to guide that awakening. The occasion arose when Ben, who had turned twelve, arrived home from school one afternoon. Maurice was there to greet him with a hug that was hurried because Ben had to hurry to use the toilet. As they sat down to munch on apples and cookies at the kitchen table, Maurice quipped, "No time for a pee during the afternoon?" Ben had grown used to sharing his thoughts. In response he recounted in quizzical tone an event that day when he had been party to innocent sexual

276

play not uncommon among boys. The encounter had left him uncertain as to propriety because it had excited his own penis. Maurice listened, his memory stirred to his own boyhood wonders and suspicions when he had been ineptly instructed in the facts of life by his teacher pretending to address him man to man, all the while presenting a false picture of matters as they stood for him.

As soon as Alec stepped in the door Maurice spoke of Ben's experience, then his own with astonishment.

"Talk about being bamboozled! Mr. Dullcie, I think that was his name. I was much older than Ben, and I knew something of desires and imagination, though little of facts. We were along the beach as he scratched crude illustrations of female anatomy in the sand. He drew a penis, nothing natural at all, more like a crooked finger, detached from any body and devoid of any possible emotions. All he would say is, 'This is the part of the male to be put here,' as he sternly pointed with a line in the sand the penis's way to the strange female part which looked like a yawning trap. Of course I was sickened by this show which had nothing to say to my own interests. He preached about the duty as a man to marry for that kind of repulsive behavior. Nothing else to be desired or done by that sexual organ no matter what my wishes! Scared me half to death so that I still have trouble looking at a woman when I imagine her without covering."

Alec was pleased with the protective stance of Maurice who was certain it was time to tell Ben more about his body and its sexual expressions.

"Ben has sexual feelings and realizes other boys do as well. Of course he knows nothing of girls and I am hardly the person to tell about that. You need to explain it all, especially possibilities with women."

Alec grinned that Maurice would speak of women with regard to twelve-year old Ben. He agreed to give some explanation "about a woman's body and the male role, but only a brief account. Nothing misleading of course. It seems what is more to the point is the ways boys might interact. We will have to tell more about ourselves, nothing in the least apologetic. I want Ben to know all that is natural."

*   *   *

After supper they dallied to engage an unsuspecting Ben. Not that he had forgotten the earlier escapade, only that Maurice had been consoling enough so that the day was no longer troubling. That invitation to sex play was already receding into memory as part of the formless substance of his sexual character. But Ben was pleased to repeat the happening for his father's benefit. He had been given permission by his teacher to satisfy an urgent need and had gone to the lavatory where he stood at the urinal next to an older Mike who was playing with his cock in hand. Mike asked Ben, "Pull it for me a few times, will you." When asked by Alec whether he had thought of joining in, Ben offered that he was more surprised than displeased. He had no reason for offense since it was a pleasing prospect for Mike who thought it something they would equally enjoy. Yet he did not think it something he ought to do. Without joining in or accomplishing his own task, Ben had quickly put his own puny organ into his pants and scampered back to the classroom. The rest of the afternoon was uncomfortable for not having relieved himself.

"You did right to leave," Maurice had earlier assured him. Now he asked, "Did you feel frightened?"

Ben had been living with two men for more than three years. He was familiar with their bodies and knew what to expect in ordinary toilet circumstances. His father's genitals even at rest had put him at awe enough to wonder whether his little cock would ever grow to such manly size. He knew in vague ways there was more to a cock than peeing.

"I didn't want to touch his cock. I wasn't afraid or anything. I have one myself to touch."

"That was right," Maurice again congratulated him. "We only touch people that way, their sexual organs, if we are pleased to do so. That is a special act when you are older and know more about sexual feelings. Something for private quarters."

Now that both Maurice and Alec were interested, Ben was eager to find out more. He would not mind doing another boy a favor if it were approved.

"Do you touch Maurice's cock to please him?"

Alec boasted with a nod toward Maurice, "Of course I do. I touch Maurice's body in every place. And he is free to touch mine. That is how we join our bodies which is our way of making love. When you want to know more, I will explain it to you. Right now, it is better to deal with Mike and your own feelings."

They had to ask whether Ben was enjoying sex play on his own. Yes, his cock got hard at times, and it felt good rubbing it, and so he understood Mike wanting a little help. He was perplexed when Alec asked whether rubbing his cock brought any outburst of liquid unlike when he was peeing. He was told that would happen soon as a sign of his body maturing. Then Maurice asked whether he thought of boys like Mike, of their private parts, or maybe of girls that he saw in school. Was there any girl he liked specially?

278

"I like Sister Carmelita."

With that Alec decided it was all right to postpone too much explanation at once.

"If anything comes up with Mike, or any other boy, let Maurice and me know about it. There is nothing to worry about, nothing you need do."

* * *

An invitation arrived by mail from Sam with exciting news.

"My latest composition, Concerto for Violin and Orchestra, will have its premiere with the Philadelphia Orchestra next Friday afternoon. I have been in the Academy for rehearsal which awakened poignant remembrance of our afternoons. I will leave tickets at the box office for you and Maurice if you will give me that satisfaction."

There was also an invitation to a reception following the concert at the Bellevue Strafford Hotel. Alec wrote to thank Sam for the tickets, but to decline the reception, "because Maurice will be engaged in business that day. Instead of his company, I will be with our son Ben at his first concert. I am proud it will be one that honors your music."

It was a thrilling performance for Ben who had heard such splendid music only on records. Now that he was so close to the violinist and orchestra he became fascinated with the making of music. Then the composer after his second bow looked their way, more to Alec but curious regarding Ben, and waved a barely detectable greeting that Ben took as an inspiration.

Ben began to spend more time at the piano, having received some earlier instruction. Maurice contacted Sister Carmelita to arrange for lessons at the school.

It would be more than a year later, a Saturday when Rosa and her girls had completed housework. They all sat down to hear Ben play a longer piece he had mastered, if such can be said of someone not a prodigy. When the performance was over there were compliments while the younger girl, only a year older than Ben, went to the piano and surprised Ben with a kiss on his cheek. Ben stood up and with a full embrace kissed her on the lips as he was used to doing with Alec. Rosa pinched her lips and extended her upward hand with a knowing toss into the air and a maternal smile, while Maurice with aplomb hurried to serve cake to everyone.

All was not well in the world in the midst of a great war, but Alec took satisfaction things were all well in the Scudder household.

End of Part I

Afterthought

If any person should presume to assert
This story is not moral, first I pray,
That they will not cry out before they're hurt,
Then that they'll read it o'er again, and say
(But doubtless, nobody will be so pert)
That this is not a moral tale, though gay.

Lord Byron, "Don Juan"